LESSONS IN MAGIC
– AND –
DISASTER

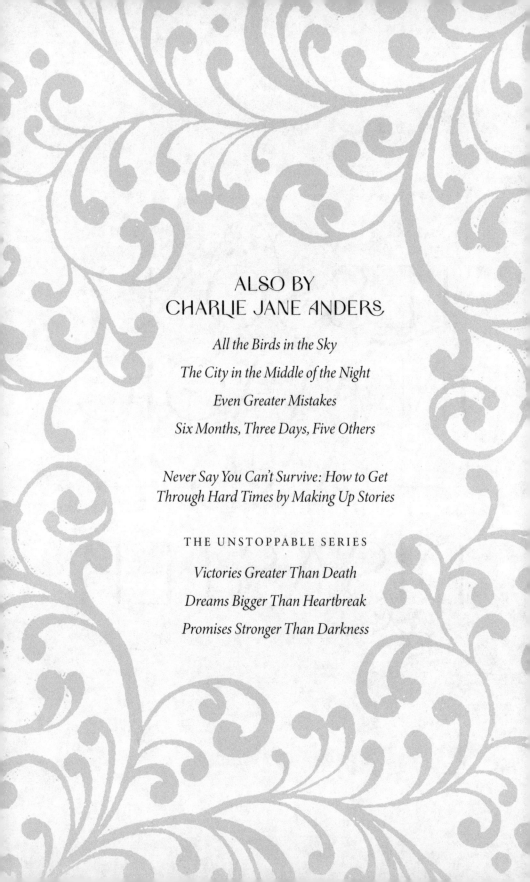

ALSO BY
CHARLIE JANE ANDERS

All the Birds in the Sky

The City in the Middle of the Night

Even Greater Mistakes

Six Months, Three Days, Five Others

*Never Say You Can't Survive: How to Get
Through Hard Times by Making Up Stories*

THE UNSTOPPABLE SERIES

Victories Greater Than Death

Dreams Bigger Than Heartbreak

Promises Stronger Than Darkness

LESSONS IN MAGIC AND DISASTER

CHARLIE JANE ANDERS

TOR PUBLISHING GROUP

NEW YORK

LESSONS IN MAGIC AND DISASTER

Copyright © 2025 by Charlie Jane Anders

A Tor Book
Published by Tom Doherty Associates / Tor Publishing Group
120 Broadway
New York, NY 10271

www.torpublishinggroup.com

Tor® is a registered trademark of Macmillan Publishing Group, LLC.

EU Representative: Macmillan Publishers Ireland Ltd, 1st Floor, The Liffey Trust Centre, 117–126 Sheriff Street Upper, Dublin 1, DO1 YC43

The Library of Congress Cataloging-in-Publication Data is available upon request.

ISBN 978-1-250-86732-2 (hardcover)

ISBN 978-1-250-86734-6 (ebook)

Our books may be purchased in bulk for specialty retail/wholesale, literacy, corporate/premium, educational, and subscription box use. Please contact MacmillanSpecialMarkets@macmillan.com.

First Edition: 2025

Printed in the United States of America

10 9 8 7 6 5 4 3 2 1

For the families that made us
and the families we make

LESSONS IN MAGIC AND DISASTER

1

A hermit's life may appear the most pleasant thing in the world—
until one requires a proper cup of coffee.

—*EMILY: A TALE OF PARAGONS AND
DELIVERANCE* BY A LADY, BOOK 1, CHAPTER 1

Jamie has never known what to say to her mother. And now—when it
matters most of all, when she's on a rescue mission—she knows even
less. What the hell was she thinking?

Somehow Jamie had imagined just marching up to the bright red door of
her mother's tiny house. She'd knock, and then proclaim: "Listen Mom, I'm
a witch, and I'm here to teach you how to do magic."

As if that was a thing a person could say to her mother, after years of
barely speaking to each other.

So Jamie stands frozen. She tries instead to gather her thoughts, and stares
at the ancient one-room schoolhouse where her mother, Serena, has hidden
from the world for the past six and a half years, ever since her life fell apart.

The schoolhouse is a box covered with flaking red paint, fifteen feet by
fifteen feet, suitable for educating half a dozen children. A narrow gravel
path skirts a garden where pansies, carrots, basil, and cilantro shimmy in
neat rows, like spectators cheering a team that's already lost the season.
In the distance, past a row of trees and a sloping lawn, Jamie can just make
out the mock-Colonial pile belonging to the Fordhams, who let her mother
live here rent-free in exchange for various favors. The air swims with grit

in the late-August wind; smoke from the first burning leaves of the season turns the world into a fireplace.

Jamie breathes and finds her center. *Time to be a witch about it,* she tells herself.

Meaning: *Time to put everything out there, with no control over the outcome.*

She marches up to the windowless front door and knocks, then hears stumbling on the inside that seems to go on for a long time. The door yawns, and Jamie's mother blinks at the unexpected visit. Serena is about to say something, some pleasantry.

As it turns out, Jamie doesn't utter the words "witch" or "magic."

Not just because of how ridiculous those things might sound—it's actually that Jamie is convinced that the mystical energy, or whatever force she cadges favors from, doesn't like to be spoken of so openly.

Even so, Jamie speaks before she can lose her moment.

"Mom. I have something important to show you. I can't explain, but I know a major secret. And I think you need to know about it."

· · · · ·

Coming to see Serena wasn't a conscious decision, not really.

A few hours earlier, Jamie was sitting in a cafe near Central Square, crafting a syllabus for her freshman composition class, and she found herself obsessing about her mother.

Back when Jamie was growing up, Serena used to stomp around and speak truth to whomsoever would rather not hear it, returning home an hour before Jamie's bedtime full of curses, like the occluded front of an oncoming thunderstorm—but now here she was, rotting away in some semi-suburban stale box. Jamie never visited, but every now and then she and her mother had the same blandly pleasant conversation over the phone.

Suddenly, with an acid shock, Jamie realized that her mother was going to die: maybe in two years, maybe in twenty. And when that happened, Jamie would do all the funeral crap you're supposed to do, go through some therapy, and maybe put up Serena's picture somewhere on her desk—but she wouldn't have a living relationship to mourn. Not like last time.

All at once, this situation felt unbearable. Jamie leapt out of her chair and bolted, leaving half a scone and most of a coffee.

Perhaps the downside of being a witch is too much awareness of your own feelings. You spend so much time trying to sink to the bottom of your own emotional lagoon so you can dredge up one honest *want*, that you stop being able to hide your feelings from yourself. This is annoyingly therapeutic, and it's ruined Jamie for Jacobean theater and Romantic poetry. Whenever Jamie experiences a strong emotion, she's the first to know, which never used to be the case. And most of the time, Jamie has to act on it.

. . . . .

"Do you want to come in?" Serena shuffles backward.

Jamie can't help feeling like a giant, towering over her mother in a fake-leather jacket and wide hiking boots.

The air in here smells like cedar, but with a musty undertone that prickles Jamie's nose. Two corners of this tiny room are never properly lit by the sun or by the single overhead bulb. A metal bedframe supports a futon mattress and duvet, near a writing desk and a single dresser with one rod to hang things that need hanging. Jamie sits at a folding card table in the center of the room, her left leg jiggling—because now that she's here, she cannot wait to get into it.

Let's gooooo.

Jamie can't untangle her feelings, looking at Serena's bony white face: gray eyes sunk deeper than Jamie remembers, brown hair steelier.

Here, in one frail body, is the person who held Jamie until the nightmares went away; who taught Jamie how to tie her shoes, skate, and dance; who once accused Jamie of stealing; who crouched in front of tiny Jamie and said, *You will always be loved, you cannot mess up so badly that you will not be loved*; who instilled in Jamie a deep paranoia about the world that still snags her when she's trying to be generous; who walked Jamie home from school when bullies were after her. Jamie was all set to breeze in and drag Serena out of this psychic prison, and now a part of her regresses to early childhood, swinging her legs under the table.

But adult Jamie can't help thinking about the trope in eighteenth-century lit where adults meet their mothers for the first time and do not know them. This gets downright squicky in Fielding's *Tom Jones* and Defoe's *Moll Flanders,* and the notion of mother-as-stranger is clearly a compelling one during a time where ideas of women's roles in the domestic sphere are shifting.

Bleh.

Jamie's brain will not stop churning, no matter how much she wants to be present.

"What's this secret you want to tell me?" Serena heads for the little kitchen counter and pours coffee. "Why show up out of the blue like this? Is everything okay?"

Somehow Jamie forgot about Serena's habit of tossing out questions like bombs with lit fuses. How is it that tenderness and annoyance go fist-in-palm? "I need to *show* it to you. I can't explain. Let's just say, it's something that could turn your life around, or maybe turn your life sideways. Do you want to see or not?"

Serena pauses, coffee in hand. Her head swivels by instinct, as if to ask Mae what she thinks.

But of course, Mae hasn't been available to ask such things for a long time.

So her head turns back, toward the one person who's living and present. "Sure. Yes."

Jamie takes a sip of bitter chicory and pushes the chipped mug away. "Okay. Let's do this."

"Where are we going?"

"I figured we could start with the woods out back."

Serena thumbs through her clothing rack and digs out a magnificent blue peacoat, with a crushed dried flower pinned to one lapel.

· · · · ·

The woods seemed an easy hike from the schoolhouse, but they're farther than Jamie realized. The wind grows colder and Serena keeps griping, to the point where Jamie wonders when her mother last left the schoolhouse for any length of time. Jamie doesn't have a plan exactly—maybe having a plan is a hindrance for the sort of thing she's hoping to do.

Once in the woods, Jamie scans in all directions. A soda can flashes candy-apple red under the maroon of dead leaves. They're close, she can tell.

"What are we looking for?" Serena sounds curious, rather than impatient.

"Hard to describe. It's a 'know it when you see it' thing." Jamie is low-key terrified that speaking out loud about magic will ruin it forever, and then where will she be? Still, she set out to teach her mom, and pedagogy is always at least partly a matter of providing a conceptual framework.

"I did a lot of trial and error." Jamie chooses her words with care. "Back in Wardmont."

"When you were in eighth grade?"

"Eighth through tenth." Jamie nods. "I used to sneak off by myself and go to the warrens. I found it only worked in certain spots."

There's a whisper of a trail between birch trees with flaking bark and a few grouchy evergreens.

"Is that why you used to disappear?" Serena steps over a bulbous tree root with caution. "We never figured out why, and we couldn't just ask, I guess."

This land once belonged to the Nipmuc Nation, but they were forcibly relocated in the seventeenth century, and this whole area was formally ceded to white settlers via the misleadingly named Massachusetts Indian Enfranchisement Act of 1869. These grungy woods were mostly chopped down by loggers in the late nineteenth century, then slowly grew back. People have hunted, gathered, played, and hidden among these trunks, but they've also sat empty for years at a time.

So this should be ideal, but Jamie can't seem to find the right spot as they walk. You need someplace that's halfway in between: neither wild nor tame, neither occupied nor unoccupied.

When Jamie was a teenager, she found a community vegetable garden that had gone to seed—plants grown out of hand, rabbits chewing through everything, bugs all over the splintering sticks that once supported vines or saplings. That garden was the best magical cauldron a girl could ever wish for. Those neat rows covered by messy greenery brought Jamie her first guitar, the first blowjob she ever gave, her first kiss—which happened way later than her first blowjob—and her ticket to the best music camp in the state.

"You were a strange child, always rushing someplace, making up your own games," Serena says. "Do you remember when you tried to give me an acorn of perfect knowledge?"

Jamie shrugs; she doesn't remember that.

Forests don't go on forever, not anymore, there's always a development or a hunting trap, a clearing or a dirt road. People have carved up these woodlands so much, they've created an incalculable number of new magical places.

Still no luck, but Jamie keeps pressing forward.

"If we get lost in the cellphone dead zone, I plan to be quite passive-aggressive," Jamie's mother says.

"We're not lost yet. Still working on it."

Serena starts quoting some Thoreau pomposity about losing yourself in the woods—as if getting lost is intrinsically better in the woods than in a suburban IKEA. The whole concept of "getting lost" implies that at some point we are in fact oriented, which flies in the face of everything Jamie has ever known about people.

Jamie finds it: an in-between place. A spot where someone had tried to build a shed, or a hut, or some kind of gazebo, but the wood rotted away and a few rusted nails splay on the peaty ground. The whole thing smells of mulch.

"Oh, this is perfect," Jamie tells her mom. "It's big but totally disintegrated."

What Jamie can't explain out loud—for fear of wrecking these perfect conditions—is that this is a spot where people tried to impose their will on the forest, but they failed, or gave up. A place between grown and built, where someone took care of things, for a while. A neglected place, Jamie calls it.

The ideal spot to do some magic.

"So we found it," Serena says in her most patiently matter-of-fact tone (the one she used to use when Jamie was a kid who occasionally made up weird stories to explain her messes). "Now what do we do?"

"Just watch."

Jamie had the whole drive down to the schoolhouse to think about what spell she could do in front of her mother, and luckily she already had the perfect thing in her rucksack. She pulls out an egg-white cardstock envelope with the Rugby College crest on one corner. Inside, a letter explains that due to changes in the college's endowment, Jamie's graduate-student stipend is being reduced by $5,000—leaving her to starve or take on more debt. (The college has wasted a small fortune on the Quantified Text initiative, using algorithms to identify patterns in classic works of fiction, so nobody actually needs to read them. A total disaster, and now belts are being tightened.)

She lays the stipend-reduction letter ("We regret to inform you . . .") in the center of the decaying structure. On top of it, she places some dandelions she picked: a good symbol of abundance. And then she adds an offering, a cow heart that she bought from the butcher. *Hope you like big hearts.*

Serena peers over Jamie's shoulder, puzzled.

Explaining a ritual is worse than explaining a joke—it makes Jamie's skin itch. But she has to try. "It's not about power. It's not. It's about knowing what you really want, in your fucking secret heart, and putting your wishes into the world in a way that can be heard."

"Heard by whom?" Serena asks.

Jamie just shrugs in response.

"And now?" Jamie's mom asks.

"Now, we forget we did this, and head back. I know the way to the schoolhouse from here."

At least, Jamie's pretty sure she can figure out how to get un-lost.

"So doing that makes you feel better?" Serena asks. "Or do you really think it has a material impact? Was I supposed to feel something? At my age, I'm used to dismissing my own sensations so I don't turn into a hypochondriac. How do you tell if you accomplished anything? How often do you do this sort of thing?"

Questions, questions, questions, coming too fast for Jamie to answer any of them.

If Mae was here, she'd be saying, *Stop giving our child the ninety-ninth degree*—but of course if Mae was here, everything would be different.

Jamie stops and wheels around to face her mother.

"Look, I can't really explain. Not properly. Maybe in a few days, something will happen—like the department secretary will tell me that they found some money for me in a research fund, or they'll change their minds about this cutback. You never get help in the way you expect, and it's best not to be too prescriptive. But I've already said too much. This thing only works if you don't think too hard about it, much less speak of it out loud." But Jamie keeps seeing the tiny schoolhouse in her mind's eye.

"The woodland exercise that can be spoken is no woodland exercise?" Jamie's mom only rolls her eyes a little.

"You're half right." Jamie turns and keeps walking. "There's more than a small element of the Dao in this practice, but it's also way too anchored on desire, want, craving, self. That's the whole reason I wanted to teach you: you need to let yourself want things again."

"Who says I don't want anything?" Serena bristles so hard, it's like a crackle of static electricity on the back of Jamie's neck. "And what's so great about wanting things?"

Jamie can't find a way to state the obvious: Serena has been unmotivated since she crawled into her box to hide, and it's heartbreaking for anyone who remembers how alive she used to be.

The woods darken. Serena's footfalls land heavier. Jamie decides to change tack. "It's not just about goals or whatever, it's about self-knowledge. A person can't really know who they are unless they know what they want. That's a big part of why I do this thing: I can read the ransom notes left by my own heart."

"Doesn't obsessing over everything you crave just lead to bitterness, though?" Serena says.

"No, no, no." Jamie hears her own voice go up, pushes it back down. "No, not at all. That's the other part, see? You put your desires out there into the world, and then you can let go of them a little bit. I never know if anything will come of it, but I find I can obsess about something less once I've made an offering."

Serena doesn't talk for a while. Jamie glimpses the Fordhams' manor through the trees.

"So how often do you do . . . that?" Serena asks when they get back to the schoolhouse.

"Once in a while," Jamie says. "Just finding the right locale usually takes forever. And then I have to get in the right headspace."

"Hm. Do you need to find a new place every time?"

"Not always. But once I've disturbed a location, it's no longer as untouched as before. So I usually can't go back to the same spot too often."

Jamie's mother is being shrewd, avoiding any awkward questions that might stray too far into demanding an Explanation. And either it hasn't occurred to her to think her daughter is delusional, or she's giving Jamie the benefit of the doubt. (Why do we say, "benefit of the doubt"? Why not "benefit of the belief"?)

Serena insists on making dinner before Jamie drives back to the city, so she texts her partner, Ro, that she'll be home late. She hasn't eaten her mom's cooking in years, and of course food is basically pure nostalgia in chemical form. Soon Serena is whipping up her healthy versions of Midwestern comfort food, all cheese curds and veggie sausage.

Jamie keeps expecting to see Mae wander in the front door, shucking an oversized bomber jacket with a grin on her round craggy face, under henna-red bangs.

When Jamie's clearing the table and getting ready to leave, Serena looks her in the eye and says, "Thanks for showing me. I think I've wondered for a long time."

And that's it.

She always knew something, and now she knows something more.

2

Grief, nobly expressed in small portions, may be the surest sign of a refined sensibility. Yet an excess of grief soon appears wicked and selfish, and none will tolerate it for long.

—*EMILY: A TALE OF PARAGONS AND DELIVERANCE* BY A LADY, BOOK 1, CHAPTER 7

Jamie keeps meaning to go back and check on her mother, to see if Serena was able to make anything out of the lesson in the woods. *I'll make the trek down to the schoolhouse in a few days,* she tells herself occasionally. They can go for another walk and do another working, and Jamie can give Serena a few indirect pointers. Jamie'll probably have to take Serena through it a few more times before everything falls into place. But meanwhile, she has a dissertation on eighteenth-century lit to finish, and Professor Zhang keeps nagging her for a chapter, and magic really *can't* write her thesis for her.

(Though, on the bright side, the department did come up with enough money to restore the full stipends for Jamie and the other PhD students. As usual, Jamie tries not to wonder if her spell had anything to do with this windfall, because overthinking will ruin it.)

Each morning, Jamie revels in the abundance of a whole day, stretched out before her—a dozen hours in which to write epic sentences and accomplish great things—and she looks up, and suddenly it's evening and she's gotten nowhere. Somehow a month and a half pass without Jamie going anywhere near the schoolhouse.

One day, a sharp pain hits Jamie mid-chest, more an impact than a twinge, as she climbs the staircase out of the basement of the Banner Library. (She has a tiny makeshift office in the Goblin Market, the warren of converted storage cages down there.) She stumbles, she almost skids downstairs.

As if her mind has been working the problem in the background, Jamie suddenly knows what she should have said to Serena in the woods: "Remember when I was thirteen or fourteen, and I went to the Mercy school where I suffered a mild concussion every other week? I used to drift for hours, playing imagination games in the railyard and the abandoned garden and the old mall. I was looking for something, I didn't even know what. And then I found it, and I was free and nobody could trap me anymore. Once I had my freedom, I could make space inside myself to want other things, and the more I could chase the things I wanted, the more I could understand what lay beneath them. Until I had a life and an identity and some of the things I had craved as a teenager, and I became too busy or too serious to want much of anything anymore, other than just safety and comfort. I became a grown-up, after a fashion. But when I remember to covet, and I go back to the sort of places where I used to pine after unattainable wishes as a kid, then . . . something happens. I can make my life a little better. Other people's lives, too. I can wake up my own heart."

It's perfect, and she only hopes she's not too late to say it to her mother.

· · · · ·

This time of year, fall creeps up on you and whacks you upside the head. One minute it's hazy and bright and your collarbone itches with the sweat trapped under your shirt, the next—bam! The sky darkens early, cold mist fills the air, and everything feels weighed down with regret, or just damp. Five layers of wool cushion Jamie's rangy, coltish arms and legs; she runs cold these days. Her shaggy brown hair, in need of a trim and some color, forms a net for snowflakes. She sets off for her mom's twee cabin in the middle of the day, but by the time she arrives, the sky is graying.

As soon as she gets to the schoolhouse, she can tell something is messed up. The door is locked, but a crack runs from top to bottom, wide enough for Jamie to nudge the bolt out of place. Inside, Serena lies in the middle of the floor, wearing a frayed housecoat, the same one she used to wear when Jamie was little. She's hugging an old throw pillow, and she's tangled in a rug.

"Why did you teach me that?" Serena's face presses against the floor, so her voice travels through the floorboards as much as the air. "Why would you teach anyone that, ever?"

"I wanted us to be friends. We're both grown-ups now, more or less. We're almost the only ones each other has left. And . . . I thought this could be good for you."

Jamie was trying to soothe Serena, but only succeeded in pissing her off—which is almost as good.

"You thought it would be good for me." Serena peels off the rug and staggers to her feet, flinging the pillow aside. "Ugh. Seems we've reached the role-reversal stage, where you know what's best for me. I am not ready to be your motherfucking dependent."

"Motherfucking" being, of course, one of those words that one uses all the time and seldom parses anew—until one hears it spoken by one's own mother, whereupon it becomes an ouroboros of obscenity.

"I don't want you to depend on me any more than you want to." Jamie speaks with care. "Until a few minutes ago, I thought you were capable of taking care of yourself."

Serena looks at her own dirty housecoat and the indentation of her body in the rug.

"Don't make this about me." The sharpness in her mother's tone regresses Jamie instantly. All at once, she's a small fry, in Trouble, looking over her shoulder to see if Mae will come to her rescue. She shakes it off: Mae is long gone, Jamie's approaching the age Mae and Serena were when she was born, and Serena is no longer the boss of her.

"I didn't teach you anything," Jamie says in a painstakingly even voice. "Teaching implies structure, a syllabus, tests, a body of knowledge."

"Didn't realize your field was semantics." Serena crosses to the tiny kitchen and starts making hot chocolate, the way she did when Jamie was a kid—one last gambit to infantilize her.

"I didn't teach, I *showed*. I can't talk about it without getting tangled up. I just wanted to share something with you."

Some primitive yearning activates in Jamie at the scent of cocoa in progress. She can taste the first sip and the last, just from one distant whiff.

"I want us to be equals," Jamie says. "Neither of us needs to know what's best for the other."

"That merely represents an intermediate state." Serena has her back to Jamie, stirring chocolate and warm milk. "A changing of the guard on the way to you looking after me as if I'm helpless."

"You've forgotten how tough you actually are." Jamie takes the cocoa, breathes in the sugary steam. "I could never lord it over you, even if I wanted to. Those bastards did a number on you, but I wish you could remember yourself."

"You want us to be equals, but you also want to be the one to remind me of myself."

"That's not even remotely a contradiction. Friends remind each other of who they are."

Serena squints. "What if I don't want to be friends?"

Jamie loses her grip on the mug, so it tumbles toward the scuffed hardwood floor. She catches the mug, but the cocoa is a puddle. Her heart is a techno song, or maybe house—the music Ro used to take her out dancing to.

"I'm your mother. We're not supposed to be 'besties.' We didn't join a study group together—you came out of me and I tried to teach you what you needed to know and now you're teaching *me* and it's awful and I can't sleep, and everything smells weird and there's clutter I don't recognize, all over the place. Everything is dirty."

Oh shit.

Never even occurred to Jamie that magic could go wrong. In her experience, either it works or it doesn't. You try enough times, you get lucky. Now Jamie's having a guilt spasm, staring at the cocoa-spill and tangled rug next to each other on the floor.

Nobody makes any move to clean up. Jamie is seeing her mother new: a sixty-year-old dyke whose skin clings too tight to her bones for wrinkles to form. She was unnervingly beautiful in her twenties (more beautiful than Jamie could ever aspire to be), with her frost-gray eyes, pale hawkish face and sleek chestnut hair. Jamie heard the stories—Serena tore through the lesbian scenes in a few cities, and people lined up to date her long after she had a reputation for breaking hearts. Jamie can still glimpse that fierce glamour through the pall that despair has cast over her.

Jamie doesn't know what to say. She can't ask Serena what went wrong, because that might make things worse. It's frustrating for someone who swims in words for a living to find herself in a situation where words are counterproductive.

At last she says, "Show me."

Serena hesitates, then leads Jamie to her cracked front door.

They trudge through the woods, on a different trajectory than last time. Serena wears a dour look, and her arm slaps against her leg as she walks. She's always been excellent at projecting wordless anger, even back when she was mostly happy.

Jamie keeps thinking they've reached the spot where Serena did her working, but she's wrong each time. There's a rotted birdbath that Jamie might have expected a novice to choose, but nope. Ditto for the decaying plot full of rusted tools, which looks fairly promising.

Serena was half-supine back at the schoolhouse, but out here she's vigorous, bloody-minded. They march until Jamie's feet ache, after which they come to a spot that looks like nothing at all. Jamie's mother gestures at some faint indentations in the grassy pine needles and whispers, "This was a road."

At this moment, Jamie begins to suspect her mother has an actual gift.

"I thought I should find the loneliest place, or rather the place that felt the most lonesome," Serena says.

Not at all how Jamie thinks about it, but Serena's way obviously works.

Once Serena locates the exact spot in the overgrown road, where somebody went to a lot of trouble to clear away the brush long ago, she peels the bracken to reveal Mae's favorite hat. Jamie's other mother.

"I just miss her."

On top of the hat rests a gently putrefying slab of smoked salmon, the kind that comes in vacuum-sealed pouches.

Seeing this woolen cap, sort of a beanie, with faded stitching that reads BRAIN COZY, Jamie feels so much tenderness, she wants to give her mother the first hug anyone has given her in several years. But Jamie is also horrified, revolted, furious—she has a powerful urge to run away, screaming and windmilling her arms.

Why in a million years would you leave a dead woman's hat in the grass of an overgrown road? What was Serena even asking for: Mae back from the dead? Some long-deferred justice for her death? Something else?

You can't do magic unless you can clearly express your profoundest craving, without equivocating but also without being greedy.

What did Serena think would happen?

And what *did* happen?

Jamie can't imagine the answer to either of those questions.

Serena wants nothing from the living. That's the unmistakable message of this dirty hat. Nothing from Jamie, nothing from the Fordhams, nothing from Ying, Spotty Dobbins, or any of her other old friends.

"You have to ask for something that is possible," Jamie whispers, deathly afraid she's going to ruin things for both of them.

"I do not know what's possible for me."

Jamie picks up the hat, though she's sure it's too late, and folds it carefully before placing it inside her messenger bag. She stares at her mother's unexpressive face and gropes for something to say.

She settles on banality. "Mae would have wanted you to go on living."

Serena rolls her eyes. "Okay."

"What do you mean, 'Okay'?"

"Doesn't that seem like a small ask? I could be in a coma on life support and that would satisfy what you seem to think Mae would have wished for me."

"Being alive and living are two different—"

"I thought I raised an interesting person." Serena snorts and walks away.

Jamie almost claps back, but she can see the fragility below the salt. Serena has always had a huge asshole streak, but she (almost) never insults her own child. She's clearly still rattled and anxious, though she's hiding it better now. So Jamie walks quietly beside her, figuring she'll lead the way back to the schoolhouse. Maybe the two of them can drink cocoa instead of drizzling it onto the floor, and figure this thing out.

They get lost. Really, really lost this time.

Serena stops and says, "Let me get my bearings." The sky goes black, and she appears more disoriented. Either she knew how to find the overgrown road, but not how to get back, or this is a consequence of her failed spell—or maybe Jamie made things worse by removing the hat. They're in unknown territory, in both senses.

They stand in the gloom, while Serena tries to orient.

Jamie turns her phone into a flashlight, while all her energy goes into not griping at her mother. Her phone's GPS is all over the place, but she has plenty of signal, so she texts Ro: *lost in the woods with my mom. gps borked.* Ro sends a bunch of heart emojis and asks if they need to call 911. Jamie says *nah, fuck that. I just need a clear sense of direction.*

Ro responds by texting Jamie a link to a stargazing app. A moment later, Jamie knows which way is south. Her phone battery is at 12 percent.

"This is horrible." Serena groans. "Is it always like this?"

"It is never like this." Anger leaks into Jamie's voice at last. "I've literally never had anything like this happen to me."

Serena nods, with a brittle formality. "Thank you for sharing this with me, even if it didn't come out the way you hoped."

They find the edge of the woods, two miles down the road from the schoolhouse.

"I know you've been lonely," Jamie says to her mom's back. "Living in that schoolhouse by yourself with nobody to talk to but the Fordhams."

No answer. Trudge trudge trudge.

Jamie is ready to stop regressing around her mother. Which ought to make her punch the sky, triumphant—instead, she feels as though she's let go of something precious. This shift goes hand in hand with the role-reversal thing Serena keeps dreading, where Jamie starts looking after her mother. At least Serena still has the power to drive Jamie to scream-town, same as ever.

"I miss Mae, too," Jamie says.

She has paperwork to complete, and she promised Ro she'd clean the bathroom, and there are five episodes of *Real Housewives* that the two of them haven't watched yet.

But she cannot leave until she figures out what went wrong with her mom's spell. Or rather, what was the fallout from it going wrong—other than being bad enough that Serena was in a fetal position, spooning a tassel-fringed pillow.

They straggle back to the schoolhouse. Serena doesn't want to let Jamie back inside, even to use the bathroom. "You're going to judge me."

Jamie looks down at her shrunken mother. "I already went in earlier, when I first showed up."

"It's different after dark."

Jamie doesn't argue, just pushes past without actually shoving Serena aside. As soon as she stumbles into the schoolhouse, she chokes on a terrible smell. She can't place this stench at first, but she can't escape it. She nearly throws up.

What sort of smell is it? Barfy, rotten, sour, soiled. Now Jamie knows exactly what smell this is, or rather what combination of smells.

It's Mae's filthy bandages, from when she started to get bedsores. It's the black bile she vomited up in her last days. It's the adult diapers. It's the stench of her cadaver when Jamie and Serena found her that last day, neither of them quite managing to be there in her last moments. The burnt stir-fry she made when she was trying to convince her family that she still had it together and nothing needed to change.

"I sprayed. I opened all the windows. I cleaned and scrubbed every inch."

Jamie looks at her mother and thinks: *Imagine what you could accomplish if you tried something constructive.*

No clue how to fix this. Jamie has always told herself a good spell is one where you are never sure if it worked—even if you get the exact thing you asked for, it could just be a coincidence.

How do you clean up a category error?

They already removed the hat, but Jamie doubts that will suffice on its own. She can't help thinking of this as a haunting, or some sort of infestation, which needs to be expunged. But that's pop culture speaking through her, not her actual understanding of magic and how it works.

So . . . what???

Solving this mess is going to require Jamie to think more deeply about magic than she ever has—deeper than she'd usually consider wise, or sane. This could ruin her spellwork forever.

Serena stares. As if she can't decide whether she's more worried that her daughter is going to think ill of her, or that Jamie can't clean up this mess.

Okay . . . Serena asked for something impossible, or just unexamined. What she got was all the horrible memories, Mae the way they both swore they wouldn't remember her. Mae on her way out.

Not Mae when she was fully alive, in her long and glorious prime. Smiling, singing, doing math in her head while also reciting a Romantic poem. Turning every odd and unlovable leftover in the refrigerator into a miraculously tasty stir-fry or casserole. Mae had her own kind of magic.

People always say *Be careful what you wish for,* as if anyone ever really chooses their own wishes. A person who could wish with care would be an irredeemable monster.

If this were a horror movie, or some gothic romance, the key would be to accept that Mae is gone and she's not coming back. But that's ridiculous: Jamie and Serena are adults who live in the real world, and they understand the nature of death and irrevocable loss perfectly.

No, the trouble here is that Serena was sloppy, because Jamie taught her sloppily. Jamie should have supervised her mother's first attempts at spellwork.

"What do you actually want out of life?" Jamie asks her mother.

Serena gets down on her hands and knees and scrubs the floor. "I want this terrible smell gone."

"What do you want that's not just a negative? What would make you happy?"

"Why are you asking me? You're my daughter, not my therapist."

"I'm trying to help you."

How to explain without saying too much? Maybe this is it. Maybe Jamie has to ruin magic for herself to save Serena from the mistake Jamie led her into. Jamie doesn't actually *know* that magic will fail if she speaks about it too freely, she just *feels* it, in some organ deeper and more obscure than her heart or stomach.

"The only way to repair this is to want something new," Jamie says slowly.

Serena looks up from scrubbing.

"You know as well as I do that the thing you did with the hat caused this—" Jamie struggles to find a word that fits. "—this infestation."

Serena doesn't try to deny it. She's always been a pragmatist, where Mae was more of a skeptic—and yes, pragmatism and skepticism are opposites, as Jamie learned the hard way whenever she heard the two of them argue. A pragmatist is up for whatever works, but a skeptic wants things to make sense and have a reasonable explanation, even if that leads to nothing but trial and frustrating error.

"You had a chance to ask the universe for something," Jamie says. "But instead you chose to register a complaint."

Serena pulls herself up into a sitting position. This foul odor is getting to her, even more than it's getting to Jamie.

"Everybody reaches a point where they have more past than future. Some people are aware when that happens, and at that point your fondest wishes are liable to become retrospective," Serena says.

"You could live another twenty—"

"Don't threaten me with longevity."

"I'm just saying. You have a future. Same as anyone who's not imminently dying." Jamie sucks in a breath and the smell of Mae's deathbed throws her.

Serena looks weary, grief-beaten, ashamed. Frightened to want anything new, after what happened to her wife and her career.

"Okay, get up." Jamie puts on her briskest speaking-to-freshmen voice.

"Where are we—"

"We're going to find another spot out there, and you're going to put down something forward-looking and hopefully plausible."

"I'm not a good judge of plausibility anymore."

"Just try."

For a moment Jamie is sure Serena will refuse to follow her back out there. But Serena is desperate enough that she gets her coat and tromps out the door.

They don't go back into the woods. Jamie doesn't much want to fall and break her neck, or get bitten by something. Instead, they get in the dirt-mobile and follow the unpaved back roads, until they find a road that dwindles to a hiking trail that they only follow a few yards before discovering a makeshift shrine that someone put a lot of work into before leaving it to crumble. Mossy candles, a porcelain figurine, handwritten notes gone illegible.

"Perfect." Jamie turns to her mother. "You got something?"

"I think so. I hope. Let me try."

Serena jots a few words on a paper and wraps it around a small cardboard box. She leaves this tiny bundle under a layer of moss at the center of the ruined shrine, along with some chocolate from Jamie's bag. "Uh, thank you and please and I hope this meets with your, uh, approval."

Neither of them talks on the crunchy bumpy drive back to the schoolhouse. Jamie's already dreading the longer haul back to Somerville.

When they reach the schoolhouse, the smell-cluster is gone. Slight bleach-Febreze scent, but other than that, nothing. Jamie hugs her mom good night. Serena feels like a sack of twigs. She yawns and sobs a little. Maybe she'll sleep now. Jamie hopes so.

Jamie doesn't know what Serena's new spell aimed for, and she doesn't want to know. But it was something that she dearly wanted, or it wouldn't have been enough to cancel out the earlier demand.

The next morning, Jamie decides: her mother shouldn't do any more spellwork without Jamie's direct supervision, or maybe assistance. At least until she's gotten a bit more control over it.

3

My being the Author is now one of those profound Secrets that is
known only to all the people I know.

—JANE COLLIER IN A LETTER TO JAMES
HARRIS, 18 MARCH 1753

The next morning, Jamie nurses an AeroPress coffee at the wooden table
near the front window of the one-bedroom walk-up apartment she
shares with Ro. She keeps replaying the moment when Serena showed her
Mae's hat in the road, and some rotten part of her feels as though Mae just
died all over again. No amount of coffee will warm her insides. Ro sees Jamie brooding and sits next to her at this wooden table, which is supposed
to unfold to seat six or seven people but has been stuck in two-person mode
for at least a year.

"You got in late last night." Ro smiles.

Jamie tries to nod and knead the back of her own neck at the same time.
"It sucked."

"Is your mom okay?"

"Sort of."

Ro doesn't get along too well with Serena. They don't complain about
her or start fights, they just keep their distance. Jamie asked about it once,
and they said Serena was just too bitter, in her cheerfully resigned fashion.
Ro felt as though cheerful bitterness was the worst kind—they could handle

fist-shaking at the sky or breakdowns, but not the Brave Face: Ro grew up around WASPs who repressed and sublimated everything, so Ro became highly attuned to the trapdoors and landmines inside the blithe silences. Jamie has tried to explain that Serena had been someone who never had cause to complain until her life was literally ruined, and she'd ironically been much better at expressing anger before there was simply too much to vent about. Ro understands Serena's quiet despair perfectly well—they just don't enjoy being around it.

Jamie and Ro's apartment isn't much larger than Serena's schoolhouse, but it's cozy: concert posters and friends' oil paintings and talismans cover every wall, except for the parade of bookcases where most people would have put a flatscreen TV. They have three hand-carved wooden chairs with cat-faced armrests, and a purple velour sofa. The tiny bedroom has a fluffy duvet and shoji screens on wheels that they can move around to change the room's shape.

"I knew my mom was still messed up over Mae, but I had no idea." Jamie stares out the window at the morning bicycle parade on Russell Street, everyone swarming to the Davis Square T. "She's just broken. It's a whole scene."

"Really? The love of her life, the person who stood by her when her career was imploding, and you're surprised that she's a wreck?"

Ro chose their name for a reason. They identified strongly with Ro Laren—a character so rebellious, *Star Trek* built a spin-off around her and she refused to show up. They've been trying to finish an econ PhD for years, they have a weird angry-seagull laugh that they only do at the most inappropriate moments, they love square dancing and line dancing because they spent their high school years in the Carolinas, they have an endless series of nerdy T-shirts and gorgeously dorky sweaters.

"It's been more than six years," Jamie says. "I was in college when Mae died, and now I'm failing to write my dissertation."

"So she should be over it?"

"No, of course not."

"Some things, people don't get over."

"I know, I know."

Ro liked Mae, a lot. The two of them met a handful of times, when Jamie and Ro were first dating. Mae taught Ro how to play card games, Ro helped fill Mae's birdfeeder, and Mae made it clear Ro was part of the family. Back when there was a family for Ro to be part of.

"I know all the grief clichés," Jamie says. "It's a process, it's work, it happens on no timetable, it's a ravenous beast that never stops eating away at you, it sneaks up on you. Did I miss any?"

"You always think that hyperawareness of tropes is equivalent to understanding the lived experience behind them," Ro says.

"Isn't it? You strip away the clichés, and what remains is the truth."

"Has that literally *ever* worked? In your experience? Like, *ever*?"

"It's just . . . my mom won't let me mourn with her. She's having this whole desolate thing, but she won't allow me to be a part of it."

Ro smiles, because Jamie's finally talking about what's really bothering her. "Have you tried telling her any of that?"

"Not in so many words. I tried to teach her a . . . technique for dealing with the grief, but it kind of went wrong."

Jamie has considered telling Ro about magic a few times. But she's always bitten her lip, because she knew magic would destabilize any relationship she brought to it, and she needs this relationship to be stable.

"One grief cliché that's absolutely true is that everybody deals with it in their own way," Ro says. "So what works for you might not work for her. I support you in trying to nudge her to work through it so she can get on with her life, but she gets to decide what that's going to look like. Right?"

Every time Jamie looks into Ro's bright blue eyes, she feels wonder-discombobu-elated. A feeling of scary joy and familiarity, like she *knows* them really really well and she's never going to be chill about that much understanding and skin-tingling closeness. It's never going to be like, "Oh yeah, that's my spouse, whatever." More like, "Oh wow, oh shit, oh damn, I still get to be with this person"—it's still somehow an uncanny surprise, even though it's also comfortable and familiar. Did Jamie use magic to get Ro to notice her? Maybe. Hard to say.

Jamie kisses them and grabs her knapsack, because she's going to be late to teach Crisis of the English Novel. Which, believe it or not, is a survey course, because the English novel has been one long crisis.

· · · · ·

Berniece the dirtmobile weaves along leaf-strewn streets, past sidewalk trees encircled by cedar chips. The tinny speakers blast Seinabo Sey at top volume, and Jamie tries to squish her brain into a shape suitable for imparting literary insight while trying really hard to avoid Memorial Drive on a Friday morning. The commute from Somerville to Allston ranges from "vexing" to "life-crushing," and even magic can barely help.

The Plaintive Gate always springs up as you round the bend on Western Ave., as if the dark gray slabs and wrought-iron wings were a fairy portal that appears only to the fae-touched. (The Plaintive Gate's imagery was inspired by some transcendentalist doggerel about pining for a life of the mind, but people started calling it the Plaintiffs' Gate when Rugby College decided to sue nearby businesses and residents.) Jamie veers left to find one of the last spots in the restricted lot, arranges her parking pass on the dashboard next to the swaying pink bunny statue, and dashes into the Tangram, the lightning bolt–shaped green space at the heart of campus with Banner Library at one end and the administration building at the other. She makes a beeline for the one beautiful building on campus, Hirschfeld Hall (made of stones from an old Scottish castle that Roy Dylan, the industrialist, had disassembled and shipped to the United States before everybody realized they didn't know how to reassemble it, so Dylan donated the stones). Jamie's ID taps three times before the door clicks open.

Jamie's thesis advisor spots her rushing to the classroom and hurtles in her direction, linen skirts swirling. Ariella Zhang traps Jamie in the hallway, asking uncomfortable questions about the state of the dissertation with a kind look on her round face, ringed with wild gray hair. "Perhaps you could stop by my office after your class." Jamie can't think of a reason to say no.

And then Jamie's in a lecture hall full of undergrads, faces hidden behind laptops or phones. She was so excited about this chance to tell the story of how technology and society shaped the most miraculous object of all:

the book. She loves nothing better than helping people understand why we tell long-form stories the way we do—but she wasn't prepared for the anxiety, not to mention the imposter syndrome. It's only a few weeks into the semester, and Jamie is already forming a mental map of the lecture hall, demarcated into friendly, neutral, and hostile areas. At one extreme, there are a handful of queer and BIPOC students who always seem to be picking up what Jamie's putting down, like Rosie Ho and Thane Briggs, and at the other . . . there are older versions of the dudes who used to bully Jamie in school. The worst is Gavin Michener, who looks like the villain of every eighties teen comedy (wavy dishwater hair, beady ice-blue eyes, letterbox chin). Gavin derails today's class for twenty minutes with his insistence that epistolary novels are inherently boring, because anyone who carries on a long correspondence simply cannot lead an interesting life. Just try writing ten pages of flowery prose while being chased by stampeding elephants! Gavin is the master of flooding the zone and poisoning the well—he'll probably become a US senator.

After class, Jamie hightails it out of there before anyone can corner her with more questions—fuck 'em, she's got office hours—and soon she's perched in Ariella Zhang's dusty lavender-scented office, the sun hitting her eyes through gauzy curtains.

Ariella doesn't offer any herbal tea or small talk, and instead launches right into asking where the fuck are some chapters. Jamie, dry-mouthed, says she's hit a snag; but soon, very soon, Ariella will be drowning in pages. Ariella seems actually pissed, her neck all tendon—but then Jamie realizes she's looking at guilt. Ariella feels responsible for encouraging Jamie to go down a rat hole that may result in no scholarship of note.

Around the same time Jamie fell in love with Ro, she was also smitten, head over bloody heels, with Sarah Fielding. And now, maybe, she's paying the price.

People go on and on about Shakespeare's sister—there was even a band with that name, back in the day—but the famous novelist Henry Fielding actually did have a sister. And Sarah Fielding was *brilliant*: she wrote *The Adventures of David Simple,* a compassionate and sly novel about a man searching for a true friend, plus she also wrote the first young adult novel in

English, *The Governess*. Sarah Fielding basically invented the YA novel as we know it! (Well, mostly.) Jamie had been taught that Jane Austen was the first woman novelist who mattered, but Sarah Fielding was one of many earlier women who were both influential and massively popular.

Something in Sarah's writing spoke to Jamie's damaged core. Put simply, Sarah Fielding was obsessed with tyranny versus mutual aid. What makes people so eager to inflict misery on anyone less powerful than themselves, when they could achieve better outcomes by working together instead? This question keeps coming back in *David Simple*, whose hero is nearly ruined by his deceitful brother and then goes searching for a true friend, only to find abusers everywhere. Again and again, Sarah's heroes expound a philosophy of kindness and cooperation, putting aside vanity and greed—and most of the time, they find themselves disappointed by other people. Little is known about Sarah's life before she published *David Simple* in her midthirties, but her father was a typical Georgian scoundrel, and the preface to the first edition of *David Simple* says that if this book is successful, it will be the first good fortune the author has ever known.

Sarah's lifelong companion, Jane Collier, also explores the theme of cruelty in *An Essay on the Art of Ingeniously Tormenting*, a satirical handbook for anyone who wants to punch down.

"You need to do more than rehash all the work that's already been done in the past few decades on eighteenth-century women's writing." Ariella shakes her head wearily. "I just don't want to see you fail."

I've cast so many spells, Jamie wishes she could say. *In some of the filthiest, most unregarded places on earth, I have focused all of my eldritch power on pleading for a scrap of knowledge.*

Instead, Jamie says, "I still think *Emily* might be something."

Ariella purses her thin lips. "I'm starting to worry that *Emily* is a dead end."

Right. So *Emily* is a novel from 1749, which Sarah Fielding's distant relation Lady Mary Wortley Montagu attributed to Sarah at the time (along with *The Female Quixote*, which everyone now knows for sure was the work of Charlotte Lennox). Scholars have debated *Emily*'s true authorship for decades, with most of the heavyweights dismissing Sarah out of hand. But Jamie had a feeling—the same instinct that guides her to the perfect magical place—that Lady Mary might have been onto something. There's just something about Emily's quest for companionship that feels like an echo of David Simple's, and the fairy tale that Emily tells to her servant is reminiscent of *The Governess*. Most of all, Jamie is sure this book is full of secrets—secrets that are meant for her specifically—though she couldn't explain why without sounding like a poor scholar.

"I swear, I will pull this together," Jamie says. "I just need a little more time."

Ariella glances at her own cluttered desk, brows twisted, as if she's trying to figure out what she can say without overstepping. "You may not have as much time as you seem to think."

Tell me about it. After the thing where Jamie's stipend got temporarily slashed, she's highly aware that the English department's funding hangs by a thread. Colleges are shuttering whole departments these days or closing down altogether, and the shot-callers view English lit as decorative but lacking in nutritional value, like a butter sculpture of Elvis.

At first, Jamie had to bite her own inner cheek to keep from thinking of Ariella as a maternal figure, because Ariella's silvery hair and assortment of colorful sweaters and paisley silk scarves made her seem nurturing and aspirational. But looking at Ariella now, Jamie doesn't see a mother-substitute at all. Neither of Jamie's mothers were ever this comfortable, and yet this far into uneasy complicity with a fucked system. Ariella has made it clear that she wishes she could offer Jamie the world she was offered at Jamie's age—but she can't, and there's no helping it.

Lately, Jamie watches other PhD students—talented, valiant souls—going on the job market and getting no offers. Grad school feels like the conveyor belt in *Toy Story 3*: Jamie can see the toys just a ways ahead of her tipping into the incinerator. Her only hope is to produce a dissertation so mind-freaking that someone scoops her off the conveyor belt, brushes her fake fur clean, and puts her into a loving home, wherein she shall befriend a spork.

• • • • •

Jamie finds a sandwich bearing her name at the back of the minifridge in the junior common room. And now, she ought to head to her nook in the Goblin Market at the bottom of the library, to keep poring over the correspondence of Sarah Wescomb for any clues about *Emily*. Instead, she gets in the dirt-mobile and drives until she finds herself in Wardmont, the suburb where her family moved when she was in junior high. Jamie didn't plan on ending up here, but soon she's looking at the one-story rowhouse where Serena and Mae used to dance, freak out, and bake chocolate macadamia-nut cookies. Looking through the side window, the kitchen looks unchanged: canary-yellow walls, with a grease-encrusted old stove and a startling turquoise tile floor. As if Jamie could climb in through that window and be a child again, plinking her guitar while her parents fussed around her.

How does Jamie feel, looking at this old house? Wistful, maybe—if wistfulness could sock you in the jaw with a roll of quarters in its fist.

Everyone says nostalgia is about suffering, because of the Greek *algos* meaning pain, but Jamie prefers to think of the *algia* in "nostalgia" as coming from algae. The longing for lost people and places grows at the bottom of your soul, brackish and salty, clogging everything with its endless fronds. Nostalgic people can never want anything cleanly.

Jamie ends up in the abandoned garden where she used to do magic when she was thirteen or fourteen, and of course it looks tiny and squalid now. But she feels the same awareness as in all the best magic places: like a breath of wind from a distant superstorm, as if here is a place where you can touch the edge of something whose epicenter would ruin you. Safe, but also in the presence of danger. Jamie often feels contradictory things, perhaps as a result of growing up in a warm, loving, paranoid household.

As Jamie sets up a spell in the same fallen-down corner where she begged for miracles as a teen, she imagines herself explaining every step to Serena, in a way that hopefully won't throw off the delicate dance of will and thoughtlessness. She homes in on the perfect spot, then lays out her ask: a photocopy of the title page of *Emily,* with "By a Lady" clearly visible. On this paper, she scatters rose petals from her jacket pocket, as if to symbolize the fame she wishes to bring to this anonymous author. And then, from her satchel, a slice of chocolate fudge cake the department secretary saved for her from a party, which she'd been looking forward to eating. She sighs and places it on top of the petals and the page. *Please,* she thinks, *please, I need to know. I can't explain this book fully if I don't know who wrote it.*

(Yes, yes, Death of the Author, but whatever, context can still matter. Shut up.)

Most of the time after Jamie does a working, she gets up and leaves right away, so she won't dwell on what just happened and ruin everything. But this time, she can't help sitting on the slimy earth, staring at the cake and the petals. Coming back to her teenage home feels clarifying: *Emily* swept her away at a time when her faith in the universe was rocky, and even though other texts have lit up her whole mind since then, *Emily* is the one that keeps featuring in her dreams. Some books stay with you even as you evolve, level up, and taste disappointment, and maybe you owe something to those books.

• • • • •

The rare books at Harvard aren't at the Widener Library, the big behemoth at the edge of Harvard Yard—instead, they're at the Houghton Library, at the bottom corner of campus, just across from the Harvard Bookstore. The guard checks Jamie's credentials and waves her inside. On a whim, she requests a box of treatises and pamphlets from this period, all of which were printed by Andrew Millar (who also printed most of the works of both Henry and Sarah Fielding). She handles them gingerly, with fresh gloves, and finds herself paging through a treatise translated by Irish minister Archibald Maclaine on ecclesiastical history, with some added defenses against the criticisms of David Hume. The theology is terribly esoteric, but then she hits pay dirt: wedged between two pages is a scrap of paper. It appears to be a partial draft of a letter from Millar himself to an unidentified person, haggling over terms for publication of a novel that she's sure must be *Emily*.

Millar, as usual, is offering a flat payment up front in exchange for all rights:

Upon perusal of yr MSS, as recommended by our mutual Friend
Mr Richardson, I am prepared to offer £700 for yr literary property,
acting as yr sole agent and bookseller in this matter. I find it indeed
a worthy Undertaking, containing many true Virtues, and appealing
greatly to all readers of the Moral Romance. I found myself quite

affected by yr heroine's instruction of her maid Tilly and by certain
moments in the Ruin'd Abbey.

Knowing as I do that you desire the greater Improvement of yr
impressionable readers, & wt every confidence in the Merit of this
History, I wonder if perhaps Mr Fielding or Mr Richardson might
be prevailed upon to provide an Introduction thereof. Such an
Endorsement cou'd assist greatly in encouraging subscribers, or engaging greater distribution. Mrs. Millar greatly desires yr company,
and please give yr regards to yr esteemed brother the Grammaticus.

The salutation is too smudgy and indistinct to read—curse eighteenth-
century handwriting!—but there are references to the notable facts of *Emily*.

But who is Millar writing to? Whoever it is, they're a friend of Samuel Richardson, author of *Clarissa,* but that doesn't narrow things down
much: Richardson supported many women novelists of the time. (Richardson even befriended Sarah Fielding, even though he was Henry Fielding's
nemesis.) Millar is hoping either Richardson or Henry Fielding will write
a preface to *Emily,* which definitely didn't happen. Jamie's eyes hurt from
trying to decipher these squiggles, but her eye keeps coming back to the
reference to "the Grammaticus." At least, Jamie is pretty sure that's what the
squiggle says, after staring for a full hour.

Jamie hoots out loud, she can't help it—the entire walnut-paneled reading
room turns to glare at her, and she raises her gloved hands in apology. She'll
need to do a happy dance as soon as she's not in the midst of old, irreplace-
able documents.

Still, there's something she's not seeing here. What in the name of Fanny
Hill does "Grammaticus" mean in this context?

She takes several photos of the letter with her phone, then tucks it neatly
back into the folio, where hopefully nobody else will stumble across it any
time soon.

• • • • •

Jamie comes home amped up, ready to tell Ro every last detail about Gavin,
Ariella, and the letter she found. Ro isn't home yet, so Jamie bustles until

Ro stomps through the front door. The look on their face tells Jamie everything she needs to know, even before Ro says "bicuspid."

(Years ago, Jamie and Ro agreed: if either of them says the word "bicuspid," the other one drops everything and goes into emergency best-friend mode. "Bicuspid" basically means, "I've had a shitty day and I don't want to talk about it yet. Please don't ask any questions." Ro's more likely to use this word than Jamie, purely because Ro often doesn't want to rehash the awful details of their bad day while they're still feeling cruddy.)

Mere seconds after Ro has said that word, Jamie has her phone out, to order delivery from Ro's favorite pizza place and to put the soothingest playlist on the Bluetooth speakers. Jamie runs a hot bath, with a bath bomb and some rose petals, and peels off Ro's boots to give them a foot rub: no pressure, just fingertips on the skin for now. As Ro takes off their glasses and lowers into the bath, they look at Jamie. "I didn't even ask how your day was."

"Mixed bag," Jamie says. "Tell you later."

The food is arriving in half an hour. Perfect timing. Jamie leans over the side of the tub, reaching into the caddy for a water-spotted copy of *archy and mehitabel* to read to Ro. They close their eyes, breathing deep through their nose; when Jamie takes her eyes off the page, she sees their shoulders loosen. Ro murmurs, at last, about the horribleness of their day: department politics, microaggressions and misgendering, minor sabotage from their archrival Bettina Quark, more microaggressions, a seminar gone cannibalistic. Jamie puts the book aside and kneads Ro's shoulders in the mulled wine–scented bathwater.

Ro's eyes pop open. "Oh shit. I was so pissed off, I think I left my phone. At the coffee place near campus. They're closing soon, I ought to—"

"Stay. Soak." Jamie lifts off her haunches. "I'll get it. Pizza's coming in fifteen minutes, save me some."

"I love you." Ro closes their eyes again, smiling this time.

It's only a five-minute drive to the coffee place, no big deal. The whole time, Jamie reflects on the paradox that she never feels more taken care of than when she's able to do something nice for her partner—maybe because that level of trust is the warmest, softest embrace you could possibly have.

• • • • •

The next morning, Jamie wakes still basking. Ro has one hand wrapped around her waist and she can feel their breath on her neck, and she doesn't know what she did to deserve this splendor. She could stay in bed the rest of the day—literally, it's Saturday—but when she closes her eyes again, something pops into her head and she's blazingly awake.

She says out loud: "Arthur Collier."

Ro mumbles, "Wha?"

"Okay, so the word 'grammaticus' could mean literally someone who studies grammar, but it came to mean a teacher of Latin and Greek. Millar is teasing his correspondent about knowing classical languages, something that was pretty controversial for a woman at the time. And wouldn't you know it? Arthur Collier taught Latin and Greek to Sarah Fielding, Hester Thrale . . . and his sister Jane." Jamie sits up, her brain on fire. "Jane Collier! Oh my god, this changes everything, I am on fire! Sarah Fielding didn't write *Emily*—her best friend Jane Collier did!"

Ro groans into their pillow, then turns their half-open eyes toward Jamie. "If you're going to talk about your research first thing in the morning, you're bringing me coffee in bed."

"It would be my greatest honor." Another minute to psych herself up, then Jamie bounces out of bed and goes into the tiny kitchen where she grapples with the eternal AeroPress-or-French-press dilemma for a heroically short time.

Jamie's brain itches. The whole way through breakfast, she pieces it together in her mind.

The year *Emily* was published, 1749, was a big one for Jane Collier. Jane's mother died, and she had some kind of falling out with her brother Arthur, so she moved out of his housing and became a governess to Samuel Richardson's children. We know Jane was close to Richardson before that—and *Emily* reads very much like a response to Richardson's novels *Pamela* and *Clarissa,* which Jane probably read early drafts of.

Pamela is about a maid who fends off the advances of her employer, Mr. B., until he finally marries her. *Clarissa* is about a woman who runs away from home and ends up at the mercy of the rake Mr. Lovelace, whose advances she rebuffs until he rapes her and she kills herself. Both stories are about women struggling to live according to contradictory rules of good behavior, while dealing with men who do whatever they want.

Emily, meanwhile, feels like a fable in which a young woman plays by the rules and still controls her own life. Jamie has been unable to shake the feeling that whoever wrote *Emily* was queer, and that the novel represents a queering of the "moral romance" genre that was popular at the time. Underneath the main plot about a dutiful daughter trying to marry well and please her father, there's another narrative, one which feels like negative space, and emerges in Emily's sly, sarcastic asides. The sarcasm feels of a piece with the vicious satire in the book we know Jane Collier wrote, *An Essay on the Art of Ingeniously Tormenting.* And yeah, there's a fairy tale about a princess and a traveling performer, which is told in interludes in between the main story and feels a bit reminiscent of some parts of *The Cry: A New Dramatic Fable,* which Sarah and Jane apparently co-wrote.

If Jamie could make a strong enough case that Jane Collier was the author of *Emily,* she could build a crystal structure around it, encompassing all of her obsessions about women's roles in the mid-eighteenth century and the shifting nature of storytelling. And knowing who wrote the book makes this whole thing feel more personal, not less, as though Jamie is getting to know an old friend in a new way—or as though untangling the roots of this book will somehow give Jamie the wisdom to get to the bottom of her own personal mysteries. This makes no sense, but it feels true nonetheless.

"My brain could eat a horse," Jamie tells Ro.

"Okey doke," Ro says. "I mean, the main thing I learned in the one art class I took is that horses have pickles for bodies."

For some reason, this brings to mind the horse field near Serena's schoolhouse. Jamie can't let too much time pass before she gives Serena a proper lesson in magic after the Hat Incident. But she doesn't know how to tell Ro that she's going back down to the one-room schoolhouse in Old Wollston, NH (thus named to distinguish itself from Wollston, the trashy neighboring town where they built all the textile mills and birch-beer distilleries back in olden times). Not that Ro will disapprove of Jamie spending time with her mother, exactly—they might think it's a little weird, and possibly symptomatic of some sort of quarter-life crisis. Or they'll suggest that perhaps Serena needs to go live in assisted living, which is way too soon and honestly would destroy what's left of her.

But when she and Ro are heading out for lunch in Inman Square with some friends, Ro pauses in the apartment doorway and says, "I think you should go check on your mom again."

"Really?" Jamie is so startled, she puts her arm in the wrong jacket sleeve. "I was thinking I should. But I don't want . . ."

Ro smiles. "I know you've been worrying about her. She's important to you. You're lucky to have a close family member left."

Jamie leans forward and kisses Ro: first on the cheek, then even more lightly on the lips. "I love you so much. You have no idea. I just adore you with every brain cell and blood vessel and nerve ending."

Ro pulls her closer and gives her one of the kisses that make her half swoon. "I love you, too. Just drive safe, okay? And get home before dark if you can."

The next morning, Ro needs to hand in more chapters of their dissertation, which gets longer and longer and is about diminishing returns. So Jamie kisses them, stuffs a bag with extra layers of clothing and protein bars, and hops in the dirtmobile. She listens to K-pop the entire drive down to the schoolhouse.

i

Sure, everyone wants to be a dyke now; they crave our freedom, guts, and knowing looks. When I saw a paparazzi photo of Axl Rose of Guns N' Roses wearing a "Nobody Knows I'm a Lesbian" tee-shirt, I didn't waste two seconds thinking about him. I looked a little closer at the picture because the woman who gave him that shirt must surely be in the background.

—*SUSIE BRIGHT'S SEXWISE* BY
SUSIE BRIGHT, CLEIS PRESS, 1995

Serena and Mae used to say they'd joined together using words that no-body would understand anymore. Serena had been a "soft butch," Mae a "stone femme," and the two of them had formed a "domestic partnership." These things had mattered, not just as labels but as statements of intent and fealty.

Serena Decker and Mae Sandthorn met in the ladies' room of a club near Central Square at a riot grrrl music show. The band was called something like Razor Maid or Monster Beauty or Death Fuck, and they clanged out the same few chords with a vicious insecurity. All of their songs were about the bass player's unrequited love for the tragically straight drummer—actually they might have been called Tragically Straight. Mae was wearing Doc Martens and a Laura Ashley dress with a shredded lower hem, and Serena had a denim jacket, *Tank Girl* T-shirt, and leather biker pants and boots, because she had an actual motorcycle parked out front. Serena was on a date with Louise, who had confessed that she wasn't attracted to women but had decided after reading Andrea Dworkin that heterosexuality was immoral. So Serena was hiding in the bathroom in the hopes that Louise would get bored and leave—because Serena was only ever good at confrontation when she believed someone deserved to be destroyed. (Or if they attacked first.) Mae kept wandering into the bathroom to pee or work on her graffiti masterpiece, and she noticed Serena hiding out in there.

"Tourists," Mae said.

"What?" Serena stared back.

"Tourists," Mae said again. "That's why I keep taking refuge in this dirty old restroom. These girls keep giving me a spiteful lip-curl, like I'm ruining their perfect Lilith Fair vibe. Why are *you* hiding out in here?"

"Bad date." Serena explained about Andrea Dworkin.

"Ah. Your bad date sounds a lot like one of the girls who keep giving me stink eye. So . . . do you want to go out there and brave the club together?"

Serena shook her head.

"Or do you just want to keep hiding in the bathroom? And if so, would you like some company?"

Serena nodded, twice. Yes to both.

A few minutes later, Serena was pressed up against the sticker-covered tile wall, with Mae's right hand caressing her face, while Mae's left hand pulled at her belt, kissing, groping, biting (gently), grinding. Louise the political lesbian walked in just as Mae had Serena's belt in both hands. (Years later, Louise became a campaigner against trans women's inclusion in women's spaces, and Serena was not terribly surprised.)

· · · · ·

Mae and Serena didn't go home together that night, but they met again a few days later at a rally to protest against the Defense of Marriage Act. A few dozen people raised a proper commotion in front of the John F. Kennedy Federal Building, a pair of brutalist wedges designed by Walter Gropius. Serena stood with some of the Boston Lesbian Avengers, holding hands with Lottie and Ying. Nearby, a smaller group of counterprotestors huddled, baleful, waving signs about the sickness of homosexuality.

Serena concentrated on staring down the homophobe contingent, especially one red-faced man who seemed to toy with hurling a glass bottle across the divide. Feet planted, shoulders plum level, making herself a brick wall. So she didn't even notice Mae at first.

And then Mae was the only thing Serena could look at—shimmying in a canary-yellow hoop skirt and a peacock-green bustier with diagonal slashes across the ribs that "bled" bright red tulle and ribbons. Curves on glorious display, round face alive and defiant, shouting about love. Serena, who never hesitated to talk to anyone, felt suddenly shy. Mae saw Serena, smiled, and then turned her attention back to the Gropius complex.

The next time Serena glanced, Mae was leaning close to Wendy Preston, as if the two of them were whispering. Serena had dated Wendy for a few weeks, until they'd had a screaming fight about nothing in the middle of Kim Airs's birthday bash (in the lull between performances by Double Dong and Chucklebucket). Well, that tore it: Mae would never go on a proper date with Serena now. Probably it was time for Serena to move again, to another city where she didn't have so many exes (yet).

But then Serena kept running into Mae: at the Milky Way Lanes, at the Lizard Lounge, at a picnic in Boston Common near the duck boats. Mae had a way of laughing behind the back of her hand, as if scandal were afoot. She moved through the world in a billow of pink flutters, exuding shyness and a deep love of trouble. Mae had written an essay in a local zine about being okay with uncertainty, with never knowing what would happen or what other people were really thinking, and it snagged in Serena's mind.

Three weeks after the bathroom make-out session, Serena realized: she was developing a crush.

Serena didn't do crushes, not since her early twenties. Her last several relationships had started with mutual attraction and grown into mutual understanding, and that's how things were supposed to work. She felt like a schoolgirl, pining for somebody she didn't even know. Time to nip this in the bud: Serena took a couple weekend trips to New York and Northampton, tried to avoid going to places in the Boston area where she would see Mae.

It didn't help—she kept daydreaming about Mae's wicked gray eyes and the way she could flip from bashful to bratty. She was stuck, it was bad.

Somebody bombed a lesbian club in Atlanta, with the same M.O. as a notorious abortion-clinic bomber. Everybody sprung into high alert, planning marches of solidarity and watching out for copycat attacks. Serena was at an emergency meeting at someone's house, eating potluck polenta fritters, and she found herself in the kitchen washing dishes next to Mae. Serena washed, Mae dried.

"It's fucking awful," Mae said as she swiped the dishcloth in crisp lines. "They'll never let us live. They want to control us, and they'll never stop. They can't stand to see us flourish."

"I know," Serena said, scrubbing harder than she needed to. "But it's not up to them. They don't get to decide. We fought too hard to be here. We marched and organized and made our own spaces, we built something real, and they can't get rid of us." The water sloshed wildly—or, wait, Serena was splashing, attacking the dirty plate with her whole body. Mae came closer and put down the dishcloth.

Mae and Serena exchanged a look, until Serena felt herself subside. All Mae said was, "Let's change places. I'll wash, you dry." Serena nodded and gave Mae the sponge and brush with mock-formality, bowing slightly. Mae did a little curtsy.

Someone had forgotten to bring paper plates, so the same plates and bowls kept getting washed and reused. Serena and Mae hung out in the kitchen for an hour, holding space over the soothing gurgle of the sink filling and emptying over and over.

"I really like what you wrote," Serena said, "in that zine. When you said that the most important things are always the things we can't know. Like, that's why we have poetry. That's why we have music, and dancing, and books of queer theory that make your head spin. We can't predict what'll happen, or whether we'll be alive tomorrow. We can't even be sure what already happened. But we can hold onto a feeling, we can all share a feeling together, and that makes us stronger. Fuck, I'm not explaining it right. You said it way better in your essay."

Serena was washing again. Mae took a plate from her but did not start drying it. She just held it, a useless mirror, dripping onto the floor.

"You read my thing." Mae breathed. "I didn't know what I was talking about."

"Well," Serena said, "it spoke to me. It's what I needed to hear right now."

"I don't really think the only reason we have music and art is because we can't know stuff," Mae said. "I think music is awesome and fun to dance to." She finally swept the towel across the plate.

"Very true. We can't let the bastards keep us from dancing." Serena scooted a woven mat with her toe, to sop up the tiny puddle underfoot. "Dancing is great. Would you . . . want to go dancing with me sometime?"

Mae bit her lip, eyes on the plate.

Serena's heart couldn't quite manage to beat, it thrummed all out of whack. She let the cup in her hand subside back into the plastic tub full of soapy water. *Please,* she was yelling inside her head, *please just give me this chance, I really really like you.* She tried to keep her face even.

"Listen," Serena said. "I don't know what you've heard about me, from Wendy or whoever. Probably all of it is true, but it's not the whole story. I don't . . . I don't know what I can say, except that I really like you, and I want to get to know you, and I promise if you give me a chance, I'll treat you right." She was very aware that she'd descended to giving Mae puppy-dog eyes. She only hoped it worked.

"Okay, fine," Mae said. "We'll dance. But I lead, you follow."

"Always." Serena smiled and whipped up suds.

· · · · ·

Serena never decided to move in with Mae. She just spent more and more time at Mae's studio apartment, until she realized it'd been days since she'd been home and it was silly to keep paying her share of rent on the three-bedroom loft she shared with Vallie and Dee.

When Serena brought her stuff over to Mae's, she faced the book dilemma: do you merge your libraries? Do you unbox all of your books? Everything else was simple by comparison. Did they really need two copies of Audre Lorde's *Sister Outsider*? But also, how should they organize their books—by topic, by genre, by vague association? Which books are close companions that need to be reachable at a moment's notice, and which are more like friendly presences you can gaze at from a distance? Torrid romances have ended over less.

Serena decided to let Mae organize the books. She hung a tapestry her friend had made, showing a virgin and a unicorn wearing sunglasses and playing musical instruments.

They settled into a wobbly routine: Serena cooked Sunday dinner, to cushion the impending blow of Monday. Most weeks they went out to a few music shows and queer spoken-word events as a couple, and once or twice a month they went clubbing. They mostly sat and watched other people dance, from a corner quiet enough to talk in a normal voice, their faces upshadowed by a single candle caught in red glass. They took every opportunity to dress up in rockabilly outfits, semi-formal wear, or whatever finery they'd scored from the dollar-a-pound bins at The Garment District.

Was Mae waiting for Serena to get bored with her and disappear? Serena couldn't tell—Mae clearly had heard about Serena's heartbreaker rep, and Serena didn't know how to prove this situation was different. In Serena's darkest moments, she was terrified that everyone was right, and she would let Mae down in spite of herself.

But no, her attachment kept deepening instead of fading. Maybe the thing she'd dismissed as childish, her "schoolgirl crush," was actually evidence that she was getting (slightly) more mature? Maybe she'd lacked the capacity to lay herself open to someone until now. This felt true, but it might be wishful thinking. Serena prayed she would have the strength to live up to the things she was feeling right now.

In any case, Serena couldn't find a way to talk about any of this without sounding corny, like a pickup line. *I've never felt like this before. You're not like the other girls.*

The only cure was time. Relationships did not grow steadily, they grew at the speed of intimacy and trust—which was to say, slowly except for the occasional headlong leap. All they could do is keep dressing up, going to puppy adoption events without ever adopting a puppy, reading to each other in silly voices. Serena did run into Wendy at a drag-king performance at Milky Way Lanes, both of them waiting to order drinks. Serena muttered something like, *Good to see you, I like what you did with your hair,* and Wendy made pleasant noises back.

Each of Serena's past relationships had ended with a fight over nothing: someone had bought the wrong kind of mustard, or said something about a television show. People spar about trivial shit when they don't want to talk about the real reasons they're fighting or they've run out of things to say. Or when the strain of proprioception, the nearness of another human, gets to be too much. Doesn't matter: you can't resolve a meaningless fight, and you definitely can't win one.

Serena was still freelancing as a journalist, writing for alt-weeklies and lefty magazines, but also for niche publications like *Knee Replacement Observer* and *Funeral Director Biweekly,* which meant a headset was always glued to her face as she typed frantically to capture everything people were telling her about housing discrimination, abusive policing, keyhole surgeries and how to upsell urns and caskets. Occasionally Serena made eye contact with Mae when she asked someone an especially outlandish question about white-supremacist terrorism, or how to keep dogs out of an open casket, and Mae would try her best to crack Serena up.

She was already starting to think about going to law school, driven by an itch on the roof of her mouth when she wrote articles about systemic violence and corruption, only to see a moment of outrage but no real change. The itch only grew thirstier whenever a knot of white men in ugly parkas tried to face down the Lesbian Avengers at one of their actions: scowling, snarling. Serena hesitated to bring up the law-school thing with Mae, a confirmed dilettante who harbored skepticism about anyone who built too much of their identity around a career. This month Mae was dabbling in fashion design, but a month ago she was a concert photographer. Every few months she was a zinester.

Given that Serena was already worried that Mae might think she had one foot out the door, the last thing she wanted to do was announce that she was going places.

. . . . .

Mae came home with a beach tote full of sex toys from Grand Opening, plus a few books with titles like *The Great Big Book of Super Hot Lesbian Sex for Lesbians*. Mae was smiling and showing off the purple silicone vibrator and the strap-on and all the clamps and plugs, and Serena felt brittle. This pile of colorful shapes was too much: the exact sort of grand gesture you make to salvage a relationship that's dying from the inside out.

Mae was doing *The Price Is Right* motions, humming, grinning. Then she saw something in Serena's face and paused. "What is it?"

"Uh, nothing." Serena stammered. Then she said, "I just wanted... You're not, like, worried about us, are you? This isn't because you think we need any help? Because you know I'm crazy about you." She had just written a whole feature about communication in relationships for a gay magazine in Atlanta a few hours earlier, but now she couldn't speak anything but drivel. Why was it so hard to talk about anything real?

Mae recoiled, as if she'd made a fool of herself. Trying too hard, coming on too strong. She started putting everything back into the tote. "I'm pretty sure I can return it all for store credit or something. I'm sorry, I didn't mean..."

Serena leaned forward and reached out, not quite touching Mae or the bag. "No, no. I didn't mean... I love this stuff. I just worry. I worry all the time."

"About?"

Oh fuck, now she'd done it. Serena was going to have to wrench open the entire can of worms and cast their wriggling bodies across the floor.

"I worry that I don't do a good enough job of showing you..." Serena shook her head. "I love you so much. I haven't ever loved anyone like this before. You're the first person I've ever lived with—the first person I've wanted to build a life with. I know I've got a bad reputation, and I earned it. I just want to find a way to prove to you that this is real, that..." She was talking in circles, repeating herself.

Mae had shrunk to the far end of the fainting couch, away from the bag of toys and Serena. Now she leaned forward a little. "That's it? *That's* what you've been stressing out about this whole time?" She shook her head and made a clicking noise in her throat. "You do realize that I dated other people before, too? I wasn't a blushing virgin when we got together. I have exes out there who could tell some stories, most of them are even true. Being a femme doesn't make me helpless, much as some butches would like to think otherwise. If anything, us femmes have to be tougher than anybody. Just remember who pushed who against a bathroom wall when we first met."

Now Serena was pretty sure she was blushing, remembering the sticky tiles against her neck and the backs of her hands. "Point taken."

"Listen, we might break up." Mae saw Serena's look of alarm, and hastily added: "Not today, I hope. Not anytime soon. But one of these days, sure, we could break up. What matters isn't that we stay together forever, but the way you treat me while we are together. If you started taking me for granted, ignoring me, going out without me all the time, *that* would be a problem."

Serena felt a weird mixture of shame, adoration, and horniness. She'd never been able to have this kind of relationship conversation before. The vulnerability was a lot—it was more than being shoved against a hundred bathroom walls. Her nipples had come alive, they could feel every cotton fiber in her long-sleeve shirt.

"How—" Serena locked eyes with Mae and let all of her insecurity show even though her mouth had a faint smile. "How am I doing so far?"

"I'd say you're a solid B, maybe B-plus. How am I doing?"

"Oh, you're an A-plus-plus," Serena chuckle-growled. "You are on the freaking dean's list." Her eye traveled to the bag of sex toys. She suddenly wanted to try them all out, right now—why did exposing her emotional underbelly make her so fucking hot?—but she'd probably ruined the moment.

"I love you, too," Mae said. "Even though you're way too high on yourself. 'Bad reputation,' my ass. I've dated people with worse reputations than you before breakfast." She leaned forward so they were almost kissing. Serena could taste that kiss, she needed it more than anything.

"What does that even mean—" Serena breathed.

"Shut up." Mae kissed her, and Serena fucking melted.

. . . . .

For the first time in Serena's adult life, she had a stable living situation. She was helping to build something, instead of just occupying space. It was hard, and exhausting, and you couldn't just walk away when shit went wrong. Serena and Mae fought plenty: Serena showed up late for dinner because of a deadline crunch, Mae bought ingredients for a meringue and let them go moldy in the fridge, they agreed to spend a weekend at the Cape with friends when neither of them actually wanted to go. But the fights felt like mortar between the bricks.

Serena felt a muscle-cluster relax inside herself, like she was letting go of the expectation of loneliness—but at the same time, she felt her senses heighten, grow vigilant, because now she had something to protect.

Serena and Mae went out to brunch with some of their friends, and Lottie had her new baby, Eve, in a sling around her chest as Ying fussed and cooed. Baby Eve was bloody adorable, fuzzy-headed and hypercurious, and Serena had never seen Lottie and Ying look so blissed out. "We haven't slept! In weeks!" Lottie sounded as though she was describing a party where the walls were made of cake. "We made a person!" Serena couldn't help holding out a finger for Eve to seize in her tiny hand, cooing like a pigeon, hiding and revealing her own face.

A man on the row of television screens was droning about healthy families, while the screen showed a book called *Heather Has Two Mommies*, which people were once again trying to ban. "Incapable of having a healthy home life." The man had a boiled-egg face and shellacked hair. "Every child needs a mother and a father." Blah blah blah.

People at a few tables yelled until they changed the channel. But Serena could see Ying and Lottie looking at their baby, as if a hurricane could yank Eve away from them at any moment.

"Progress always brings a backlash," Serena said. "It's like physics."

"It doesn't feel like a backlash," Mae muttered. "It feels like the same shit forever."

Ying was leaning on Lottie's shoulder, so her face was close to Eve's. "I know there'll always be people who hate our family," she said in a low voice. "But they can choke on their hate for all I care."

It wasn't that long ago that a Virginia court had taken a child away from his mother, purely because she was in a relationship with another woman. Massachusetts had come down on the side of supporting lesbian moms, but it might not take that much to turn the entire country to Virginia's side of the argument. (Which made Serena think, once again, about law school.)

Serena and Mae agreed: they never wanted to bring a kid into this ugly world.

A few months passed. Serena found a pamphlet about artificial insemination, and she started touching her own stomach, trying to imagine. Mae found the pamphlet sitting in a pile of Serena's stuff, and raised an eyebrow. And then somehow, in one conversation, they went from debating the idea to discussing logistics.

"I was scared to tell you how much I wanted this," Mae said.

"Me too," Serena said. "It's okay to be scared. Sometimes fear is just a signpost to the thing you want most."

. . . . .

When Serena was pregnant, she and Mae finally scrounged up enough to get a place with a bedroom. (Doesn't matter who the sperm donor was; they're not part of the story.) Serena had to keep working right up until the eighth or ninth month, because Mae's several careers were not lucrative enough, but Serena did give herself permission to take naps for once. "It turns out naps are resplendent," Serena drawled as she woke up one afternoon. "Why did nobody tell me? I feel like an empress."

For months, Serena and Mae were stalked by the Larkin Prophecy. It was Mae who first quoted that notorious Philip Larkin poem about how your mum and dad will inevitably fuck you up—or in this case, your mum and mum. They stayed up late one night swearing that wouldn't be them, or at least they'd do a better job than their own birth families. Eventually, it became a verb. "Stop Larkining," Mae would say. "You Larkined first," Serena would respond. "I'm just Larkining your Larkin." At night, Serena would burrow as deep as she could into Mae's big spoon, and whisper promises to her own belly button that she might not be able to keep.

Here's the thing: neither Mae nor Serena had grown up in ideal situations. Serena was the classic surprise final child, born when her parents had already raised nine others, and her father had died when she was small. Serena's mom had immigrated from Estonia as a child, and she used to say during bouts of severe depression that she could never go home because of the Soviet occupation. Serena wound up being raised by siblings who acted like capricious gods: sometimes spoiling her, more often tormenting. *You're so lucky, you're the baby of the family, you get to do whatever you want, plus you never had to deal with Dad's bullshit,* they'd say before launching her downhill in a shopping cart. Mae, meanwhile, had grown up in an evangelical household where her behavior was endlessly policed, and at age fifteen she'd caught the eye of the son of one of her father's friends, so her family started talking about wedding plans for her sixteenth birthday. Mae had ditched before she could get hitched, and by age seventeen she was an emancipated minor.

Mae's theory was that all they had to do was keep their queer community close at hand, so Jamie would always have a million aunties and nuncles around. Serena, though, had grown up in an unconventional family, and couldn't shake the sense that at a certain point, all the aunties go home and leave you alone with your kid. "What we need," Mae said, "is accountability. To each other. To our friends. No secrets. We'll share everything, the good and the bad."

Once Jamie was born, they just wanted to hold her all the time—they went all in on attachment parenting—and they stopped worrying about the Larkin of it all. Instead, they speculated endlessly about whether their child would turn out to be straight. They comforted each other by pointing out that no matter what, Jamie would be "culturally queer," having been brought up in a gay-as-hell household and exposed to positive queer role models. (Jamie's parents thought they were raising a boy named R____, and didn't realize their mistake for years.) Serena never wanted to admit out loud that she kind of hoped this kid would wind up being cis and hetero, because she didn't want her child to have to wade through all the sewage that still clung to the legs of every queer person she knew.

Let this baby have an easy life, she prayed as Jamie nursed. *Peaches and fucking cream.* But she'd already seen what life did with her fondest dreams, so she wasn't exactly getting her hopes up.

Dearest Sally,

Since the moment you stepped onto that coach to London with your esteemed brother, my whole heart has yearned toward you. My love for you is of the purest kind, as South writes: such a love that is *the great instrument of nature, the bond and cement of society, the spirit and spring of the universe.*

Yet am I not the only one who thinks of you. Harris asks after you with every breath, as he desires nothing so much as your conversation, and my brother likewise mentions you often. I have also seen your sisters Ursula and Kitty around town, and they wait eagerly for your every letter. They hope, as I do, that you have been able to visit with your great aunt Cottington in Westminster.

This current separation is the longest that you and I have had since my calamitous stint as a Companion to she who shall not be named. I know you will understand my earnest sobriety when I say your absence vexes and taxes me near as much as the teazing I experienced in the service of her Ladyship. I read books and scribble my silly thoughts as always—but without you here in our reading circle, ready to discuss every last thing, I scarce feel as though it matters.

Have I truly read a book, if you are not here to discuss it with me?

I comfort myself in your absence by reading every worthy text that my hands may lay claim to; and yet every word my eyes scan, I only miss your conversation all the more. Pray do not take this to be any form of reproach, for I am so pleased that you have been able to introduce yourself to the much greater society in London; yet, know that there are those here in Sarum who love you and think fondly of you.

Now I must ask the most pressing question on everyone's mind: have you heard Mr. Handel's *Atalanta*? Did you somehow attend the premiere performance? They say sheet music will be printed soon, but to appreciate Mr. Handel's genius needs must require hearing his work given voice by those who are among the greatest singers of our time. I have read that fireworks accompanied Mr. Handel's lofty melodies, and he so affectingly captured the story of a king disguised as a shepherd who falls in love with a princess disguised as a huntress. How ornate were the costumes and the furnishings? If you saw it, pray share every last detail, that I may imagine the spectacle for myself.

I fear that after spending so much time in the greatest city in the World, you will upon your return find Sarum rather mean by comparison. I hope one day to know London as you now know it, as one who dwells therein and grows familiar with all of its delights. But more than anything, I await your return here with the greatest eagerness.

As many varied sentiments as a heart may feel, from the most sublime affection to the basest malice, there surely exists a flower for each and every one. Tho' the antient goddess Flora has scarce furnished enough flowering shrubs and plants to express the fullness of my regard for you—every nosegay in the world would scarce suffice.

And yet, I find that no flower exists, nor could exist, to represent the wild and inexpressible wonders you and I have brushed against. I fear that language itself may prove insufficient, or that the proper words have yet to be invented. Perhaps a jonquil, or a sprightly hyacinth, may signify that which cannot be spoken, or even understood? A sweetbriar? Nay, I shall choose the lowly daisy, that flower which grows everywhere and is scarce regarded.

I have chattered overmuch already, and I regret I have no real news to share as yet—you being only a short time gone, no matter how long my heart may insist your absence has already lasted. Please write back and tell me everything of London, sparing no detail. I await your correspondence and remain always,

Yours more than my own, JENNY COLLIER

4

Mr. Toby Langthrope attracted admirers wherever he went, displaying as he did the most elegant and graceful fashions and a notable air of worldly wisdom, borne of wide travel and varied experience. O handsome man!—Ah, how charmingly he speaks! cried all the ladies who had occasion to see him. Even Emily's normally forthright maid, Tilly, lowered her eyes and blushed in his presence. Alone among the gentlewomen of her acquaintance, Emily mistrusted Mr. Langthrope, whom she believed a most profligate rake whose designs could end only in ruin.

Emily was attending Divine services at church, listening modestly to the lessons and sermons therein, but upon her departure found Mr. Langthrope directly in her path, as an oxcart might block the progress of a carriage. Said Mr. Langthrope: My heart, which until now withstood the beauty of many most illustrious ladies, finds itself helpless, agonized—in the presence of your innocent grace. He entreated her to send him hence and give him permission to die, for if he had no hopes of her favour, much less her esteem, he could have no prospect of remaining alive.

One who is as hale as yourself should not jest about mortality, Emily reproached with the merest hint of a smile—I fear you mock me, sir.

Nay, protested he. 'Tis cruelty on your part, to refrain from compassionating the depth of my suffering.

Emily saw that he would continue in so dramatic a fashion until evening had descended, so she resolved to cut short this interlude. I pray you, sir, trouble me no further, said she—for my father has schooled me from a young age in the seven cardinal virtues, both natural and theological, and I would not upon any consideration disgrace his lessons with imprudent intercourse.

Ah, virtue, said Mr. Langthrope. Know you the dual meanings of the word? For the wits of London speak not of virtues, cardinal or otherwise, but rather of virtu, from the Italian, which forms the root of the word virtuoso, and refers to the good and wholesome appreciation of works of art. How, he asked, can the love of beauty be wrong, or the pursuit of aesthetic splendor? Such virtue as denies the pursuit of embellishment is indeed no virtu at all. Thus, mightily pleased with his own wit, he took his leave.

—*EMILY: A TALE OF PARAGONS AND DELIVERANCE*
BY A LADY, BOOK 3, CHAPTER 17

Jamie leads Serena down a dirt path through a tangle of rusted farm equipment, then a moss-eaten graveyard and a grapevine gone wild. They keep passing spots that are *almost* abandoned enough, but not quite. Jamie can sense her mother's gaze, her troubled hypervigilance, so familiar from all the making-it-work-the-best-I-can parenting when she was little. It's weird: one moment, they're two adults hanging out, and the next, they're mother and daughter.

"What?" Jamie says without turning around.

"Are you unhappy? I thought you were having a good life, up there in the city. Ro, your students, your research . . . you seemed to have found your place." Jamie's mother scrutinizes her, same as when eleven-year-old Jamie insisted that she'd done all her homework, and Serena suspected Jamie had been playing video games. "I just want you to be happy. Tell me you're happy, I will back off."

Neither of them really knows how to talk to the other without Mae in the mix. That's why all of their conversations have been so empty, so polite, the past several years.

"I am, Mom. I am happy."

"Because if you're not—if you need anything—I know I've been a hermit, I haven't been a resource, but I'm still your mother, and I would do whatever it takes—"

"I'm *fine*. My life is good, I'm doing well."

"But . . . then *why*?" Serena stops in her tracks. "Why do you need to do this? If you're happy, then what's the point?"

"It's a spiritual practice. It's a cool thing that almost nobody else can do."

"You get lost in the woods, you root around in the dirt, you dig through other people's trash. I could understand if you were miserable and needed a way out."

"I'm happy. I'm not content. There's a meaningful distinction. Henry Fielding says—"

"If you're going to start quoting one of your theory nerds at me, then never mind."

"Henry Fielding was not a theory nerd! He was perhaps the greatest comic novelist who ever lived."

"I thought Alison Bechdel was the best at comic novels."

"That's *graphic* novels, and—" Jamie realizes Serena is trolling. She knows exactly who Henry Fielding was, and what the term 'comic novel' means.

"So you didn't decide to teach me how to make wishes because you thought I was unhappy?" Serena asks.

Jamie doesn't know how to answer that. So she retreats into pedantry.

"We're not making wishes. That would imply there's someone out there who grants boons: some sort of djinn, or faerie. And that there's a transaction taking place, with fixed rules. This is more like, you figure out what you really want—not what you think you should want, or what you're willing to settle for, or what you let anger and resentment prod you into grasping at. And then you have to find something, an object or a symbol or a synecdoche, to represent that desire in its purest form. And then leave a small offering to the universe, and get out of the way, and try to forget what you just did."

Serena stands still and regards Jamie with wonderment, or admiration. Or just pity?

"You spent a lot of time figuring this out."

"I had my whole teenage years to try things."

Jamie spies the perfect location: another abandoned garden, ringed with shredded chicken wire and full of withered and denuded shrubs, except for one gorgeously blossoming pea vine. She gestures for her mom to shush, and crouches in the dirt, feeling for the right level of softness, the faint tingling that says potential.

There, in the far corner: a spot where someone dug a furrow, and a splintering Popsicle stick pokes up out of the dirt.

Jamie talks through every step, methodically, out loud. Her neck and forearms tighten, because she's trained herself never to speak this secret to anyone—to the point where she's had nightmares about letting something slip—but in the wake of the Hat Disaster, there's nothing for it.

"I find the spot that someone put a lot of themself into, which nature is reclaiming, or maybe it's halfway between natural and artificial. There's a kind of hum. You can feel it. Then I try to see what the space is waiting for."

"Waiting for?" Serena wrinkles her nose.

"Like, unfinished business. Just, what could have become of this place, if either side of the push and pull had won? What sort of entreaties is it likely to be open to receiving?" Jamie gestures. "Depending how you look at it, either this garden is being reclaimed by the local ecosystem, or it's been overrun by weeds, which are kind of a mixed bag. Like I'm sure that's poison oak, but over here are some gorgeous dandelions."

"So which do we do?" Serena frowns at the mess. "Do we uproot the weeds, or tear down what's left of the garden? I didn't bring my gloves."

"Neither. We leave it as is. We offer something else to channel all of that tension into—a different sort of overgrown garden to revitalize."

Jamie rummages in her messenger bag. She never leaves home without some potential spells, because you never know, plus a lot of her "spells" are just random artifacts of her life. In any case, it falls into her hand: the paper assignment she gave her students last week, all about George Eliot, William Thackeray, and Elizabeth Gaskell, social realism and upheaval. In a couple days, she'll have seventy-seven essays to grade. So she folds the assignment page and concentrates on what she wants: for those essays to be decent and not too painful to read, or else for some miraculous last-minute help with grading, if Walmouth suddenly has time. Then she draws a crude picture of one of the dandelions on the paper and sits a moment longer.

"Is the picture part of the process?" Serena jolts her out of her blank mind-state.

"Not really, I guess. I like to give a little encouragement." Jamie places a piece of vegan teriyaki jerky on top. "The main thing is to be very specific and yet incredibly vague about what I want. Like in this case, I don't want to be overloaded with half-assed papers to grade. The papers could turn out to be dandelions instead of poison oak, or I could get some help weeding them, or something else could happen."

"So . . . why not just ask for something bigger? Like some kind of fancy fellowship? A job at Harvard? Or even winning the lottery, so you don't have to worry about money?"

"I don't know. That sounds greedy. I'm not sure if I want any of those things, so it probably wouldn't work. And if it did, I could never explain. It would be weird."

Serena nods, though she clearly still thinks that Jamie's being too timid. She had this same look when Jamie was afraid to get in the shallow end of the swimming pool, after all the lessons she paid for.

"Listen, Mom. Remember when I was eight or nine and you tried to teach me about delayed gratification?"

Serena nods.

"I thought you were just being mean, and even Mae was kind of taken aback. I heard the two of you whispering about parenting styles. I really wanted a My Little Pony, and it would take weeks to save up my allowance, and I was sure they would sell out, and I kept walking by Toys 'R' Us and hitting refresh on all the websites. You insisted I had to learn to wait, or life would swallow me whole."

"Didn't I buy you that toy? After about a week, if I recall."

"Yes. You found some excuse to bump up my allowance, or 'reward' me for something. And once I had the toy in my hands, you sat me down and told me this wasn't only about teaching me to save up for things I wanted, though it was partly about that—thanks for indoctrinating me into the petite bourgeoisie—it was also about making sure I really wanted the thing. Because if I still wanted it after a week, then I must have a sincere desire, rather than a passing fancy."

"Always wondered about that phrase." Jamie's mom chortles. "What happens to the fancies that *fail*? So . . . you're saying I need to delay my gratification? You do realize I've spent the past six years doing nothing but obsess. I think my gratification has been sufficiently delayed."

"You're engaging in rhetorical shortcuts again. I just explained—it's not the delay, it's the certainty of what you really want."

Jamie knows all of her mother's discursive modes by heart. There are the questions without good answers, the silent treatment mixed with non sequiturs (which is usually when she's pissed or preoccupied), or the rambling anecdote, a sign of a super-good mood. Sometimes, when she's feeling contemplative or sleepy, she'll bust out with these bizarre little koans, at least half of which Jamie has realized are half-remembered song lyrics from her youth. Jamie long ago developed coping strategies for dealing with her mother, and she got so good at deflecting and counter-deflecting and counter-counter-deflecting that no amount of actual content actually slips through. Jamie and Serena might not have had anything real to say to each other, but Jamie has helped to engineer a stalemate in which they would never have to find out.

"What if all I want is to stay in bed forever?" There's no self-pity in her voice, just curiosity.

"I'm sure part of you does. Just like part of me wants to eat every donut I see, and there's a tiny sliver of me that fantasizes about jumping every time I stand on a high balcony. But those things aren't about intent, right? I don't *intend* to eat twenty donuts a day."

Serena nods. "You really think it's possible to want something with any purity? I feel like I've been ambivalent for as long as I can remember."

"I would never shit on ambivalence. If you're ambivalent, it's okay to wait until your feelings come clear. But . . . I don't think you *are* ambivalent. I think you just aren't willing to admit what you want."

"So you think I'm repressing my desires, and that's why I did bad magic before?"

She said the "M" word. Out loud. Jamie braces for a thunderclap. A shattering.

"Why are you looking like that? You have the same look you had when your pet ferret ran away. Mobley."

Mobley was a good ferret. Everyone told her that she would forget about him soon enough. They were all wrong, as usual.

"I just never say that word out loud. 'Magic!'" Jamie braces again.

"You're almost as clueless about all of this as I am." No scorn, just . . . relief.

"I've been doing it for a long time, but I had to figure out a lot of stuff on my own. Until now, I never even knew there was such a thing as bad magic, until you did some."

"So I'm ruining everything?"

"No. We're both learning. Some days I love teaching, when I learn something new by seeing through my students' eyes."

Serena fidgets. "But all I've taught you is what *not* to do."

"Which is the first step to greater mastery." Jamie is feeling itchy, because she's done leaving an offering, and she doesn't want to overstay. "I miss her too, all the time. Mae."

"Are ghosts real?"

"Hell if I know."

"I hope not, at least in her case. She would hate being a ghost. She could never stand to be in a scene without being part of it, right at the noisy center."

"She would find some way to make her presence felt. But . . . I think she's gone. Like, *gone* gone. Except in our memories or some shit."

"I don't know who I am without her."

"You're . . . the person she turned you into? I mean, you're still the product of that relationship, she's still shaping your life."

Jamie hauls herself to her feet, leaving the paper assignment and the vegan jerky surrounded by quivering dandelions. "Come on," she tells her mother. "There's still time to find another spot."

· · · · ·

The plan for today's field trip was for Jamie to do a spell herself and walk Serena through everything she did—so far, so good. But then Jamie was going to help Serena do a spell of her own, and that's where she's hit a snag.

Serena stalls, every time Jamie tries to coax her to figure out a good second spell. She's already managed to do something that was at least good enough to get rid of the curse she'd unleashed with Mae's hat. But that's no guarantee of future performance, as Ro would say.

The sun shies behind some clouds and the afternoon fades to evening, as she and Serena pick through the ruins of other people's dreams. An old World War II gun battery on a sea cliff is overrun, cement placements stripped of their guns and suffocated by bracken. A caved-in barn on a back road, a single diesel pump teetering in the dirt, the walls tag-teamed by mold and ivy. An archery range near the satellite campus of the nearby boarding school, where the targets disgorge their straw guts onto the knee-high grass. They wander until the scent of decay clings to their clothes and hair. Sometimes pungent, sometimes kind of . . . loamy?

You don't even have to reach for the metaphor: these places were loved once, and the neglect only makes the love more palpable.

They drive and walk and drive and walk, and the whole time, Jamie tries to get Serena to think about a plausible future where she comes back to life. Little sidewise hints, innocuous questions . . . Jamie knows better than to pressure her mother, or box her in.

They're following a hiking trail past a waterfall—there's got to be an abandoned campsite around here—when Serena turns to Jamie with her face washed out by the sunlight reflecting off the water.

"Do you really think there's any point?" she says.

"Any point in what?" Jamie knows what Serena means, but wants her to say it. Plus answering a question with another question has always been a good way to get under Serena's skin.

"Any point in all this spell-casting, in my case. What can I possibly aim for? I've been out of work for nearly seven years, and I left my last job under a cloud. I doubt I could get re-hired in the housing equity space, and as for journalism . . ." She scoffs.

"Journalism, no," Jamie says. "The news media is even more fucked than academia lately. Anything that helps the world make sense is being sabotaged."

"So it's a lost cause?" She's seeking confirmation rather than asking Jamie's opinion.

Jamie stops walking and looks at her. She's fully present: her eyes are clear and focused, with the sustained attention that Jamie used to take for granted. Her mouth slightly pursed, her brows knit—she's curious to hear what Jamie is going to say next.

"Capitalism wants to assign a value to each of us, based on our ability to generate profit for the owner class." Jamie is trying not to lecture, but it's easier than staring down at her mom's lean face, her waterfall-gilded wrinkles, and speaking like a human being. "They want to turn each of us into assets, pieces of capital, and decide whether we're worth investing in. But we don't have to live that way, none of us does. We can live for ourselves and the people we love."

"Rousing speech. What's it mean?"

"You don't need to restart your career, or rebuild your résumé. You just need to have a life once again. Which means getting money and finding things to do that make you feel fulfilled. Right? And maybe you can combine those two things, and get money for doing something you enjoy. But you don't have to think of your job as your life, or try to be 'high-powered.'"

Serena stares out at the white-foam base of the waterfall. "With one breath, you tell me to make sure I only ask for what I really want, deep down. Like with your My Little Pony toy. And with the next, you're telling me what you think I ought to want. So which is it?"

Jamie stumbles and nearly topples into the rocks facing the waterfall. Her head is an old-fashioned car radio turned to two stations at once. One station shrieks, *You screwed up, you fool,* the other croons, *Your mother is a niiiiiightmaaaaare,* and she wants to turn them both off but oh dear, the knob is broken.

She tries to psych herself up to feel desperate. To make up her mind to freak out, instead of doing what she kind of wants to do, which is to give up and drive Serena back to the schoolhouse in a cordial near-silence, never to mention the topic of spell-casting again.

Why is it so hard to tell love from obligation? Maybe because humans are not really built to sustain an intense emotion for hours and years, so we need connective tissue to carry us between the moments when we can feel. Or maybe it's that the people we love always seem to need us at the most inconvenient times.

But then Jamie remembers being little, and Serena saying, *You cannot mess up so badly that you will not be loved.* Some part of her has carried that promise this whole time.

"I know you too well, Mom." Jamie strains not to raise her voice. "I know you want more, because you've always wanted more, and yeah, it's up to you to tell me what 'more' means in this context. I cannot believe you are ready to spend the rest of your life wasting away in a tiny box, and it has to have occurred to you that the Fordhams might one day change their minds about letting you stay there." (Serena winces, because of course it's occurred to her.) "You asked me if I thought you were unhappy, and honestly I don't know. I know you're not joyful. You're not excited, you're not fucking *thrilled,* to see what the day is gonna bring. I think you're scared, after how screwed up everything got before—"

Ouch. Too far. Serena gives Jamie the gaze that would have destroyed her at one point. Jamie has to take a step back, dangerously close to the rocks.

"—but you're stronger than that. I know you are. Jesus, Mom. I think you're severely depressed and whatever you've been doing isn't helping, and so here I am trying to help you the only way I know how."

Serena doesn't reply. The silence isn't silent: Jamie becomes acutely aware of the water droplets spraying on her arms, and the cackles of the birds, and the raucous wind.

"Fuck," Serena says at last. "This is an intervention, isn't it? I thought those things only happened on television."

"I just miss you, okay? I miss the real you, the you that you had spent all those years constructing. And yes, I believe the 'real you' is a construct, because it's all constructs. We build ourselves to fit our environments." Why is Jamie more comfortable nerding out than expressing her feelings? She's talked about this in therapy: the ease with which she slides from the visceral to the theoretical, without even noticing that she's doing it.

Serena sits down on a wet rock. After some hesitation, Jamie does, too. They're going to have watery moons on their pants.

"I already borked my first spell," Serena says. "What happens if I get it wrong? Let's say you're right and I want more, or better. Let's say I want to be challenged again, but some part of me is consumed with doubt, what happens then? Do I get another terrible odor?"

Serena holds her hands on either side of her face, as if gearing up to play peekaboo with a small child.

"No," Jamie says. "There's a lot I don't know, but I know with certainty that nothing bad happens if you harbor doubts about the thing you're asking the cosmos for. Maybe the spell works, maybe it doesn't." Jamie can't help remembering when Serena used to push her to go to guitar lessons, swim camp, karate lessons, coding camp, always telling her that she would be glad afterward. Mae would've been happy to let Jamie lie around playing games and re-reading *Private Eye Grabote*. Tough love.

Serena rests her cheeks on the heels of her hands and stares at the froth of the water feature.

It's late and they've been at this for hours. Jamie wonders if they should come back another day and try again. But she has a feeling it's now or never.

"Okay," Serena says at last.

"Okay what?"

"I will try." Serena makes a noise in her throat. "All I want is a low-key job where I can help people who are devalued by the 'owner class,' as you put it. Maybe find solidarity with other people who are lost causes."

"I know you helped a lot of people before," Jamie says. "I still run into them sometimes, you know. They ask about you and they get this look in their eye, which I can't describe. It's like, something opens up inside them to release a tiny amount of a bottomless reservoir of trauma with a sheen of gratitude on top. Just remember: this spell may not work, and even if it does, it might make someone glance at your résumé a second longer, but it won't write the application for you." Jamie swings one leg too wide and kicks herself, which feels appropriate, because she just realized they're going about this all wrong. "Ugh. In fact, I don't know if we can do a working yet. The best one would be if we could leave a page of job listings with an offering."

Serena fishes in her leather purse, so old it's gone saggy with cracks, until she finds a paper football. No, wait, it's a piece of paper that was folded and then wadded, under all the other random detritus in her bag. "Would this help?" She unfolds a pay stub from the Housing Now Foundation, dated eight years ago.

Jamie squints. "Yeah. I think so."

"I didn't keep it for sentimental reasons." Serena glares, as if Jamie was about to jump to conclusions. "I didn't even mean to keep it. I just never got around to cleaning out my purse."

Jamie hands the old pay stub back to her mother. "Don't do that."

"Do what?"

"You need to be honest about why you have this thing, and what it means to you, or this spell won't work."

Serena hunches and stares at the grubby, almost illegible token of remuneration long past. Her lower lip pulls inward, her upper lip creeps up.

"You break me down and break me down. Like some drill sergeant. But will you build me up?"

Ugh. So we're back to self-pity. When Jamie decided she wanted a living relationship with her mother, this was what she signed up for.

"Fine." Serena is shrinking right in front of Jamie, who used to ride on her shoulders. "I kept it as a talisman, a keepsake from a time when people still valued me for something. Maybe I didn't intend to keep it at first, but I found it in my purse and didn't throw it away. Have I stated the obvious enough now?"

"I'm not trying to torture you, Mom. I just want this to work."

They find the half skeleton of some structure in the woods: a clubhouse for local kids. A plywood framework, badly nailed together, covered with branches and mud that mostly washed away long ago. The weather turns chilly. Serena places the pay stub at the dead center of the rickety wooden parallelogram, then hesitates before placing a cannabis gummy on top. She closes her eyes for longer than strictly necessary, stock-still on her haunches.

"You know that there are lots of ways of knowing that people value you besides pay stubs, right?" Jamie says softly. Serena nods.

5

"School me," beseeched Toby Langthrope. "Pray teach me how to be good. I make no jest. I know I do not deserve your aid, but I ask it nonetheless. I wish only to be a man of honor and decency, could you but show me the way."

"I shall teach you," replied Emily after a moment's consideration. "But in return, you must teach me how it is that so many people dwell in iniquity and yet are esteemed by all the world to be near unto saints."

"We have a deal," replied Toby with alacrity. "Tho' alas I fear my tutelage shall be much less pleasant than yours."

—*EMILY: A TALE OF PARAGONS AND
DELIVERANCE* BY A LADY, BOOK 6, CHAPTER 4

In the fall, New England peels away its green skirt, revealing petticoats in a patchwork of ochres, browns, and yellows. Jamie loads up on Dunkin' Donuts and drapes a crimson snood around her shaggy brown hair, freshly streaked with blue. She suffers winter, but she luxuriates in autumn.

Serena has gotten a ride to Boston with Tanister Fordham, so she can meet up with some of her nonprofit contacts and whatever old friends are still talking to her. She wants to have an early dinner with Jamie at the Indian place where she and Mae used to eat all the time—the Royal Indian Garden was already going downhill when Mae was alive, and Jamie hasn't eaten there in years, but Serena is craving their version of baingan bharta.

Jamie keeps telling Ro they don't have to come to dinner, but they insist that it's fine, they want to come.

The day, predictably, starts off awful. Jamie was assigned at the last minute to teach an Intro to Creative Writing course, with no time to prepare a decent syllabus. She's making the best of it—or so she's told herself—but today's class is an actual shitshow. Three white students have handed in stories that are racist and/or full of cultural appropriation, one of which also flirted rather aggressively with transphobia. It falls to Jamie to lead the class—at nine fucking A.M.—in a discussion of whether this is Your Story To Tell. Jamie can feel her brain cells pop like soap bubbles. Her hatiest student, Gavin Michener, isn't even one of the problem authors, but he's raring to play "devil's advocate." Is Jamie saying that white people shouldn't try to walk in someone else's shoes? People are always telling Gavin to check his privilege, but when he tries to see things from the viewpoint of a less-privileged person, they call him, basically, a thief. "What happened to empathy? What happened to breaking down barriers?" Gavin has a gleam in his eye, while Jamie has a stabbing pain in her frontal lobe. Some of the other students argue with Gavin, but everyone is talking over everyone else.

The heartbreaking thing is, Gavin is a smart person who chooses to use his faculties for trolling—it would be comforting, in a way, if he was a meathead. Rugby was his safety school, and he didn't get into any of his top choices, including the Ivies. He's let slip a few times that his family, back in Stamford, Connecticut, is terminally disappointed in him, and now he won't be on the glide path to corporate greatness.

Anyway, Jamie tries to explain why powerful people shouldn't annex the lived experience of the historically disempowered, and she might as well be reciting Celine Dion lyrics underwater. After class, Jamie sticks around long enough to chat with Zelda Duckworth, who could make a go of it as a writer.

The headache does not fade with the footsteps and chatter of departing students, but Jamie remains determined to get some pages under her belt, so she staggers into the Goblin Market. She should thank the makers of Tylenol in her acknowledgments section, assuming the diss ever makes it that far. Her cubby smells faintly like rotten banana bread, and a rattling noise comes from the bowels of the slowly reactivating central heating (though it's still cold and drafty).

Okay, think. If Jane Collier really did write *Emily,* what does that change? Leaving aside the story-within-a-story about the princess and the player, *Emily* is a fantasy about a woman who has enough status to seek the perfect husband, something that was emphatically not the case for most women at the time. Jane herself never married, and neither did Sarah Fielding, probably because they couldn't afford dowries. Jane's satire *An Essay on the Art of Ingeniously Tormenting* devotes the largest amount of space to methods of harassing and demeaning the many unmarried gentle-ladies who were forced to become live-in "companions" to wealthy women in order to survive.

Jane and Sarah were lifelong friends, meeting as children in East Stour and then living together in Salisbury (which was still called Sarum at the time). They collaborated on an odd experimental novel called *The Cry* in 1754. As far as we know, they lived together starting in 1750 or 1751, until Jane's death in 1755. Sarah lived on until 1768, but her spirit seems to have been broken by loss—all her sisters died young, and her brother Henry died around the same time as Jane. Jamie can't help wondering if Jane's death, in particular, brought Sarah down. (Is Jamie projecting her own mother's situation onto the long-dead Sarah Fielding? Maybe. We always bring our own scars to the party.)

Now Jamie thinks about a letter that appears to be from Jane Collier to Sarah Fielding, which Yolanda Troutman at Brandeis found and shared with Jamie a year earlier. We hardly have any of Jane's or Sarah's letters, so Jamie had been disappointed to find nothing but Jane wishing Sarah well on a visit to London with her brother Henry.

But now, the letter feels more significant, especially the parts where Jane is geeking out about flowers and their possible meanings. (Lady Mary Wortley Montagu's husband had been ambassador to the Ottoman Empire, and while there, Lady Mary had become obsessed with the idea that Turkish people used flowers to send messages without needing to write a word. She had carried this notion back to England.) In one part, Jane writes to Sarah:

I find that no flower exists, nor could exist, to represent the wild
and inexpressible wonders you and I have brushed against. I fear
that language itself may prove insufficient, or that the proper words
have yet to be invented. Perhaps a jonquil, or a sprightly hyacinth,
may signify that which cannot be spoken, or even understood? A
sweetbriar? Nay, I shall choose the lowly daisy.

Jane seems to be thinking about nature and the sublime, and maybe
starting to explore the themes that will culminate, years later, in *Emily*?
But Jane can't make sense of parts of it, no matter how much her eyes blur
from staring.

So. The phrase "queering the moral romance" sounded cool in Jamie's
head—but what does that actually mean? Umm, well.

"Moral romance" was the label Sarah chose for her novel *The Adventures of David Simple,* and it describes a lot of popular books of the time.
("Romance" didn't necessarily mean "love story" back then.) These are
philosophical stories about human nature, and what it means to be good
in a corrupt world—but even when they highlight the ways men mistreat
women, they don't question traditional gender roles. Or patriarchy, of
course. They're bound up in "sentiment," meaning a kind of genteel sensi-
tivity.

Emily is about heterosexual courtship—but all the power belongs to Emily, and her love interest Toby becomes her student, dependent on her. The
narrator describes Toby in feminizing terms, too: he has "flaxen auburn
hair," a "pleasing countenance," and "a most tender, gracious sensibility." In a
moment when novels were full of adorably clueless himbos like Joseph An-
drews and Roderick Random, Toby has a surprising amount of emotional
intelligence, which is what enables him to win Emily's hand. Maybe "queering" is too strong a word, but . . . complicating? Challenging? Fuck, Jamie
really wants to write "queering" if she can justify it.

Jamie looks up from her laptop screen and realizes two things. First, she's
going to be late for dinner with Ro and Serena unless she hauls ass. And
second, her headache is gone. Obsessing about the meaning of a juicy text
is dang medicinal.

Ro is texting about dinner—Ro does not want to arrive at the restaurant before Jamie and sit alone with Serena, so maybe they could head there together? Jamie texts back an enthusiastic *hell yea,* and soon Ro is meeting Jamie on Mass Ave. They kiss in front of the fading tiki bar and then walk hand in hand, chattering about all the minor epiphanies they've had since morning.

· · · · ·

"What's it actually about?" Ro asks as they walk toward the restaurant. "Your eighteenth-century lady book. *Emily.*" Jamie has tried to tell them the whole story before, but right now they seem to be in a listening mood (or in need of distraction).

"Uh . . . Emily is a girl who was a foundling—they're all foundlings in those days. And she's raised by a wealthy man who wants to teach her perfect continence."

". . . He potty trains her?" Ro snorts.

"Um, not exactly. Continence in the St. Augustine sense. In this context, 'continence' means chastity, but also modesty, forbearance, patience. So anyways, Mr. M. is determined to shape Emily into a paragon."

"And then it all goes terribly awry?"

"Um, not exactly? For about five hundred pages, Emily is perfect, and a lot of the first half of the book consists of her expounding on the value of submission to God's will. She impresses everyone with her steadfastness, though she hardly ever leaves her house."

"Sounds like a page-turner."

"It was the *Fifty Shades of Grey* of 1749. Bear in mind, this was before the gothic novel, before the Regency romance, before most of the storytelling tropes we're used to."

They're almost at the restaurant. Jamie can feel Ro tensing, involuntarily.

"So this lady is hiding in a house in the middle of nowhere?" Ro says. "Sounds familiar."

"Um. Slightly different. She's under the protection of Mr. M. The problems only crop up when he wants to marry her off, and he can't find a man deserving of her purity. The second half of the book is all about a parade of men trying to court her and win Mr. M.'s blessing, but they are all vain peacocks, rakes, playboys, wastrels. By creating the perfect woman, Mr. M. has put her beyond the reach of any man alive."

"So . . . he has to marry her himself?"

"Nah. Not a gothic novel. He realizes she can only marry a man who is her equal in virtue and accomplishment, so she helps him to devise a series of tests. Back then, men were expected to be scoundrels, so this was actually revolutionary."

"Soooo, using these tests, they find the most perfect gentleman to marry Emily?" Ro sounds genuinely curious.

"Not exactly. There's a dude who shows up at the start of the novel, a foolish libertine named Toby Langthrope, who becomes utterly smitten with Emily, and he sets about doing whatever it takes to win her hand. Depending on which reading you believe, either Toby learns to become a man of virtue with Emily's help, thus finally earning her love and respect, or . . ."

"Or . . . ?"

"Or the reading I prefer, which is more complicated. Emily grows to like him, incorrigible dipshit though he is, and she sees him as a route to a kind of freedom, an escape from the prison of being a total paragon. So she conspires with him to help him pass the tests and 'prove' he's a man of virtue. It's probably a little of both, honestly. She does make him better, while also helping him to cheat. She escapes from the virtue trap, while also bringing virtue out into the world. It's ambiguous, because it's so lengthy that you can cherry-pick whatever meaning you like, and so many of the words are deliberately double entendres. Language was more slippery before Samuel Johnson went about shellacking it down, and a lot of words could mean their own opposite, the way 'cleave' does now. Oh, and over the course of the novel, Emily tells her maid Tilly a long fairy tale about a princess and a strolling player."

Okay, Jamie has slipped into lecturer-speak. She glances at Ro, and they're half smiling. "I can see why you're obsessed."

· · · · ·

The restaurant door jangles and Jamie and Ro march inside. The restaurant is dark and homey and appears empty, until Jamie spots Serena at a booth in the back. She's been waiting a while, judging from the empty chai cup.

As soon as Jamie sits down and makes apologies, Serena puts on a taut smile. "You made it! I can't wait to hear all about your day, but first I have some news. I met up with Spotty Dobbins—you remember her, she used to babysit you—and she told me there's a job opening at Spectacles, the feminist bookstore where Mae used to work."

Jamie remembers that store, all right—because Mae used to complain endlessly about work drama. But Serena is in a good mood, and Jamie almost forgot what that looked like.

Serena leapfrogs straight to logistics: she'll need to get her old suit dry-cleaned and find a pair of slightly uncomfortable shoes for the interview, and if this works out, she'll need to go apartment-hunting. "I'm looking forward to seeing the landlords' faces when they look at my credit report."

"We'll help," Ro volunteers. "Now's not the worst time to look for housing."

"I'm so happy, Mom," Jamie says. "I hope this works out."

The restaurant is playing a mix of Celine Dion and Tori Amos, instead of the Bollywood soundtracks they put on at the Punjab Spice House. The wailing layers a tragic lassitude over everything, but meanwhile the chana is actually quite good: not too sweet, with a nice crunch.

Jamie comes back from the ladies' room to hear Ro explaining their research to Serena. "So in economics there's a lot of work on market failure. You know what that is, right?"

Serena rolls her eyes for comic effect. "I am quite familiar with failing markets, yes." Everyone laughs. It's good.

"Most examples of market failure involve a breakdown in supply and demand, or a speculative bubble where everyone pours too many resources into something that can't possibly sustain that level of capital flow, right? Or people make strategic decisions that don't pay off, because they misjudged the market, like if a shoemaker decided that everyone wanted a revival of platform shoes." Ro is getting that gleam in their eyes that sets off a sympathetic glow deep inside Jamie, because nothing stokes her love for them like hearing them geek out. "But I'm interested in the mechanism of diminishing returns. What makes people keep doing something, when it's not working anymore? How do you identify the exact moment when a product or a practice is no longer worth pursuing?"

Serena smiles and orders another mango lassi. It's weird in a positive way, seeing her smile again. "It all comes down to human nature, doesn't it? People can't let go of the memory of when they knew what they were doing. It's probably the same phenomenon that makes us so good at guarding against the bad things that have already happened to us, but so bad at bracing for dangers we haven't seen yet. Right?" She laughs. "I often think economists and philosophers should be forced to talk to each other once in a while. Or psychologists, maybe."

"I've been thinking lately that memorization is the first step in forgetting." Jamie speaks for the first time in ages. "The moment you know something by heart, you stop thinking about it so much, and it's no longer front of mind. I think organizations are kind of the same, maybe? That's certainly how academia is. Nobody knows why we do anything."

They chat for ages, and Jamie's habitual anxiety melts a bit. This feels weirdly like family.

· · · · ·

Jamie only met Ro's parents one time, at a funeral for a beloved grandma who kept talking to Ro after the rest of the family decided on a polite distance. Ro didn't fight with their parents or go through a dramatic break—they just never spoke, and it suited everyone fine. Their father was a structural engineer for large infrastructure projects, someone who talks easily about torque and striations, and their mother was a microphotographer. Ro once told Jamie that their parents were convinced that all of their life choices were about rebuking their birth family, as if Ro couldn't just try to be happy on their own terms without implicitly passing judgment on their mom and dad. Ro became especially unsettled—their version of "pissed" most of the time—by the notion that their relationship with a flaky trans woman was motivated by a wish to mortify their mother and father, rather than just because Jamie is a clever flower (their words).

We so often talk about "chosen family" as if it's the lack of choice that's the problem. Maybe instead of trying to replicate familial structures, especially that of the nuclear family, we could find something new, a paradigm that allows us to cherish each other without staking any claims—something with room for more people, and many types of relationships at play.

Anyway, Jamie was at this funeral, only the second or third she had ever been to, and everybody was being super quiet inside this Presbyterian hall where the minister quoted the Bible verse about a great secret: we shall not die, but shall be changed. Nobody threw dirt on the coffin, because this funeral wasn't the dirty kind.

After, they all went up the grassy slope road from the main road, to the big house—Ro told Jamie all the neighborhood kids used to toboggan down that hill in the winter. There were thumbprint cookies, mulled wine, and sweaty cheese. Ro's father Hugh, whose mother had just been buried, stood with the cookie plate as if it were his job to make sure the cookies got taken care of. Ro's mom, Inga, held court in the sitting room, a brace of high-backed chairs clustered around her. Neither parent spoke to Jamie, but both of them looked first at and then past her. So maybe Jamie's never really met Ro's parents at all.

· · · · ·

"Your mom seems better than in the whole time I've known her," Ro says as the two of them hang up their jackets on the door hooks at home. "I'm proud of you."

"Thanks." Jamie leans forward and kisses their lips—kissing Ro is a tactile experience unlike any other kiss, like their lips have so many shades of texture, and they're so warm and soft, and she can feel their hand on her neck—and then she makes tea for both of them. "I just hope Serena doesn't get her hopes up, in case this job fails to pan out. Rebuilding her life could be a long process, especially at her age."

"Either way," Ro says, accepting ginseng tea from Jamie. "You've done a good thing."

"You don't think it's weird that I'm spending so much time with my mom?"

The insecurity in Jamie's own voice catches her off guard.

They've both participated eagerly in conversations about acquaintances who are unnaturally close to their parents—not necessarily living-in-the-basement close, or letting-their-parents-cut-their-hair close, just not having formed a separate identity as an adult.

"You can be friends with your mother," Ro says. "You don't need my approval."

"But I doooooo," Jamie mock-whines. "I need your approval aaaaaallll the time, in every context! Am I brewing my tea right? Does this shirt explicate my hair?"

"You have my stamp of approval." Ro pretends to hold up an invisible rubber stamp and boops Jamie's arm with it. "You should get a tattoo, my forever seal."

"That's the most romantic tattoo idea I've heard today." Jamie has two tattoos already: an art nouveau lady on her left shoulder, and on the right, a quote from *The New Atalantis* by Delarivier Manley: *nature has made nothing in vain.* "But I have questions. What sort of stamp are we contemplating? Is it a rubber stamp, or a perforating stamping machine? Also, does it come with some official document that explains the provenance of the guaranteeing authority?"

As much as Jamie gets a thrill from kissing Ro, she enjoys being married. Actively, continuously. Being married is a goddamn nonstop thrill, in a way that dating somehow never was. Dating made Jamie anxious and the fun parts were laced with uncertainty—unsteadiness—like she could lose her footing at any moment. Jamie never tried to cast a spell to make herself a babe magnet, because she never wanted that in her deepest core. She always wanted this: a spouse who loves her and sees through all her crufty subterfuge.

There used to be an internet meme about the ordeal of being known, or something like that. But Jamie has always believed the truest joy in life is when someone else holds in their hands a relief map to all your most errant nonsense. Money is fake, fame is bullshit, but intimacy is bloody treasure.

. . . . .

Ro slaps a flogger made of recycled rubber against their left palm. "So. Which cardinal virtue are we to expound today?"

A shiver starts in Jamie's scalp, she can enumerate every follicle on her head. They're doing the cardinal virtue game! Corporal punishment for cardinal virtues—it's the tits.

She gasps and blurts: "Forbearance."

"Forbearance. Excellent choice. A lesson must be taught. How able are you to forestall satisfaction for the sake of a greater reward in future?"

They pull out the padded cuffs, and soon Jamie is secured to the attachment points that screw into the hardwood floor. On her knees, naked, with her back arched. (On a pillow, so her knees don't get jacked up.) The cardinal virtue game is a mash-up of their two preoccupations: eighteenth-century morality tales and twenty-first-century economic theories about marginal utility.

"You understand your situation, young lady." Ro puts on a stern voice. "You have only to say the world 'frailty' and your torment shall cease. However, should you prove able to endure this rough and malign treatment, then you shall have earned a most bountiful reward. Do you understand me?"

Jamie gasps as much from excitement as from pain—the pain, thus far, is pretty pro forma, to be honest. "Yes, yes."

Ro fetches a riding crop, and a lappy-flappy toy that Jamie doesn't know the name of.

Jamie is not much of a masochist. Sure, she enjoys being flogged, because who doesn't, and she loves clamps and plugs and wax and slaps and spankings and sometimes canings. But she views pain as a means to an end, for the way it brings her closer to whoever she's playing with, and exposes a well of vulnerability in her, which can be filled with affection, tenderness, care. The little caresses and ministrations, the fingers wrapping around her ear, the thumb against her lips inviting her to suckle—all of these things become sweeter once the pain has awakened her skin, and set her heart to rolling downhill like a runaway rock.

She's floating, lost in sensation, eyes focused on nothing, ears hearing only her own hah-hah-hah sounds, when a voice cuts thru her dazzlement.

"What do you want?" Ro asks.

She can't think of the right answer, the correct catechism for this role-play. So she says what comes to mind: "I want to please you."

"I see." They make a noise with their tongue, and a sharp gust through the roof of their mouth. "And what are you willing to do to please me, young miss?"

It's a trick question, but only slightly. If Jamie says, "Anything," or "Everything," that's clearly a lie, because she's not an amoral monster—there are things she couldn't, shouldn't, do to please anyone, even Ro. So she says, "Whatever lies within my power."

"What if I ordered you to disobey my previous instructions? To use your safe word early, and display a lack of forbearance?"

Ahhh. So we're doing the rapacious master and the innocent maid.

Jamie is about to say something fairly eloquent about how she can best please Ro by being true to her own devices, but at that moment Ro lays into her with a single tail.

"Confess that you are a dirty girl with loose morals, unable to control your urges, and I will grant whatsoever you wish," Ro says. There's an edge to this game that Jamie didn't expect, like the two of them are working out something to do with trust or desire or her own selfishness.

"Can a person gain their fondest desire"—Jamie moans involuntarily, from unexpected pleasure whose source shall be left for you to guess—"by surrendering that which makes them themself? Is it not in enduring privation that we form a self that may harbor desires?"

"If you start quoting that John Donne poem, I'm going to add another dozen strokes to your tally." Ro knows Jamie too well.

Jamie can't help snorting, but then it turns into a squeal.

"How easy it is to lose or gain a reputation," said Mr. Langthrope. "How vain, the chatter of gossips who would cast down the worthy and exalt the rotten! Reputation is but a phantom, a spectre in whose shape we may imagine any and all fancies that may come to us. I have known Gentlemen of impeccable behavior, who never trespassed with the fair sex, of whom the world gave a miserable debauched character; and others, the most lecherous rakes, whom all and sundry saw as the very image of decency."

"Oh," said Emily, "you would think so! Nothing would serve you more than to see reputation become as worthless a conceit as many craven hypocrites already believe. Then would we live in a world where everybody shared equally the presumption of spotlessness or wretchedness."

I scarce can describe the expression that passed across Toby Langthrope's face at these words. He had not the mocking look of a seasoned rake, willingly caught in his own devices, but rather it was as if a dark cloud had passed over his mind.

"I can tell you for certain," said he, "that there are those who gained widespread infamy, in spite of utterly innocent conduct. I myself know of several ladies whose lives the whispers of envious and jilted fools have destroyed. One such lady, I consider a friend, and found to my sorrow that my every attempt to rescue her honor succeeded only in making her situation worse. Unscrupulous men will pretend to have had intrigues with women whom they scarce have seen, and the whole world will believe their tales."

"O, such wickedness," said Emily, who began to fear for her own character for perhaps the first time, recognizing the peril into which she had placed herself merely by conversing with this young scoundrel.

Mr. Langthrope went on in this vein for some time, discoursing to Emily on the cruelty with which the idle and malicious will use those whose reputations they wish to destroy. Where someone is charitable, accuse him of being a pinchpenny. Where someone is learned, tax him as a dullard. And none is more easily damned as a harlot than the purest vestal virgin. In a world full of hypocrites, you will all the more easily be believed, the more perfect may be someone's behaviour.

"I must thank you, for you have done me a great service," Emily proclaimed.

"Indeed?" asked Mr. Langthrope, who appeared startled at her good spirits.

"Indeed," said she. "For you have convinced me that the only true recompense of virtue is the knowledge of one's own inner peace, and the inward satisfaction of having done well. To pursue the good opinion of the whole world is pure folly."

But even as she spoke, and laughed, Emily's heart was sore troubled, and she felt herself in great distress.

—*Emily: A Tale of Paragons and Deliverance* by a Lady,
book 4, chapter 3

6

I returned the borrowed Hat, and went Home triumphant in my own—Paid my Landlord, and, as long as the Money lasted, was the worthiest Gentleman in the County.

—*A NARRATIVE OF THE LIFE OF MRS. CHARLOTTE CHARKE* BY CHARLOTTE CHARKE, 1755

Serena and Jamie have a picnic, with all the foods they used to eat on long road trips with Mae. Dinosaur-shaped fruit pops, Cool Ranch chips, samosas, vegan corn dogs, apple fritters, juice boxes. Amazing how the more revolting the food, the greater the comfort. They drive until they find a small town with a memorial to something mossily illegible and a store that sells "sundries" (which seems an odd business model; the sun will dry things even if you don't pay anyone), and they sit on a bench where a pit bull–collie mix keeps pestering them, even though the dog knows that none of what they're eating would taste good.

"I never knew when I was little, why we took all those road trips," Jamie says after a chewy silence.

Serena sighs. "Depends? When you were little, I was still doing journalism and I had no clue how to find a story. I would go someplace to do research or interview someone, and I'd haul you along. There were also the trips where our marriage had hit a rough patch, and Mae and I thought going somewhere as a family would help us reconnect."

Jamie puts down her gross pickle sandwich.

"A rough patch? I never realized."

"It's a parent's job to obfuscate."

"How rough are we talking?"

"On a scale of *Mad About You* to *Real Housewives,* probably in the middle? We never stopped talking to each other or broke anything, and I don't think we were ever actually about to part ways. But did we have issues? Yeah. I was ambitious, I had all these heroic dreams of changing the world, and Mae always identified as a dilettante."

Jamie's earliest memories were of walking around the neighborhood with her hand in Mae's, as Mae said hello to everyone. All the neighbors loved Mae, and she seemed to know about every random tribulation and ambition, as if she thought of nothing besides Mrs. Jenkins's bad knee or Mr. Gulliver's model train set. While Serena practiced law, Mae had a half dozen part-time jobs, including designing sets for the local theater company and building holiday displays at the mall and the downtown center. And nobody except Serena knew that Mae was also working as a pro domme at a fancy dungeon in an old industrial building; Jamie thought Mae maybe did social work or something, which wasn't far from the truth.

"You were gone a lot when I was little," Jamie said. "I remember one time you came home and I didn't recognize you, and I started screaming."

Serena closes her eyes a second, then nods. "I was off reporting out my big story about domestic violence among first responders. I had shaved my head and you thought I was a mysterious intruder."

"I was like, 'Who's this lady kissing Mommy?'"

They eat in silence for a while, watching the dog wander off.

Then out of nowhere, Serena says, "It's all just strange without Mae. I was a pretty poor excuse for a parent, but I was a decent co-parent."

"All I ever wanted was to be like you," Jamie says in a low voice. "It's still a lot of what I want. You were always charging off to light some fires."

"If I had known you could do magic this whole time, I would have lost my shit." Serena reaches for some lychees.

"Um . . . yeah." Jamie flushes happily but there's a weird undercurrent, too.

"No, I mean really," Serena says. "You have this relationship to the world that is just so much healthier than I had when I was your age, or even twice your age. You opened my fucking eyes."

You can tell Serena is speaking from her heart when she starts swearing like a drunk burlesque performer.

"It's just, how do you ask the fucking universe for what you fucking want?" Serena shakes her hands like a raver. "I always thought I had to punish myself to get the least little thing. Who taught you to just ask for stuff you wanted? For happiness? I know it wasn't me. Maybe it was Mae. She trusted the universe, even when it fucked her. Even when it fucking killed her. Always catches me off guard, how like her you are. Even after all this time, it throws me for a fucking loop. She's not gone, not all the way, as long as you're here giving me that 'shut up you dumb fucking cunt' look."

"That is not the look I am giving you, Mom," Jamie blurts between sobs.

Serena's baring her soul, but Jamie's the one who's crying.

"Nobody taught me," Jamie says once she can talk again. "Not exactly. I was a lonely kid. I wandered and played where nobody else was. Lots of kids build funny shrines in the woods—I just had a knack for finding them."

"So . . . do you want to try and do one together?" Serena speaks in a low voice, like when she used to entice Jamie to go get ice creams, when Mae probably wouldn't approve of all that sugar before dinner. Funny how your first experience of politics, of conflicting authorities and checks and balances, comes from your own family.

"You . . . want me to do a spell with you?" Jamie says. "Not just give you moral support, but actually participate?"

Serena doesn't answer. Instead, she says, "I'm sorry you were a lonely kid."

Jamie starts to say that Serena needn't apologize, because none of it was her fault—but of course, some of it was her fault. She raised Jamie to be the sort of child that other children want nothing to do with: a grown-up in a child's body.

"But," Jamie drags the conversation back on track. "What kind of . . . what kind of working did you want to do?"

Serena looks at her daughter with her head tilted to one side, exotic bird of prey. "I don't know. I just think it could be fun. This might help me understand better. Is there something we both want?"

"World peace?"

"I don't want world peace." Serena stiffens. "There's been too much of the wrong kind of peace, for too long. A great many situations won't get better until someone is willing to break some heads."

"We both want Mae back," Jamie says in a tiny voice. "But you already saw how that turned out."

"We want to become better friends, don't we? And yet that doesn't sound like something we need outside help to accomplish."

Jamie doesn't know about that, honestly. But she lets it go.

"We both want justice," Jamie says. "It's the main thing we've always had in common, besides blood. But let's start with something smaller. Justice feels huge and abstract. What I want is to understand what happened back then. We had everything, we were a family and things were going well, and then we lost it all while I was in college. I wish there was some way I could see the whole thing now, with the distance of time."

"There's nothing to see, you already saw it all," Serena says. "They took everything from us."

"Yeah, sure. It just felt . . . sudden."

"When you're young, everything is a confusing mess, right? You just get blindsided constantly."

"I guess," Jamie says. "One reason I do what I do, grad school and everything, is because most of our stories about who we are are garbage."

Serena shakes her head. "Journalism taught me that honesty is contingent, at best. People tell their version of the story, and they usually don't know how much they're slanting the truth. I always learned more from the stuff people let slip after I kept them talking a long time. I ended up feeling as though the whole concept of objectivity was problematic at best, because it's subjectivity all the way down." She starts packing up what's left of the picnic—they'll have unhealthy leftovers for days. "I just think . . . if one person can make something happen by focusing on what they crave, then two people focusing on the same intention should be twice as powerful. Or maybe there's a multiplier? I just think we should try it."

Jamie keeps chewing over this notion the whole time they're packing up and taking everything back to Berniece the dirtmobile. Serena is probably on to something, and this is one reason it's good that Jamie shared magic with her—she can see possibilities that Jamie has been overlooking. So why is Jamie so nervous about this idea? Maybe because it could put a lot of weight on a relationship that maybe can't bear it, after all.

But also, Jamie can't help noticing that Serena keeps saying the two of them combined could be twice as powerful—and she replays in her head what she told Serena before their first lesson: *It's not about power. It's not. It's about knowing what you really want, in your fucking secret heart.* But what if Serena is right, and Jamie is wrong?

They barely talk on the drive back to the schoolhouse, both of them chewing over separate versions of the same conversation. The road unspools on its own, and Jamie zones out until they pull up to the gravel drive.

*   *   *   *   *

Jamie can barely see the Fordhams' manse across their big lawn as she climbs out of Berniece and walks through the misty October rain to the old schoolhouse, her feet squelching on muddy leaves. The gravel walkway feels like pebbles at the bottom of a fishbowl. She could be on the moors, or the downs, striding toward an old many-gabled house to conspire with a gamekeeper or a rogue chaplain.

Jamie raises her fist to knock on the front door when it whirls open and Serena rushes out, so briskly the rain seems to part around her. She's wearing a long leather duster, almost a trench coat, that Jamie has never seen before, and the sides of her head appear freshly shaved. "There you are," Serena says. "We've got a lot to do, best get going." Jamie expects to get back into her car, but Serena walks right past Berniece and heads down the driveway, then across the road to a drowned pasture with one stoic goat tied to a tree. A boggy scent thickens the air. Jamie has to rush to catch up; she'd almost forgotten what Serena on her highest setting was like.

"I've been saving them for when you got back down here," Serena says over her shoulder, and Jamie doesn't clock at first that she's talking about neglected places. "I found so many of them within walking distance of here—it's like I've become a magnet for them."

On the other side of the soupy pasture, a stand of trees borders something akin to a proper forest. Ears of fungus cling to rotted planks that look as though they'd coat your fingers with slime forever if you touched them.

"I remember years ago there was an obsession with 'ruin porn,'" Jamie says. "It's some 'Ozymandias' shit: 'Look on my works.' People are so prone to infrastructural masochism."

"I disagree." Serena carves a path through the sodden brush, never slowing down. "I think we love modern ruins because we wish we could pull down the towers of the wealthy with our bare hands, and we know we can't. We look to entropy and hubris to save us."

Serena stops and raises her arms in triumph. As Jamie gets closer, the mist parts and she sees something out of a low-budget horror movie: a makeshift shrine with wind chimes inside a wooden frame, with two piles of mossy slate on either end. Serena produces something from her jacket pocket: a printout of the GoFundMe page for Teena Wash, with the picture blurred by ink streaks even before the paper grows damp on the shrine's mossy surface. Neither Jamie nor Serena can afford to give enough to make even a tiny dent in Teena's staggering medical expenses, but they'd move mountains to see Teena okay, after everything she's done for the community. Plus a queer woman getting fucked over by the medical establishment? That cuts close to the bone for both of them. Still, Jamie has no idea if this'll work—neither of them has met Teena Wash in person, and Jamie's never tried to bless a stranger. Just that word, "bless," makes Jamie cringe, maybe because it sounds religious. Or presumptuous?

Serena crumples a dollar bill until George Washington's eyes gaze upward from the apex of a pebble. Jamie has a random, unexamined urge to take Serena's hand, so she does, and Serena squeezes. "Make it rain," Serena whispers, even as droplets spatter on her face and the paper in front of her. Jamie doesn't know what to do, so she mutters "Make it rain" as well. There's a shift in the air, like a high-pressure system, and every hair on Jamie's arms and legs takes on a static charge. Her anxiety turns, somewhat, to exhilaration.

She closes her eyes, lost in the wild sensation, then forces herself to release Serena's hand and turn away, gazing into the darkling wood with ribbons of water hanging from each branch. *Put it out of your mind,* she tells herself. *Don't dwell on what just happened, or you'll curdle the spell.*

Jamie opens her mouth to say this was intense and a great start to their experiment, and they should head back to the schoolhouse now. But Serena pushes farther into the woods. "Come on, there's another place that's even better." Jamie tries to follow, but her legs wobble. On the second try, she succeeds in rushing after her mother, sploshing and squelching.

The air sings with rain showers, and a white haze overlays Jamie's vision, like she's high or sleep-deprived, though she is neither of those things.

Turns out having another person to do spells with, someone with whom she's shared so much joy and bereavement, is incredible. For maybe the first time ever, magic is more than a Band-Aid over a hole in the world.

. . . . .

By the time Jamie gets back to Somerville, she's teetering with exhaustion: she and Serena did three spells together in the increasingly hard-driving rain. Both of them wired, enervated, thirsty even with water deluging onto them, until Jamie got the hangover to end all hangovers. When Jamie staggers inside the apartment, Ro exclaims.

"Oh, thank Laser Perkins. I was starting to worry. You weren't picking up your phone." They rush toward her, one arm in a hugging stance and the other in a judgy *where were you* arc.

Jamie glances at her phone and realizes she somehow missed a dozen texts and calls from Ro—she was trying so hard to focus on the road, wishing she'd made time for a get-home-safe spell. Also, it's somehow nine o'clock already.

"Fuck, are you okay?" Ro is staring.

"Uh, long day. I just realized I haven't eaten since midmorning."

Apparently she's swaying unbeknownst to herself, because Ro rushes to guide her onto the purple sofa, wrapped in the handwoven blanket, and they fetch a cup of fragrant tea and a sandwich.

"Listen," Ro says, when she's had some food. "I know you've been reconnecting with your mom, and it's been good, and you feel like you know her better. But we never really know our parents, not the way we know other people. There's a veil, or a distortion, in the way, and you can't separate the reality of them as people from the ways they shaped you. And there has to be a way you can help your mom fix her life without wrecking your own. Seriously. You have to teach tomorrow morning, right?"

Jamie nods, thankful the sandwich is keeping her mouth too busy for anything else. Warmth flows back into her body.

"Oh!" Ro claps while Jamie takes her last bite and reaches for the mug. "Did you see? Freaking Teena Wash's GoFundMe got a huge surge in donations, after the actor who played Dirty Man in that Netflix series boosted it. She's almost at her goal now. If this keeps up, she'll be able to get a private hospital room and everything." Jamie spills tea all over herself.

An hour or so later, they're getting ready for bed, brushing their teeth side by side like an old married couple. Jamie spits toothpaste and says, "You're right. Today was intense, because . . . I don't know, my mom is my mom again. She's full of vim, and I'd forgotten how exhausting it can be when she's firing on all cylinders. And how easily I get sucked into her energy vortex. It makes me so happy, but . . . I need boundaries. Plus she doesn't need my help so much anymore."

Ro sighs and their shoulders lower a bit. "Yes. Thank you. I told you I'm proud of you, right? I'm proud of you. But you cannot go on like this. The time will come when your mom really can't take care of herself, but let's hope that's a long way off. For now she's a healthy adult who's on a good path, and you have a lot of stuff of your own to deal with. Like, I heard you have a really high-maintenance partner." On that last bit, their voice takes on a flirtatious tone.

"Oh yeah?" Jamie puts her toothbrush away. "How high-maintenance are we talking about?"

"Sooo high-maintenance." Ro laughs, their toothbrush also back in its nest. "I heard your partner is a total *utility monster,* with a near-limitless capacity for enjoyment."

"Oh dear." Jamie leans forward and nuzzles her face against Ro's neck. "My hedonic calculus is utterly undone. However are we to maximize the pleasure of the masses with such an egregious outlier in the mix?"

"There's nothing for it." Ro places their hands on the back of Jamie's head and the small of her back. "For the sake of the world, you must endeavor to satiate the insatiable. John Stuart Mill demands it."

"Oh, my." Jamie pauses to nibble Ro's earlobe, with lips rather than teeth. "I cannot possibly disappoint John Stuart Mill!" They grind against each other, Jamie in her nightgown, them in their union suit. "I must take extreme measures to ensure the greatest good for the greatest number." They fall onto the bed, Jamie's nightgown disarrayed like a scene from *Fanny Hill*, and she tugs at the waistband of Ro's union suit.

Jamie goes to sleep with a smile plastered on her face.

• • • • •

Jamie wakes up with a crushing headache that starts in her neck and jaw, like she was sleep-gnashing again. Ro holds a cup of coffee under her nose like smelling salts, and she groans to life. Shit, she has to teach in one hour, and her actual brain hurts.

Somehow she makes it to Hirschfeld Hall in time for her Crisis lecture, which is dealing with *Moll Flanders* and *Vanity Fair* and the female hustler. Gavin Michener sits in the front row again, raising his hand constantly like a cocker spaniel, because everyone has to know all the time how clever he is. Jamie finally calls on him and he launches into a whole thing about women's bodies as the loci of reproduction and receptivity, nurturing, and how these male authors were imagining a rapacious femininity. He gets a little evo-psych, with a touch of Lacan, and Jamie starts to suspect he's fucking with her on purpose, playing on her lack of a uterus. "These women— Moll and Becky Sharp—are using their low status to hide in plain sight and advance through trickery and manipulation, which are traditionally feminine powers, yeah? But the only thing they cannot be is fertile. They transcend their social role as women by denying the most quintessentially female part of themselves."

She fixes Gavin with a baleful stare until he runs out of bullshit. Then she says, "If you put a twenty-first-century gloss on these narratives, you could come to all kinds of conclusions about reproduction and fertility, except context matters. We're talking about a period where childbirth was often fatal, and the problem of unwanted pregnancy hangs over Moll Flanders and leads to her not knowing her own son. I don't think you can discount the role of class and—" Jamie can hear her own voice climb into a grating register, while Gavin smirks through half-lidded eyes.

Then—huzzah!—Jamie escapes from campus altogether and makes for the Houghton Library at Harvard. She hasn't forgotten Ariella's warning, and she wishes she could bring the flow of time to a halt, or a gentle trickle, while she pores over every scrap of eighteenth-century correspondence. She parks near Dana Square, nearly a mile away, because she needs the steps and parking near Harvard Square is a fool's game, even if one does have a tiny amount of magical juice. (And then she remembers: Teena's GoFundMe. What the hell?)

On her way to Harvard, Jamie finds the most unlikely thing of all: in the midst of manicured lawns, hedges, and wrought-iron fences, a Greek Revival townhouse rots from the inside out. Someone must have started to renovate this beauty and then run out of money, and it's sat with its guts torn out, long enough for grass and weeds to spring up, and for the remaining beams to molder. How has Jamie never noticed this decomposing shell before? She must have passed a hundred times. Some part of her wonders if this house wasn't here yesterday, until the universe decided to offer it to her, but that's not how . . . she stops herself from saying, even in her own head, *how this works.* The more she teaches, the less she knows. This place seems almost too ideal, but Jamie hesitates: yesterday's spells took a lot out of her, and maybe she ought to hold off for now, plus she could break her neck in this deathtrap. Then she remembers Ariella telling her that time is running out, with an urgency that she could not entirely parse. So she slinks through a gap in the chain-link fence and treads carefully onto what remains of the floorboards over an earthy pit. At the dead center of the structure, she finds an explosion of fungus—"explosion" is the only word, it's so violent—and she freezes, unsure what to do. She gropes in her satchel and the first thing she finds is a printout of the last page of her list of research sources, which she had grabbed in case Ariella wanted a visual aid. She lays the paper on top of the fungusplosion as neatly as possible, and adds her last Ferrero Rocher, which she'd been saving for a post-grading treat, but oh well. She almost turns to leave, until she remembers her mom's habit of always saying something at the end of a working. She half closes her eyes and murmurs, "The pursuit of knowledge for its own sake"—the closest she knows to magic words. She's even more careful getting out than she was going in.

Inside the library reading room, Jamie hesitates, because she's already looked at everything obvious. She finds herself thinking about why *Emily* clings to the inside of her mind so much—it's pure wish fulfillment, a fantasy about a woman who gets to marry for, if not love, at least mutual esteem, and yet the text is riddled with compromises and confusion. Emily is caught in a feedback loop of soul-searching, to make sense of her own tangled desires, which she wishes to speak into the quiet of the nearby ruined abbey.

If Jamie didn't know better, she would say *Emily* was a book about witchcraft—and now she thinks of the letter Yolanda Troutman shared with her, the one where Jane hints at some sublime wonder that language can't describe, not even the language of flowers. (Or maybe Jamie is just projecting.)

Jamie closes her eyes, right there in the quiet of the reading room, floorboards protesting under her feet. Everyone will think she's dozing off; it happens all the time in here. The same instinct that led her to the Andrew Millar letter is tugging again, and she can't help opening her eyes and heading to the reference desk to ask for pamphlets from the 1730s and 1740s— the "pamphlet wars" in those days would make social media look like a tea party.

Hours pass. Jamie's eyes unfocus. So many feuds, so much vitriol. Whigs versus Tories, Jacobites versus Georgians, Pope and Swift versus everybody. On impulse, she switches from the 1740s to the 1730s, when the Walpole government was fighting to shut down the seditious and scandal-ridden unlicensed theaters. Back then, the theater was a vital public forum, bringing together everyone from the royal family on down, and scribblers dissected every tiny controversy over which actress should play a popular role. Actors rubbed elbows (sometimes literally) with cutpurses and sex workers, in a sewer that shaped highbrow culture. Jamie squints at pamphlet after pamphlet, barbs tossed back and forth.

She finds something curious in the middle of an especially ranty pamphlet from late 1736:

> Gentlemen who know me best will affirm my great Candour, sometimes to the detriment of my own Interests, but pray believe that I speak the unstinting Truth in this case. The Enemies of good Judgment think their worst Excesses their greatest Merits, but they will soon see the truth. Mr F—g and his Associates strive to bring Dis—r and Ruin upon us all with their coarse Jokes and salacious Displays. The late production of P—q—n serves as proof enough of a ruinous Hubris.
>
> We have in our hands an Opportunity to restore good Sense to the City, after years of wandering in the Wilderness like the Israelites of Old. No longer can we tolerate such Mischief. Even now the self-styled Impresario believes himself untouchable as he spreads Tr—n against the Government and soils the good name of Mr C—r. The less said of Mrs C—e and her late Follies the better, particularly the recent escapade at T-m K–ng's Tavern, cavorting in men's Attire with a supposed Gentlewoman whose close connexion with the Impresario must give rise to Commentary. How much longer can such Improprieties be countenanced? Nay, the breast of every Gentleman must swell with Indignation.

The mid-eighteenth-century habit of putting em dashes in the middle of words, including proper nouns but also certain abstractions, never fails to vex. And yet, Jamie's eye gets stuck on this passage. "Mr. F—g" is clearly Henry Fielding, who at the time was running the Great Mogul Theater Company at the Little Theater in Haymarket, where he proceeded to mock his enemies. (Henry was never happy unless he was at war with as many people as possible.) *Pasquin* was Henry's scandalous play, in which the infamous actor Charlotte Charke played a man's role, as was her habit. It seems very likely that "Mrs C—e" refers to Charlotte Charke, especially with the mention of men's attire, and she apparently lured a supposed Gentlewoman to Tom King's Tavern, a notoriously debauched alehouse off Covent Garden. Who was this Gentlewoman? Based on the mention of a "connexion" to the Impresario, this could be Sarah Fielding herself. It's all maddeningly vague but important, Jamie feels it in her teeth.

Charlotte Charke didn't just play men's roles onstage—she also dressed in men's clothes in her regular life, and went by the name Charles Brown. (But she still seems to have used she/her pronouns, and it's a dodgy idea to impose twenty-first-century labels like "trans" on someone who lived three hundred years ago.) When acting work dried up, Charlotte worked in male garb as a waiter, as a butcher, and even as a valet to an Irish gentleman—jobs that were reserved for men. She was openly married to a woman, for years, who was known only as Mrs. Brown. And according to her memoir, Charlotte started dressing in her father's clothes at the age of four, and Little Charlotte went to great lengths to have everybody see her strut around in a man's wig, hose, and coat.

As an actor, Charlotte was part of a whole eighteenth-century tradition of women playing "breeches parts" in male clothing, but she didn't stick to playing female characters who disguised themselves as men, like Viola in *Twelfth Night*. Instead, Charlotte made a habit of playing men's roles, taking parts away from established male actors and poking fun at the most famous actors of her time. Her targets for ridicule included her own father, the superstar actor/playwright Colley Cibber—and Colley ended up disowning her because of it, condemning her to live from hand to mouth for the rest of her life. (Colley became famous, in part, for playing an over-the-top parody of a peacocking man named "Lord Foppington," so Charlotte was following in dad's footsteps with her silly portrayals.) Small wonder that when Henry Fielding was launching his own theater company in 1736, doing satirical plays aimed at tweaking the powerful, he seized on Charlotte as his lead. When she couldn't act onstage anymore due to politics, Charlotte ran a successful puppet show, staging Punch-and-Judy plays where she did funny voices. Later in life, Charlotte traveled the country as an impoverished "strolling player," with the mysterious Mrs. Brown always at her side, and finally turned to writing, producing a wonderful memoir and some undistinguished novels.

Basically, Charlotte Charke/Charles Brown was an unsung transmasc icon, though she paid a heavy price for it, living on the edge of starvation and dying fairly young. She was also a notorious chaos goblin who broke all the rules and blurred all the lines—and maybe she convinced a young Sarah Fielding that she could do the same?

Not much is known about Sarah's whereabouts for most of the 1730s, though that letter about flowers has her leaving Salisbury to stay with her brother in London in 1736—when Henry was riding high as a theatrical mogul. So it's possible that she met Henry's star actor and fell under the spell of Mr. Brown. Jamie can almost imagine it: the dashing Charlotte, dressed as a fashionable young man, charming Sarah and coaxing her to visit a tavern in disguise. Well, everyone always said Sarah had a deep understanding of the inner workings of human nature, and *David Simple* betrays a detailed knowledge of London's geography—she had to learn these things somewhere, right?

Even if Jamie's right about Sarah and Charlotte—and she recognizes it's a huge leap—her questions only proliferate.

Like, why has nobody ever heard about this scandal? Sarah had real claims to being a gentlewoman, so if she was seen at a place like Tom King's Tavern with a notorious actress like Charlotte Charke, it should have been enough to destroy her, and probably her brother as well. Henry's enemies certainly would have seized on such ammunition with both hands, so how did this get hushed up? Also, could Sarah and Charlotte have been more than friendly acquaintances? Most of all, what does any of this have to do with *Emily,* which was published a good dozen years later? There's just not enough to go on. Charlotte's memoir is no help—it's heavily sanitized, of course, and mostly aimed at soliciting a reconciliation with her father that never came to pass.

This tidbit is probably nothing—but the figure of Charlotte Charke lurks in Jamie's daydreams: strutting, playful, brash, utterly alluring. When she was alive, Charlotte had a way of injecting a boisterous note of gender anarchy into every narrative.

Is it any wonder that Jamie can feel Charlotte Charke/Charles Brown setting up shop inside her mind?

· · · · ·

Jamie's head buzzes like an old-fashioned alarm clock when she walks out of the Houghton Library, too many thoughts at once. She's exhilarated, jumpy with pleasure—she can't wait to tell Ro, not to mention Ariella. This could be a paper in a top-flight journal before she even finishes her diss, just to whet everyone's appetite. *The pursuit of knowledge for its own sake.* The cold damp air, laced with wet grass, cedar shards, and manure, tastes like single-malt Speyside Scotch in her mouth. She nearly walks into a group of barefoot undergrads playing Ultimate Frisbee on the grass. Maybe she'll treat herself to ice cream from J.P. Licks or Toscanini's. Holy flaming shit, life is full of wonders when you let it open up to you.

Jamie's phone blarps as she reaches Mass. Ave. Serena's name pops up, and Jamie's convinced something must be wrong because her mother never calls out of the blue. Except when Jamie picks up, Serena is ecstatic—the flood of words out of her mouth whooshes over Jamie, too intense to parse, until she says, "I got the job." She got the job! She's going to be working at Spectacles Women's Bookstore near Inman Square, where Mae worked a decade earlier. Of course, now the bookstore is circling the drain financially, but it has a proud legacy and lots of community support, and Serena believes she can help turn it around. Serena starts in a few weeks, so she has time to find an affordable place to live and get some new outfits.

"Damn," Jamie says. "I'm proud of you, Mom. You did it."

"We did it," Serena replies. "I wouldn't have made it if not for you."

The sun sinks through bare branches, pinking a corner of the sky, and even with a chill wind, the world feels utterly new.

After Jamie hangs up the phone, she goes back to thinking about Charlotte Charke, aka Charles Brown. Her mind drifts to the fairy tale that is told in installments throughout the middle of *Emily*, about a princess who becomes entangled with an actor, and nearly loses everything.

Emily found herself unable to refrain from thinking upon the affrightful notions Mr. Langthrope had shared with her, and wondering how one might remain pure in the eyes of a world whose judgments were so easily swayed by slander. Her maid Tilly, too, professed a great unease, saying "O, what a wicked world, O these deceptive tongues." Declared Tilly with great heat, a society that prized seeming virtue over real devotion to goodness would deserve naught but scorn.

To calm her maid, but in truth also to soothe her own anxious breast, Emily decided to read a diverting fairy tale that had of late come to her attention—a story in which goodness is tested and greatly wronged, but triumphs at last thanks to the generosity of friends. Tilly cried out with great eagerness to hear such a tale, and so with no further delay, Emily began.

THE TALE OF
THE PRINCESS AND THE
STROLLING PLAYER

A great many years ago, in the time before society was so worldly-wise as it is today, there lived a Princess who was admired by all who knew her. She brightened each room with her sweet Countenance, her Understanding was perfect and matchless. She knew languages of old and had a mind that made connections between diverse Subjects. This admirable Lady lived in a grand house surrounded by verdant lands whose front window had a prospect of a sunlit meadow wherein deer and pheasant wandered at perfect ease. Every person who visited paid tribute to her gracious Nature, and her Reputation spread far and near.

One day, a group of strolling players came to the nearby town, to perform the most suitable plays in the most current style of the time, carrying a resplendent host of Costumes on their persons, along with such Scenery as they might require. They marched into town and posted bills and notices advertising that they would be performing the latest Entertainments from the Capital, and all in town were transported with a great Fervor to see them play.

Among these players was a young man named Cleverly, whose voice lilted like a flute playing a high, dulcet melody, and whose eyes sparkled with gay mischief, like a cat at play with a moth. Master Cleverly stood out even in a group of fellow actors, for the liveliness of his Disposition and the versatility of his Attire—for his Coat was of a patchwork that seemed to adjust itself into any pattern, any shape, he might require, appearing one moment an exquisitely tailored garment fit for a Gentleman of Fashion, and in the next a Highwayman's dark Cloak. With this magic Cloth, Cleverly could so Transform himself that you might scarce recognize him from moment to moment, and he could inhabit several Characters on the same stage.

The Princess was curious to see these players, including the infamous Cleverly, perform the newest and most widely approv'd Plays, along with older classics by Shakespear and Jonson. But fearing as she did the merest breath of Impropriety, she hesitated to venture into the theater, where she heard common wretches gathered and immodest Behaviour was often seen. Her friends implored her to reconsider, promising an evening of most excellent Diversion, in which they would shelter her and preserve her Innocence. Reading the great works of dramatists alone, they said, was a fine Education, but a poor Substitute indeed for the Opportunity to hear those immortal Words in the mouth of a skilled Actor.

At last, the Princess agreed to go with her Friends, and there was much Merriment and lively Conversation as the Company prepared to venture out to the theatre. It is well known that nothing is more agreeable than a pleasant Recreation in the company of one's dearest Couchfellows.

The Company passed a delightful theatric afternoon, and partook of several fine Performances in which the Versatility of the players was much admired—chief among them the mercurial, omniform Master Cleverly.

When the plays were completed, the Princess's friends implored her not to let their Amusement cease so soon, but to meet with these actors, and perhaps invite some of them for Revels. For players who travel will savor the Opportunity to visit with folk of good Lineage, and to bide an Evening with some sublime Conversation (and the possibility of Patronage).

That is how the Princess found herself discoursing with the star of the troupe, Cleverly, who charmed her with his keen Observations on many pleasing Topics and paid her subtile Compliments without an excess of fawning. Hours passed in the company of Master Cleverly and the Princess found that she could listen to his mellifluous voice forever.

And yet the next day, when the Princess rose up, she found she no longer fit into any of her shifts, aprons, skirts, hoops, or stays. None, nay not one item, of her clothing would settle onto her, instead hanging loosely around her. With the most acute Distress did she conceive that she was shrinking away. As the day went on, she found herself growing tinier with each passing hour, in fits and starts.

—*Emily: A Tale of Paragons and Deliverance*
by a Lady, book 4, chapter 9

ii

We've gone from dot-coms to palm readers... The summer
of 2001 will be remembered here as the season San Francisco
returned to normal, or at least its own version of normality.

—"A CITY TAKES A BREATH AFTER THE DOT-COM
CRASH," *THE NEW YORK TIMES,* JULY 24, 2001

We should have put our stuff into storage back East." It became a refrain: every time Serena and Mae shlepped a giant box of zines or
their bowlegged fainting couch up two flights of winding bald-carpeted
stairs to their new apartment in San Francisco's Presidio district. "I'm just
saying, we didn't need to lug all of our junk across the country," Mae said.
"We could've sold it off."

"No argument." Serena panted.

To make matters more complicated, one of them had to keep at least
one eye on Jamie the whole time—and now that she was a toddler, she'd
become an escape artist, even wriggling out of the straps in a car seat.
Mae kept wondering out loud if Serena had given birth to a hairless cat
instead of a human being. The first thing they'd done upon arrival was
run around putting plastic covers on all the power outlets, like an odd
scavenger hunt.

Serena and Mae lay on the fainting couch, with Jamie cocooned between
them, staring up at the rococo bullshit in the plaster moldings overhead:

fruit, flowers, goats. "Looks like a wood nymph projectile-vomited onto the ceiling," Mae said.

"We should take the moving truck back to the company before they close for the day." Serena groaned.

"We should, yeah."

"We should unpack all of these bloody boxes."

"We certainly should."

Neither of them moved.

Jamie started fussing and crying, so Mae and Serena just looked at each other until Serena rolled off the fainting couch to find the bag of Jamie-related supplies.

The sun went away twice: first due to a fog the color of dryer lint, and then because of an actual sunset. Once they'd fed Jamie, Mae and Serena ventured out into their new neighborhood to find something for grown-ups to eat, and they eventually stumbled on delicious cheap sushi, which they ate straight from the carton, sitting on the floor in between the non-functional fireplace and the space where they had laid down their futon. They were still too exhausted to unpack, but Serena was starting law school at USF in just a few days. Jamie ran around touching every box, shrieking and whooping, until Mae dug out Jamie's stuffed muskrat, Woople, and then both Jamie and Woople sat on the floor with identical grins.

Serena would later look back on this period as the happiest time in her life—but at the time, she was just aware of being caught up in a high-pressure system: doing, doing, doing. She sometimes felt as though happiness was inherently retrospective, like the past could be happy or sad, but the present was always complicated. Also, when Serena looked back on her three and a half years in San Francisco, the memories jumbled up so that one moment, Jamie was in first grade, and the next, she was still a toddler.

Jamie was the happiest kid anyone had ever met, which came as a huge relief to both Serena and Mae. She went through a phase where any time she entered a room, she would go and stand in the corner, facing outward, arms akimbo—because someone had once told her to stand in the corner and think about what she'd done, and she'd decided this meant taking a moment to be proud of her accomplishments. If someone asked her what she was doing in the corner, she would announce, "I am Thinking About What I've Done!" and then proceed to list everything she had done lately: she found a snail, she gave a crumb to some ants, she told a fire hydrant to cheer up, she climbed *five hills*.

Serena was starting to suspect this kid had inherited her talent for disrupting authority.

Luckily, San Francisco was full of people with kids around Jamie's age, because an internet bubble had burst and people could afford to breathe (and breed) again. Serena and Mae started meeting other queerdos, and soon they were getting invited to gay brunches, daytime drag parties, poetry readings, and roller-skate excursions, where kids ran around in feral packs with hands full of candy. Some queer shindigs were only kid-friendly until sundown, which suited Serena and Mae fine because they were no longer night people.

. . . . .

Law school was exhilarating and only slightly terrifying. Journalism had taught Serena to retain random facts in her head so she could deploy them strategically, either to win over reluctant sources or to trip up people who were trying to bullshit her. And the ability to cram her brain with case law and statutes, along with a certain agility of thought and a talent for creative bullshit, turned out to get her surprisingly far in class.

Her cohort included a couple dozen white men with names like Zane and Bertram, who exuded competitiveness and spoke in clipped, unaccented sentences, like they'd practiced talking like the men in *The Firm*. Serena was prepared for the microaggressions—nothing new, really, after growing up queer in rural New Hampshire—but the actual sabotage caught her off guard, all the small-ball acts of cheating like cutting in line and taking credit for other people's brainwaves. Playing slightly dirty just for the principle of the thing. Serena soon learned to spot the tiny number of other students who were interested in public interest law instead of big corporate jobs: they had a hangdog, disheveled look to them. They also tended to be more visibly queer and feminist—like Tariq, who was interested in cyber-liberties, and Anita, who obsessed about antidiscrimination lawsuits. Serena was remembering how much she'd enjoyed debate club in high school, the willingness to put every topic through the crucible of argument, the satisfaction of immuring your opponent behind a wall of passionate logic.

At home, Mae hurled facts at Serena: their kitchen-sink trash disposal sometimes gurgled like a beast with indigestion; the only laundromat was two blocks away and Mae had found drug paraphernalia stashed in the tiny space on top of one bank of dryers a couple times; even with Serena's loans and freelance journalism, Mae was having to work three part-time jobs to pay their rent, on top of childcare.

Serena sometimes had a hard time switching out of righteous-argument mode, in which case she would simply remind Mae of the countervailing facts. They had both agreed that law school was a good idea, and Serena would be able to support them once she was done. Serena was working more than the twenty hours a week that USF recommended as the maximum for full-time law students. With a law degree, Serena would be able to help so many people.

The two of them would go back and forth, trying not to raise their voices because Jamie was sleeping or playing. Mae would usually be the one to lose her cool, disturbing Jamie—which meant that she'd won or lost the argument depending on your parameters.

"Law school is for single people," Anita said, as if she was stating a basic fact of the universe.

They got Jamie into a daycare center three days a week: a sun-drenched loft where the floor was paved with foam letters and numbers, full of toys whose edges had already been chewed away. Jamie actually made a friend: a mop-headed hyperactive boy named Ramon who was really into *Sponge-Bob*. Some days, they went on playdates supervised by Ramon's mom, a dietician named Xenia.

Meanwhile, Mae was making decent money doing phone sex, whenever Jamie was at daycare or out with Serena. People would phone a special 1-900 number and pay a few bucks a minute to talk to the woman of their dreams, or a reasonable facsimile thereof. Sometimes Serena would sit on the fainting couch, reading her law textbooks, while Mae perched on the bed, purring and drawling into the phone. Mae had different personae for her phone clients, with whole different voices, depending on which "line" they chose to call. There was Daisy the innocent schoolgirl, Lavinia the frustrated housewife, and a flamboyant domme named Mistress Impatient.

She started getting regulars, including one guy in the Midwest who kept her on the phone for an hour at a time, just talking about all the sensuous fabrics she was wearing on her body: a skirt made of taffeta and tulle, a velveteen bustier, a diaphanous satin slip. Mae would do nothing but list textiles for several minutes, and this man staggered his breaths. Once or twice, Mae would run out of things to say, while Serena frantically searched on her Dell laptop for more luxurious-sounding types of cloth, rushing the screen over to Mae's perch just in time for her to say the word "chantilly," like "CHANNNNNN . . . tilly." (Another time: "Organza," which Serena had to admit sounded dirty.)

In addition to the phone sex, Mae was picking up shifts at a yarn store, a tiny organic grocery, and a Buffalo Exchange where she used her employee discount somewhat liberally.

The first year of law school was a never-ending grind of coursework about the fundamentals, but the second year was where the pain really began. (Serena interned with a cyberlaw nonprofit the first summer, but she was already realizing she ought to intern with a big law firm next time, to pay off more loans.) She got sucked into trying out for the *Law Review,* which involved proofing a mind-numbing article, and she was also taking more specialized courses in environmental law, labor law, and other stuff that might help accomplish something meaningful with this degree. Most of the other students who'd started out wanting to do public-interest law were slowly waking up to the reality of needing to make money, and Serena's little clique kept shrinking.

Serena kept doing journalism on the side—she was chasing a story about a group of doctors who were running a clinical trial for a new weight-loss drug without disclosing that they owned a piece of the drug company. Picture Serena, with Jamie perched in her lap and a law textbook wide open on her knee, lobbing questions at a medical administrator through her phone headset. "So you admit that Breckington Medical Group purchased a stake in Klinika Pharma *before* you signed on to recruit patients for a clinical trial of their drug? It's a yes-or-no question," Serena barked. While the administrator answered, she highlighted a passage in the labor law textbook while also waggling a finger puppet for Jamie. "Did you have any internal discussions about disclosing this conflict of interest?"

After the freaked-out administrator ended the call, Serena turned off her recorder, and told Jamie, "Your mommy just nailed the bastards. Yes she did. Yes she did." Jamie clapped.

From the other side of the apartment, Mae said, "You would be terrible at phone sex, dear."

• • • • •

Jamie's fifth birthday was a disaster. She and Ramon had stopped talking to each other, though nobody was quite sure why. Nevertheless, Jamie's party needed to be *SpongeBob* themed, and Serena swore she would get some *SpongeBob* decorations. Mae decided to invite a bunch of her friends' kids: those feral ramblers who showed up at the queer brunches and drag garden parties. Jamie wanted everyone to play *SpongeBob,* role-playing the plot of some episode she'd just watched.

Serena kept promising to go to the big party superstore, but there was a cram session and a practice for a mock trial, and the copy editor kept calling with fact-checking questions on Serena's clinical trial exposé, and oh bugger, it was party time. In a feverish daze, Serena ran to a housewares store and bought an assortment of sponges—kitchen sponges, loofahs, plus one mop cartridge—and some paste-on googly eyes. She would make some DIY SpongeBobs on the bus ride home, it would be fine.

When Serena got home, Jamie was already in tears because half the kids didn't want to play *SpongeBob* and the other half were all insisting they had to be SpongeBob or Squidward, and nobody wanted to be Mrs. Puff. Mae was smiling but her eyes looked murder in Serena's direction, especially after Serena tried to sell the sponge-and-googly-eyes thing as a fun craft project the kids could do. Everyone ended up playing *Mario Kart* on the janky secondhand Nintendo. At least the cake was delicious and contained an accurate representation of Bikini Bottom, because that had been Mae's job. Jamie hid in her bedroom for half an hour—she had a tiny bedroom now—until Serena and Mae coaxed her out with endless bribes.

This was probably the day when Jamie learned the lesson every kid learns at some point: adults suck, and so do other kids, and you can't ever have whatever prize you've yearned for, except in the sanctity of your own imagination.

Everyone finally went home, the other adults probably congratulating themselves on being better parents than those messy lesbians. And then Jamie ran around for two more hours, amped up on sugar and existential angst. After they finally got Jamie down, Serena and Mae ate cold party snacks and stared at the mess they were too tired to clean up. Frosting was smeared all over the Nintendo controllers: a reminder that Mae had at least gotten the cake right.

The air felt heavy, freighted with unspoken words. Not just today's birthday fiasco, but a host of recent incidents besides. A week and a half ago, Mae had been telling a cute story about Jamie to some friends, and Serena had corrected her facts over and over, until Mae threw up her hands and said, *Fine, you tell it,* at which point Serena had gone silent. Serena had been late to pick up Jamie from daycare a couple of times in the past month, and had flaked on a brace of promises to Mae. But most of all, Serena had been throwing elbows a lot, any time Mae asked a question or pointed out an issue. Sometimes five minutes later, Serena would realize she'd handled things for shit, but it was too late. And now, it all felt like a giant pattern.

Serena sighed and rubbed the whole upper half of her face with the heel of one hand. "How do I fix this?"

Mae faced her with a grave look. "I'm not sure you can."

"Can't we just hang in there for one more year? I'll be finished with law school, and then—"

"—and then you'll need to work nonstop to pay off the loans. I can't do this. I'm not interested in recapitulating patriarchal family structures through a queer filter."

Oh dear. Discourse had infected the conversation. Serena's eye traveled to the crammed-to-bursting cardboard box of zines that she and Mae had never quite unpacked. Every zine was full of rejoinders to Andrew Sullivan and other "respectable," "normal" queers who just wanted everybody to act as straight as possible, as if blending in would make everyone else hate them less.

"What happened to supporting each other as we chased our dreams?" Serena struggled mightily to keep her voice down, because the last thing they needed was to wake Jamie up again.

"What happened to us sharing childcare equally? What happened to carrying all the burdens together, as a family?"

Serena didn't have much of an answer for that.

The next few days, Mae barely spoke to Serena, who in turn tried her best to be home more and help out with childcare and household chores. When the kitchen sink broke, Serena was the one who called the landlord three times and then stood around watching the handyman futz with a wrench for an hour and a half. Serena carried Jamie on her shoulders through Golden Gate Park, gawping at hummingbirds and gophers, while Mae sat at home and talked on the phone about cashmere.

A few days after that, Serena was trying to bang out a Memorandum of Law for her class on how to write like a lawyer, and Mae asked if Serena had bought any milk. Without looking away from the screen, Serena said that there was an easy way to find out. The next day, she and Mae had a completely pointless argument about whether Kathy Acker could be considered cyberpunk, or cyberpunk-adjacent. (Neither of them was entirely sure how to define "cyberpunk," which made it worse.)

The two of them kept butting heads, no matter how desperately they wanted not to Larkin their child. Every interaction with Mae put the hot prickle into Serena's nape. Serena was aware, deep down, that Mae's questions brought back ugly memories of her army of older siblings constantly tearing her down, but she didn't know how to explain that, and they weren't having a sharing kind of dynamic right now.

Serena came into the tiny kitchen area of their apartment one day and found Mae reading an article about a celebrity lesbian, who'd split up with her longtime partner not long after they'd had kids via artificial insemination. The newspapers and glossy mags were having a field day, including snide quotes from all those bigots who'd insisted that lesbians couldn't provide stable environments for kids—never mind the sky-high divorce rate among the straights. Anyway, Mae gazed at the photo of the last time these famous dykes had been happy in public: swaddling their newborn twins.

Serena felt as though she ought to say something, like *That won't be us,* but she drew a blank.

When Serena looked back later on this moment in her life, she wasn't sure how long it had gone on, or how bad it had actually gotten. There was just a collection of asynchronous sense memories: the feeling of Mae's hand slipping away from hers, the fleeting satisfaction of having "won" an argument, the self-loathing that settled in afterward.

On a rare day off, Serena took Jamie to Golden Gate Park, holding hands as they walked past the roller skaters and the hippie drum circles. Jamie was clutching Woople, the stuffed muskrat, and exploring on her own while Serena brooded on a bench. She looked up and couldn't see Jamie—heart instantly Klaxoning!—but then Jamie walked toward her with a solemn expression, hugging Woople with her right arm and holding a tiny object in her left palm.

Jamie held up a dirty nugget to Serena's face: an acorn. "Woople says it's a magic seed."

She held the acorn, expectant, until Serena took it and held it gingerly between one finger and a thumb.

"Thank you," Serena said. "This is a lovely gift."

"It'll make you the smartest person in the world," Jamie explained. "So you'll always be right. You'll always be right about everything."

Oof. Serena's heart, which had been panic-spiked a moment ago, now sank. It was clear what had happened: Jamie had overheard a conversation the day before. Mae had accused Serena of needing to always have the right answer, which was a major drag to be around. Serena had replied that the homophobes were determined to win at all costs, so we needed to be equally determined. Mae was like, ugh, just don't bring it home with you, okay?

Jamie was still telling Serena to keep the acorn with her always, to ensure perpetual correctness.

Serena gazed at the acorn, rolled it around in her palm. Then she handed it back to Jamie with care. "Thank you. That is the greatest gift. But you should keep it."

Jamie stared, eyes wide. "Why???"

"If I was always right? That would be so boring!" Serena said gently. "I would never learn, because I would already know everything. Life would be so dull. Plus other people would have to be wrong all the time, and that wouldn't be fair to them. If I was right and everyone else was wrong, I'd be very lonely."

Jamie thought about this, looking intently at the acorn. Then she tossed it in the grass, under a branch with a scampering squirrel. "Okay," she said. "I guess it's okay to be wrong sometimes."

"Sometimes, yes," Serena said. "Sometimes people will try to tell you that you're wrong because you're saying things they don't want to hear. Like sometimes things are unfair, and people don't want to know." She worried she was going to confuse Jamie, but the kid was nodding seriously and soaking up every word. "But sometimes you can be sure you're right, but you still need to listen to other people who say you're wrong. It's complicated and confusing, even for grown-ups."

By the time Serena got home, she was pretty sure she owed Mae a huge apology.

* * * * *

"I've been the biggest jerk." Serena tried to maintain eye contact with Mae no matter how much she wanted to look down, or away.

"Mm-hmm." Mae gazed at her, not smiling or scowling, just being present. They were facing each other in their sidewalk-scavenged 1950s foam-cushioned chairs, across their tiny breakfast table, which had also been on the sidewalk. Jamie was at daycare, and Serena was blowing off a study session.

"I told myself I was going to law school so I could help vulnerable people. I had this whole righteous mission in my head, and it turned me into a selfish person. I've been mean to you. I've flaked on stuff. I've sparred with you instead of talking to you. I'm going to do better."

Mae nodded: she already knew everything Serena just said. She leaned forward and said, "How?"

Serena breathed deep. She'd been expecting Mae to make a speech back. "The law school has a part-time option, which is less of a nightmare, but it'll take longer. At this point, it'll probably just be a semester extra. But I could work more, so you can work less, and I can also do more childcare.

Also, I'm going back into therapy. I've already found someone and I made an appointment. We could also do couple's counseling, but I don't want to ask you to do more work, and I can work on myself for now."

There was a chipped mug of coffee in front of Serena, which she didn't remember making, but now she was glad it was there. She lifted it carefully and breathed in the gentle pungency.

"That's all really good," Mae said. "I love you, and I love this family. So much. But . . . you don't even realize that we keep on having the same issue, with variations. Like, first you were a player and I was supposed to be scared that you were going to get bored with me and take off. And now you're getting to be a high-powered lawyer and I'm supposed to beg you to make time for me. That's not a healthy dynamic, sweetie. Not in a million fucking years. I appreciate you, I adore you—but you're not the bloody center of the universe."

Whoa. Serena felt like she was falling, but also cradled? She had that vertiginous perspective shift that only happens once in a while, where you get to see yourself from outside: the truth you never glimpsed even though it was obvious to other people. It was scary, a diminishment. But she also felt weirdly grateful, relieved even. Serena had seldom needed anyone to see the best in her, but on some level she had searched her whole life for someone who could see her worst garbage and still stick with her.

Serena leaned forward and extended a hand across the table, hoping fervently that Mae would close the remaining distance. Took a few seconds, but then Mae's hand and hers made a coracle of lightly enmeshed fingers.

"You're right," Serena said over and over, "you're so right. I love you, too, and I love this family."

They talked for another hour, before they realized they had one hour left before Jamie's daycare let out, and they ended up in bed with the toys Mae hid under a pile of tax documents in a hat box labeled FINANCIAL AFFAIRS. They were both sticky with lube and sweat and other things, and Serena raised her head and realized it was time for someone to go pick up Jamie. She smiled at her wife. "I'll go," she said. "It's good to take a break from being the center of universe every now and then."

Mae whomped her in the head with a pillow. "Too soon." But she was smiling.

7

MISS JENNY: Pray, Miss Sukey, do answer me one question more. Don't you lie awake at nights, and fret and vex yourself, because you are angry with your school-fellows? Are not you restless and uneasy, because you cannot find a safe method to be revenged on them, without being punished yourself? Do tell me truly, is not this your case?

MISS SUKEY: Yes it is. For if I could but hurt my enemies, without being hurt myself, it would be the greatest pleasure I could have in the world.

—*THE GOVERNESS; OR, THE LITTLE FEMALE ACADEMY* BY SARAH FIELDING

Serena is in a good mood. Jamie sees it in the folds of her neck as she bends over a bowl of lockets, and the loose set of her arms and shoulders. She's humming to herself.

They're antiquing together. There are seven or eight tiny stores within a dozen miles of Old Wollston, with names like the Ribbon Drawer. Cutesy hand-painted signs, that almost guarantee an elderly proprietor with excellent sweater game and at least one sleek, complacent cat. Officially, they're buying stuff for Serena's new apartment—which they haven't found yet, but Jamie figured having some old-timey knickknacks, or even some old-fashioned furniture, would ease the transition. *Un*officially, though, they're goofing off, taking the opportunity to paw through detritus and speculate on the intimate lives of people whose possessions ended up in the Heirloom Barn. Or Bygone Treasures.

They smile at the round-faced, gingham-clad shopkeeper, who's probably only in her early thirties after all, then shuffle along the aisles, playing the "censer or funeral urn" game. They marvel at the array of brass doorknockers, medicine flasks, duck calls, goblets, and teapots. Everything radiates, everything whispers that their homes could have character and mystique. They could display this bronze bottle-holder engraved with the initials MED and pretend it had been in their family for simply *ever*. You cannot look at an old teapot and feel alienated from the world, it's simply not possible. Here are old keys, which could open a chest full of gemstones, or an ornate secret door. Who can feel even ambivalent while looking at a basket of keys?

"I think that lamb figurine is trying to steal my soul." Jamie gestures at the limpid eyes which have been following her around the cramped space. The porcelain lamb is carrying a basket full of wool, which is probably why none of the other lambs want to be its friend.

Serena laughs, but then her face breaks into sadness. Like all this old stuff is touching a nerve, after all.

"What if we wanted to take someone down?" Serena whispers.

At first Jamie is sure Serena's talking about the lamb, which to be fair is getting creepier by the minute. "What?"

"Like, a hex. Can we put a hex on a person? Or an entire organization?"

"Like . . . JawBone?" Jamie says. This is the first time in years that either of them has mentioned that name.

The shop owner is definitely staring. Jamie hustles her mom out into the muddy parking lot, where Berniece the dirtmobile is the only vehicle other than an old pickup.

"I can't believe you're seriously talking about revenge." Jamie keeps her voice low, even out here.

"Hypothetically, if I did try to take McAllister Bushwick and his 'boys' down, it would be justice," Serena says. "I would be doing everyone a favor." She seems to realize she sounds like a vigilante from a terrible movie, and resets. "I'm just saying, have you kept up with what they've been doing since they went after me? It's a bloody trail of wreckage."

Jamie hasn't wanted to give those trolls any more attention than they've already stolen from her. But she's seen the headlines: McAllister Bushwick posed as an LGBTQIA+ activist and tricked the first gay high school principal in Tennessee into saying something that could be twisted into sounding borderline pedophilic, even though in context it was a harmless remark about looking for cute boys at the gay bar. The JawBone crew also manufactured a scandal around a journalist who'd broken some stories that damaged far-right candidates: they got him on tape mouthing off at the bar about his political views. They've besmirched a string of activists, online personalities, and minor cultural icons, through a mixture of social engineering and other dirty tricks. The world is demonstrably a worse place because of them, even aside from what they did to Serena.

"Not saying they don't deserve it," Jamie says with extreme care, like when one of her students thinks they've caught her in a contradiction. "But this thing I've been teaching you? It's the wrong tool. You remember what happened when you mixed it up with your grief over Mae. Just imagine what'll happen if you try to bring in vengeance and anger."

"Wasn't the problem before that I wasn't definite about what I wanted? This is crystal clear. I want to destroy that piece of shit and all of his friends."

"Sure. But . . . that's not a pure desire, right?"

"I think it is. It's the purest desire anyone can have. You just don't think it's worthy. You think it's wrong."

"No, I think it'll backfire and you'll get hurt. If even a tiny part of you blames yourself for what happened rather than JawBone, you could bring a rain of almighty shit down on your head. And there might not be a way to take it back this time."

"You keep changing your story."

"That's because it's not set of parameters, it's a feeling. And you have to go with what feels right."

Serena snorts. "The humanities."

"Yes, the fucking humanities. Not everything is exact, or a science. The world is full of flukes, and whims, and unpredictable crap, and that stuff is the most important of all, no matter how much people want to double down on machine learning and statistics and the bloody quantified text. The things that are hardest to talk about are the things most worth talking about."

"Did I sign up for your TED Talk?"

Mae would have gotten what Jamie is trying to say here.

"You are finally getting your life back." Jamie feels chilly—numb, even. The wind picks up, but also the desolation of this parking lot is seeping into her soul. "We got you a job, you're getting an apartment, you're rejoining the world. Don't risk everything on a vendetta. Seriously."

"So you think justice is a luxury." Serena spits.

Jamie has seldom been on the receiving end of one of Serena's ugly-bug looks, but she's seeing one now. (Mae called them "ugly bug" looks, as if Serena had just turned over a rock and uncovered a truly revolting insect. Her nose wrinkles, her lip curls a bit, her eyes turn an icier shade of gray. A few seconds of that look have been known to make people shrivel to half their size and whimper-scamper away from her.) Jamie makes herself hold eye contact, gritting her teeth.

"I think if you want to go after McAllister Bushwick and the JawBone crew, you should do that—using legit means." Jamie is trying not to raise her voice. So, so hard. "I bet you could make contact with some of their other victims. You could band together, tell your stories, drum up support. All the stuff you're good at, basically: community-building and muckraking. You don't need magic to make him regret messing with you."

"An alliance of the discredited." Serena shakes her head, her body half-turned away.

The image of a soggy hat in an abandoned road pops into Jamie's head and she can't get rid of it. And meanwhile, her actual vision is washed out by late-afternoon sunbeams.

"Nobody's discredited, Mom. That's such bullshit, and I know you know it's bullshit. You did nothing wrong, and neither did any of those other people." Jamie reaches out to her, and she walks a few paces away.

Jamie felt cold a moment ago, but now her ears are hot.

Serena is stomping toward Berniece the dirtmobile, as if Jamie is the one who's trampled across a line. "Take me home. We're done here."

Jamie stares. Every tendon in her body clenches.

Everything Jamie has been trying to teach Serena is about moving forward, but here she is again, digging through the trash pile of her past. This was a mistake, all of it.

"Fine," Jamie says. "Let's go."

For some reason, the drive back to the schoolhouse—hopefully, almost Jamie's last time visiting this shack—feels more hazardous than usual. She clutches the steering wheel as if it could slip out of her hands and swerve them off the road at any moment. Somehow Jamie rolls up to the schoolhouse without wrecking anything or anyone.

Serena's last words before she strides inside her tiny domain are: "You'll see that I'm right. This is just how you are: you always hate any change at first, until you embrace it."

"If you're about to bring up the purple blanket—"

When Jamie was seven, Mae and Serena decided her beloved quilt had gotten too ratty to keep using, so they cut it into rags and got her a purple blanket as a replacement. Jamie cried and refused to sleep with the blanket for a week, until she decided she loved it more than anything.

"I wasn't going to." Serena shakes her head. "You're not a child anymore. These days, you're the one who holds things over my head, not the other way around."

She walks inside the schoolhouse and the dead bolt clunks into place.

· · · · ·

To the extent that Jamie thinks about Serena's plan to curse JawBone, it's only in flashes. She spends most of her time trying to pull together a proper thesis statement that situates *Emily* in the middle of mid-eighteenth-century debates about women and marriage—and wondering about that strange pamphlet she found. Did Charlotte Charke and Sarah Fielding have a scandalous connection in 1736? And did Jane find a way to write about it in that fairy tale, with Sarah as the princess and Charlotte as Master Cleverly? (And if so, who's Lady Sagacious, the princess's friend? Is that Jane herself?) If any of this is true, it could turn the whole meaning of the novel sideways.

But also, Jamie has to grade stacks of papers that may or may not have been written by machine learning. The grad student union is once again talking about going on strike, which Jamie hopes will come to pass, and a conservative student group is inviting transphobic legal scholar Wanda Bock to speak. Ariella Zhang keeps sending Jamie messages hinting that she's out of time, she needs to produce scholarship right away, because something is arriving soon. Jamie has run into Ariella in the hallway twice lately, but hasn't been able to gather any hints about the nature of this oncoming storm, other than to say that the trustees are awake and you can see the shreds of old dreams between their teeth. The trustees are cosmic antigods; Ariella's eyes unfocus when she mentions them, as if she is trying to unsee the unseeable. *Just hurry,* she tells Jamie.

So Jamie scarcely has time to think about Serena's invitation to join forces and curse their enemies. Instead, she recalls the scornful way Serena said, *the humanities.* As if Jamie is clinging to a decadent fantasy, and her commitment to liberal arts is clouding her view of magic—like, what if the correct approach to spellcraft is one of bold experimentation, instead of sticking to what "feels" right, the way Jamie does?

"But feelings are all we have," Jamie says to Ro as she cooks dinner. "The scientific method is about empiricism, but no matter how good your experiments are, you rely on your senses to interpret them. And there's all this slimy brain-meat between observable reality and whatever conclusions you draw."

"We agreed: no Descartes after seven P.M.," Ro rumbles from their favorite chair.

"I'm just saying: there's always an observer with their own biases, and flukes happen, and maybe every science is a little bit art."

"And every art is a little bit science?" Ro only rolls their eyes a little.

"Yeah, maybe. I guess I feel like everything in the world is trying to keep us from getting lost in thought lately. There's endless pressure to make enough money so you can keep paying sky-high rents, and anxiety is our natural state. All of our culture is demanding that things be clear-cut and simple, when messiness is beauty." Okay, Jamie is ranting. At least dinner smells and looks delicious.

"I feel like I'm hearing one side of an argument with your mom," Ro says after they both sit down to eat.

Jamie groans. "I'm sorry. That is a totally uncool thing to do. Serena has a way of getting in my head."

Ro gives her a look, like: *Uh-huh.*

Lately whenever Jamie complains to Ro about her mother, she has to skip over all the details pertaining to spellwork, which leaves every anecdote full of holes. Jamie can tell Ro is noticing—she usually overloads them with details, so this comes across weird—and Jamie is a terrible liar.

"Let's change the subject," Jamie says. "I've been dumping too much of my mom drama on you lately."

But she can tell that Ro is troubled.

. . . . .

Wanda Bock has written anti-trans articles for major publications and the national media has fawned all over her for her brave stance against the Trans Menace—so of course she's here on campus to talk about how her voice has been silenced. Jamie gets roped into taking part in a protest against her campus visit, which gathers a slightly bigger critical mass than anyone hoped. There are nearly forty people present, including a bunch of bright-eyed undergrads.

As one of the few trans grad students, Jamie is expected to ululate into a megaphone, possibly shout "What do we want?"—though nobody ever answers truthfully when an amplified voice asks what they want, or protests would be a shambles.

Jamie huddles with the organizers: a transmasc sociology grad student named Markus Vance and a genderqueer math geek named Gigi Yang. They know that whatever they do, Wanda Bock will spin it into victimhood and an assault on academic freedom—but if they do nothing, it'll "prove" nobody supports trans rights.

A single news crew shows up, from the Channel Seven Eyewitness News Team, and the presence of a camera is enough to elicit larger-than-life performances, of a type that Charlotte Charke would have approved. Jamie notices a few of her students standing with the pro-Wanda Bock crowd, including Gavin. He glares with his eyes and smirks with his mouth.

As she waits to speak, Jamie finds herself telling Markus the whole story about JawBone and Serena. McAllister Bushwick sent a young woman to become an intern at the Housing Now Foundation, and she managed to record Serena talking shit, the sort of stuff that you could take out of context if you were a master manipulator. It cost Serena her job and a lot of her friends, right before Mae died. "I think my mom will never move past it," Jamie says.

"That sucks." Markus shakes their head. "I guess that's why I'm so keen on seeing everything in terms of collective struggle. Individual people get burned out or broken, but we keep moving forward." Markus is half Senegalese, half Irish, with a round face, warm dark brown skin, and a smile that's impossible not to reciprocate. A little fuzz on their chin, from a brief experiment with testosterone. As usual, they're wearing a silk bow tie and cashmere sweater.

There's a bullhorn in Jamie's hand, everyone can hear her breathe. "Nobody is trying to silence Wanda Bock, or anyone else," Jamie says as clearly as she can. "But the world needs to know that we don't welcome her, because if she had her way we would all be erased from our own lives." Some cheering, some boos—as usual when Jamie addresses a crowd or a lecture hall, she gets fish-eye vision, everyone appears both too close and too distant. She can't tell who's cheering and who's booing, and she's not entirely convinced that the syllables coming out of her mouth are actual words.

When Jamie gets home, Ro asks how the protest went—but when she answers, they stare at their pile of econ notes, and she can't tell if they're listening. A chill sweeps over her, like a wind across a frost-limned canyon.

As she and Ro are getting ready for bed, Jamie says, "Here's what gets me. How do we keep our activism focused on doing positive things for our community, instead of getting sucked into hating our adversaries?"

"I don't believe that hating our enemies is always bad, to be honest." Ro speaks through a cotton veil as they pull their pajama top over their head. "When people want to take away your rights and turn you into a non-person, hate is the only honest response. I don't think we should take any tools for organizing off the table."

Jamie wants to ask Ro's advice about the whole "curse JawBone" idea, but the closest she can come is to say, "I just feel like . . . if you put negative energy out into the world, maybe that's what you get back? I know, that sounds woo-woo, but you know me: I'm a fluffy bitch."

"I really don't know. It's complicated." Ro sounds tired, like it's too late at night to have this conversation, or maybe too late in their relationship? "On the one hand, I think worrying about 'negative energy' is a luxury, or a privilege, that not everybody gets to enjoy. On the other . . . you have to do whatever allows you to keep doing the work, and not burn out, right? Everyone has a different comfort level."

"Yeah." Jamie can't help hearing Serena in her head, talking about *a rough patch in our marriage.*

"I need to crash." Ro smiles, but without any hearth light in their eyes. "I have a big day of marginal utility tomorrow."

The night turns cold and rattlesome, as if the wind is reminding the leafless trees of a duty they've already shirked.

· · · · ·

"I'm okay if you don't want to push it any further. The, uh, workings, I mean," Serena says after the server places shallow bowls of pasta in front of her and Jamie. "I'm in a good place now, or I will be when I find an apartment that's not a roach motel." Jamie and Ro have been helping Serena look for a flat within commuting distance of her new job, and thus far every place has been a bit depressing. "I can keep doing small things on my own. You've already done so much for me, I don't want to push you to do something you don't feel is right."

The first bite of shrimp fra diavolo peppers Jamie's tongue, with a sweetness that turns tangy as she chews. She breathes easier as the garlic soaks in. She'd been bracing for Serena to push the idea of casting a curse.

But . . . there's a part of Jamie that wishes Serena would.

Anxious as Jamie is right now, she can't help basking in the sight of her mother come back to life. *I did this,* Jamie thinks. *I hauled her out of her living tomb and showed her a filthy miracle, and now she's herself again.* Jamie imagines Ro squeezing her hand and saying, *You did good,* except of course Ro doesn't know the half of it. The fact that she shared this secret with her mother and not her partner is dragging her soul, when she allows herself to think about it.

Serena looks at Jamie through the lens of a half-empty wineglass. "You seem sad. What's going on?"

"Nothing," Jamie says. "Just . . . I think Rugby is getting ready to screw us over, more than before. And we did a protest against this transphobic campus speaker, and it felt worse than useless. I can't help thinking I'm going to spend the rest of my life beating my hands against walls, when there's a sledgehammer at my feet."

Serena's brows come down and her mouth purses as she chews. The room darkens abruptly as the sun slips away.

"You know what?" Jamie says. "Maybe you and I should try doing more workings together. We could try to afflict the comfortable a little."

Serena smiles. "I'd like that."

. . . . .

"I still think this might be a bad idea." Jamie follows Serena through the outskirts of a dilapidated textile factory complex.

"It's a good idea," Serena says. "As long as we believe it's a good idea, then it is one."

"That's not how . . ." Jamie shivers and trails off. She's taught Serena everything she knows about magic, so she doesn't get to keep saying, *That's not how it works.* "I just think this has a huge risk of going catastrophically wrong."

They've already passed two spots that Jamie would have considered ideal for spell-casting.

"You were the one who said we should try to afflict the comfortable," Serena says.

"Yes! But this isn't quite what I had in mind for our first effort."

"They treat people like rotting garbage at that college of yours. They own endless amounts of real estate and don't care about their local communities, they treat their students like a revenue source instead of their mission, they overinvest in middle managers instead of professors, and they exploit an army of service workers. And now you and your fellow grad students are asking for just enough to survive, and they're spitting in your faces."

Serena is only parroting all the things Jamie has told her, which makes it hard to argue.

"Sure," Jamie says. "There are huge systemic problems in higher education right now. But systemic issues and magic don't mix."

"Why not?" Serena glares/smiles. "If magic is about moving energy around, and systems are made of energy, shouldn't it be ideal?"

Both of them identify the perfect spot at the same moment: an old water wheel from a nearby mill has become a sideways planter for big thick bearish weeds. Serena nods and Jamie nods back. They're suddenly in tune, moving together as if they'd rehearsed for hours: a mother-daughter dance squad.

Jamie has the latest ominous letter from the administration about funding cuts and restructuring, and we deeply regret blah blah blah. She places it at the center of the water wheel, then hesitates. Clarity and honesty: what is she hoping will happen as a result of this? What does she want from, or for, Rugby College? If she can't sort out her feelings, she shouldn't be doing a spell right now.

But Serena is already moving, putting a roll of quarters on top of the wadded-up letter. Jamie spreads the quarters around on top of the crease at the center of the letter, and then for good measure she plucks a few leaves off the weeds in the wheel. She focuses her thoughts on the ruined mill: first flowing with water, then consumed by earth. Cleansing, fecundity. Maybe Rugby College can make soil for good weeds. Jamie's love for her future alma mater is a flower among filthy splinters. Serena is saying something, too quiet to hear at first, then Jamie hears: "Make learning free." Jamie chimes in: "Make learning free. Make learning free." She's not even sure what that means: should college not have tuition, should we rethink how we define education? She only knows it feels right in the moment.

Jamie has never done a spell quite like this before, but Serena gives her a smile that's different from the smiles she saw as a child—conspiratorial? Cahootsy?—and Jamie feels like the two of them can accomplish anything.

Afterward, Jamie doesn't feel the usual post-spell emptiness, as if she just poured out her dreams and now she's suffering a dream hangover—instead, she feels wired. She can't stop picturing the quarters and the weeds and the letter, all of it crackling with something akin to static electricity. Jamie can't obey her own biggest rule of magic: to avoid dwelling on a working once it's finished. *What did we just do?* She doesn't know, she can't stop wondering.

Neither of them wants to quit now. Jamie's mouth is dry and electric and all the smells in the world are turned up to a hundred. Sweet and warm and pungent and yeasty seeds, everything bursting with life.

"Can't believe I spent so many years hiding away in a schoolroom," Serena says. "Like I was just waiting to follow Mae to the other side or some shit. That whole time, I could have been breaking things wide open."

They wander until they find another perfect locale, a hiking trail that rocks and bracken have closed off, with thorny slender branches and spiky flowers over what appear to be some discarded camping gear and an old half-melted doll. Probably teenagers were fucking around here, setting shit on fire, back when this trail was still a trail.

Jamie and her mother move in sync, preparing the site, and then Serena gives Jamie a look—like, *my turn?* Jamie nods. Serena digs in the inside pocket of her gray tweed coat and pulls out a kazoo. Jamie doesn't need to see the logo on the side to know: this is a promotional item from the early days of JawBone, when it was more pranks and less full-on misogynistic sabotage. Serena pauses, as if composing a mise-en-scène, then places the kazoo right near the melty doll.

Jamie's heart flaps, like the loose skin-lid after a thumb-slicing accident.

This is it: they're going to cast a curse.

Nobody could deserve it more than McAllister Bushwick, that smug bolo-wearing dipshit who probably never even thinks about how he ruined Serena's life (and Jamie's).

Serena pauses, just a second, not looking at Jamie at all except a quick side-eye, like: *Is this going to be a problem?* Jamie no longer feels things are as simple as her being the teacher and Serena the student.

Now is the moment for Jamie to say, *This is not going to work. We cannot cast harm upon anyone, even the most deserving and disgusting predators.* Her mouth has gone gluey, speechless. And honestly, she's curious. What if this works? What if there's a whole category of magic she's been cutting herself off from all this time? Plus deep down, Jamie hates this guy as much as Serena—maybe more, because he put an abrupt stop to Jamie's youth, to her happy(ish) family, to all her sweet illusions about the world. Screw McAllister Bushwick, he can't possibly get the full measure of what he deserves.

Jamie doesn't speak, just finds some mud that could maybe have dog poop mixed in. She scoops with a forked stick, smearing it along one side of the kazoo. Serena finds burnt cones from some kid's long-ago bonfire.

"Get it," Jamie mutters. She doesn't know where those words come from. Saying them feels right.

"Get it," her mother says.

For a moment, Jamie thinks this is going to turn into a chant, but nah—Serena is already muttering something else, something like, "So good I want this," and Jamie joins in without meaning or choosing. Swept? Whisked? Unmoored by the intensity of the moment and the poopy, polleny, wild scents of the overgrown trail. "So good I want this so good I want this." Jamie feels drunk but clearheaded. Drowning but also swimming, water-dancing even.

When it's done, Jamie wants to starfish on her back in a nest of dead leaves, staring up at the lymph-white sky.

Instead, she and Serena go for onion rings and milkshakes. Jamie can't believe she lived for years before realizing that you don't need to have a burger or any meat-adjacent centerpiece in a meal—you can have onion rings and a milkshake by themselves and nobody can judge you. Serena gets the same thing, but also a Chicago dog with salt, celery, mustard, and sauerkraut on it. They're both hungry as condemned men.

They don't talk until the meal has been reduced to dregs and a few bready shells.

"It's a miracle you didn't blame me for what happened," Serena says out of nowhere, while Jamie is trying not to burp. "A lot of people would have—most people, even."

Jamie stares. It never occurred to her that she had the option to blame Serena for anything.

"I let that dickface get the better of me, I walked into an obvious trap and blew up your life as well as mine. And meanwhile . . ." Serena shakes her head, alluding to something else, something too painful to say. "Teenagers are supposed to be vindictive, even if adults have only the best intentions. You had plenty to hold against me, if you'd wanted."

"What? You were my hero." It comes out matter-of-fact, rather than sappy. Jamie could be pointing out a stain on the vinyl tablecloth. "Those dicks went after you because you were doing good in the world. I was pissed at that Bushwick guy and those doctors and everybody else who took a blowtorch to our lives. You were fighting the good fight and it fucks me up to hear you even suggest that I could have held it against you."

Serena puts down the stub of Chicago dog she's been clutching in both hands.

For a moment, Jamie thinks her mother is going to cry or make some declaration. But Serena just pooches her mouth and says, "Well, okay then."

They drive back to the old schoolhouse in near silence, except a little bit of small talk. When Jamie drops Serena off, she smiles and says she'll see Jamie soon. Then Jamie has the long drive back to the city to feel every feeling she has ever felt in her entire life, all at once. Like, she's terrified, thinking of the way she and her mom felt in perfect sync, and the fact that they just crossed a major line without even slowing down—*we cursed a guy!*—but also so so so churned up with adrenaline and blood and and and joy and pride. Pride! This family was, is, a force not to be fucked with. Plus Jamie keeps remembering the vulnerability in Serena's voice when she said Jamie could have blamed her. Jamie can't honestly remember Serena ever showing weakness like that, even after Mae died. Halfway home on the highway, Jamie is shaking and misting so hard, she needs to pull over and hug herself on the dirt gully for a while. Jamie makes up her mind around the time she spies the clown-head liquor store: she's not going to do any more mother-daughter spells, she's going to tell Serena it's too intense and weird. Someone could get hurt, maybe someone already did? But when Jamie gets home and she's standing on the frayed-carpet stairway of the apartment building, she knows that she absolutely wants to do more magic with Serena. They had so much power together, and Jamie's wasted her time doing small-ball shit, and she wants to find out what she's capable of. Plus who knows what Serena might get up to without Jamie there to provide adult supervision?

Ro is already asleep and they don't so much as grunt when Jamie crawls into bed. In the morning, they hand her a warm mug and say, "Late night?" Jamie tells them she was helping her mom to sort stuff out, and they shrug. "Didn't ask. All good." Jamie seriously almost tells Ro the whole thing, starting with stumbling on a crumbling gazebo with a powerful sense that something could happen here, back when she was thirteen going on fourteen, and ending with smearing poopy mud on a kazoo. But she knows Ro will start pointing out logical fallacies and rational explanations, and may wonder why Jamie never told them before, and honestly she just can't right now. So she just thanks her spouse and drinks the coffee.

You do me a great injustice, professed Tilly, and I wish you would not teaze me so.

Indeed Emily had no idea what Tilly meant, until the maid could be prevailed upon to explain that she had been in great suspense since Miss Emily had left off the fable of the Princess and the Strolling Player in the middle, and she could not rest until she learned the fate of the poor wronged princess.

Emily laughed and proposed to resume the tale immediately.

THE TALE OF
THE PRINCESS AND THE
STROLLING PLAYER

(CONTINUED)

Everyone was mystified as to the cause of the Princess's grievous Distemper. Physicians and Druggists could make no sense of it, this being a time when our understanding of Medicine was less advanced, and they prescribed her aught from purgatives to drams of metheglin, to no great Effect.

At last, though, the cause of her Malady became plain: after her delightsome interlude with Master Cleverly, which had consisted of nothing more than lively Conversation about the merits of various Dramatists, the local Gossips set to work, imputing all manner of Impropriety to the two of them. The Princess, whose Reputation had been peerless ere now, was all at once touched by Infamy.

In Despair, the Princess wrote to her oldest friend, Lady Sagacious, explaining the Situation and beseeching her Aid. Lady Sagacious arrived via coach drawn by her fastest horses, and was greatly distressed at the state of her lifelong friend. That Ill Repute had touched the Princess was dreadful enough—but that scarce explained the strange Diminishment of Her Highness, who seemed to grow lesser each time her name and Master Cleverly's were spoken together. Lady Sagacious was wise in the ways of Faeries, and soon found out the Truth: Master Cleverly was a half-Faerie, son of the Faerie King, who had offended his royal

Father with his poor Behaviour. The Faerie King had placed a Curse upon his child, ordaining that anyone who formed an Association with Master Cleverly would suffer a Reduction in both Stature and Status. Moreover, because of the strange Laws of the Faerie Realm, the Princess, having supped and conversed with Cleverly, was now presumed to be his Bethrothed.

Lady Sagacious resolved to do aught that she could to rescue her friend from this Fate. Thus, at the next full Moon, the lady ventured into the Forest and sought an audience with the Faeries. When she met with a Faerie Duke, a noble of the King's court, she struck a Bargain: the Princess would be freed from this Curse, but in exchange Lady Sagacious would return at the end of one month and thereafter must remain in the Custody of a member of the Faerie Court.

The next day, the Princess was overjoyed to find that she had returned to her former Size, and what's more, she had been freed from all those invidious Whispers. She could scarce credit her Fortune—but as the day wore on, she began to wonder how she had been saved, and she noticed the sadness behind the pleasant expression on the face of her oldest Friend, Lady Sagacious.

8

Let him who would choose honesty consider first his own motives, such that disclosing the reasons for speech needs must colour the response to such speech.

—*EMILY: A TALE OF PARAGONS AND DELIVERANCE* BY A LADY, BOOK 3, CHAPTER 17

Jamie doesn't hear from Serena for a few days after their big cooperative spell-casting blitz. That whole excursion—the melted doll head, the chanting—it all feels like a TV show Jamie dreamed about watching, except that from time to time she snaps to attention like a soldier who dozed off on guard duty, and gets a panicky flash of her mother and herself with their faces flushed. She compartmentalizes like a fucking spreadsheet.

Jamie sits in endless meetings about a possible grad-student strike along with Markus, the sociologist. A sense of doom flutters in the air: *the trustees are awake.* Everyone has heard similar things. Markus distracts themself by jotting lines of poetry in a thumb-sized journal, like golf scores: their handwriting is gorgeous, and the lines that Jamie glimpses chime in her head for hours afterward. She's not surprised when Markus mentions a love of the poetry of Christopher Smart, especially all the stuff about his cat.

Serena sends a text one afternoon: she's found a place near the Alewife T stop, and it's perfect, judging from the photos. There's a tiny bedroom, with closets along one wall, and a kitchen that you could fit two people inside—

there's even a nice main room with a spot for a sofa, an article of furniture Serena hasn't owned in so long. The front windows look out on a pleasant street with an oak tree on the opposite sidewalk. Jamie texts back: *looks perfect, go for it.*

While Jamie still has her phone in her hand, she can't resist searching for any news about McAllister Bushwick and the JawBone organization. And . . . nope. If any misfortune has befallen Bushwick himself, or anyone connected to his organization, then he's kept it quiet.

Even though Jamie does magic sometimes, she's not sure she believes in magic. It's a useful practice for thinking deeply about what she craves the most, and the actual process of spell-casting soothes her, but who the fuck knows if these tiny rituals are doing anything real. What Jamie does believe is that the things you pour energy into will grow in your life, and she's never regretted pouring her energy into love and community. But especially love.

So Jamie's working in Diesel Cafe, and she finds herself thinking about Ro. She can't imagine what her life would be like if she hadn't found them when she did—it'd be like speculating about what kind of life might have developed on Earth if our sun had been a blue giant. Ro makes her brain do a wild and gleefully uncoordinated dance, makes her skin tingle, brings her heart to life. Joy is always present, just at the edge of the frame, even in the bleakest times. The world seems huge and undiscovered. People talk about relationships in terms like, "I like who I am when I'm with them," or "They make me want to be a better person," as if the purpose of love was self-improvement. But fuck that—the purpose of love is love.

The scent of coffee and baked goods, the winter sunlight slanting through the window, the acoustic singer-songwriter playing on the cafe sound system—all of it feels brand-new. All Jamie wants to do is embrace Ro, whisper sinful virtues in their ear, keep her skin close to theirs until both their skins have softened with age. She wants to tell them *Love me all at once or I shall die,* like "The Miller's Tale." She feels swept away with sugar-brain. She texts Ro that she wants to take them out tonight. Fancy restaurant, tablecloths, wine list, rich dessert, all of it. Ro texts back: they'll meet her there.

• • • • •

The Forager is the only restaurant in Cambridge or Somerville that has both tablecloths and food that Jamie enjoys. In her experience you either get cool décor and sedulous waitstaff, or you get delicious cuisine. She makes a big deal of getting all the things Ro likes, including the fancy truffle fries and a salad with endives. Ro is stressy and a little grumpy, and keeps nattering about deliverables. At last, Jamie takes their hands and say, "Hey, I know I've been gone a lot lately, helping Serena get back on her feet. I swear on my thesis that this is almost over and I won't need to visit her as much anymore. Soon, I promise."

"It's fine, I get it, I don't want to be the shitty partner who gets mad that you have family responsibilities, it's all good."

"It's not all good, not at all. I don't want to be the selfish jerk who takes her partner for granted just because I'm on some kind of mission to reconnect with my mom, or repair my birth family. That's not who I want to be."

Jamie has a burning desire to tell Ro everything. Magic, the whole shebang. *Go on,* a voice somewhere in her pulmonary system urges. *Tell them, give them the whole story.* Jamie hesitates. And thinks of the scene in *Emily* where Emily and her maid Tilly debate the imperatives of honesty vs kindness, and it turns into a lot of wordplay about "kind," as adjective, as noun, and its Germanic roots, meaning "child."

Why would Jamie trust her mom with knowledge she's not ready to entrust to her life partner? That's kind of the question and answer, both in one. Jamie has way more to lose with Ro than with the woman she's barely spoken to since she turned twenty.

Jamie realizes she's been staring at the dessert menu for ages, zoning out and maybe even muttering to herself about transparency vs purity of motives. Ro is giving her a hard look, wondering what the fuck is up. If the goal of not telling Ro her secret was to avoid awkwardness, then that boat just burst into flames and drifted out to sea.

"I think the tiramisu sounds sexy as fuck. Want to split it?" Jamie says, as if she really was lost in dessert thought.

"Are you bored with me?" Ro doesn't give Jamie time to protest that no, of course not, she is more fascinated and lovestruck than ever. "You're barely paying attention to me tonight, you're incommunicado for hours at a time and coming home late, and I've just been taking it for granted you're visiting your mom, but either way you're going to pretty extreme lengths not to be home. Perhaps reconnecting with your mother is part of some quarter-life crisis, and this is the sort of dinner you only take someone out for to assuage some unshakable guilt. Either way, sharing a goopy dessert is no substitute for communication."

Jamie looks away from the suddenly cloying descriptions of gelatos and pastries. All desire for confectionary bonding has vanished, and in fact her lower gut is a fucking anvil.

She flings too much cash on the table and pushes back her chair. Fuck it.

"Come on. I need to show you something."

"What— Where are we going—"

They follow her out of the restaurant, still asking a million questions.

"I'm going to show you what I've been doing with Serena this whole time. You just need to promise me that you'll keep an open mind, and trust that it'll make sense soon enough."

"Why can't you just explain—"

"Because—" Jamie starts out with an edge in her voice, then dials it back to sweetness. "Because it can't be explained. It's like in *The Matrix*: you can't be told, only shown. Just like that. One of the ten thousand reasons I love you is because you always want to explain or form a working hypothesis or figure out exactly how something works. But with this, that won't fly. I promise you'll get it soon, but for now let's just say it's . . . it's a kind of a mindfulness technique. More or less. You'll see when you see."

Ro grumbles but follows Jamie to the car. She drives a short distance to the start of the Minuteman Bikeway, near Alewife. They go off-trail right away, into the dense bracken along the banks of the Little River, which leads to the Little Pond. They wander, semi-aimlessly, away from civilization.

"So what, you've been doing mother-daughter yoga?" Ro says.

Jamie leads as if she knows where they're going. Which . . . if she knew where they were going, there would be no point. She wants to do better this time, not throw Ro in the deep end the way she did Serena.

Half an hour later, they're still going in circles. The moonlight only filters discreetly through the canopy overhead, and Jamie keeps seeing a bit of detritus that she expects to be the remains of someone's project—a plank, a rotting branch—but nothing intentional enough for her purposes. This would have been much easier in the daytime or at least the early evening.

"Okay, look," Ro says. "I'm cold and exhausted and we have a meeting tomorrow morning, at which I am expected to speak, and I wish you would just tell me what we're doing out here."

They are very lost. Her phone has zero bars. Some of the art of finding the in-between places is absolutely subjective, and tonight everything looks wild and forbidding. Shit damn shit.

"This was a mistake," Jamie says out loud. "I'm sorry. I just got a fire lit under me and I wanted you to see for yourself, but this is a bad idea, and I'm sorry, I will just have to show you some other time. Come on."

Jamie starts tromping forward, but Ro does not follow.

"A: you're going the wrong way. That way just leads farther into these damn woods. And B: you dragged me out here, you can at least give me an executive summary, or a few hints about whatever the hell this is."

Jamie heads back toward the sound of Ro's voice, nearly snagging her ankle on every other tree root, while she tries to come up with a half-truth that will hold them for now.

When she gets back to where Ro was standing, there's no sign.

"Uh, Ro? Where did you go?"

No answer.

They were right here, a moment ago.

Not panicking, not yet. They probably got sick of Jamie's bullshit and stormed off, or just walked back to the car. Except they're as lost as Jamie is, and they wouldn't just abandon her in the woods without saying a word, however much she might deserve it.

The air feels colder all at once, seeping through Jamie's clothes, and oh god, she is lost in the woods under unbearably vague moonlight with no cell signal at all.

She's starting to think this is some magical shit, but it's not a kind of magic she's ever come across, and she's beyond out of her depth. She was supposed to be the wise mystical teacher who knows all the ropes and the bells to which the ropes are attached, and she really knows nothing, and she's lost Ro.

Bloody hell. They were right here, right next to Jamie, a few obnoxiously visible breaths ago. This is just like in *Emily,* where the author keeps finding excuses for people to get lost and separated from each other, and to become disoriented in various ways. It's Collier's way of transiting from one set piece to the next, but also of commenting on the unsteadiness of her tragicomic hero, the futility of plans and fixed ideas. Here, a highwayman attacks Emily's carriage; there, a freak hailstorm during her evening constitutional causes her and her companions to sprint for shelter. She goes from interlocutor to interlocutor, bridged by a series of bewildering encounters and misadventures. Jamie forces herself out of her dissertation reverie, and back to her actual dire situation.

"Ro!" She shouts herself hoarse. "Jesus, Ro! Are you out there? I promise I will tell you whatever, I'll explain all the shit, if you just come back and tell me to my face how bad I messed up." No answer but the bloody wind.

Jamie should get out of these woods, assuming she can even find her way out. Get to someplace with signal. See if Ro left her any texts or voicemails, or if she can get some help.

But . . . some instinct? Some feeling, some sense of magic, tells her that if she leaves the woods now, she will never see Ro, ever again.

THE TALE OF
THE PRINCESS AND THE
STROLLING PLAYER

(CONTINUED)

Days passed, and the Princess and Lady Sagacious took their Ease, now that the Princess had been restored to her usual Perfection. They drank tea and strolled in the gardens as usual, and played merrily on the Harpsichord, and enjoyed all of the Pleasures at their Disposal.

The Princess rejoiced to be so free, and to spend so much time with her Friend from whom she had not been used to much Separation, except that she worried for Master Cleverly. The strolling player had departed once again on his endless Peregrinations, and the Princess could scarce enquire after his well-being without the risk of reigniting the fires of Scandal that had only recently been doused. Despite the grief Master Cleverly's curse had caused her, she still pitied this wretch for having suffered his father's immoderate Wrath, such being the singular Generosity of her heart.

At the same time, the Princess noted on occasion a Shadow passing across the heart of her beloved Lady Sagacious, and she could by no means discover what had caused so much Grief to her friend. A generous heart will more readily trust in the Honesty of Friends, yet will a true Friend not also strive to learn the truth of one's most vexing Maladies, by any means that lie within its power? Thus the Princess sent her most gracious lady in waiting,

Penelope, to befriend Lady Sagacious and gain her Trust. The first three days, Penelope reported back only that Lady Sagacious sighed grievously when she thought herself Unobserved—but on the fourth day, the lady at last broke down and told Penelope the entire story.

The Princess at once summoned Lady Sagacious, who confessed all, but lamented that there was no helping her Situation. The only way to save the Princess from the Curse that afflicted all who came close to Master Cleverly was to offer herself—and now Lady Sagacious herself was Faerie-touched, and must belong to one who is of the Faerie Court. No Recourse, no Refuge, was available. At the end of two short weeks, Lady Sagacious must present herself in the forest, to be gone forever. The Princess's heart was sore grieved, and she wept freely at the thought of losing her Friend.

But when a few days had passed, the Princess began to think of a way that Lady Sagacious's Sacrifice could be redeemed without losing her forever.

9

The snares and traps laid by libertines and scoundrels are well understood in this day and age; less so, indeed, are the chains within which the most ardent students of virtue may find themselves entrapped, should they suffer their friends and family to use them ill too often. The wits have said a surfeit of virtue can do as much ill as a dollop of vice, and I believe it to be so.

—*EMILY: A TALE OF PARAGONS AND*
DELIVERANCE BY A LADY, BOOK 1, CHAPTER 19

Jesus, the wind out here is like a fucking hose spraying Jamie with frigid water, she's in the world's shittiest wet T-shirt contest even under four layers. Every direction looks exactly the same and the moonlight is ambient rather than focused, thanks to all these damn trees, and Jamie just wants to cry, she wants to howl and beat her head against the trunk and weep like a drunken sorority pledge, she's so tired and scared and alone and she misses her bae, and whatever she did she takes it back, she will do anything in her power to undo it.

Jamie tries to breathe knife-cold air and get herself together. If this really is some magical shit, then she needs to finish whatever it is that she started.

So . . . what the ever-fucking fuck? Did she somehow cast a spell that made Ro disappear? Was she . . . wishing for them to vanish? No, no no no. Can't even think that. She was definitely dreading this conversation, and wishing she didn't have to confess that she'd kept this huge secret from them for so long. All this time, she kept telling Serena that you have to be very precise and exact about what you desire, what intentions you focus on, all of that. And then she goes and puts a completely wrong and contrary and self-destructive want out into the world, a shitty garbage impulse that is the total opposite of what she would actually want, ever.

She didn't think she was actually doing a spell—like, she hadn't found the right spot and put down an offering/petition or whatever. She had done exactly none of the steps. But then, she thought she'd figured out exactly how this worked and what the limits were, before she and Serena started experimenting so much. That's the whole reason she's out here in the first place: she got scared, she got wise, she realized this thing that she had chalked up as just a weird practice that maybe netted her a twenty-dollar bill every now and then, and maybe made her teaching assignments slightly less shitty, was in fact scary powerful, and she was a shitbird for keeping it from the love of her life. And now look at her.

She's hugging herself, hunched over, hyperventilating, and she realizes she's mentally composing the email she's going to send—Facebook post??—explaining that Ro disappeared and is presumed dead. Talking about how she met them at a college career fair where neither of them was even remotely trying to think about careers, and something in their smile, their goofy laugh, just seized hold of her, like their spiky hair had a halo, and she felt her heart rise up and open into a pair of wings, each chamber flapping and catching the updrafts, and she chattered awkwardly and tried to flirt without having her head explode or seeming too sweaty, and she had this feeling, this urgency inside her godfisting core, that she wanted to spend all the time it was possible to spend with this person, and maybe even a little more time than that. She would steal extra time from sleep or death or office hours or her friends, or just make time slow the fuck down so she had more of it with this luminous human. Usually when someone cracks wise, it's as foolish as eating a chili dog on a moped while wearing white satin—but Ro's wisecracks were actually wise, and she would rather be the butt of their jokes than hear a soaring compliment from anyone else. She says, in this imaginary email that she finds herself scripting in her head, that she would give literally everything she will ever own, all her senses, her career, even the secrets of Jane Collier and *Emily,* to have them back with her again.

Jamie is the kind of frozen where she cannot tell if she's sobbing or shivering, and the distinction does not feel meaningful.

She turns slowly, a complete revolution, looking at every spooky-ass branch and trunk, orienting. Fills her lungs. Ow cold air ow. She closes her eyes and gathers her strength. She's supposed to be a witch. She might not be a natural like her mother, but she can do a working. She can put her will into the bloody universe.

She marches until she finds it: a fire pit, the indentations of tent poles. Someone camped here, and they did not leave the campsite the way they had found it. Thank all the fucking goddesses of the fuck pantheon. She kneels in the middle of the firepit, muttering *please yes please, I know, yes please, just this once, for me*—she gets louder and she's just going *please please fuck please. I need this.* She places her favorite picture of Ro, from her wallet, along with a pair of handmade glass teardrop earrings, and she closes her eyes as it all goes into the long-cold ashes with a melted beer can poking out, she keeps saying *please I swear please I'm begging.* She still doesn't know any formal rituals, but verbalizing seemed to help when she and Serena did it. Her hands are filthy with ash, her face is soaked, and her heart is louder than a construction site. *Please I swear please, this time, just once, I swear please.*

"Jamie, what the fuck?" Ro's voice comes from behind her. "What are you doing?"

She staggers to her feet and crushes them in her ashy, filthy embrace.

"This has been the weirdest night of my life, and I went on tour with a few show choirs." Ro seems extremely disoriented—no huge surprise—but they have a weird memory of coming into the woods with Jamie, and then they were caught in a shaft of moonlight, and it was like they became moonlight, and it's really hard to explain, but they were weightless and so cold, ghost cold, and then they were back to normal, except they were watching Jamie chant and keen like a cult member.

"Uh, I wanted to give you a demonstration, but that was not the demonstration I had in mind. I have this, uh, hobby, ever since I was like thirteen, and until recently I didn't think it was that big a deal, but I don't know how to say it."

"You're some kind of chaos wrangler," Ro says. "Ugh, everything is making a whole new sense now. You make chaos your bitch."

"Um. Sort of. Yeah. Actually. Wow, you're taking this really well, considering. Oh god, it's just hitting me, I almost lost you. I really did not know what I was doing. This is a fucking nightmare." Jamie feels exhausted and also amped, like she pounded a dozen Red Bulls.

She keeps talking talking talking, but no sentences are coming out, just disordered strings of words—as if she cannot stop spell-casting, no matter how she tries. She's still so cold, even with their warmth next to her.

"I really want to understand," Ro says. "And I have a feeling I'm never going to. Because chaos. And maybe that's why you held off telling me? I'm not saying I get it—I sort of get it, but also I hate it. Having something in your life that I will never understand, that can never let me in, is possibly a deal-breaker, and I can't even tell right now." They are sounding just as rational, calm, and sober as ever, but also shivering and quaking harder than Jamie is, which is a lot.

"Come on." Jamie manages to sentence. "Let's get out of these woods. I think I can find the way." Usually, when a spell is concluded, she has a much easier time finding her way back to the "civilized" world of cars, lights, convenience stores, and cell signal, and she prays that rule will hold when all the others have been splintered.

She and Ro cling to each other like wounded soldiers: stumbling three-legged, root-tripping every other step. When they see a streetlight and hear the hum of a generator, Jamie wants to cry and sing and barf.

"You have to understand," Jamie says in the car. Oh fuck yes, the car. Heater going, stereo softly playing Laura Mvula. She loves this car so much right now. "You have to understand, I have a whole superstition that if I talk about this thing I do, this practice—"

"Magic."

"—If I put a label on it or dissect it, then it'll stop working. It'll lose all its power. And I've been trying to teach my mom without speaking too plainly about it, and it's been tough, and I did have to explain more than I wanted. And maybe that's why everything is so weird, like what just happened to you."

She's driving fifteen miles per hour, because it's so dark beyond the yellow thread of her lights and she doesn't trust her reflexes for shit right now.

"If you can do it, you can think about it," Ro syllogizes. "And if you can think about it, you can talk about it."

"I try not to think. I've trained myself to do it without thinking too much."

"You're sounding like a serial killer right now, and it's not as sexy as I thought that would be."

"Listen, like I said the other day, I believe the things that are the hardest to talk about with any precision are the things most worth talking about."

"And it's your job, your actual job, to find ways to talk about them. You wouldn't write your thesis saying it's too hard to explain the Hogarthian tableau in *Emily*, so you're just going to draw a cat picture instead."

Ro stops and stares at Jamie, driving fifteen miles per hour on a sleepy road near Malden.

"What?" Jamie says without looking away from the road.

"You're smiling. Why the fuck are you smiling? Did I say something funny?"

Jamie glances in the rearview. Yes. She is smiling. What. How.

"I guess . . . I can't hear you say the words 'Hogarthian tableau' without having to smile. It's all I've ever wanted from my life, ever: hearing the most amazing beautiful person in the world talk about my obsession like it matters."

"This is serious," Ro stammers. "It's not a joke."

"I promise I will find a way for all this to make sense to you. I got you to accept my obsession with the epistolary mode versus the discursive narrator, this practice should be easy to understand by comparison."

"Just say the goddamn word. Magic."

"Okay." Breathe, unclench. "Magic."

They sit in their separate feedback loops until they're almost home, no sound but music and the tick of the engine.

"So." Ro hesitates. "You didn't . . . plan for me to vanish. In the woods. When I turned into moonlight. That wasn't on purpose."

"What? God no. I hadn't even started to do a spell yet, I was still search-ing for the right spot. That just happened—like, on its own. Nothing like that has ever happened before, ever."

"So . . . what? Magic doesn't want you to show me how it works?"

Jamie hadn't considered that weird thought. She almost veers off the road.

"I mean . . . magic doesn't *want* anything. Magic reflects our wants, if we share them in a way that makes sense, in the right place and time. I mean, I clearly know less than I thought I did, but . . ."

Ro goes, "Huh." They fall back into a reverie.

Back at the apartment, in bed, Jamie tries to explain more, make some vow, build a blanket fort around the two of them. Ro hugs themself, turned away from her in a non-spoonable fashion.

"Too tired," they say. "I can't do this right now."

Jamie thinks that's it, they're done talking.

They turn back to face her. "So . . . things started to get weird after you showed your mother how to do magic."

Jamie grunts like, yeah, sure, uh-huh.

"That's interesting." Then Ro is either asleep or fake-asleep; either way, they're not talking anymore until morning.

Jamie takes a sleeping pill. It helps a little.

In the morning, Ro pops a vegan toaster pastry into the toaster with-out offering to make one for Jamie. She's torn between joy/relief/gratitude that they didn't vanish forever, and inky guilt that gets all over everything, smearing her fingers, impossible to scrub. She hunches on the edge of the bed, hands between knees.

"Would you ever have told me?" Ro asks between pastry bites. "About your 'hobby'? If things hadn't started getting intense with your mother? Would you ever have let me in on it?"

"I can't ever tell anybody anything." Jamie sounds drunk to herself. "I don't know how to talk about it. Probably I'll never know how. I wanted to show you, but I knew you'd want me to explain first and show after, and I cannot do that. I can only demonstrate, not analyze. Some things resist analysis."

"Your pedagogy leaves much to be desired." Ro scowls, but at least they're teasing her, not shutting her out. They pull out their phone and start tapping.

"What are you—"

"I'm going to your Rate My Prof page and leaving a review. 'Professor Sandthorn did not provide the syllabus or make her expectations for the class clear, and instead led me into a dark forest where I turned into mist. Two out of five stars.'"

Jamie is so relieved they're making jokes, she wants to cry.

"I'm really sorry," Jamie says again. "I never . . . I would never want that to happen. I had no idea. If anything had happened to—"

No more jokes. Ro shakes their head, wearily. "I don't need any more non-apologies where you explain your lack of intent. I want you to fix it."

"Fix . . . Fix what? You're here. You're safe. I got you back."

Ro stares, like they're waiting for Jamie to catch the fuck up.

"Ugh." Jamie clutches her head between her knees. "You don't think . . ."

"Doesn't matter what I think. You keep telling me your 'practice' is about intent. I believe you when you say you didn't intend for me to get erased like that. I have to believe you, because that would be so unthinkable, I would never recover for as long as I live. But so, if you didn't intend for that to happen to me . . . Who did?"

Goddamn logic.

Jamie almost gets into the dirtmobile and drives straight down to the old schoolhouse right away. But she has a class to teach, and no time to find a sub.

"Foundling" is one of those words that nobody uses anymore, though it has a really cool ring. It suggests a very different relation to family, to self, to the body—as if a foundling is forever defined by having been discovered in a basket or bassinet as an infant. Once found, never to be lost. But also, never to be desired in precisely the same way as someone who was always where they were supposed to be. A foundling is eternally out of place, othered, not of any true family. Actually, maybe to be a foundling is to be forever lost, after all. The word "foundling" also reminds Jamie of "changeling," as if the heroes of all these eighteenth-century novels were at one remove from the spawn of faeries, like Master Cleverly. Maybe part of what attracted Jamie to the eighteenth-century novel, in the first place, was that odd combination of innocence—optimism even—with alienation and the otherness of orphans.

The whole time Jamie natters about the birth of the novel to blank-faced teens, her mind is trying to untangle the thing that happened in the woods, and what Ro said this morning. She's wide awake, she can't wake all the way up, she's dreaming on her feet. The moment when Ro vanished keeps coming back, not like a flashback in a movie, but like a sense-memory. She can see the scene, a terrible Hogarthian tableau: Jamie marching bloody-minded into the moon-silted trees, Ro slowly fading to moonlight. And Jamie's mom . . . what? Sitting in her one-room schoolhouse, sipping rum neat, with a placid look of triumph? Jamie can't picture Serena's slice of the triptych.

As soon as all the young minds have been molded, timeless wisdom dispensed, the crisis of the English novel explored, Jamie grabs her shit and bails so fast, nobody has a chance to corner her and ask what will be on the final.

Back home, she puts down her school shit and grabs her driving shit. Ro sprawls on the couch, watching some reality show about people who aren't genetically related but still believe they are identical twins. Apparently this happens in Nebraska.

"Hey," Ro says, in a friendly but not spousely manner.

"Don't wait up. I need to go talk to Serena. She's still at the schoolhouse."

"About . . . what happened last night?"

Jamie nods. On the television, two people who look nothing alike are insisting that they have all the same quirks and nobody can tell them apart when they dress the same.

"You said it," Jamie says. "It would be a super weird coincidence if there was no connection between me teaching my mom and you vanishing like that."

"I don't think Serena is evil or anything," Ro says slowly. "But she's been through some stuff, and you put her on a pedestal. Pedestals make people do wack shit."

"I'm really really super sorry. No matter what the explanation turns out to be, even if it was a thing with my mom somehow. I'm sorry that happened to you. I was a fucking goon getting lost with you in the woods in the middle of the night. I promise if you keep me around, I will never put you in harm's way again."

Ro closes their eyes, as if watching a private movie. "It will be difficult to feel safe with you. For how long, I cannot say. Longer than a day, less than a lifetime, I hope. I didn't know I could be scared like that."

Jamie is still standing, they're still sitting. The TV blares, faux twins refusing a DNA test.

"So you're just going to ask your mother if she made me vanish?"

Sort of, not exactly. That's close enough to the plan that Jamie nods.

Ro turns off the television and grabs their jacket and keys. "I'm coming."

"I don't think that's—" She can't come up with a reason why it's a bad idea, it just seems self-evidently bad, like she needs to have an intense mother-daughter conversation about mystic shit, and she knows her mom won't open up if a third person is in the mix. Serena has never known how to talk to Ro, and it's always been awkward on both sides. Plus Serena's wary of what she says to almost anyone, after JawBone.

"I'm coming with you." Ro might as well be explaining a fact of nature. "Or else I won't be here when you get back."

Oh god. Now Jamie is the one turning into frozen moonlight. Nothing is solid, everything is gray.

"Calm down." Ro grabs her hand, gently. "Not trying to scare you. It's me, okay? You look as if a ghost is chewing up your butt. I still love you, okay? But I'm the one who turned into mist, and I need to be there when you get to the bottom of this. Plus you should not have to face this alone."

"You're—" Jamie chokes. "You're giving me an ultimatum."

"I'm setting expectations and limits, because we are in a fucking relationship."

Her heart is fucking head-banging, all of her insides shook up to shit, she can barely think, she tastes dry mouth. But also? She feels loved, recognized. They're pissed, for good reason, but they're right.

"Okay," Jamie says. "I wouldn't wish it otherwise. Let's go."

10

Emily's father, Mr. M., wished nothing more than her happiness, and for her to flourish—so long as those things did not conflict with the strictest rules of good conduct, which of course they always did.

—*EMILY: A TALE OF PARAGONS AND DELIVERANCE* BY A LADY, BOOK 5, CHAPTER 9

On the drive down there, Ro keeps trying to make sense of this whole deal.

"So your mom has been hiding from the world in a schoolhouse for the past several years," Ro says. "And you thought she needed to be empowered?"

"Well, yeah. Everybody needs empowerment. Right?"

"Uh, no. You're smarter than that. At least I thought you were? Plenty of people, plenty of white women even, do not need to be empowered. They need to use the power that they have more responsibly. Power is only as good as your willingness to lift everyone else up with you. You told me this thing you do is all about intent, right? Focusing your desire in a particular direction? So it matters what your wants actually are. And maybe someone who's been living in the middle of nowhere stewing and brooding might not be the best person to entrust reality-twisting power to? Because she's literally out of touch with the world? I don't know."

Jamie doesn't say anything. She keeps replaying the Hat Incident—and then the poopy kazoo, the intensity, *Get it.* She's never felt anything like that.

"I just wanted to bring her back to the world," Jamie says at last.

"Sure, yeah. But people don't always return to the world in triumph, right? Sometimes you come back humble and work your way back in."

The road putters under their wheels. The steering wheel jerks.

They're almost at the schoolhouse. Jamie feels a sudden weird urgency, like they could be too late. For what? She doesn't know. She just feels unmoored.

They pass by the old gamekeeper shed. The road turns to gravel. Crunch crunch grrr.

She lets go of the gearshift long enough to hold out her hand to them. They squeeze it.

"I'm glad you insisted on coming with me. I'd be shitting myself if you weren't here."

They crank around the corner and the schoolhouse appears on their right, gray-pink in the twilight. The white columns of the Fordhams' house are faded by mist in the distance.

The schoolhouse door is locked but not dead-bolted, so there's just a clackety rickety latch that dislodges with a bit of a jiggle and push. Groans inward, and Jamie steps inside. For some reason, she's expecting a face-melting stench again, but there's only a pine-scented must. No sign of how long Serena's been gone, or what she's doing.

Ro looks around, wrinkling their nose. They've been inside this house once before, a long time ago—Serena doesn't like entertaining here, so when the three of them have hung out, they've mostly gone to the rustic train-themed restaurant a few miles away.

"It's smaller than I remembered. And, I don't know, sadder."

"I think her plan was just to waste away here."

Ro keeps looking around. "Just promise me something, okay? If something happens—more than what has already happened—and everything goes to pieces, promise you won't hide from the world like this." Jamie gives them a helpless look, still wanting to defend her mom, and they add, "I'm *serious*. I can't bear the thought of this happening to you. You need noisy people around to remind you of yourself. Even more, now that I know you sneak off to do conjurings or whatever, on a regular basis."

The truth is, it wouldn't take that much to make Jamie retreat into a tiny box. All it would take is what it took for Serena: being disgraced, losing the love of her life.

What hubris, what smugness, for Jamie to assume she had stable ground on which to stand and help her mother. She thinks of Wile E. Coyote realizing mid-ravine that he is running on air. And then Jean-Paul Sartre's famous thought experiment: a voyeur stands in a hallway, looking into someone's bedroom through a keyhole—only to realize that someone is standing behind him and watching him in turn. Both scenarios are about a startling shift in perspective, the illusion of imperviousness ripped away. Subjection.

Jamie looks at Ro, still kind after what (almost) happened (and still could happen) to them.

"I'm sorry," she says. "I've been proud. I've made decisions that I should have known would end up affecting you, and I didn't consult you. I've had this power, this thing that shapes my life in so many ways, and I never wanted to let you in on it."

Ro retreats into the darkest corner of the schoolhouse, suddenly far away.

"I think you just put into words something I was struggling to piece together for myself," they say.

"I keep saying that a witch needs self-awareness, or this will never work."

"Just enough self-awareness, though. Not *too* much, or you'll be enervated into inactivity. Right? If you have perfect self-knowledge, you'll be too swept up in your own contradictions to cast a clean working," Ro says. Jamie gives them a helpless, sputtering look, and they add, "I'm paraphrasing what you said to me before."

"Nobody ever achieves perfect self-knowledge. That's impossible."

"But so you thought your mother was more capable of knowing herself than I am. Or anyone else in your life."

Jamie wants to explain that it has more to do with need than ability. And she was hoping to help her mother *gain* self-awareness, rather than make use of self-awareness she already possessed. Except before she can voice any of this, the flaw comes clear in her mind. You don't hand cosmic power to someone who doesn't know how to handle it, and *hope* that they'll learn the hard way.

"She was always there for me, she sacrificed so much. I needed to pay her back."

"So magic isn't strictly transactional. But relationships are?"

Ro is starting to realize how angry they are. It's a weird feature of their relationship with Jamie: they often fail to recognize their own anger until she helps them to figure it out, and then she catches hell.

Serena's cellphone still isn't picking up. She tends to drop it into the bottom of her purse and ignore it unless she's digging for chewing gum or lip balm. It's getting late, visibility is for shit. What if something happened to Serena? What if the same thing that made Ro vanish also affected her?

Jamie stands up. "She's not coming back, there's no point hanging around here. It's a long drive back to Somerville." She feels Ro's lack of forgiveness on the back of her neck and the most goose bump–prone skin on the sides of her upper arms.

"Are you sure?"

"We can keep trying her cell just as easily back at our place. She's probably roaming the woods or shopping with her phone off. I feel creepy lying in wait here."

Right when they get in the dirtmobile and start the engine, Serena turns up in a Range Rover Jamie has never seen before.

"Jamie? Ro? What are you doing here? I've been out doing errands. The movers are coming on Tuesday, and I need to get set up in my new place." Serena sees both their faces. "What? I thought you'd be excited."

Jamie sits behind the wheel of the dirtmobile, like a crash-test dummy waiting to collide.

Ro opens the passenger-side door and places one foot on the gravel while their left leg remains ensconced.

"We were just heading back to the city." Ro sounds stiff, their Midwestern roots showing. "We should have called before we came out here. Jamie wanted to check on you."

Serena stares back. The canvas bag on her shoulder droops until it slumps onto the ground. "I'm sorry we missed each other. We should make plans soon."

Ro gets their right leg back inside the car and shuts the door. Seat belt snaps into place.

Jamie starts the engine, puts the car in reverse, everything. Then she turns it off and palms the keys.

"Did you put a spell on Ro?" Jamie blurts as she gets out of the car.

"Did I—" Serena looks at each of them in turn.

Ro hesitates, then gets out, too. They stand on either side of the vehicle like the Winchesters circa *Supernatural* season 3.

"So you told them." Serena folds her arms. "I thought magic was our thing, you and me. I thought we had something that was just for us."

"Are you seriously jealous? I told my spouse about an important thing in my life. I should have told them a long time ago." Jamie kicks gravel as she closes the space between her mother and herself.

Serena goes stiff, and the skin on her face seems to tighten. "What are you accusing me of?"

"Just answer the question." Jamie can feel Ro's gaze on the back of her neck. "Did you put a spell on my partner? Because I can't think who else it would have been."

Serena is giving Jamie the ugly-bug look again. "I can't believe you would accuse me of that."

"That's not a denial."

Until this moment, Jamie did not believe, in her gut, that Serena could have had something to do with Ro disappearing. Now, facing her mother's scowl, she's sure it's true. Jamie ought to feel furious, bitter; instead, an ice helix burrows inside her, delicate but unbreakable. She searches her memory for when she's felt this wretched chill before, and then it's obvious: she is grieving for the mother in front of her, the same way she once grieved the mother who is long gone.

"What is it you think I did?" Serena is frantic, hopping like a crow in the frozen air. "If you're going to stand and accuse me—I need to know the particulars—I can't defend myself—"

"You don't get to claim victimhood this time." Jamie can hear her voice rising. By now, she's sure that Serena knows exactly what she did.

Ro speaks for the first time in a while. "We're not solving anything like this. I've barely eaten since that wretched dinner yesterday. But I deserve, we both deserve, an explanation."

"Fine." Serena gets right in Jamie's face. "We'll talk in a civilized manner, over dinner at the Bohemian Express."

Groan. The Bohemian Express is the aforementioned train-themed restaurant, a few old converted train cars on a tiny stretch of track, with soggy beef Wellington, dry Yorkshire pudding, and other stodgy old-white-people foods, plus a generous selection of beers, wines, and aperitifs. Trust Serena to turn her own hideous crime into an excuse to strong-arm Jamie into taking her to dinner.

When the three of them get seated in the "dining car," Serena insists on ordering drinks and eating bread rolls before she'll talk about the subject at hand. It's late and Jamie is starving, and Ro clearly is, too.

"Very well." Serena butters a half roll that she already got butter on earlier. "Ask me what you would like to know."

Jamie hates that her mother's power move has worked so well.

She's about to snap—Serena knows what they want to ask—but Ro speaks first.

"As I understand it, the practice of spellwork requires a great deal of intentionality. One cannot simply decide to achieve a particular end, one must desire it, and that desire in itself becomes a form of currency, or perhaps current, to power a working." Ro sounds so calm, it's spooky. "So I would like to know why you wanted me gone so badly. So deeply."

"I . . . didn't. At all." *Now* Serena flinches. "I like you, even though you regularly work my nerves. You're good for my daughter. Her happiness is more important to me than my own."

"Then . . . why?"

Serena destroys her last bread roll with index fingers and thumbs. "I don't know. I never did a spell to make anyone disappear, because why would I do that? In what world would that make sense? Doesn't it seem more likely that all of this was an accident?" She's still flinching. The questions are a flimsy barricade.

"You did a spell, Mom. Probably more than one." Jamie strains not to snarl. Her hands are full of tablecloth. "You have a history of doing magic with uncertain motives. We just want to know what you did this time. Stop protesting too much and tell us what you did."

"You told me never to talk about workings after they were—"

"I know what I said. I don't care. What did you *do*?"

"It wasn't anything." Serena looks out the train window at the parking lot. "I just . . . I was worried. Because we were moving mountains, you and me. The two of us were working justice. I could feel something happening. For the first time in nearly seven years, I had a family and a purpose, you gave those things back to me. Happiness? Happiness scared the shit out of me."

Jamie can't tell if Serena is laughing bitterly, or choking on a bread roll.

"I just . . . I wanted to cover our tracks. I wanted to make sure nobody could find out what we were accomplishing together. That's all." Serena turns to Ro. "It wasn't aimed at you personally. I swear. I never imagined that Jamie would confide in you, or in anyone, after all the time she spent lecturing me about secrecy."

"So anyone who learned about your spellwork would have been erased? I'm not sure that's better, to be honest." Ro keeps Serena in sight.

"I honestly wasn't sure what would happen if someone triggered the spell. It's never exact or definite, right?" Serena turns to Jamie, as if expecting her to launch into teacher mode.

Jamie's throat is sealed.

The waiter brings drinks on a trolley, as if they were halfway across the Alps.

Jamie takes a glass, not caring whose it is, and tosses it back. Speech unlocked. "I don't understand how a spell like that would work." She chokes on booze-throat. "We've gone over it so many times, you can't be vague or clever with the spellwork. So what desire could you possibly have put out? Was this just a cry of raw paranoia? Because I am struggling, I really am, I'm struggling to see how that would—"

"It was you." Serena gives Jamie a look that goes all the way through her. "The need, the want, that I put out into the world, it was for you to be safe. I'd do anything to protect you. You've always made yourself easy to notice and hard to understand, ever since you were little, and I've always worried. And now I think of you out there in the city, trying to do magic in the half-wild spaces under, I don't know, freeway overpasses or something, I imagine you getting hurt and taken advantage of. You're still the only part of me that hasn't gone rancid. I don't mean to be self-centered, but it's part of being a mother. Before you taught me to do mystical things, I just sat in that schoolhouse imagining if something happened to you, if I lost you the way I lost Mae, and I was stranded, trapped in my own uselessness, so yes—as soon as I had the ability, I wanted to hurt anyone who might try to hurt you. I wanted to keep you secret. I never meant anyone to suffer."

That moment Serena was so afraid of? The one where the roles reverse and Jamie becomes a species of parent to her? Jamie is pretty sure it just arrived, and she hates it. She feels too drunk and not drunk enough. "You had no fucking right." Her voice doesn't sound like her voice. "You're incapable of doing constructive magic, after all. I made a mistake teaching you. I don't know what to do about it now, I can't take the lessons back. I taught magic to a broken woman."

"What do you—"

Jamie can't look at Serena and she doesn't want to look at Ro, so she picks a server in a train-conductor uniform to direct her gaze at. Probably creepy af, but what can she do.

The wrinkles and folds in the tablecloth are a relief map of a doomed planet.

"You and I share a goal," Ro says in a quiet voice. "I would give almost anything to see your daughter safe, healthy, unmolested by this putrescent world. Even now that I know she was keeping me in the dark about such a huge part of her life, even with all the fury I know will consume me a few days from now, I would give a flight of organs to ensure her well-being. You didn't even try to ask anyone else for help with safeguarding Jamie."

"Let's say for the sake of argument—" Serena falls back on her attorney training.

Jamie pushes her chair away from the table. "Let's go. We wanted an explanation, we got one. Sometimes you have to accept the impossibility of epistemic closure."

Ro sits frozen for a moment. Then they throw a wad of bills onto the table and follow Jamie out of there onto the train track—rusted, except for one gleaming stripe along the top. They slouch back to the dirtmobile.

Ro drives back to Somerville, while Jamie stares out the passenger window at the ghosts of maples and oaks. Her only consolation is that Serena's spell is probably played out for good. It already took effect, on Ro, plus they just analyzed it to death—so if anything Jamie understands about magic still holds, that spell has been fully neutralized.

When they stagger into their apartment, Jamie is wiped to the point of delirium, but she can feel all of this unprocessed crud between them.

"We should—" Jamie can't finish. She pours vodka into a *Sesame Street* cup.

"I don't have the spoons for guilt right now," Ro says. "No spoons for regret. Absolutely out of spoons for explanations or expiation. I know what happened now, and I need to sit with it for a while. Maybe a long time. You'll have to give me space. Can you do that?"

Jamie nods. Finishes her vodka and brushes her teeth.

THE TALE OF
THE PRINCESS AND THE
STROLLING PLAYER

(CONTINUED)

A month passed, all too quickly, and the day arrived when Lady Sagacious must surrender herself to the Faerie Court. That last day, she and the Princess took tea and played the Harpsichord one last time, then took a turn around the Gardens, and the Lady thought her heart would burst with Sadness at the thought of leaving her beloved Sister once and for all. But when evening descended and the Lady gathered a small bundle of her things, preparing to leave, the Princess stood in her path.

"You shall not leave," the Princess insisted.

The Lady protested that she must—she had made a Bargain and must honor it, or the Princess might forfeit her very Life. But the Princess smiled, and took her hands, and said that she on no account would suffer her dearest Companion to make such a Sacrifice on her account. Instead, the Princess said, she would redeem the Lady's Promise herself, and all would be well.

The Lady might have pressed her Case until her breath ran out, but Time was scarce and the Princess would not be argued with. All the Victory the Lady could claim was that she might accompany the Princess to the Faerie Door and observe the Princess's Gambit in close Quarters, though she must promise not to Intervene in any way.

The Moon sat high overhead when the Princess and the Lady

reached the Faerie Door, and the Lady was sorely affrighted at the Fate she imagined might await her Beloved, whom she considered a Sister in all but blood, and she tried every Argument she could imagine to sway the Princess to return home. But soon they were faced with the same Duke of Faerie with whom Lady Sagacious had dealt before. The Duke smiled, showing Teeth that gleamed in the Moonlight, and welcomed Lady Sagacious to his Court for all Eternity. He reached out to take hold of her.

"Stay your hand," said the Princess. "You cannot take my Friend."

"Oh?" said the Duke. "And pray why not?"

"Because," said the Princess, "she is already a member of my Household, and as I understand it I am now considered to be betrothed to Master Cleverly, who is a son of the Faerie King. Your deal with her stated that she must remain forever with a member of the Faerie Court, and my Claim on her company precedes yours by many years."

The Duke blustered and protested—the Princess was a mere Mortal—but she insisted, and her Arguments held. The same Circumstance that had caused her so much Grief, her Association with Master Cleverly, now gave her the Right to hold fast to her Friend. The two Ladies returned to the Royal Abode, with no ill Effects. Lady Sagacious felt no Compulsion to travel to Faerie, and the Princess did not resume shrinking.

Except, of course, that both of these Gentlewomen were now touched by Faerie, and on clear nights the waxing Moon bathed them both in a Glow that looked quite Uncanny. Even to this day, if you visit their lands, you may see the two of them wandering the Meadows, gathering Flowers and laughing, for now they shall belong forever to each other.

I found that lesbian mothers scored higher on the moral attitude scale than their heterosexual counterparts and were more likely to create opportunities for their sons to examine moral and values issues. They were also more likely to talk about morality in terms of broader social implications.

—*RAISING BOYS WITHOUT MEN* BY DR. PEGGY DREXLER
WITH LINDEN GROSS, RODALE BOOKS, 2005

Serena managed to unlock the front door of their new apartment in Jamaica Plain with one hand while holding three bags with the other. The door swung inward to reveal a hallway with blond hardwood flooring, leading to a sunlit kitchen/front room/nook, with doorways leading to small bedrooms and a bathroom along the right side. This was the nicest place she'd lived, and she felt the residential equivalent of imposter syndrome, mixed with dread that some nasty surprise awaited, like a locust infestation or a neighbor who held noisy midnight rituals.

They had moved back East just as California—California!—was passing a state proposition saying that marriage was one man and one woman. At least here in Massachusetts, the state supreme court had recognized gay and lesbian marriages, in a case which Serena had written one of her last papers about.

Once inside the apartment, Mae took charge, because even though Serena was good at organizing people, Mae was better at logistics, which meant certain rules were observed. Upbeat music blared at all times, everyone had easy access to snacks, and the whole family took regular fifteen-minute breaks.

Jamie was going through a sulky phase, and of course hadn't shown any signs of transitioning yet, so Mae had told her with mock-sternness, "R___, your job is to move in your own stuff and also make sure the entertainment system is set up to your exact specifications. If I hear that you're unable to excel at *Mario Kart* due to a bad entertainment setup, I will be Deeply Concerned." Jamie kind of smiled, kind of groaned, *Maaaamaaaa.*

Halfway through unloading, Serena got annoyed at Mae's bossiness, which verged on micromanaging, but then she saw a twinkle in her wife's eye, and her grouchiness melted away. Moving was always going to suck, but thank goodness Mae was taking on the hardest part without complaining. Mae smiled at Serena, and Serena smiled back, and later the two of them spooned on the fainting couch while Jamie played games. Mae had a whole herd of charley horses, to which Serena applied careful pressure until they had been gentled.

Jamie was starting third grade, so she'd have to make new friends in a new place—or rather, she'd have a second chance at finding even a single friend at school. The exact same qualities that made Jamie such a delight for the adults in her life—her dream logic and flights of fancy, the invention of the Floppy Game, her habit of talking like a little professor—made her an instant pariah among the elementary-school set.

Mae and Serena debated in whispers if they should do something to help Jamie, but "help" in this instance basically translated to "crush her spirit and try to turn her into a different person," the way adults had done to them when they were little. "Literally all we can do is let her know that we're here if she needs us," Mae said. "Like, if she had a bad day and wants to talk about it." Serena couldn't help wondering about other options—like, she kept reaching out to queer people she knew with kids around Jamie's age, hoping they could all hang in the park together or something. But she agreed with Mae that they could not, should not, tell Jamie to conform, or even to stop offering to teach people the Floppy Game within five minutes of meeting them.

(Serena was never quite sure what the Floppy Game involved, especially since the explanation was different each time she heard about it. There was a lot of making your arms and legs as loose and wobbly as possible without falling over, but also keeping a stuffed bunny airborne without touching it with your fingertips. Sometimes there were words you had to recite, sometimes there was a thing with your nose.)

Jamie read at a middle-school level already, but she wouldn't read anything except for this one series of horse-camp books that were basically the same book with minor variations. Lottie had given Jamie a copy of a really great kids' book about robot hairdressers who defend their barber shop from hair-eating monsters, but Jamie wouldn't even look at it. She sometimes blurted out facts she had learned on the internet about Roman aqueducts, but she spent most of her time playing Nintendo and nobody could get her interested in anything. Serena and Mae took her to a child psychologist, who agreed with the pediatrician that there was no reason to worry yet—but more parental attention was always good.

To pay down her loans, Serena had used one of her USF professor's connections to score a coveted job as a first-year associate with Yeager, Furst and Bullman, a healthcare-focused firm that promised they did lots of pro bono work. She seemed to spend most of her time on the kind of contract-law stuff she'd gritted her teeth through in first year, combing through M&A deal terms and HIPAA compliance.

Serena was a proper grown-up for the first time ever. She wore crisp business outfits that hadn't come from the deepest-discount rack at T.J. Maxx, she talked precisely and with understated confidence, she nodded at her colleagues and they nodded back. As a mostly freelance journalist, she'd learned to say "hed," "dek," "lede," and "slug" in casual conversation and navigate journalistic ethics (making sure her sources were fully tenderized before burning them). But this was a different level of professional. Stressful and constricting, for sure, but also weirdly comfortable? In the same way that being a goody-goody teacher's pet had comforted Serena back in middle school, before she'd gone full rebel in high school.

There was a whole other self buried inside Serena, that she'd forgotten was there.

At the same time, Serena barely hit her minimum billable hour requirement (which somehow didn't account for a huge chunk of her work hours) and she felt like she was multitasking in her sleep to keep up. They were constantly tossing her new cases and inviting her to more networking events, and she caught everything she could. The promises she'd made to Mae back in San Francisco tugged like a piece of string around her wrist, so she was constantly running from the office to hold up an equal share of solo childcare. Sometimes she snuck out of bed at four in the morning to catch up on paperwork before the rest of the family woke up. She reminded herself every day that this big-box law firm was not her career—just a way station, a chance to balance the books.

Work remained the clean part of Serena's otherwise messy life, a space where she could be self-assured without complication. At first, at least.

She was at lunch with her coworkers, and another first-year associate, Greg, started parroting everything the man had said on television about *Heather Has Two Mommies*. You had to admit that the critics had a point, he said with a half smile on his pale horsey face. Our society was doing an unprecedented experiment, dismantling the family unit, and what if we knocked down something that turned out to be load-bearing? Middle-class (white) American values had created the greatest civilization the world has ever seen, and now we were treating those same values as disposable.

Serena didn't want to be the bitch who got into fights at work, plus she couldn't figure out how to respond to Greg without pointing out the racism twisted around the strands of homophobia. (So much of his argument seemed to come down to the idea that Black people struggled purely because of broken families, and they were a cautionary example for white folks.) But Serena knew the moment you brought race into a conversation like this, you'd lost the argument even if you won—especially if you won. Luckily, Serena's work friend Jessamyn just rolled her eyes and told Greg, "Dan Quayle called, he wants his potatoes back." Which was honestly the perfect response to this foolishness.

Did Serena dream every night about debating Greg properly? Or better yet, facing him in a courtroom somehow? Putting him in his place once and for all? Not, like, every night. Just . . . a lot of nights.

· · · · ·

Mae and Serena went out, leaving Jamie with their friend Spotty Dobbins, and had dinner at a new Italian place where starch vapors, garlic, and olive oil turned the air warm and viscous. While they dipped focaccia in oil and vinegar and waited for salad, Mae gushed about the poetry she was writing, and the thunderous reception she'd gotten when she'd read at GenderCrash, and all the stuff she was doing to help out with the Princesses of Porn and the Dukes of Dykedom, a local troupe of drag kings and femme burlesque performers. Mae was having the time of her life—she even enjoyed all of her part-time gigs right now—but there was a toxic undercurrent, something she wasn't saying.

Serena kept her hands busy with spongy bread and bit her tongue to keep from firing off a spread of questions. Mae would tell Serena what was bothering her eventually. Coming in hot would just make her close off. Thus did Serena build a titanium wall between her work self and every other version of herself.

When the pasta showed up, Mae picked at it, suddenly morose.

"I'm here," Serena said in what she hoped was a soothing, even voice. And waited.

"It's such stupid bullshit." Mae waved a forkful of linguini, like a conductor's baton. "But it's gotten under my fucking skin. You remember Hettie? My coworker at Spectacles Women's Bookstore, with the rainbow candy-floss hair?"

"Yeah." Serena poured wine. "You're friends, right? You said you were happy to have a new friend."

"I *thought* she was my friend. She was so nice at first, and we had a ton in common. We're the only two people I know who've read all of Sheri S. Tepper's books. It was great for the first month and a half, and then she turned on a dime. I don't even know what happened. Now she hates me and tries to sabotage me all the time. I feel like such a fool for opening up to her."

Serena shrugged. "I don't know where I'd be right now if you weren't somebody who gives people the benefit of the doubt."

Mae picked at her food and shared a ton of upsetting incidents. Hettie had found ways to blame her own mistakes and some random mishaps on Mae. She'd started saying little quips in front of their boss, Billie, that sounded innocent but would get under Mae's skin, specifically—so if Mae reacted, *she* was the one who was having drama. She'd taken to adjusting every chair to make it less comfortable for Mae's wide hips, forcing Mac to readjust each chair laboriously in front of her coworkers, disrupting staff meetings.

"And before you say it, talking to Billie won't do any good," Mae said. "She loves Hettie, and she's made it clear she doesn't want to hear about any drama. And you know me, I get shy."

Serena nodded. For ages, she'd thought of Mae as someone who went around shoving people against bathroom walls, because that's the version she'd met. Took her a long while to realize there was a whole other side to Mae: anxious, withdrawn, not particularly great at sticking up for herself when she was outside her queer comfort zone.

So instead of offering advice, she asked, "How come you didn't tell me about this until now?"

"Because like I said! It's petty bullshit. I should be above it. And you've already got so much on your plate."

Serena gestured at her plate, which was empty.

"You know what I mean," Mae said. "Your work is crazy and actually pays our rent. You're walking the walk as a co-parent. There's real important shit to deal with, like those fuckers who keep trying to shut down the abortion clinics, and those other fuckers who want to make our relationship illegal. Like that coworker you told me about, Greg."

Serena suppressed a wince at the mention of Greg.

"If we can't talk about the stuff that's bothering you," Serena said, "then it doesn't matter if our relationship is legal or not, it's already a sham. Seriously, your problems are way more important to me than wrangling over whether HIPAA allows physicians to take laptops home."

Mae groaned. "I don't even know what's in it for Hettie—if she drives me away from the bookstore, she'll just have to work harder and train a new person. Maybe I did something to piss her off? Or maybe she just hates seeing a fat queer take up space? We're supposed to be a fucking feminist bookstore."

"I know you'll figure this out," Serena said. "You got to the bottom of that one guy's lobster fantasy when you were on the phones. This is nothing."

"Honestly, I'd take a dozen lobster fetishists over Hettie," Mae said. "But thanks. Ugh, I have garlic mouth."

"I'm kissing you anyway."

When they got back from dinner, Mae paused at the doorway, composing herself almost like an actor entering a scene, and put on an easygoing smile. Inside the apartment, Spotty Dobbins and Jamie were watching a *Xena: Warrior Princess* DVD with a bowl of homemade popcorn and an empty soda bottle in front of them. Jamie had a rapturous look, like she'd glimpsed the secret of endless wonder. Spotty was smiling, proud that she'd introduced this kid to a new fandom. Serena was pretty sure she was going to be buying Jamie some *Xena* paraphernalia soon.

If Serena hadn't just seen Mae freaking out, she'd never have suspected. Mae bantered effortlessly, and asked Jamie lots of questions about the *Xena* episodes she'd just watched. But Serena saw something in Jamie's face, or maybe her body language: a flicker of hypervigilance. Jamie studied Mae as if making sense of a puzzle. Maybe Serena and Mae had messed up somewhere, to make their kid such an intense watcher.

· · · · ·

A noise startled Serena around two in the morning: a bird, a cat yelling outside the window? Her dream-brain summoned a bestiary. Then her mom-brain woke up and she recognized Jamie, crying. "Your turn," Mae mumbled, not fully awake. Serena nodded and rolled out of bed.

Jamie was awake in a fetal position, hugging her blanket, cringing out of a bad dream. Serena sat down on the side of the bed, moving the crew of stuffed animals aside instead of displacing them with her body. "It's okay," she said. "Everything is okay. You're safe. Your mama and I are here." Jamie stared, unspeaking.

Serena tried everything she could think of to comfort her kid, or to learn what had freaked her out. She arranged the stuffed animals, including the by-now-extremely-threadbare Woople, into a garrison that could watch over Jamie as she slept. She plugged in the night-light, which Jamie hadn't needed lately. She cuddled Jamie and even tried to doze next to her in the too-small bed. She crooned that Sarah McLachlan song about ice cream in a low voice, and even hit a few of the notes. She repeated, *You're safe. Your family is here.*

Sleep was falling away from Serena; she was whip-alert now, probably up for the rest of the night. Welcome to middle age. Jamie hadn't settled, she was still whimpering and muttering, and she couldn't explain what was wrong, like if she was getting bullied at school.

"You can tell me anything," Serena said. "You can always tell me anything."

"It's just . . . what if I do something bad?" Jamie said, haltingly. "What if I do something really bad, and you and Mama won't love me anymore?"

Serena crouched on the floor in front of the bed, with Jamie sitting up, their faces close together. Serena's outstretched arms flanked her child.

"We love you so much. No matter what, you will always be loved. You cannot mess up so badly that you will not be loved. We love you with our whole hearts." Serena went on in this vein for a long time, and she saw something soften in Jamie's tiny face, her eyes widening and her body language slackening.

Jamie probably wouldn't remember Serena saying any of this stuff later, she was still at an age where things just flowed through you. But she did go back to sleep, and she slept through the night for weeks afterward.

· · · · ·

Jamie was definitely getting bullied at school. A group of thick-necked white kids had decided to make an example of the weirdo new kid, led by some towheaded bruiser named Zeb. Every morning, Jamie's posture changed, hunching even before she shouldered her bookbag, eyes cast down instead of looking straight ahead. In the afternoons, Jamie came home worn out from stress. Both parents noticed it around the same time—they were going to have to talk to her teachers, maybe the principal.

This was where it started: the perpetual motion machine. Kids learned from an early age to punish difference, to enforce stigma, by any means necessary. Kids like Jamie learned to spare themselves pain by hiding. That's how you ended up with assholes bombing lesbian bars and beating up queers in the street.

Mae, too, was getting bullied. Hettie kept escalating, until by now other coworkers had noticed. *Ooh drama,* they whispered. Mae couldn't leave food in the employee fridge for any length of time without finding it in the trash, or on the floor. Hettie was making remarks in staff meetings.

Serena wasn't naive or egocentric enough to think that she could wrap a giant bulletproof cloak around the people she loved most. Helplessness was a huge component of loving anyone.

Well, mostly. Serena managed to finagle a half day at work, so she could be standing on the front steps when Jamie got out of school. She wore her bulky leather jacket and scuffed Docs, though on reflection her "corporate lawyer" drag might've been more intimidating. "Hey kiddo," she said, and Jamie nodded shyly.

Jamie shambled away from the school, and came back to life one block at a time. Once they were a third of a mile from the school, Jamie was clowning, pretending to be a pirate whose parrot had turned disloyal. Serena took Jamie to the comic-book store, the toy store, and the candy store, mostly window-shopping apart from some chocolate doubloons and a rubber finger puppet. At the used bookstore, Jamie surprised Serena by picking out a *Captain Underpants* book instead of yet another horse-camp book; maybe this kid was branching out at last.

Serena wanted to say something reassuring about how once you grow up, there are no more bullies, except she didn't want to lie to her child. The truth was, people were garbage at any age—but school was an institution, no different in principle than prisons, the military, mental hospitals, or other places where society warehoused entire classes of people. Once school was done, you might never again be trapped in an ugly building with a large number of shitbirds—if you were lucky and played your cards right. This felt like an overcomplicated argument to make to a little kid, and probably unhelpful.

A finger puppet, a handful of melty coins, and a book about a grown man running around in his underwear felt like a poor substitute for actual words of consolation, but this was what Serena could manage right now. And Jamie seemed happier for a few days.

A couple weeks later, Jamie started saying Zeb was her friend, and she was part of Zeb's crew. Mae and Serena were like, didn't Zeb throw your new sneakers in the toilet last week? Jamie had freaked out about those shoes, almost howling with rage. But now Jamie deflected like a politician: the shoe thing didn't happen, or maybe it happened but it wasn't Zeb, or if it was Zeb then he was just messing around and who cared. Serena had never expected to be gaslit by her own kid. What made things worse: Jamie started repeating misogynistic, homophobic jokes she'd heard from Zeb in front of her moms.

Serena had only just sworn she'd always love Jamie no matter what, and now she kept biting back the thought: *I don't like this little creep.* Mae said it was a phase, and peer pressure was a fucker. Give Jamie time, she'd find a new crowd. She was in third grade, she barely had a prefrontal cortex yet. As usual, Mae was right, but . . . goddamn, this hurt.

Did you ever feel like there was a thermostat in your life that you couldn't reach, but someone else could crank it up or down? Like, you're just hanging tight, and everything is going okay—but suddenly the temperature rises and everyone is low-key homicidal, at your work and at home and in your social life. Or the temperature drops and nobody anywhere gives a shit. This mostly isn't anything to do with actual seasons.

That's how Serena felt. Right after Jamie started kicking furniture and making crude remarks about *lezzies,* Serena's coworkers turned more hostile and gave her more side-eye, especially Greg but not only Greg. The local queer orgs were all having more drama, too. And Mae was stressed, because of Hettie and Jamie, and a few other things besides.

Serena finally sat Jamie down one evening and said she wasn't allowed to say certain things. About women, about gays, about disabled people.

"Why?" Jamie asked.

"Because it's disrespectful. Because these are human beings who deserve to be seen as actual people." Serena glanced at her wife, praying that Mae wouldn't be rolling her eyes at Serena's attempt at play-acting a disciplinarian.

"But everyone says those things at school," Jamie retorted.

Serena said she didn't care, but also, she was sure not everyone said those things.

Jamie looked down, then looked Serena in the eye. "You say mean things all the time. You hurt people's feelings, too. Mama said you were a jerk."

That was true. Mae had said that, the day before. Serena couldn't remember why, but she'd probably run her mouth. As usual. Serena swallowed the first three responses that came to mind: *I'm allowed to say stuff because I'm a grownup. Don't change the subject, we're talking about you. Quit lawyering me.*

Mae was giving Serena a look that encompassed a whole semiotic cluster of *This is on you, good luck.*

God, whoever said you had to handle judges like children had never tried to talk to an actual kid. Judges were easy.

"It's true," Serena said. "I was a jerk yesterday. I said I was sorry, which means it's on me to do better. Listen, how do you think I know that it's bad to say mean things? I learned the hard way. That's the worst way to learn. Why would you want to learn that way, when you could learn by listening to people who've been through it?" She went on in that vein. Jamie's face turned stony, as if she was resolved to sit through this nothing lecture.

When Serena ran out of steam, Jamie's expression had not changed. Serena sighed and climbed to her feet, to make herself some damn chamomile tea. If only she had a mug that read WORLD'S WORST MOM, the scene would be complete.

When Serena was on her way to the kitchen, she heard Mae say in a quiet voice, "You made me sad."

Those four words accomplished more than Serena's whole speech. Jamie teared up and said she was sorry, and she didn't understand.

"You don't know what the word *lezzie* means, do you?" Mae said.

Jamie shook her head.

"It means people like your mom and me. It means families like ours."

"Oh." Jamie's face fell. "I didn't mean it."

"I know you didn't." Mae sat on the old fainting couch and gestured for Jamie to scoot next to her. "Listen, sometimes it's hard to be part of a family like ours. Kids are going to say mean stuff, including your friends."

Jamie looked down. "I can stop being friends with Zeb and the others."

Serena wanted to jump in and say, *Yes, please, kick those fuckfaces to the curb.* But she kept making tea.

"You should be friends with whoever you want," Mae said. "We won't tell you who to be friends with. And we don't need you to stick up for us if someone says something. It's our job to protect you, not the other way around. But please don't say stuff like that, because you don't even know whose feelings you might be hurting. Do you understand?"

Jamie nodded.

Later, in bed, Mae hugged Serena and said, "I think I need to talk to Billie, about Hettie's behavior. It's gone too far. I love that job otherwise, but I can't deal with this anymore."

Serena squeezed Mae's hand. "I'm proud of you. Lemme know if you want to practice."

"Nah. Just . . . thanks for listening. You helped a lot."

"Anytime." Serena hadn't done anything, just let Mae work it out on her own. But maybe that was the point. She'd always thought of herself as someone who knew how to ask the right questions, but now she was realizing her best skill could be creating fertile silences. Food for thought.

11

"You may indeed be too good for this wicked world," said Toby Langthrope with a grave expression. "And yet, you still must live in it."

—*EMILY: A TALE OF PARAGONS AND DELIVERANCE*
BY A LADY, BOOK 7, CHAPTER 5

Giving" someone "space" sounds like a gentle process, a forbearance. You are bestowing a gift of your absence, yet staying available in case you're suddenly needed or wanted.

The actual process of leaving a loved one to their own devices for an indefinite period is a violent struggle against habit. You cannot resist all of your deepest-seated impulses that clamor for you to reach out to the one who always made sense of a host of nightmares, and you don't want to excise your favorite human from your life completely, for fear this separation might become permanent.

So. Ro isn't talking to Jamie, beyond the minimum, and Jamie is not talking to Serena. There's nobody else Jamie is especially keen to talk to—most people just spout platitudes, and report on whatever distorted reflections they've noticed in the glossy surface of the world. Jamie might be turning into a bit of a misanthrope.

Jamie tries to focus on work, especially since she's way behind and she really cannot afford to blow her one chance at academic relevance. She's consumed, now, with the idea that she's been missing the heart of *Emily*. All the time, she's thought of Emily as a paragon who yearns to be imperfect, and conspires with Toby Langthrope to break free. But now she's obsessed with the idea that Sarah Fielding, a shy book nerd who thought endlessly about morality and family, got sucked into actor drama with Charlotte Charke, and the awareness that anybody can be destroyed—anyone, at any time!— soaks through every page of *Emily* like kerosene. But so many questions remain. And lonesomeness distracts her, a cacophonic soundtrack drowning out her thoughts.

One weekend, Ro needs help running an errand at the big hardware store at the mall off Route 44, so Jamie volunteers to drive. On the way back, she gets an idea as they're driving along a back road with unruly forest on the other side of the muddy buffer along the road. She slows down and jerks her head at the woods. "We could try right now, if you want. I bet we could find a spot around here."

"Try what?" Ro sounds flustered, until the truth hits home and their voice turns brittle. "Oh. Oh, no, thank you."

Jamie sputters. "I thought . . . I thought I could give you a lesson. I could help you master it, understand better how it works . . ." She gestures at the rocky fringe of a sparse woodland dappled by the late-afternoon sun. She can already tell there's some excellent spots in there.

"Why would I want that? Why should I retraumatize myself? I have a feeling I might never go into the woods again."

"Oh god." Jamie shrinks into the driver's seat. "I know, I'm sorry. I just, you've been handling it so well, and I thought you might want—"

"I really don't want to be reminded of what you and your mother did to me."

"It was my mom, I had nothing to do—"

Ro gives Jamie a look. She shuts up.

It's still sinking in: Jamie could lose Ro for good. And it would only be fair.

"I've been handling this well because I'm only starting to process my feelings," Ro says. "I don't have a road map."

The air pressure just dropped to way below sea level. In Jamie's head, Serena says, *Our marriage had hit a rough patch.*

Jamie puts the car in gear and speeds back up. "Come on, let's drive home and we can talk over s'mores."

Ro seems to hesitate, like they suddenly don't want to be in a car with Jamie. Then they nod. "Sure."

Jamie feels drained of some essence she took for granted. The skin on her face is too tight, her extremities feel like reclaimed items. She doesn't think she can operate a motor vehicle, but she makes it work.

Ro stares out the window, face turned away from her.

· · · · ·

Jamie finds herself behind a lectern speaking about *Frankenstein*, Sir Walter Scott, and Jane Austen, her "*Pride and Prejudice* and not exactly zombies" lecture. Gavin keeps raising his hand every time she finds her rhythm, and the harder she tries to ignore him, the more urgent the thrust of his palm until it fully resembles a grotesque salute. She finally calls on him, and he launches into a rambling comment about artificial life, and reproduction, which is juuuust skirting the edge of calling Jamie herself a Franken-woman. She shuts him down, but he's succeeded in derailing her lecture, and he's opened the floor for a series of interjections. Her head is throbbing again.

Jamie probably ought to stop drinking vodka out of that *Sesame Street* glass every night. It's just too funny to count the shots in the Count's voice: "THREE SHOTS OF VODKA, HAHAHAHA!"

After class, Jamie walks across the Tangram and her phone thrums with a number she doesn't recognize: someone in Richmond, Virginia. She hesitates a second, then picks up because maybe she's been closing herself off from too many voices lately.

"Ms. Sandthorn?" It's a man's voice, low and confident in a way that sounds natural, but also well-rehearsed. Jamie can't place it, but it sounds familiar.

"Uh, yeah?" She's standing in front of the Banner Library, with an eye-line on the spot where they did the anti–Wanda Bock protest.

"I was wondering if I could ask you some questions about a class you're teaching," the man says, smoothly, as if this is just a routine matter and he won't take much of Jamie's time.

Fuck, Jamie is a grad student. She's a hired birthday clown. Why is this guy calling her?

Her heart is thudding in EDM time, and she doesn't know why.

"Uh, what is this in reference to?" she stalls.

He starts to say something else—but now Jamie knows that voice. From YouTube videos, from endless tweets urging boycotts of anyone who gave this man a platform.

McAllister Bushwick is cold-calling her.

Her mind spins. Does he know Serena is her mom? Does he even remember what he did to her? He's had so many victims since. And then Jamie thinks about the spell Serena and she cast, the smear of dirt and dogshit. They put something out into the universe, and now something is coming back.

Bushwick is still talking, then he stops. "Ms. Sandthorn? Are you still there?" He hasn't said his name yet, or given a fake name.

"Um, yeah." Shit shit shit. What to do? "I need to call you back. I'm in the middle of something."

"I'm on a deadline," he says, as if he's a journalist writing a story. "Can you get back to me soon? I really want to get your perspective."

"Perspective on what?" Jamie says, because she can't help being curious to see the jaws of the trap.

"I'm interested to learn more about your approach to gender ideology in education," he says smoothly. If you weren't paying attention, you'd miss that phrase: "gender ideology." So this is a trans thing. Someone—probably Gavin—has been nudging right-wing provocateurs to look into the obnoxious trans woman who's putting wokeness into the study of the literary canon.

The EDM beat inside her head is louder and now she's seeing flashing lights and smelling dry ice, and basically these college library front steps are a rave now.

"I'll call you back." She hangs up. She won't call back, of course.

What the hell? What does she do now?

In the end, all she can do is block that phone number and hope that this was a lone fishing expedition. Actually, there's one other thing she can do: drive out to the same woods where she offered to teach Ro magic. She only falls and scrapes her knees a couple times before she finds a good spot to do a simple spell of protection. (Probably not too different from the protection spell that made Ro vanish into moonlight, a thought that brings back the chill.) She puts everything she can into begging the universe to keep the bastard from her door.

Then she tries to forget about that phone call, since she can't tell Ro about it, and she refuses to have anything to do with Serena.

She goes into the library and gets lost in reading three-hundred-year-old emails, and soon the only drama she's obsessing about is Laetitia Pilkington getting dissed by Jonathan Swift after Laetitia's husband contrived to catch her cheating and then kicked her to the curb, leaving her penniless.

Still there's a gnawing anxiety in Jamie's lower gut and the sinews of her neck and shoulders.

· · · · ·

Days pass, solitary confinement without walls. Ro speaks pleasantries and occasional logistics. Serena makes no effort to reconnect, though she must have moved and started her new job by now. Also, not a peep from McAllister Bushwick, possibly because Jamie blocked his phone number—but he makes no other attempts to slime her that she's aware of. Life settles down and she finds a queasy equilibrium: working until late in the library so she won't bother Ro, doing office hours, and trying to avoid looking at Gavin and his buddies as she teaches. You really can get used to almost anything.

Which is worse: when someone you love doesn't want to talk to you, or when you don't want to talk to someone you love? Maybe it doesn't make a difference after a while, and "want" isn't even the right word. Jamie couldn't call Serena no matter what—she would choke on her own tongue before she finished dialing.

When Serena learned about magic, she just shrugged, took it in, and jumped straight to the possible applications. Much later, Serena demanded to know if Jamie was unhappy, as if unhappiness was the only reason a person could have for casting spells. Mae would have looked deeper, asked better questions.

Mae would have understood that happiness does not stagnate, but rather it flows, and yes, it can be blocked or diverted, or just dry up, but we can find the source again. Mae would have nudged Jamie to see whether she was addressing her real issues, and if maybe instead of bending the prongs of reality, she might need to retrace her steps away from true. She definitely would have nudged Jamie to confide in Ro before it was too late. Mae *got* people, in a way that neither Serena nor Jamie ever will. That's what made Mae a good mom, and a good friend to everyone in the neighborhood, and, yes, a good pro domme, too.

Jamie wishes more than ever that she could talk to Mae.

So she does.

Jamie finds a quiet spot at the edge of the Gravelhurst Preserve, with a grassy slope on one side and a few trees on the other. One tree has a broken tire swing, like a crescent moon, hanging from it. She spreads her floral skirt around her and settles onto a grassy dirt patch, facing the green hillside.

"Uh, hi. Mae. Other Mom. Mama. Been a while. I miss you so much, like I miss you more as time goes by, and I'm pretty sure that's not how it's supposed to work, right? But every passing day brings another thing I wish I could share with you and get your reaction to, and they just pile up, like a conveyor belt to nowhere. I have no idea what you would say if you were here, which makes it so much harder, makes you more absent in a way. I . . . I have used everything up, like everything, and I don't know what to do about any of it. I tried to help Mom get out of the rut she's been in since you went away, and I know you would have told me to be careful, right? And not give her another rabbit to chase after, because she gets carried away. Right? Or maybe you would have told me to go for it, because the woman you loved was hurting and alone and stuck, just mired, in heartsickness. See? I have no idea what you would say if you were here. I think maybe I had impure motives, after all? I did want to help her, to rescue her, I did, I know. But I also took pleasure in being her teacher, knowing more than her for once. Maybe it was a kind of revenge, I don't know. For what, I'm not even sure. Anyway, I could play at being a wiseass for a minute, but I'm no match for Serena, I never was. She's surpassed me in magic now. I'm paying the price. I feel so lost. I don't, I don't know how to walk any of this back, or how to move forward, I just don't know. I so wish there was a spell I could do, that would let you speak to me one more time. A séance, or I don't know, something. But I don't believe in life after death—to be honest, right now I barely believe in life before death. And I don't want to talk to ghost you, I want to talk to everyday, running late for the bus, getting your period and forgot a tampon, paying attention to a million things and still somehow keeping a space open for me, you. I lost my place in the book of fucking life. What do I even do now?"

Jamie sits: spent, silent at last, making all of the motions of weeping with none of the sounds or fluids. Trembling violently enough that her vision decoheres. No ghost shows up, she doesn't feel Mae breathing on her neck, there's no *presence* or whatever. She feels more alone than before.

But. She also feels a touch of clarity. Like, what would Mae want? If she was here, alive, and not just in Jamie's head? Mae would want Jamie to be okay, and for Jamie and Serena to be there for each other. It would break Mae's heart to think of the two of them not on speaking terms. And Mae would want Jamie to be brave and humble, two virtues that oft keep company. Which might mean a certain amount of vulnerability and willingness to make everything not about Jamie.

In any case, Jamie feels better, but also worse. Clarity. And now she's struck by the tire-swing crescent, and the gently decomposing toys around the tree roots. Someone lit a fire nearby, and there's a wilted fast-food clamshell and some possible drug stuff. This would be a perfect spot for a working—she's only done one since Ro vanished, and she's scared to do one now. What would she call out for? What does she actually want?

She digs in her bag and finds a piece of jerky, and the cover page from Ro's dissertation, which she kept as a joke after she did some photocopying for them. She takes the jerky and lays it in the midst of the toy pile, near the burnt area, then adds the cover sheet, sprinkled with a few wild daisies that she picks nearby. She hopes the message is clear enough: bless Ro's research, may they prosper. She wants Ro to be happy, even if she might not get to witness up close.

Jamie rubs down her grass-stained legs and heads back into town.

12

In truth, the rake pursues his pleasure by much the same means that a lady might employ to plague the mind of a hated rival: flattery and promises, followed soon thereafter by teazing and an accounting of her faults.

—*EMILY: A TALE OF PARAGONS AND*
DELIVERANCE BY A LADY, BOOK 3, CHAPTER 2

Everywhere Jamie goes, she sees the bones of long-gone infrastructure. Right now she's standing on the edge of the old Farmington Canal, which ran through rural Connecticut 150 years ago but now looks like a dry gully, overgrown with wild grass and surrounded by rock walls. The Farmington Canal Heritage Trail goes right past the Lewis Walpole Library, where Jamie has come to scrounge any and all info about Jane Collier, Charlotte Charke, Sarah Fielding, and other persons of interest in her investigation. The air is that kind of New England crisp where you wish it would snow, because then you might feel less bitterly cold. She's only a couple hours' drive from Boston, but she feels much farther away; she's barely spoken to anyone since she arrived here a couple days ago. She's settled into a soothing routine, waking up in the famous white cottage, a nine-bedroom Colonial house where they put up scholars working in the library, and she makes coffee in the shared kitchen before going for a walk in the neighborhood, or on one of the dozen nearby hiking trails. All the houses around here scream "Ye Olde," from the colonnades to the gables to the dark shutters. Jamie doesn't know why the place she's staying is called the white cottage, since every building around here is painted blinding white, with a white picket fence out front just for extra measure. Sometimes when she goes out on one of the trails, she does a tiny working, to beg for help finding something in this massive archive of eighteenth-century letters and literature.

A hundred years ago, a Yale man named Wilmarth "Lefty" Lewis became obsessed with Horace Walpole, the youngest son of England's first ever prime minister, and the result was a massive collection of Walpole's papers and assorted other eighteenth-century documents. The Lewis Walpole Library is technically part of Yale, despite being nowhere near New Haven.

Jamie should "throw herself into work," right? That's what you do, when your personal life is a ninety-nine alarm sewage conflagration. Except, that "throwing yourself into your work" means falling into a story about the Puritan work ethic—a story that has devoured countless people only to spit out their bones one at a time, over a long period. The rise of the English novel in the eighteenth century is inseparable from the rise of Calvinism and capitalism, which formed an unholy alliance to spread a gospel of industry and productivity (after chattel slavery and stolen land in the Americas made England rich and created a glut of resources). Calvinism focused on individual salvation, and a vision of "stewardship" in which every person needed to work hard to improve their situation on earth—which dovetailed nicely with capitalism's new emphasis on relentless production. At the same time, capitalism gave rise to an urban petite bourgeoisie who had (some) leisure time for reading, including merchants and bureaucrats, but also apprentices, housewives, and some of the fancier household servants. This created an audience for stories about "everyman" heroes who deal with challenges in their own lives, instead of the noble-born protagonists contending with huge issues who'd starred in previous works of literature. So yeah, the novel as we know it is inseparable from the cult of hard work—even though ironically, the mid-eighteenth century also gave us the notion of reading for pleasure.

Jamie suspects capitalism is a huge part of the reason why magic is so difficult: nobody knows what they want, because we've all been brain-washed to want garbage.

But still, she "throws herself into work." She paws through Horace Walpole's correspondence, but also the masses of other papers that Lefty Lewis amassed. She doesn't find any more serious proof that Jane Collier wrote *Emily,* or anything more about Sarah Fielding and Charlotte Charke, but she does find a few stray allusions to the novel in letters by London taste-makers, buzzing about that sexy motherfucker Toby Langthrope. Fun fact: everybody loves a bad boy. Since Jamie needs to prove that *Emily* is important and worth discussing, she scoops up these tiny shout-outs up like a basket of kittens and cradles them in her arms, cooing and covering them with little kisses. *Who's a good citation? It's you, it's you.*

Jamie spends only six and a half days at the Lewis Walpole, but her sense of time goes out the window as she's sucked into archival dumpster diving. She barely speaks to another living person, except when she runs into Praveen Gupta in the kitchen and exchanges small talk. She falls into a routine of scholarship and hiking trails, broken up occasionally by a quick trip to the one strip mall nearby with a convenience store and two small restaurants. One morning she wakes early and gazes out her bedroom window at the vista of a leaf-swept meadow, with the barn in the distance and the woods beyond. And she can't help thinking that she's home, that she's always been here and will stay here indefinitely.

And then the spell is broken and she's cut loose. She crams all her belongings into Berniece the dirtmobile and heads south to Philadelphia, where she's decided to attend a conference about the state of literary classroom instruction. She probably won't learn much, but there might be some good networking for her inevitable job search, and the department's research budget might pay for her hotel room and meals. Mostly, it'll keep her on the road and out of Ro's adorably mussed hair for longer. And she misses Philadelphia, which is one of those cities where you can still find endless secret treats: strange tiny bookstores on the top floor of rabbit-warren malls; gay bars sneaking between the stained-glass blades of civic institutions; base-ment music venues whose air has gone thick with the trapped exhalation of uncountable drunken cheers and whose floors are tarry from years of spilled drinks. Though of course, the conference is happening in a Marriott somewhere outside of town.

The moment she drops her bag in her hotel room and wanders down to the common area of the conference, with its handful of tables promoting obscure but lavishly printed journals, she realizes coming here was a mistake. She keeps running into other grad students as well as junior faculty, and having the same conversation: how are things going? *Oh, there are cutbacks. Oh, the state is slashing funding. Oh, there's no more tenure and everyone is a contractor now, we're all getting paid a subsistence wage while tuition has doubled, and the students think we owe them blood.* It's not just the words, it's the bedraggled tone of voice, the mismatched eyes (one screwed tight, one bug-eyed), the hunched body language. The scent of furniture polish and stale Danishes clings to the hotel's dining area, and this place feels like one of the middling levels of perdition. The first evening, Jamie gets a whiskey sour from the hotel bar and soaks up gossip about the few lucky jerks who've gotten real jobs, before she finds herself talking to the one person who doesn't look like an academic: a skinny middle-aged white man in a white-collar shirt and sweatshirt, who turns out to be an editor from Pimlico Books named Gordon Fairwood. Unlike literally everyone else she's met today, Gordon asks how her research is going and what she's working on, so Jamie finds herself telling him in great detail about *Emily* and her theories, re: authorship and relevance. Instead of going glassy-eyed, Gordon seems fascinated, his well-shaped eyebrows going up and down as he asks questions. At last he says, "On the off chance you don't want to go with a university press, we'd love to take a look at that when it's done. The line between mass-market and academic publishing gets thinner all the time." Jamie smiles and nods politely, though she doesn't want to throw away her chance at a university job by publishing for a mainstream audience. Gordon has clearly heard this before, so he shrugs happily. "Just think about it. Let me give you my card." The card goes in the bottom of Jamie's purse, probably to be tossed in the next recycling bin she sees.

The next day, Jamie lurks in the back of sessions about Teaching in the Social Media Age and Storytelling in the Late Anthropocene. The third time she hears someone mumble about how to cope with the culture-war outrage vortex, she finds herself standing up and slipping out of the audience. She sneaks out a side door onto a cement walkway to the parking lot, where she climbs into Berniece the dirtmobile and drives.

She almost finds a spot to do a working, but she has no idea where to look for a neglected place in the Philly sprawl. So instead she takes a random exit and drives around.

The randomness is what makes Jamie realize: there's someone following her.

She saw this navy-blue sedan in the parking lot of the conference hotel, and now here it is again, taking the same random exit, heading into East Kensington near Temple University. She picks a side street, driving past endless two-story rowhouses made of brick or plaster, crowned with decaying eaves, and the snub-nose blue car keeps three spots behind her at all times. Pace for pace, turn for turn, no matter how erratically on purpose she drives, this blue shape haunts her rearview. Her heart ransacks her chest cavity, tossing the place frantically, while her thoughts play a loop of, *Oh fuck yourself, stalker.* Roaming the outskirts of an unfamiliar city, with some creep on her tail: this is the sort of situation where she would normally text Ro. But she is Giving them Space, and screw it. The sun shines high, and nothing bad ever happens in daylight, right?

Jamie only knows about being tailed from movies and books, and she gathers the two main strategies are to lose your tail, or to stop and confront them. (Ro's voice chimes in her head: *You always think that hyperawareness of tropes is equivalent to understanding the lived experience behind them.*) She can't drive well enough—or badly enough—to get rid of her pursuer, and her appetite for pyrrhic interventions is at its weakest. She needs a third option.

Miracles still exist: she finds a tiny cozy used/antiquarian bookstore called Peacock & Todd Rare Books Inc., on a street that otherwise contains nothing but rowhouses and one small bicycle repair/rental shop. This is perfect. Jamie doesn't believe in much, but she always believes that bookstores are sacred, and enough books in one place will ward off almost any evil.

The young Black bookseller nods at Jamie before returning their gaze to an old hardcover of Graham Greene's *The Quiet American.* Jamie makes

note of the front door's jangle: the driver of the blue car will have to announce their arrival if they chase her inside. Deeper inside the store, past
the front rows of recent stuff, a maze of dusty shelves pulls at Jamie, and
soon she's lost in browsing.

Holy cow, there's a bookcase full of eighteenth-century books, including
a copy of *The Fair Moralist* by Charlotte McCarthy which looks like it could
be a first edition. Jamie almost skips past *The Fair Moralist*, because she's read
that book several times and she's worried it'll disintegrate in her un-gloved
hands. But some instinct—the same tingle that guides her to magical places—
makes her slip it out of its nest and cradle it in her dry palm. She pages with
care, and . . . it's full of scribbles. Marginalia? Someone who owned this
book back in the day wrote all over it. She'd have to get an expert to look it
over, but the ink looks old, maybe even dating from around the time this
book was published in 1745?

On one blank page in the exact middle of the book, someone has written
a few lines, crossing out words and correcting. She blinks and looks again:
it's the opening lines of *Emily*. She forgets to breathe. Her heart is gonzo,
she's grown a few inches, she thinks of all the desperate spells she's cast. She
exclaims out loud: "Hot damn. The hottest damn."

"Good afternoon," a voice says behind her.

Jamie turns, realizing that she's been so absorbed in book-finding, she
totally forgot about the blue car and her stalker.

McAllister Bushwick is standing a foot and a half away, close enough to
grab her in one lunge.

Jamie hugs the marked first edition of *The Fair Moralist* to her breast,
like *You can't have it*—as if Bushwick could possibly know or care what she's
holding in her hands. To him, it's just an old book. She knows this, and yet
she can't help shielding it with her whole body.

He says, "My name is," and Jamie is morbidly curious to hear what name
he's about to say.

But Jamie can't help saying, "I know who you are. You're pretty famous."

McAllister Bushwick smiles and raises an eyebrow. He's an attractive
man, unfortunately: brown curls swept back from a high forehead, short

sideburns, a slender nose and full lips. He looks Irish, or maybe Jamie just read somewhere that he's Irish-identified.

He takes a step back, hands raised, showing he's no threat. Which Jamie knows is a lie. Now she can get a better look at him: checked shirt, hoodie with a faded logo on one breast, blue jeans. Jamie can't help searching for signs of cursedness, or some indication that she and Serena had any effect on him with their dog-poop-mancy. He looks fine—just as jovial and deceptively sweet as ever—but he's the first and only person Jamie has ever cursed, so she has no idea what to look for. A facial tic? A haunted expression? For all Jamie knows, their spell made him stub his toe for a few days, or caused his milk to go sour faster.

Jamie backs away from him, still clasping the first edition McCarthy in both arms. "I don't have time to talk to you right now," she says in her most professorial voice. It takes all of her self-control to avoid adding that she has office hours. "I'm already late getting back to a conference." She leaves unsaid, *As you know, since you followed me from there.*

"It's in your interest to speak to me, Ms. Sandthorn," he says smoothly. "If you know who I am, then you know what I do, and you'll understand that someone like you is of great interest to my readers. One of my people is preparing a Media Awareness Package about you, and I thought I would give you the opportunity to respond."

"Media Awareness Package," or "MAP," is what these ghouls call the dossiers they give to right-wing media outlets and big social-media accounts, to try and create a toxic narrative. If they can get mainstream outlets to pick up a story and run with it, they've won—but even if it's only spread by their own people, they can still unleash a gutter-flood of harassment against their targets.

A wave of cold sweeps over Jamie's skin. In her head, she and Serena keep chanting, *Get it.* She's absolutely certain they summoned McAllister Bushwick with that spell, as sure as if they'd conjured a demon into a broken circle.

Jamie's usual impulse in stressful situations is to talk a blue streak, make lots of noise, raise her voice, say things that can be used against her. Thank all the Blue Stockings she's in a bookstore and the importance of quiet browsing is seared into her soul. She stares at Bushwick, surrounded by flaking spines that remind her that beauty (and meaningful ugliness) endure long after the noise and brutality have died down. So even though her instincts are yelling for her to run, flee, get back to Berniece and drive away, she stays right here.

She forces herself to move slowly, walking around the bend in the shelves, until she gets in the eyeline of the bookstore clerk. She makes eye contact, and they look back, with a clear *Is this guy bothering you?* in their eyes. She nods, gently.

"From the information we've gathered, it appears you've been spreading a hazardous ideology," Bushwick says. "We just want to get at the truth."

"What ideology would that be?" Jamie sidles closer to the counter and lays down her copy of *The Fair Moralist*. She hasn't even looked at the price tag—doesn't matter, she'll buy it no matter what. The clerk rings it up and she hands over her card.

Bushwick looks at the clerk and then at Jamie, realizing he's outnumbered. "You know what ideology. We have recordings of you in the classroom, talking about gender fluidity, spreading negativity toward traditional masculinity."

Jamie's rib cage shrinks to the size of a walnut. He's got her on tape! She runs her mind frantically over a half dozen lectures where gender and sexuality came up, and all she can remember is being so cautious her teeth always hurt by the end of class, because she could feel Gavin and his crew staring at her. Still, her nightmare-mind cooks up images of herself screaming *Fuck the patriarchy* in class, or just tearing off her clothes and running around the lecture hall making screech-owl sounds. Of course, for some people, just the specter of a trans woman daring to stand in front of impressionable young adults would be horror enough.

Jamie already knows she's going to spend pointless hours trying to figure out what this toolbag and his people might have on her. And she'll never know, and that's part of the point. They want to scare her.

The clerk hands back her card, and wraps the book inside a paper bag, neatly. The receipt has one too many zeroes, and Jamie prays the research budget will cover this purchase, or else she's eating instant noodles for the rest of her life. Worth it.

"Please leave me alone," Jamie says to Bushwick, in her best impression of Serena. "I'm not interested in whatever your issue is."

He looms until Jamie stands under his shadow. Then he turns and walks away, with a thin smile on his face.

When the door jangles shut, the clerk turns to Jamie and exhales. "That man had serious mass-shooter energy."

"You're not wrong," Jamie says.

Turns out the bookseller is named Danica, and she uses she/her pronouns, and she's finishing an English degree at Temple. She didn't know there was an English lit conference here in town, which says something about the state of the field. Okay, sure, Danica's an undergrad, but Jamie can tell after a few moments that she's passionate about poring over old stories. Like recognizes like.

Jamie stays and chats with Danica for twenty minutes, and not just because she's waiting to make sure Bushwick is gone. When she finally goes back to the dirtmobile, there's no sign of the blue sedan, and her drive back to the conference hotel is uneventful, except for Philly drivers. She pulls into the parking lot, punching her own leg and subvocalizing, and then her eye falls on the brown-paper package from Peacock & Todd.

She's found a precious piece of evidence, come this much closer to solving the puzzle of *Emily*. The world may never recognize her—may soon try to finish her—but she is on fire.

By the time Jamie heads inside the Marriott, she is convinced that she has earned, and desperately needs, a slew of strong drinks. She sees Gordon Fairwood at the other end of the bar, chatting with a couple other people, and he raises a glass in her direction.

When she gets back to the hotel room, she opens her copy of *The Fair Moralist* with all the delicacy she can muster, and finds something flattened between its pages: a bundle of letters, two of them. No, three. It's a snippet of correspondence—Jamie's heart sets to galloping—between Jane Collier and Sarah Fielding (where they address each other as Jenny and Sally, as they commonly did).

She photographs them with her phone and then puts them back, touching them as little as possible. Then she crawls into bed and starts reading.

My dearest Jenny:

I am ruin'd, utterly. I hate that I must relate this awful tale, and I have torn this missive to tatters a half dozen times—because I would sooner play with stinging wasps than cause you the least grief, and I fear this tale will grieve you abominably. There is naught that you, or anyone, can do. I am utterly destroyed, my life lies in shards, and I can blame nobody but myself. I have chosen my friends unwisely.

As you well know, I have been staying with Harry and his family on Buckingham Street these past months, and delighting in the company of Charlotte and the baby. Charlotte has needed much help with the newborn, as weak and sickly as the child is, and Harry can scarce keep a servant from day to day, so at times I have been greatly occupied with helping Charlotte care for her little namesake. Jenny, a baby is so tremendous a charge, requiring such fastidious delicacy and so little sleep, I know not how mothers survive.

Please burn this letter immediately upon your reading it, Jenny. I cannot bear for any record of these events to remain in your possession, tho' the whole world may know of them already.

I must confess to having experienced some exultation at the thought of spending time in London, a city of which I had heard much and seen little. O Jenny, it is a wonderful place! Filthy, yes; noisome with ballad singers, hawkers, patterers, and beggars, certainly; but also stimulating, fascinating, bursting with all that life has to offer. All of human nature, Jenny, is laid bare in this city, as if everyone's breast were crafted of fine-blown glass, the workings of their hearts exposed to the careful observer.

So after I had been some time in Harry's house on Buckingham Street, I hungered to see more of this great city, instead of spending all of my hours minding the baby. Harry lamented that his new Great Mogul Company at the Little Theatre, Haymarket, was woefully not furnished with sufficient assistance in a dozen employments, from costume-maker to prompter. Upon the third such complaint, I ventured that I would be pleased to assist in any capacity.

Jenny, I know you will think me a fool. To go into the theater, a place of utter dissolution, so near to the taverns and establishments of the worst repute, could only be seen as a disastrous choice. Especially for a lady to frequent such a place and be employed within, rather than being safely ensconced in a box as a spectator. And I am accustomed to extreme caution, remembering as I always do my lessons from Mrs. Rooke in my youth. And yet, I could scarce resist the chance to see Harry's plays being rehearsed and performed, and the opportunity to witness the fulness of London's varied life. And indeed, life at the Little Theatre was a rich pageant. I met Mrs. Eliza Haywood, author of *The Distress'd Orphan,* now acting onstage. (I also met Miss Betty Careless, notorious courtesan and madame of the "Coffee House" at Prujean's Court. As I have said, utter folly. What have I done?)

To reach the Little Theatre for my strange apprenticeship with Harry's company, I needed to walk through the filthiest part of Covent Garden—Harry accompanied me most days, but on some days, I must needs venture on my own, with extreme caution. To enter the theater from the street, one must pass through a narrow hallway, before emerging into a wide, chilly space. Once inside, I set about doing whatever small tasks required an extra pair of hands.

I bustled earnestly, happy to be of use, until I found myself gazing upon the most extraordinary creature I shall ever see.

Mrs. Charlotte Charke was the featured player of my brother's company, and she dressed, even offstage, like a perfect young gentleman

of fashion: clean hose, well-scrubbed boots, breeches in the
latest fashion, a handsome greatcoat, and a powdered periwig tied in
the back, with a tricorn hat perched on top. Mrs. Charke was playing the role of Lord Place, a foppish gentleman modeled on her own
father, in my brother's play *Pasquin*. When she ventured onstage,
to the hooting of the students and rascals in the pit, she was trans-
formed, delivering the comedy prologue with a fluttering handker-
chief and an affected demeanour. The whole audience roared.

Bowing deep onstage, bathed in the light of hundreds of candles,
she shone with such radiance, I could not bear to close my eyes for
a moment. Her performance was intended to provoke amusement,
but Jenny—I was enraptured. I can scarce explain. My heart—my
very soul—twittered like a nest of new-hatched chicks.

I was yet too shy to address Mrs. Charke, of course—you know
me well—and remained in my quiet corner, sewing some buttons on
a costume piece. I had thought myself beneath her notice, but Mrs.
Charke made note of me straight away. She introduced herself, her
eyes sparkling with mirth. She and her young daughter lived with
her sister in a lodging on Oxendon Street, and she declared that
those with whom she lodged viewed her as a sort of mischievous
cat, or perhaps a monkey, fond as she was of following her own mercurial impulses.

Upon learning I was Harry's sister, she avowed her esteem for
my brother and her gratitude for her present employment in his
company. I told her that her praise and thanks were better addressed
to my brother, who knew far more than I how to receive a compliment. I expected that would be the end of our intercourse, but
Mrs. Charke continued asking me questions. She had heard that I
had learning, in Latin as well as Greek, and she wished to know if I
would one day write plays, or even prose romances, like Mrs. Haywood. I owned no such ambition, but she pressed me, saying that if
I possessed even half my brother's talents, I could achieve greatness.

Mrs. Charke told me that from her earliest days she had preferred
men's garments, and she had obtained an education more suitable

for a boy than for a girl—as she watched me apply yet another button, she confessed that she could not sew a single stitch. Should the theater fail her, she said, she would chuse to pursue a man's employment. And then she said something I can scarce drive from my thoughts, even now: she could see that I was another such as herself, someone who had no place in this world of cruel misapprehensions and censorious tongues. Someone who must make her own place, by whatever means present themselves.

Even as I attempted to keep this bewildering creature at a distance, I found myself longing to converse further with her. I had never met anyone like her, and I told myself that as a student of human nature, I was merely curious about such an odd creature— surely, I told myself, my curiosity could do no harm.

If Harry noticed his sister keeping company with his lead actress, he chose not to remark on it. For her part, Charlotte commented that she, too, was good friends with her own brother—tho' she was not above cruelly teazing her Theophilus on occasion.

The more I conversed with Charlotte, the more fascinated I grew. She carried herself so much like a man in publick that few could discern her true nature, and she moved with an assurance that even most men could scarce emulate. Few men have stirred in me the sensations I felt when she gazed upon me with that quirk of a smile on her lips. Oh Jenny, you must burn this letter! Let not a soul read it beside yourself.

Charlotte had written plays herself—tho' she saw no great purpose in uplifting anyone's understanding or morality, but used her wit solely to settle scores with her rivals. Her very soul was made of mischief, and yet she saw in me what few others have: she entreated me, constantly, to think of writing my own words, to fashion tales that could make strait the crookedness in men's hearts. I replied each time that I had no desire to be such a figure of derision as her friend, Mrs. Haywood, who indeed seemed little better situated than Betty Careless herself. But Charlotte (you see now I use her familiar name!) saw through my protestations. And she insisted that I could not write the great romances of which she knew I was capable until I had tasted what the world had to offer. Her eyes, alight with mirth and tenderness, captured me, and I was helpless to resist.

Thus it was that I found myself, in a feeble disguise, visiting first coffee houses and then taverns—places of ill repute, all—alongside not only Charlotte Charke but Betty Careless and other women of low reputation—I should have known—I should never have left Sarum! With Harry's enemies besetting him from every quarter, the tale of his sister's indiscretions could not fail to arouse attention. I have seen only one brief mention thus far, in a pamphlet, but the deluge is soon to come, I am sure. I have not spoken of any of this to Harry yet, for tho' I know he relishes a public brawl, I also know his stature as a gentleman is of paramount importance to him.

Jenny, you cannot help me—none can—save through your prayers and your constant friendship. I pray I may remain yours always, Sally

———————————

My dearest Sally,

I scarce know what to write in response to your letter. I have ruin'd four sheets of paper and much ink with the deluge of my tears at the thought of you suffering so. You, the gentlest person I know—the kindest and most gracious—you, who would rather read your Xenophon in peace than seek the world's attention. The unfairness of it, that one brief adventure should cause you such lasting misery, is an injustice my soul cannot bear.

Listen to one who knows you best: You are not at fault. You have scarce erred in any particular. Your only mistake was to find yourself in the middle of a slow battle between your brother and Mrs. Charke's father, with many other combatants beside. You and Mrs. Charke are both pawns on their board, I am sad to say. You possess such a panoramic imagination, I have no doubt you will be able to envision many ways in which you are to be blamed, or in which

your accusers are correct—but let not your breadth of mind lead
you to accept these cruel judgments.

You have done nothing wrong.

Mrs. Charke was correct in one particular, my dear Sally: You
must write, one day. I know you have the capacity to transport a
reader, for your thoughts have transported mine so many times. In my
short time alive so far, I have witnessed so much rotten behavior—as
if the greatest pleasure in life, for so many gentlemen and gentlewomen, must be to torment those under their power. Yours could be
the pen that helps people to reach for grace instead of cruelty.

I can promise nothing, but—I think there may be a way that I can
help you, after all. I cannot, should not, write of it in a letter, but
there is a means by which I believe wrongs can be undone. I pray
I have the ability. I shall try. Dear Sally, write me again and let me
know how you are, or better yet, come back to Salisbury. I shall be
miserable until I know that you are well.

Praying for your safe return, yours always, Jenny

Dearest Jenny:

I cannot write a long letter, for I must depart on a coach home
tomorrow. I write merely to say that I am better, and the expected
scandal has not arrived. Perhaps your intervention, whatsoever it
may have been, has helped. I am returning to Sarum, and hope to
see you soon.

Yours, Sally

13

Misfortunes, to which all are liable, are too often the parents of forgetfulness and disregard in those we have, in happier times, obliged. Too sure I found it so!

—*A NARRATIVE OF THE LIFE OF MRS. CHARLOTTE CHARKE* BY CHARLOTTE CHARKE, 1755

I have chosen my friends unwisely. Jamie rereads these letters, almost committing them to memory, and each time they feel like a tectonic shift in her worldview. Now she knows for sure: Sarah Fielding met Charlotte Charke/Charles Brown in the spring of 1736, and they were briefly friends. Were they lovers? Doubtful, but of course Jamie will never know. What's certain is that the sheltered, studious Sarah was swept away by the devil-may-care Charlotte Charke, with disastrous consequences. And then Jane did something to help—though she had no power, and certainly no money, to help by conventional means. What happened next? Did Jane accomplish anything on Sarah's behalf, and what did it cost her? And how does this relate to that fairy tale, in which Jane is clearly Lady Sagacious? Jamie needs to know.

Jamie's so obsessed, she barely registers at first when Ro offers her a toaster pastry one morning and asks how the work is going. Jamie looks at the pastry in Ro's extended hand and tries to be chill about it, rather than breaking down in tears and bawling, *I'm so sorry I hurt you.* This tiny moment of generosity makes Jamie sorrier than ever, because she can so clearly see the love of her life standing in front of her, making a mighty effort to reconnect a little.

You will always be loved, you cannot mess up so badly that you will not be loved.

But Jamie doesn't want to make this weird, so she just takes the pastry and says thanks, and that the work is awesome, because she's had some lucky breaks.

"Well," Ro says without any bitterness or anger, "except it's not really luck, is it?"

"No." Jamie tries to smile at this. "I suppose not. I've definitely had an advantage that I ought to find a way to confess in my footnotes."

"I would very much like to see that footnote." Ro cocks their head. "You might be the only researcher in your field who can use magic to find primary sources, but some of your peers might have other advantages, like a bigger travel budget or access to private libraries."

Jamie keeps her cringe on the inside. This is one of many reasons she never told Ro her secret: she knew they would be unable to resist puzzling out the ethics.

The pastry is warm inside, just on the edge of burning Jamie's mouth. She doesn't quite taste it, but afterward she has the memory of sweetness.

"I'll see you tonight," she says to Ro.

"Yes. See you." Ro smiles.

"I love you." Jamie hopes she can say these words in this moment without being passive-aggressive.

"And I you," Ro says. Which is the closest they've come to saying *love* in a while.

· · · · ·

When Jamie touches the first edition of *The Fair Moralist* (with gloves on, she's not a monster) she gets a sense-recall of standing in McAllister Bushwick's shadow. The prickle in her arms, the fear in her guts. She represses that memory, since Bushwick wants her to live in fear—as if she cast a spell, and now she must put it out of her mind. When she does think of Bushwick, she rationalizes that he wouldn't have gone to so much trouble to chase her down, literally, if he had anything worth publishing.

But also, Jamie low-key obsesses about the idea that magic doesn't give you what you want, after all—she did not want Bushwick chewing up her ass, but she and Serena put a lot of energy into thinking about him.

She'd much rather think about Charlotte Charke/Charles Brown. She pictures Sarah Fielding coming to the Little Theatre at Haymarket, on the edge of the most disreputable part of Covent Garden and the Strand, where the streets ran with muck and fashionable ladies needed to wear special platform shoes everywhere to avoid befouling their clothes.

She pores over every scribble in the delicate rag-paper pages of *The Fair Moralist,* which she's already matched with the handwriting in Jane Collier's commonplace book. On another blank page between sections of the novel, Jamie comes across a tangle of neat lines, with a crude daisy shape drawn in a couple of places off to the right. Is this . . . a map? And if so, a map of what? Jamie squints, because it looks familiar. If the neat lines are a street plan, then Jamie's seen it somewhere before, though it's definitely not London. But what does the daisy icon mean?

It's not until later that Jamie thinks of the letter Jane Collier sent Sarah Fielding, where she says the daisy will represent the wonder that no language can describe.

•　•　•　•　•

Jamie is doing errands in Brookline and she passes by the redbrick shopping mall that includes a feminist sex-toy store, where every vibrator and plug comes with an education (if you want it). She shouldn't go inside, because she's broke and sexless, but what the hell. She has time to kill, she might as well browse silicone body parts.

There's just something soothing about a clean space that is both chill and sex-positive, where all the design choices say that your pleasure is valid but that consent and kindness are important. Jamie hardly notices the one other customer, because yet again she gets lost in browsing, until someone is standing right next to her. (She's forever doomed to be Sartre's voyeur.) The stranger is dark-skinned and bright-eyed, with wide cheekbones, wearing a lot of scarves and skirts, and locs down to their shoulders, and they're looking at the same mermaid-shaped vibrator as Jamie.

"I don't like vibrators shaped like people." Jamie's own voice sounds a bit husky, all of a sudden. "Even fish people. Feels weird."

"I think the mermaid is supposed to represent the person using it." When the other customer speaks, Jamie can see a tiny gap in their front teeth, and oh dear, they just got cuter. "Sort of synecdoche, or metonymy? I get them mixed-up."

"That just makes it worse, though." Jamie's voice is definitely husky. She hasn't flirted in so long, and she's not sure if it's happening now, but even the possibility feels wonderscary. "That's like using an effigy as a sex toy. It just feels way, too, I don't know, solipsistic."

The other customer laughs. "'Sex Effigy' is my new ska band name."

They wander off, looking at floggers. Jamie tries not to stare as they heft a velvety-thuddy flogger, medium sized; their biceps crest. Their smile says *I know how to use this.* In spite of her best efforts, Jamie keeps checking this person out, and can't help noticing the way they flick their eyes, as if they're in the habit of looking out for the best places to do a working.

All at once she's sure: this is a fellow witch.

Okay, time to leave. On the handful of occasions when Jamie has run into another witch, she's given them lots of space, because nobody needs her in their business.

Jamie doesn't leave. She can't, while this person is still swinging floggers and smiling.

So instead she introduces herself and tries to find some way to hint that she's a witch, too. Clumsily, as it turns out. "Some great hiking trails around here," Jamie babbles. "I've found so many spots that are nearly untouched, but with lots of, uh, potential."

Turns out the other witch is named Delia and uses she/her pronouns, too. Delia smiles at Jamie, still holding the flogger. Jamie wonders if it's written on her face that she's a giant submissive bottom? Probably not, right? Definitely not.

"You practice the Beige Arts as well, do you?" Delia says. "That's wonderful."

"Yeah. Ha. The Beige Arts." Jamie smiles and squirms.

Jamie is about to make a graceful exit at last. And then Delia says, "Ohhhh. You're Serena's kid, right? She's told us so much about you."

Jamie can't process what she's hearing. At least the sexual tension is gone, replaced with a sinking feeling. Jamie always thought "sinking feeling" was a metaphor, but now her cochlea and gut both inform her that she is descending, even though her eyes say there's a floor under her feet. This feels like a dream. Her brain calls a cab, and it shows up with the judgey, making-sense-of-things part of her, carrying a message: Serena's been networking with other witches.

Delia is giving Jamie a curious half smile. Her heather-gray eyes are kind.

"Yeah," Jamie says after an uncomfortable silence. "Serena can be a lot sometimes. I hope she didn't freak you out too much."

"Are you kidding? Your mom is a delight." Delia's voice has a lilt that Jamie can't assign to an accent. British? Caribbean? Or perhaps it's a variation on the educated Boston patter that everyone learns to affect. "She says nothing but good things about you."

"That's . . . great. That's really great. How did you two become acquainted?"

"Oh." Delia seems startled by the depth of Jamie's ignorance. "A mutual friend introduced us. I only knew one other person who does 'the thing we all do.'" The air quotes are almost visible, like haloes. "Your mother has been tracking us down, and it always turns out each of us knows about one or two others, and soon there's a whole extended family. Serena—your mom—keeps saying we'll all be better off if we have more people to compare notes with and call on in times of trouble. She's talking about unionizing, and I'm not entirely sure it's a joke."

Heady mix of feelings right now—pride and anxiety are thumping against the walls of Jamie's psyche.

"That sounds like my mom. She's been a community organizer since before I was born. I taught her to do magic so we could reconnect, and she could maybe snap out of the rut she was in."

"You're clearly a proficient teacher." Delia smiles wider.

"That's not what my class rating forms say."

Something makes Jamie want to trust Delia, even if Jamie can't trust her own mother right now. Maybe it's the flogger perched in her beautifully manicured hand, with iridescent nail art.

Nobody has talked for a moment. The store is playing someone's idea of sexy lady music, Berlin or the Cardigans, breathy moans over synthesizer spunk.

"So . . . how many are there?" Jamie tries to steer the conversation back on track. "Of you? I mean, of *us*. How many"—she searches for a word other than "witches"—"members?"

Delia laughs. "There's nothing to be a member of. Not yet, anyway. But there are . . . I don't know, eight of us. If you count Wardin, he's sort of peripatetic. We're still sorting out our goals and principles and suchlike."

Jamie has so many questions, but this just became too weird a conversation to have in a sex-toy store. And she needs to process all of this.

"You haven't talked to her lately, have you?" Delia's eyes widen a little. "Your mom? I guess I hadn't realized. She talks about you like you're close."

"We were. We have been. It's . . . it's a long, weird story." Jamie glances at her phone—she's late for everything. "Listen, maybe we can meet for drinks sometime. You could meet my partner, Ro." Jamie is conscious that she's shoehorning Ro into the conversation as a way of pushing all this *want* out of the frame, and it only makes the *want* more salient, not less. Plus of course, Jamie and Ro are poly, and Delia might be as well.

"Oh sure. Let me give you my number. Also, we have a Discord server, if you want to chat with some of the others."

There's . . . a Discord server for witches. Of course there is. Jamie gets Delia's number and the link to the server, and they go in opposite directions.

Jamie is breathing too loud.

Halfway home, something makes Jamie stop and pull over. Right near the road, she finds a clearing where some kids built a fort and set off some blasting caps a long time ago. She puts down candy and another page of Ro's diss, and then she jets home.

• • • • •

A couple days later, Jamie has an invite to a meeting of the witch union, at someone's house in Nashua. She also joins the Discord, where three people are sharing memes and links to articles about the Supreme Court. There's no mention of witchery, or the group's purpose, apart from one person asking if they should bring their gluten-free nut clusters to the meeting. The group must be pretty new, since Serena didn't mention it the last time Jamie saw her.

My mother is building a cult, Jamie thinks. *Or a coven, with herself as leader.* Except that Delia didn't seem especially brainwashed.

In any case, Jamie resolves: she won't go to her mother's group. (Although some wicked voice inside her whispers that she wouldn't mind seeing Delia's smile again. Ugh, stop.) She's got classes to teach, and the field of eighteenth-century literature to revolutionize, and she can't spare the time to shlep all the way to Nashua. And even if Serena's group isn't an actual cult, this is yet another example of Serena trampling past all of the limits Jamie has tried to set. Jamie is convinced this group will end in tragedy, though she has no mental model of how that'll happen.

Jamie remembers kneeling with her mother, the two of them moving in sync, smearing shit on a kazoo, and then a genteel predator looming over her in a bookstore. Teaching Serena may actually be the worst mistake of her life.

Time to be a witch about it, Jamie tells herself. This time, meaning: *Time to step away and let Serena take the consequences of her own actions.*

The day of the "witch union" meeting, Jamie stands in her usual lecture hall, teaching Crisis of the English Novel, in front of some of the best minds in English lit . . . plus Gavin.

Jamie cannot look at Gavin without seeing McAllister Bushwick, and not just because she suspects Gavin of siccing Bushwick on her. Both of these dudes see words not as a way to convey ideas or information but as traps to be set. Jamie realizes she's been zoning out in front of the class, while Luisa, one of her favorite students, is in the middle of asking a question about Thackeray and Hawthorne and female agency in an American versus British context. Jamie tries to answer, but she can't see past the image of Serena and her new friends (acolytes?) doing the same feverish spellwork that Jamie and Serena did when they were in sync, swaying and chanting and getting swept away.

With mediocre pedagogy comes a modicum of responsibility. Jamie owes a duty of care to these students, but also to her mother, whom she taught badly and then set loose on the world. Jamie finds an excuse to end class early.

Jamie drives too fast, and her mind channel-surfs from thought to thought. She braces for a dozen different things she might find in that Nashua cul-de-sac, but also: she needs to find a way to restore her relationship with Ro, because she's in a permanent tailspin without them. Not that she can't function—she can, and that's the problem. She just doesn't have any center of gravity.

She drives in circles for a while before she spots the lane that leads to the cul-de-sac with five houses in a semicircle. A handful of cars, with Planned Parenthood stickers and messy back seats, are parked in front of a canary-yellow house with an assortment of figurines on the stoop. Jamie rings the bell, and the door opens to show a white person in their fifties, with a guarded warmth in their brown eyes. "Oh, you must be Jamie. I'm Bee. My pronouns are they or she." Bee ushers Jamie into a room ringed by bookshelves, where Jamie immediately covets several books. A homey smell clings to the old carpet and the cozy-shabby sofa and armchairs. Sitting in a circle are Serena, Delia, and three others: a middle-aged Asian lesbian named Martha, a young Latinx punk queer called Paola, and the one token straight person, a thirtyish Asian lady named Yvette, who gives teacher vibes, or maybe nurse. Serena waves, like Jamie is right on time. "We were just about to break into Bee's cookie stash," Jamie's mother says. Jamie learns all about Bee's garden, Paola's experiments with baking, the dance classes Yvette has been taking, Serena's hunt for little touches to make her new apartment feel more like a real home. This could be any book club, or support group. Jamie was prepared for everything except banality. Are they avoiding talking about the juicy stuff in front of Jamie, or did they already discuss it earlier? Nah. They're just . . . hanging out.

At last, Delia looks at each person in a way that makes the room quiet down. "So, maybe it's time we talked about 'that thing we all do.'"

Jamie feels herself tense up.

"I have some mindfulness techniques that I want to suggest," says Martha. "I find that having a focus point helps me to listen to my breathing, and that in turn helps me to concentrate on what I really need."

Yvette starts discussing aromatherapy, and Bee shows off the mandolin she plays to get into an aware state of mind.

At a certain point, Serena starts sharing some of her tips for finding the best liminal spaces, and they're genius, of course.

Jamie notices that nobody is discussing the particulars of the spells they've done, which tracks.

"Jamie taught me everything I know." Serena casts a beatific look at her daughter. "But I'm very glad to have all of you to learn from as well."

The group is so low-key and comforting, Jamie can't help relaxing and munching on Petit Écolier cookies while listening to friendly tips. But there's still a queasy feeling, and she can't figure out why. Then she gets it: this group is about claiming an identity—witch—that previously was just a tiny secret corner of Jamie's life. The same thing happened, sort of, when Jamie psyched herself up to attend a trans support group when she was fifteen, except that everyone here is claiming a label they'll always hold secret.

The meeting ends without anyone getting naked or slaughtering a baby goat in Bee's herb garden. Once everyone is milling around, Delia approaches with the smile that makes Jamie all skin and blood. "So, what did you think?"

Jamie chews a cookie, collecting her thoughts. "Everyone seems nice. I was worried it would be . . . I don't know, more coven-y."

"Coven-y?" Delia snarks.

"You know. I mean, my mom has a really strong personality and she's good at inspiring people, but also at getting people to do things. She used to tell me that journalism and activism both entailed a lot of social engineering. And she's lost a lot in her life. I sort of pictured everyone helping her do some honking big spell. Or something."

Delia frowns. "How would that even work, though? Every participant in a working needs to desire a particular outcome in their deepest soul. Right?"

Jamie shrugs, then blurts: "Serena is very good at convincing people to want things."

"Even so. People might think they wanted something, but it wouldn't be a heartfelt desire. Right? The working would go wrong, absolutely."

Damn. Delia's right, and Jamie can already tell that she's not likely to let Serena manipulate her, or push her around. None of these people feels like cult-member material, for that matter.

At last, Jamie says to Delia, "There are a few basic things everyone seems to agree on. Like, everyone is queer, or queer-friendly."

"I'm not saying we couldn't all do a working together someday," Delia says. "We've talked about it, once or twice. But it would have to be some-thing pretty benign and low-key, I think."

Jamie wants to believe that. She almost does.

Serena is outside, watching Yvette smoke a cigarette. "Glad you could make it."

"Me, too," Jamie says.

"It's lonesome being a witch," Yvette says, between puffs. "Sort of like any other creative pursuit, except worse because of all the secrecy. This group is a lifeline."

Now that Jamie's out in the fresh air, the uneasiness is back. This is the closest she's been to her mother since right after Ro turned into moonlight. Serena looks cheerful, and this pisses Jamie off—even though she would've given almost everything to see her mother like this.

Yvette and Serena are making plans to go to an art gallery opening to-gether. It's all so fucking wholesome. Then Yvette wanders back inside, and Jamie is alone with her mother.

Serena sighs. "You don't approve." She flashes a shrewd look, like when Jamie used to swear she'd done all her homework. "You think this is a bad idea."

Jamie kicks gravel. "I don't know. Everyone seems nice. I'm just . . . I'm just surprised. First you disappear my partner to make sure my magic stays secret. And then you go recruiting, creating a support group, and setting up a Discord server? I've got whiplash, Mom."

"Where's the contradiction?" Serena shakes her head at the ground. "Isn't that what every stigmatized group does? You build ties with other people who share your same interest, while trying to keep the outside world at a remove." Long brash sigh. "I'm really sorry about what happened to . . . what I did to Ro. I screwed up, horribly, and I hate that I used something you taught me to hurt the person you love. I hope you and Ro are doing okay."

"We're not." Jamie tries to keep self-pity out of those two syllables.

"I'm sorry," Serena says again. "For what it's worth, that's part of why this group exists. The longer I thought about what I had done, the shittier I felt about it, and the more scared I got of screwing up again. You had cut off contact, so I realized I needed people to check in with about magic. I shouldn't be alone with this secret. I don't think it's healthy."

Getting late. Jamie's breath mists. "So *now* you're sorry."

"I was sorry before. I just didn't know how to say it." Serena chews her nails the way she hasn't in years. "I was in shock. I couldn't process what I had done at first. I was sucked back into the moment where I had blown up my own life by talking trash to the wrong person. Can you understand that? I'm not proud. Anyway, I truly am sorry. This is me trying to do better." She gestures at Bee's house, and the witches inside.

Mae would have been calling all kinds of bullshit right now. But Jamie doesn't have it in her.

"I'm glad you have new friends." Jamie kicks a pebble with her boot-heel. "Just don't let this cozy basket-weaving, farmers-market-shopping vibe make you forget that this shit is dangerous. You've already found out twice. You don't always get what you ask for, but sometimes you *do*."

Jamie almost tells Serena about McAllister Bushwick, but then Serena will freak out and make it about her. Or she'll offer support that Jamie can't accept from her right now. Plus Jamie is trying to convince herself that Bushwick has probably given up.

Serena nods. "Having these people around can only help me do better."

It's late. Jamie promises to call, and probably means it. She gets in the dirtmobile and drives back to Somerville. On the way home, she stops and does one more working to bless Ro, to smooth their path and light their way.

When Jamie gets home, it's after eleven. So she takes off her shoes outside the apartment door and tiptoes in, so as not to wake Ro.

They're sitting in the front roomlet, in one of the wooden chairs, reading by lamplight. They've been waiting up for her.

A sudden surge of gladness intoxicates her, but it's laced with a little guilt that she kind of, sort of, flirted with Delia without talking to them first.

Jamie feels shy. She's working her way up to saying, "Hi, you're up late," but the words are stuck in the pipeline.

Ro breaks the silence. "What did you do?"

"What do you mean?"

"I know you did something. I can tell. Things have been going well for me. Abnormally, improbably, well. As if someone greased the wheels of the universe."

They noticed. Jamie smiles.

But they aren't smiling.

"I might have done a small working, or a couple."

"Did I *ask* you to do that?"

"Um, no . . . but you haven't said anything one way or the other in weeks. I thought—"

"I've been trying to see my way to giving you another chance. But this . . ." They fall out of the pool of lamplight. "You don't think I'm capable of handling my shit without your help. You think I'm incompetent. Or something."

"What? I don't think that at all."

Jamie is having a panic attack hidden inside a scare. The immediate scare is that Ro is going to wise up and kick her to the curb at last, but there's also an existential dread of sorts—Ro wants to process about the spells Jamie did, and that means she has to think and talk about them, something she instinctively knows is a way to make them go away. The good luck she secured for them could even turn bad, if she dwells too much. Maybe. Uncharted territory.

Jamie chooses each of her words as if she's reaching into a box of broken glass dipped in poison. "You should know by now that I believe in you and I admire and respect you, and I would never think you can't crush the paradox of thrift. But I can't talk about my workings. I just can't. I promise not to do it again. But I can't talk—"

"Oh yeah, it has to be secret. Except when it comes to your mom."

Jamie repeats the thing she said to Serena when she first started sharing magic with her. "It's not about power, it's about knowing your own desires. I didn't stack any decks or put my thumb on any scales for you, it's not that potent or goal-directed—I just wished you well. I put a tiny grain of my boundless love for you out into the universe, and hoped it would help a little."

"There are other ways to show you love someone. You could have just been patient with me. You knew I was traumatized by magic, but you chose to do more magic that affected me."

"You're right. I should have just chilled out. I just . . . I didn't think it would be a big deal. It was small-ball, minor-league stuff."

Now Jamie is really teetering on the edge of overanalyzing what must never be analyzed. She tells herself she's willing to risk her secret joy for the person she loves, but especially after having just been in a roomful of witches, all carefully speaking in generalities, this is a lot.

"I can't talk to you when you're like this. Ever since I . . . since I disappeared, you've been a guilt monster. You keep acting on guilt but calling it love, and you have the nerve to talk to me about self-knowledge."

"All I really feel is helpless."

"What if I asked you to give it up for now?"

Jamie thinks about this for a moment. In some ways, it would be a relief to let go of this burden. But she can't let go of anxiety about Serena's new group, and the path Jamie started her mother on. At this point, Jamie's not even sure what she's worried about, except that Serena keeps catching her off guard.

"I don't think I can," Jamie tells Ro. "Somebody needs to be a check on Serena. You saw what she's capable of."

Ro sighs. "I think you should sleep somewhere else for a while. I don't want to kick you out, but—I need to be on my own, to figure out some stuff. I can't go into the woods and put some junk down to connect with my emotions, the way you and your mom can."

Cold wave hits, as if Jamie is already out on the street. Part of her is trying to figure out where the hell she can crash—who'll put her up with zero notice—and part is busy feeling utterly lost. As if she herself is becoming a neglected place.

"Promise you won't do another spell that involves me, not without my explicit permission."

Jamie nods. "I won't. Promise."

She's fairly certain her relationship just ended, but she can't cry yet—that's for three days from now, for the long low point. She drags herself through the motions of putting personal effects into an overnight bag. Brain replaying her conversation with Ro, making the whole thing realer with each iteration. Probing each moment to find the false note, the part where she could have avoided this. The conversation passed quickly in the moment, but she's going to be living in it for days or maybe weeks. She'll relitigate it until she can't breathe.

We learn to fight from our parents, and the fighting style Jamie learned from Serena and Mae was stoic, withholding. Mae would retreat into hurt feelings, Serena would get tight-lipped with anger, neither of them admitting fault or showing vulnerability, until much later when they finally felt up to processing. Jamie learned from the best how to be a brick wall in a crisis.

. . . . .

Outside the air is chilly and full of smoke from a dozen nearby chimneys, the kind of acrid that only makes the cold bite harder. Jamie stumbles to the dirtmobile with her bags of crap. It would serve Ro right if she crashed and ended up in a ditch. Who would be sorry then? Ugh, *stop it*. Ro is the injured party here, if anyone is.

She ends up in the Goblin Market, cocooned in her tiny cubby, staring at the first edition of *The Fair Moralist*. Her gaze falls on the scribble-map, with the daisies that she's sure have something to do with magic—and this time it twigs something in her memory. There's an oven mitt of streets, with a hockey-stick river off to one side . . . Jamie pulls up maps on her phone, until she finds it. This looks a lot like the famous Thomas Thorpe map of Bath, the ancient Roman spa town where Sarah Fielding ended up living. Some radical women, the Blue Stockings, tried to create their own utopian community in Bath, based on Sarah Scott's novel *Millenium Hall,* and Sarah was on the fringes of their group. Some scholars believe Jane was also part of that Bath group during her lifetime. So if this is Bath, then those daisy shapes are off past Bathwick Meadow, among some ruins, where the delightfully named Sham Castle was built in 1755. Could the daisies be neglected places?

Somehow deep down, Jamie has always known: Jane Collier was a witch. Maybe Sarah Fielding, too. All of a sudden, those letters make a whole different sense. *Whatever relief my feverish entreaties can obtain is yours.*

But what kind of spell can erase a scandal in the making? What could you possibly offer? How does this connect with the fairy tale? Jamie can't wrap her mind around it, no matter how hard her bleary eyes stare at each squiggle in the margins.

At some point in the wee hours, Jamie dozes off in her uncomfortable chair. She wakes disoriented. She hears a noise and raises her head.

Gavin is standing in front of her, wearing a baseball cap and aviator glasses. Oh fuck.

"Office hours are Tuesday," Jamie mumbles.

"Have you been here all night?"

She sits up straighter. "No."

He's about to point out all the evidence to the contrary, then he shakes his head. "Whatever. I don't care. I'm glad I caught you. I need to pick your brain."

The entitlement.

"Office hours are Tuesday," Jamie says again.

"I'm a customer. I pay your salary."

"What salary?"

Why is it that people who would never dream of telling a cop or a judge "I pay your salary" feel at total liberty to say that to a professor (or in Jamie's case, grad student lecturer)? Forget it, she knows why.

"You chose this life. So listen, I'm having a crisis here. I'm supposed to write a personal narrative for your creative writing class, but I can't make sense of it. The memoir thing, I mean. When we cook up a narrative out of all our life stuff, aren't we automatically falsifying? I mean, you keep saying the structure of the novel is a kind of false consciousness. Right? A novel reaches a crescendo and then everything is resolved, and that's fake! But it's so embedded in our minds that we can't tell a story without it. Right?"

"Um. Yeah. I mean, real life is messy, and the whole Western idea of a narrative progression is, uh . . ."

Jamie is going to throw up all over Gavin. Seems like a victimless crime, except it'd live forever on her Rate My Prof page.

"Yeah, so . . . how do you avoid that? Because I wanted to write about something super personal and intense, and I can't stop worrying about the prison of structure."

"Well. Uh. There are many alternative structures. There's the shaggy dog. There are false climaxes. There's good old *Tristram Shandy*. Or the pomo time-jumping narrative, like *Infinite Jest*. I think it depends what response you're trying to evoke in the, uh, the . . ."

"My girlfriend lost her eye."

". . . What?"

"She's not my girlfriend anymore. She dumped me, right after I vowed I would always stand by her. She had this crimson eye patch, it was stunning. But she threw me away, I don't know what happened. I would have been her man forever, you know? She just tossed me aside."

"So this is a story about how you got dumped."

"What? No. That's not part of the story. The story is about how she lost her eye. It was gruesome. I feel like I can say that now because I'm not her boyfriend anymore."

"I don't get why this is your story."

As soon as she says those words, Jamie regrets them—she already wasted an hour in the classroom debating appropriation with Gavin.

"Whose story is it, then? I was there." Gavin scratches his head.

"Yeah, but . . . I think your crisis might be about something beyond the tyranny of structure. Fuck, I need coffee. I will see you in class."

"But—we're not done."

"We kind of are. I'm sorry. I do not think you should write about your ex's mishap. If you ever lose an eye of your own, maybe you can write about that."

Jamie gathers all her stuff and hustles out of there before he can harangue her about her salary again. There's a cold pit where her soul used to be.

She sits in the Grounds for Rejoicing, the only coffee shop on this side of the freeway, and thinks about Gavin's conversation. She's pretty sure she didn't dream it. The structure of the English novel is the structure of war, or perhaps courtship? Conflict is introduced and intensified, until at last a victor is crowned and the conflict ends. Or, a potential relationship is introduced and tested, until at last the status of the lovers is codified and stabilized. In real life, of course, wars drag on and on, ending only when one or both sides become disgusted/disheartened. Love affairs stop and start, fueled by a shared love of the Jonas Brothers and derailed by an argument over the best way to cook an eggplant. If anything, structure is the enemy that none of us can fully defeat. We can't experience life as it is, because we cannot resist adding rising action and climax and denouement, pouring reality into a rigid shape. When we glimpse the world making a mockery of our tidy expectations, we instinctively flinch away. The only structure that really approximates our lives as we know them is the episodic, the picaresque, the travelogue. Or the epistolary novel in which everyday life proceeds at its own pace.

Maybe this whole notion of desiring something, chasing an ambition to the end, is a product of that delusion. What would magic look like without that imposed framework?

And that brings Jamie back to the map with the daisy shapes on it. Women of that era never would have called themselves witches, of course: the main anti-witchcraft law was only repealed in 1736, and witch hunts still went on after that. But what if Jane Collier had stumbled on the same secret Jamie had? Now she's remembering all the times in *Emily* when Emily visits a ruined abbey or a dilapidated bridge, scatters petals or cake crumbs, and pines for a way out of her cloistered life. And then there's that fairy tale . . . Jamie is sure fairies aren't real, but the stuff about finding a fairy door, an "eruption of decay" in a grotto, feels very much like the process of finding a magical place in real life.

Magic led Jamie to *Emily*, and maybe this book has something to teach her. Or maybe this is just wishful thinking, because magic just destroyed Jamie's marriage, and she's pretty sure there's worse to come.

Jamie keeps going back to Lady Sagacious: she saves the Princess, but is nearly consumed in the process. Take away the fairies, and you're left with something even scarier. But what actually happened to Jane in 1736? Was it similar to what almost happened to Ro? How did Jane survive? This mystery is going to keep eating away at both the personal and academic sides of Jamie's brain. If only she could gather her thoughts enough to solve it. For now, she needs to find a place to crash for a while. To hunker down without the love of her life.

iv

And now back to the simple part of this story and the most important truth of my life: I gave birth to a healthy baby, a human being, not a prepackaged promise of a predictable gendered life.

—"A MOM'S LETTER INTRODUCING HER TRANSGENDER DAUGHTER" BY LIZ HANSSEN, *HUFFPOST*, 2014

Jamie was missing—she hadn't come home after school, and it had been hours. Serena and Mae were texting each other nonstop with updates, and Serena's phone was stacking notifications like cordwood. Serena was trying to put out a dozen fires at the Housing Now Foundation, while scouring every possible location where Jamie might be found. Serena wasn't sure what she regretted more: agreeing to let Jamie have more unsupervised time now that the kid was in eighth grade, or getting a smartphone for herself.

This shiny little rectangle in Serena's right hand was a stress multiplier. Cora was emailing about the Wrigley case—a dozen low-income families being pushed out of subsidized housing—and there was a new draft of the white paper on mixed-used spaces that Housing Now was co-authoring with HomeStart and two other orgs. Two random people had left voicemails asking for help with legal problems, and there was static on Housing Now's new social media accounts. None of this stuff was urgent, but the buzzes and chimes from Serena's iPhone felt like a panic attack that never let up. You'd have thought that after three (!) years at Yeager, Furst, this level of pressure would be nothing, but it was harder to leave at the office.

Where the heck did Jamie spend her time? Serena rushed through the redbrick mall with the anime/manga store and the thick tang of pizza grease in the air, then into the park where Jamie used to take her pet ferret, until Mobley had run away.

Mae was combing through the strip malls near the community college, a hop and a skip from Jamie's middle school.

They had moved to Wardmont (a suburb out near where the Charles River snaked around and ambushed the turnpike) to get a bigger place and some sleepy streets where Jamie could walk on her own during the day. Neither parent knew all the enclaves where kids hung out, though Serena had seen teens smoking near a railway bridge and skateboards whipping around an abandoned parking lot. There were so many quiet lanes behind houses, so many bike trails. But even worse than the impossibility of finding all the cracks and gullies under the glossy surface of Wardmont, there was the fact that they had no idea what was going on with this kid lately.

Jamie had bemused her parents so many times before, but always in the past she'd held to a gentle sweetness, even during those moments when she'd flirted with toxic masculinity. (Besides the brief alliance with Zeb the bully, there'd been a vaguely misogynistic nerd club in fifth grade, and some seventh-grade brawls.)

Mae kept telling Serena this was part of growing up: you had to let your kid try on different identities, screw up and bruise up, and parents shouldn't hold a full topography of a healthy child's inner world. "We have to let R_____ grow up and grow apart," Mae said. "Don't be a helicopter parent, be a bus parent. Or a ferry parent, maybe. Show up regularly, be there if you're needed, hold your space." Serena had made a silly pun about ferry parents and fairy godparents, but Mae was right of course.

This particular day, Serena and Mae combed the whole town and even some bits of the more upscale Newton, but no sign of Jamie—until they got home and Jamie was sitting on the couch eating peanut butter from the jar with a big spoon.

"If we got you a cellphone, would it even help?" Serena asked. "Or would you blow us off and just use it to text your friends?" Jamie shrugged.

A few days later, Jamie had a guitar. A plain case opened to reveal a pristine Fender acoustic six-string, varnish gleaming. How in blazes had Jamie managed to buy a new musical instrument? She'd have to have been saving her allowance for a year, or gotten a babysitting job that Serena didn't know about, or . . .

Serena found Mae doing laundry in the cheap washer/dryer in the closet, and whispered, "I think R_____ might be shoplifting."

Mae shrugged. "We kept saying that kid should get a hobby outside the house." Before Serena could protest that this was serious, Mae added: "Okay. Yes. I hope you're wrong, let's not jump to conclusions. And yet if you're right? This could ruin our kid's life. So what do we do next?"

"I don't know." Serena tried to put her reporter hat back on. "There's only one music store in Wardmont, so I could stop by and try and find out if they remember selling that guitar, or having it stolen."

Working as an attorney, even mostly not in criminal cases, hadn't increased Serena's faith in the system—quite the reverse, she'd seen how fucked the system was, and the wreckage it left in its wake every day. Evil people had worked overtime to create a shape-shifting razor-blade maze out of being "tough on crime," and those fuckers especially thirsted to see families like Serena's destroyed. Result: paranoia.

The knot-bearded guy at the music shop took one look at the photo on Serena's phone of Jamie's guitar and confirmed he'd sold that guitar a week ago. *Nice kid,* he said. *You should be proud your child is taking an interest in playing an instrument, most kids these days are all about Auto-Tune and canned beats,* and on and on. Serena wanted to walk out in the middle of his lecture, but she was too embarrassed to have slandered her own kid in front of a total stranger. Mae just rolled her eyes and walked out while Knot-Beard was still mid-rant, letting the door jingle on her way out. Serena muttered *Thanks* and followed Mae.

"So now we do what we should have done in the first place," Mae said, "and talk to our kid. Maybe she's just figured out a lucrative situation."

Serena nodded. She wouldn't put it past Jamie to figure out some weird money-making opportunity that made no sense to everyone else—maybe she was charging people to learn how to play the Floppy Game. One way or another, she hoped Jamie would have a good explanation, so Serena could feel marginally less like a cop.

"I can't tell you where I got the money," Jamie said that evening. She looked out the window at the unclaimed garden and bit her lip. "I didn't steal it or do anything bad, believe you me. But I can't really talk about it."

(Jamie had taken to peppering her speech with phrases like "believe you me," and "I kid you not," like some kind of old-timey wiseass.)

Serena and Mae kept asking Jamie where the money came from, every way they could think of, but no further answers were forthcoming. Eventually, they had to drop it, and hope Jamie didn't come home with a grand piano next week.

As if to rebuke Serena's mistrust, Jamie took to practicing the guitar in the dining room/kitchen area when Serena was trying to make morning coffee or Mae was doing her stretches. Jamie didn't know the first thing about playing guitar, so she kept making twonk twank noises or plucking the same three notes over and over again, each of them sounding out of tune. Serena offered to pay for guitar lessons just to make the torture stop, but Jamie said it was all good, she was watching instructional videos online.

Also, Jamie had a new best friend, named Nope. Nope was some kind of goth, or bohemian hippie, whose pale face was covered with dark smudgy makeup, which in turn was engulfed by a cavernous black hoodie. Serena was pretty sure Nope was genderqueer or something, but she didn't feel comfortable asking for details. Nope used he/him pronouns, but reserved the right to ship a pronoun update in the future. He just hung around Serena and Mae's house, studying random objects on their kitchen shelves, like an appraiser.

Yay for a friend who wasn't going to push Jamie into heinous male bonding—but Serena literally could not have a conversation with Nope. You might as well try and shmooze a brick wall, except that Jamie and Nope were always whispering and laughing about something in the corner.

How do you keep your kid safe when you have no idea what's going on in their life?

. . . . .

"Okay, what's weighing on your soul?" Mae said one morning a few days later. "That look on your face is making me want to bake cookies, and it's too hot to run the oven."

Serena looked up from her computer on the tiny dining table and forced a smile. "It's nothing, I just . . . okay, look. I've been stewing."

There were two obstacles to explaining to Mae why Serena had been hunched over the laptop screen with her fingers pressed against the sides of her face. First, Serena would have to reconstruct the brainhole she'd tumbled down while she was staring at office emails. And then she'd have to find a way to put her irrational fears into words.

"It's . . . you know the executive director job is opening up at the foundation?"

"You've only mentioned it every day for the past month or so." Mae placed a pint glass of medium-sweet lemonade on the table next to Serena's computer. Then she sat across from Serena with her legs spread and her big hands clasped.

"I think I've got a really good shot at it. Which would be great: I get to do more good, steer the organization in a better direction. But maybe it'd be better if they picked Alice Whitley instead." Serena sipped: perfect tartness. "Alice is a natural politician with a boringly straight family. Right now we're pissing off a lot of powerful people with these housing discrimination and 'covenant of quiet enjoyment' lawsuits."

"The covenant of quiet enjoyment." Mae tasted each word. "Sounds like a perfect Sunday morning."

"It does, yes. It's also a way to nail big real-estate firms to the drywall and make 'em squirm. They'll hit back any way they can, including a smear campaign." The back of Serena's neck prickled, or maybe it was light sunburn from yesterday.

"So you think Alice's boringly straight family could be less of a target than our . . ." Mae paused to hunt for antonyms. ". . . entertainingly queer ménage?"

Serena got up to make them breakfast, Jamie already being off to school.

"I think ratfucking is becoming a varsity sport." Serena didn't have to remind Mae about the whole ACORN thing, where some nice voter-registration workers had been slimed by a sting operation and a deceptively edited video. The internet and a new far-right media ecosystem were making it more tempting for every young white failson to go after anyone working for progressive change. "And we've got some fuckable rats."

That was the rabbit hole Serena's brain had been going down when Mae had interrupted. Their kid might be a petty criminal, and Serena herself had done some light vandalism and civil disobedience in her younger days as a queer activist. Mae was still pulling down the occasional shift as a pro domme. There was tons more. Serena was about to say that she was just spiraling for no reason.

But Mae spoke first: "Maybe I should give up my job at the dungeon."

Serena was cracking eggs over a bowl, and she coated her whole left hand with yolk and shell fragments.

Part of her wanted to jump in right away and say yes: Mae should definitely stop working as a pro domme, because if anybody ever found out, it would be a whole rat king of fuckery.

But . . . Mae always told Serena how much she loved getting into character as Mistress Ravenna: putting on her shiny black dress, applying severe makeup, strapping on shoes that elevated her a full six inches, and most of all fixing her posture so she radiated poise. She looked and felt like a whole different person, an avatar of femme power. A goddess awaiting her worshippers. She and her clients worked together to create something pure, in a world of bogus garbage. A dungeon might be the only workplace on earth where power was given freely, not extorted by evil clowns.

She couldn't take that away from Mae and keep calling herself a wife.

"Listen, I know how careful you are," Serena said. "The whole setup you have, nobody comes to the dungeon without being vetted. All of you, you take such care. I don't know, I really think it's fine."

"I'm only going in occasionally now, seeing a few regulars," Mae said. "The stuff we're doing is downright wholesome by dungeon standards. But maybe it's time to pull the plug."

"I don't want you to give up your job for the sake of mine," Serena said into the steam rising gently from the yellow sprawl of scrambled eggs in the frying pan.

"I don't know. I'll think about it." Mae sounded sad, barely looked at the eggs Serena slid onto her plate. "All those times we talked about not compromising who we were, all of those promises. We were kidding ourselves, weren't we? People get older and they just want to hold back the tide of shit any way they can."

Serena grabbed another plate and served herself. She tried not to think about the ways she was serving herself.

"There's seriously no pressure," she said, "if you want to keep that gig for another year or five, we'll make it work. Of course we will."

"Just as long as you're never ashamed of my sex work," Mae said. "After all, my sex work paid for your law school."

That wasn't entirely true; Serena had gone sleepless for three years to pay off those loans. But also, not the point. She leaned forward and touched Mae's hand across the tiny dining table. "I could never be anything but proud of you." And she meant it, with every tendon and sinew and muscle fiber that crunched when she tried to bend over at the kitchen sink. If it came down to Mae's happiness versus Serena's career, she only hoped she'd always have the guts to choose Mae.

And yet, that conversation put both Serena and Mae into a weird space. Serena had that sticky nugget of guilt and resentment at the back of her throat—she'd had it plenty before, but would never get used to choking on it. Mae, too, seemed to feel a certain way.

Jamie, always hypervigilant, seemed to notice something was bothering the two of them, even putting the guitar aside for a blessed moment to listen to the silence. All through dinner that evening, Jamie cast little glances at her parents, lips pursed as if trying to solve a mystery or brace for trouble.

The next day was Saturday, and Mae headed out to help a friend move house. Serena made a nice breakfast for Jamie. While they sat eating misshapen dinosaur pancakes, Jamie leaned forward and said in a low voice, "I can help."

"With what?"

"I can help keep this family safe. I can . . ." Jamie was about to say something else, but stopped and gazed at the shaggy garden outside. "Never mind," Jamie said, arms folded like the guardian of some holy secret.

"You know you can tell me whatever, right?" Serena said. "I'll always listen."

"Yeah," Jamie said without smiling or looking directly at Serena. "Thanks, Mom."

Serena couldn't imagine what Jamie could do to *keep this family safe,* and she wasn't sure she wanted to know. She had a gnawing sense that she'd instilled in her kid a conviction that their gay little family was under siege by hostile forces, and she probably shouldn't have done that, but Larkin Larkin Larkin.

· · · · ·

Why did Serena bother to go to this LGBTQ+ community forum? Everything in this nondenominational meeting hall smelled sour, and the Costco veggie platter wilted aggressively. Half the people there nursed some obscure drama with the other half, and nobody Serena wanted to see had shown up. Too many reheated conversations, not enough cheap box wine. She decided to slip out before anybody could slide behind the rickety podium.

When she turned to leave, a familiar horsey face was beaming in her path. "So pleased you could make it," said Greg.

Fucking Greg, the attorney that Serena hadn't seen since her paying-off-loans stint at Yeager, Furst, was here.

Serena couldn't help herself. She stared him down and said, "What are you doing here? You made your views on queer people abundantly clear."

"People change," Greg said, smoothly.

Turned out he was running for Congress—as a Democrat!—in a safe seat. And he was favored to win the primary.

"You would not stop talking about the danger we posed to traditional middle-class values," Serena said. "In essence you said families like mine were going to lead to people running naked down the street lighting things on fire. And now you're here, what, courting the gay vote?"

Serena had not thought it was possible for Greg to get any paler.

He started to rattle off some platitude, only to trail off when he could tell it wasn't landing. His bland good-natured expression vanished at once, replaced by a sadistic gleam in his eye, and his body language took on a predatory lean.

"One would think you of all people would understand," he whispered in her ear, "the importance of staying in your lane. People who live inside a glass mansion should be very careful about picking up a rock."

"What's that supposed to mean?"

"Think carefully before you set about flinging other people's dirty laundry into the wind, lest your own see the light of day." Now Greg's bland facsimile of a human face had been replaced by a howling vortex ringed by naked flames.

Serena lost track of her footing for a moment, nearly took a dive. She hadn't felt this particular variety of fear in so long, she couldn't recognize it at first.

Then the good-natured expression was back, and he was gripping her hand. "So good to catch up with you. If you'll excuse me." He still had that gleam in his eye, as if he'd put her in her place.

Serena turned and walked out without saying anything to anyone.

· · · · ·

Greg was an iceberg lettuce side salad in human form. He was the soiled, footprinted, watery slush of winter's final day. His threats plodded as dully as everything else that came out of his mouth. Such an undistinguished man should not have been able to put Serena on the back foot. She kept trying to reconstruct just how much she'd overshared about her personal life at lunches or after-work drinks, when she was at Yeager, Furst, but it was all a blur.

"Why did I let that guy get in my head?" Serena groaned after she got home. An untouched tumbler of Scotch oxidized in her hand. She perched on the side of the old fainting couch, which had lost all its nice brocade and whatever you call those stitched roses on the foot-end.

Mae shook her head. "You've been obsessing about that job and all your liabilities. You had already furnished a room in your head and left the door wide open. No wonder he moved in." Mae leaned in and sipped the glass in Serena's hand, since Serena wasn't drinking it. "I hate seeing you like this. I still don't get it. What are you so afraid of?"

Serena finally tilted the glass, liquid smoke searing the inside of her mouth. "I don't even know. I love my job, I love my family. I'm the happiest I've ever been in my entire life, so of course I start looking for an eighteen-wheeler coming my way."

Mae nudged Serena's legs. Serena moved enough to make a space for Mae on the fainting couch. "Would it make a difference if I quit the dungeon gig?" She kept her voice low, since Jamie was doing homework in the next room and the walls were thin. "I mean, maybe it's time I grew up, right? Stopped trying to be some kind of goddess, and just settled for being a regular person."

"Don't you fucking dare," Serena said. "I never want you to be anything less than a goddess. I want everyone to see you that way, always."

"Come on. I know you want me to quit that job. You've been saying so with your eyes ever since I brought it up. I'm putting this whole family at risk, they could use it as an excuse to take R_____ away. It's selfish of me."

"It's not. Your beauty, your strength, they're too wonderful, too wonderful to contain . . ." Serena realized she was ruining her whiskey with foolish tears. "I can't say words anymore. The selfish one would be me, if I wanted to cut away parts of your life. Fuck those fuckers, they can fuck themselves, if they come for our family, we'll meet them in the road with chain saws and flamethrowers."

"I get scared, too," Mae said. "But I'm not so scared when you're with me. I think that's part of staying in love."

"I don't want to change you. I just want to celebrate you, forever."

Mae's feet were in Serena's lap and at some point, she'd put down the whiskey glass and started massaging them. Her thumb dug into Mae's instep as she talked about chain saws, and Mae purred.

"You wanna know what scares me?" Serena said. "I'm scared that I'm the one who's going to mess everything up for this family. My ambition. My bloody hero complex. I'm the one who's going to bring an army of Gregs to our door. I want to do good in the world, on a meaningful scale, but maybe it's better to keep my head down."

"Eh," Mae said. "Your ability to piss off wannabe petty dictators is one of the things I love most about you. Hey, let's make a deal. I won't tell you not to sue people over quiet covenants, and you won't tell me not to spank my regulars."

"Deal." Serena grabbed her whiskey glass and held it out. Mae clinked it with a mug of lukewarm Constant Comment.

And that's when they realized that Jamie's bedroom was empty.

• • • • •

Mae had last checked on Jamie ninety minutes ago, before Serena had gotten home from the forum thingy. Jamie had been ensconced, headphones on, math textbook yawning flat. During the intense conversation about Greg and the dungeon and everything, Jamie had slipped out into the thickening darkness.

They called Jamie's new cellphone: nothing. Nope's parents hadn't seen her, and Nope was sitting at home playing *Halo*. There was nothing for it but to search for Jamie again, but this time in the dark with no clue where to start. Serena suggested Mae could stay put in case Jamie came home, but Mae responded that two pairs of eyes were better. They settled for leaving a note on Jamie's bed: *Call us if you see this.*

Nope's father said one last thing before Serena hung up: "Your child has a rich inner life." He made it sound like a not-great thing.

Jamie's words from earlier kept coming back to Serena's mind now: *I can help keep this family safe.* Serena wished she'd said more in response, like: *You just focus on being a kid. You let me and your mama worry about everything else. We will always shelter you the best we can.* But she'd gotten all Socratic instead, trying to figure out what Jamie was even saying. Fuck. How much of the conversation about stupid Greg had Jamie overheard?

Somewhere between the skaters' parking lot and the smoker pit under the river bridge, Serena slipped on duck shit and landed on her right knee. Like a hot poker to the meniscus. She limped forward in the dark, clutching her leg with the hand that didn't hold a flashlight, just hoping the damage was temporary. She'd ice her knee when she got home. For now, she yelled "R_____" again and again until her voice started to fail. Once or twice people yelled *Shut up!* from the darkness, and she ignored them.

Mae kept texting with updates, and Serena responded, not mentioning the knee.

I can keep this family safe. What if Jamie thought the family was safer without her? Had Serena missed a warning sign? She was never going to forgive herself if that conversation with Jamie turned out to be a last chance.

Serena's knee kept giving her hell, and it was closing in on midnight, and she had a meeting first thing in the morning. The flashlight didn't illuminate the mist so much as decorate it with wet sparkles. *Just let R_____ be okay, I'll do anything, I'll never let her out of my sight.*

A text from Mae: *starting to freak out over here, what are we gonna do?*

The wet wind picked up, it was after midnight. Serena had no ready answer for Mae's question, which wasn't really a question so much as a call for reassurance. This night felt merciless.

Serena wrote and deleted a text back to Mae, numb fingers sliding into typos, drizzle blurring the screen. Every message she tried to write felt platitudinous.

Just before she hit send on the least bad response, Jamie's voice came. "Mom? Is that you?"

Jamie sat in a half-lotus position in the middle of a decrepit community garden, bugs and dirt and worms crawling around her. Framed in the beam of Serena's flashlight, she looked like a weird statue, with the rain pelting around her. Her face and hair were drenched, her clothes unrecognizable.

"What are you doing out here?" Jamie tried to rise, but wobbled. "Oh, my leg fell asleep. I must have lost track of time. I came out here to do a quick . . . it doesn't matter. Are you okay? Is Mama okay? Is everything okay?"

Serena erased the text she'd been about to send, and wrote instead that she'd found the missing kid. With their location.

Then she threw her arms around her soaking wet child, holding on tight, as if every iota of strength in her hands and shoulders could defy loss itself. "You gave us a fright," she choked out. "What were you thinking? You are grounded for two months. We love you so much, please don't ever disappear like this again. I am revoking your video-game privileges. You're okay, you're okay, I've got you. Don't ever vanish like this again." She kept alternating endearments and punishments.

And then Mae showed up and had to hug both of them in the rain.

Back home, Serena discovered they were out of the fancy cocoa, but there were foil-lined packets of Swiss Miss from some conference Serena had helped to organize. Oh well. At least her knee felt better.

As usual, Serena's attempts to get some information out of this kid came to naught. She and Mae weren't so much Good Cop and Bad Cop, more like Literal Cop and Figurative Cop. Mae had a talent for getting Jamie to talk about everything that made no sense to Serena, which was a lot of things when it came to this kid.

"We're not angry," Mae said, though Serena was screaming on the inside. "At least, not seriously. We'll get over it. We just want to understand. Did something upset you? Is there anything that we can do to help? We're always here."

Serena dearly wanted to add whiskey to her own cocoa, but she didn't trust herself not to hand the spiked drink to Jamie right now. So she brought three identical mugs to the fainting couch where Jamie was wrapped in a blanket like the survivor of some epic disaster.

"I promise you, everything is fine," Jamie said, face utterly placid, eyes bright and clear. "I was testing a theory."

Serena wanted to ask, *What the hell?* But Mae shushed her.

"And did your theory pan out?" Mae asked.

"You know, I'm not sure," Jamie said. "It's a work in progress." She looked at Serena, who was cradling an untouched mug of cocoa because her hands still weren't warm. "I heard the two of you talking, earlier."

"We're fine," Serena said. "Sometimes I get in my head."

Fuck, it was past one in the morning. Serena could feel the first pulses of the headache she was going to have all day tomorrow.

Mae kept saying, "You can tell us anything."

"Okay," Jamie said, just as Mae was getting up to clear the mugs away.

"Okay?" Mae sat back down.

"I do have something to tell you guys. I've been waiting for the right moment, or freaking out about how you'll react. It's a lot, it's more than you can guess."

Serena perched on the low end of the fainting couch, so Jamie was flanked by both parents. They waited, trying to stay present but not crowd Jamie.

"Uh, so, okay, so . . ." Jamie took a deep breath, and suddenly there were tears in her eyes. She quivered. "So I'm not a boy, I'm a girl, okay? I'm a girl. And my name isn't R_____, it's . . . I don't know. I was thinking Rosie. You can call me Rosie for now at least. I hope, I mean, I hope, I don't know." Her voice stayed level and reasonable, even though her body was shaking and her eyes had gone red.

"Rosie," Mae said. "That's a lovely name."

"It really is," Serena said. "Thank you for trusting us with this. We'll call you Rosie until you tell us any other name. We're so proud to have you as our daughter."

For the second time since midnight, the three of them were embracing, holding on as tight as they could. Jamie was still trembling, and Mae brushed her forehead and said everything was good, Jamie's parents were proud of her.

But some tiny part of Serena couldn't help thinking: *Fuckable rats.*

14

Doctor Swift told me he once dined at a person's house where the part of the tablecloth which was next to him happened to have a small hole in it, which, says he, I tore as wide as I could; then asked for some soup, and fed myself through the hole. The Dean, who was a great friend to housewifery, did this to mortify the lady of the house; but, upon my word, by the general love of scandal and detraction in Dublin, one might reasonably imagine they were all to feed themselves through the holes which they had made in the characters of others.

—*MEMOIRS OF MRS. LAETITIA PILKINGTON,*
1712–1750, BY LAETITIA PILKINGTON

After Jamie came out to Serena and Mae as trans, they got a birthday cake a month later with pink frosting spelling out Jamie's new name (which wasn't Jamie; for seven months she experimented with being Rosie), and Jamie cried a lot.

A few weeks after that, Jamie noticed Serena sneaking glances and closing her laptop whenever she approached—as if Serena didn't want Jamie to see what she'd been searching for. Jamie's mind immediately went to, *Oh, she's caught a nasty case of transphobia,* and a bitter root snarled around Jamie's intestinal wall. She started to shy away from Serena, until Mae noticed and asked what in the sainted name of Betty Dodsworth was going on. Mae sat Serena and Jamie down at the kitchen table and grilled the two of them.

"Oh, sweetie," Serena said. "Oh, *Rosie*. I never would presume to know you better than you know yourself. I love you and support you, you should always know that. I just . . . I never worried like this before." She struggled to find some words, her throat tightening and releasing. Steam from the plain red mug curled and twisted in the air. "It's just . . . how can I keep you safe? I'm sorry, it scares me what this world will do. You're so beautiful, you always have been, but there are people out there who won't see how beautiful you are. I don't want you to have to go through the same thing Mae and I went through as queer women back in the day—except worse, because transphobia is everywhere now. I just wish I could make the world treat you like you deserve. I know it's not my fight, but I wish it didn't have to be anyone's fight."

Something inside Jamie chimed, *You will always be loved.*

Turned out Serena had been going down a rabbit hole of reading about violence against trans people. And bathroom bills. And the rates of home-lessness and unemployment and discrimination and everything else. She'd driven herself into a frenzy of worrying, because Jamie wasn't a white cis boy after all, and that meant America was not going to clear a sunlit garden path for her.

"This is why you don't look at the internet after nine P.M." Mae tugged the closed laptop farther away from Serena, even though it was midafternoon. The three of them went for a walk and got something sweet, but Jamie no longer remembers what.

After that, Serena made sure to show up at every school board and PTA meeting. When other parents complained about Jamie, or tried to get her banned from using the girls' bathroom, Serena stared them down, without raising her voice. When some boys ambushed Jamie after school and gave her a black eye and an ugly bruise along her right thigh, Serena sat Jamie down and asked if she wanted to press charges or get those kids suspended. Jamie looked at her mother and finally shook her head: it would only make things worse. Serena looked at her a long time, and finally said: "They *hit a girl.* They are cowards, and they are rotten inside, and they're going to grow up to be the worst kind of men. I hate that you have to breathe the same air as them." Serena hugged Jamie for a long time, and she and Mae cooked Jamie's favorite foods for dinner.

For some reason this skein of memory rises to the surface while Jamie is on her way to meet Serena for lunch, though Jamie hasn't thought about it in several years. Serena was never a fighter—she was always a protector, which is different. But protectors can go dark, the same as fighters.

• • • • •

The Spectacles feminist bookstore hasn't changed since Jamie last visited. Mae worked there part-time for years, and Jamie used to sit in the corner sometimes reading Roberta Gregory comics. The space feels dusty but cozy, with recent books by women and queers in the window and on tables out front. Serena is sitting at the register, right where Mae used to sit, and an older woman with rainbow curls is tidying up. "I'm going to take my lunch break, Hettie," Serena says to the other woman, who nods and waves at Jamie. Hettie seems familiar, and then Jamie remembers: Mae used to complain about her all the time.

Jamie opens the dirtmobile and Serena gets in, smiling only with the half of her face that Jamie can see easily. Serena's shoulders hunch, and her hands seem unable to let go of the legacy of fists.

Neither of them can afford a fancy lunch, so Jamie drives to Whitney's Beef and Beer, a diner near Malden that does a decent hot sandwich with a thick pickle slice and a free bag of chips. It's a twenty-minute drive, and the whole way Jamie asks Serena neutral questions.

How's Serena's new apartment? Fine. Okay, it's small and anoxic, and there are weird smells and a parade of cockroaches, and one of her neighbors sometimes watches hockey games too loud late at night.

How's the job? Great. Except the store has been dying forever, and Serena is trying to help them reorganize and clean up, maybe get some newer furnishings and a wider focus. They desperately need a new customer base, but Hettie is resistant to change. At least Hettie's microaggressions roll off Serena's back.

Jamie can't help thinking about what Ro said: sometimes you need to come back humble.

At the restaurant, Serena pulls her bag of chips open with one hand on each side, making a soft percussive sound. She looks smaller, but she has a glint in her eye.

"I think this is going to be good for you," Jamie says. "You've been needing a challenge."

Neither of them can have the conversation they wish they were having right now. Jamie can see that Serena is struggling and starting over sucks, and Jamie wants to be able to say the things she was saying a few months ago. *You're my hero, you're fighting the good fight.* But Jamie can't pretend to exalt Serena anymore. And Serena would like to bite Jamie's head off for suggesting that Jamie knows what's best for her, but she's lost the right.

There's a terrible silence, apart from the sound of other people eating and a Los Lobos song on the kitchen radio. In Jamie's mind, Ro vanishes into a shaft of moonlight.

Jamie still doesn't know how Serena made Ro vanish. She can't stop trying to figure it out, not just out of a tinkerer's curiosity but because it seems important. It continually freaks her out, the notion that magic could be that powerful in the wrong hands. She certainly felt an unaccustomed level of power—ecstasy even, in its classical Greek sense—when she and Serena were doing spells together, which is one reason why the new witch union still makes her nervous. But she's pretty sure Serena made Ro vanish all on her own, and she can't wrap her head around how a spell of protection could have gone so dark, could have become about paranoia, secrecy, revenge. Jamie pictures Serena in the Fordhams' woods at night, on her knees in front of moldering garbage. She must have put such a clear intention into the world: not just *protect my daughter,* but *if anyone uncovers my daughter's secrets, make them go away.* It's lucky that the spell had run its course before Serena started talking to Delia and the others about magic. Annnnd this train of thought leads straight back to the mystery of Jane Collier and Lady Sagacious, which she is still no closer to solving.

Jamie drives Serena back to the bookstore. "I'll see you soon," she says, because the two of them will be going on a weekend excursion with the other witches.

· · · · ·

They march through tall grass, spiked with wheat-like patches of ryegrass or foxtails, toward the beach. The ocean glistens, a wet lattice crowned with foam, and everything smells like kelp. When Jamie was small, Mae and Serena brought her to the beach near here to dig for clams, and she shaved some skin off her left hand. Jamie bled for what seemed like hours, and she cried so hard and so long that her tears became a self-reinforcing spiral—like, she was crying because she was crying. Jamie dimly remembers Mae holding her and cooing at her, while Serena tried to distract her with jokes and song fragments. It's beautiful here, but in a glossy way, like a marble, or when someone puts colored sand behind glass.

"So where exactly are we going?" Serena walks right behind Delia and squints at the glare coming off the waves.

"Yeah, I'm cold," says Paola, kicking the dense sand with her fists in her coat pockets.

On the drive down here, Paola said her parents want her to move out of their two-bedroom apartment in Waltham, so she's been staying half the week on various friends' couches while she searches for a better situation. She wants to go to school to become a phlebotomist, because she knows about blood, but her parents won't pay and she can't get financial aid because her parents have too much money. And fuck living in debt forever. In the meantime, she's "liminally unhoused," working three part-time jobs and some occasional gig-economy shit. Paola stumbled on magic after she escaped from a disastrous party in the woods, where everybody else got wrecked and the vibes grew unsafe, and she found a dilapidated cabin out of a horror movie that seemed to whisper promises—for months she thought that cabin was a uniquely magical spot until she realized there were many others.

"I swear it's around here somewhere." Delia scans the horizon, where they can almost make out Martha's Vineyard. She's the only one who dressed for the cold, including a square fake-fur hat with earflaps attached to a cord tied under her chin. "There's a whole bunch of beachfront cottages, time-shares, which had to be evacuated three times over the past couple of years due to flooding. They're more or less abandoned at this point. The houses themselves might not be liminal places yet, but the leisure areas and gardens and playgrounds could well be. Coastal areas will all become suffused with magic within our lifetimes."

Paola hunches her shoulders and sniffs the salty air. "When I was a kid, I got obsessed with stories where civilization falls and magic comes back. Like, there's a nuclear holocaust, and in the ashes everyone becomes a wizard or an elf. Like *The Sword of Shannara,* or *Adventure Time.* I used to wish I could live in that world. Now maybe I will."

"I seriously doubt there will be talking donuts." Jamie speaks for the first time since she got into Delia's car. Her mind has been going through the same thoughts over and over, like when you do repetitive tasks in a game to level up.

Jamie hadn't realized how nice it would be to belong to a community of witches, instead of doing this on her own forever. She and Delia have private jokes, and she feels like a big sister to Paola.

Even with her senses turned way down, Jamie is ferociously attracted to Delia. She has a gleam in her eye, her ears stick out a little when she's not wearing a big fur-trapper hat, she smiles wickedly, her bone structure is outstanding.

But Jamie is also starting to like Delia a lot, as a friend. Familiarity is slowly dialing down the intensity of Jamie's attraction, so these thoughts are no longer front of mind. She's learned more about Delia, who found magic five years ago, in the summer before senior year of Yale, when her jerk boyfriend took her camping and then abandoned her in the middle of nowhere with no phone. She'd loved the great outdoors but had never camped properly, and now she was skinning her knees, bruising her palms, drinking with her whole face from a shallow stream, scared she would never find her way home. Then she found an abandoned pheasant-hunting blind: a box with a slit window, on stilts with a broken ladder. She felt a stillness in this place, and you can guess the rest: she found a road, got a ride, made it home fine. Before the woods, she'd planned to go into digital marketing, but after, she'd decided to become a therapist instead.

"You okay, Jamie?" Delia gives a sidelong smile.

"I'm fine." Jamie glances ahead: Serena has walked over the next rise, soundproofed by this wind. But Jamie doesn't want to talk shit about her mother to Delia or Paola, lest she make this trip weirder than it already is. So instead, she talks about the other thing that's driving her nuts. "I just miss Ro. And I wish I could explain to them, but they don't want to talk to me. I waited too long to tell them about magic and when I finally shared, it was an epic disaster."

"Ugh. Been there, lived that," Delia says. "It sucks. I'm curious as to how dating as a witch compares with dating as a trans person. Like, how long do you wait to tell someone you're trans? Or poly, for that matter?"

Jamie doesn't know whether to be flattered that Delia thinks she would have to tell people she's trans—like, wouldn't anyone know just by looking at her lanky frame and chunky jawline? The politics of "passing" are such a noxious bog that this doesn't land as a compliment, merely an assumption. Trans is beautiful, so to be visibly trans is to let your beauty show through. But also, yeah . . . Jamie never knows what people see (or don't see) when they look at her, and she tries not to obsess about it.

"I wouldn't know," Jamie says to some seagulls. "I've basically never dated. I hooked up with people, but that was it. I was an ugly duckling in high school, and Ro and I got together in college."

Jamie does not want to look at Paola's face right now. Paola is eighteen or nineteen and has mentioned a handful of exes in passing.

"I always find a way to mention being poly in the first conversation if I'm attracted to someone," Delia laughs. "Honestly, it's embarrassing. I can't help waving a big 'I like you' flag."

Well, now Jamie is searching her memory, trying to remember if Delia mentioned being poly in their first conversation. Jamie isn't sure, but probably not? So that settles it: Delia has a tell, and she didn't show her tell, and therefore Jamie needs to hold all of her horses.

"Ro and I were poly in theory, but never got around to doing much about it," Jamie says—and then it hits her that she just used the past tense in talking about her marriage. Oof.

Jamie's phone buzzes in her pocket. It's a message from Ariella, marked urgent. *Please call me as soon as possible. I'm deeply concerned.* (Which is her version of writing HOLY FLAMING SHIT in all caps.) There's a link to a right-wing agitprop site, and Jamie can already see her own name in the URL-slaw before she clicks. At the link, there's a slickly produced video: Jamie speaking at the Wanda Bock protest, talking in the classroom about how novels depict family structures in the nineteenth and twentieth centuries, and chatting with Markus and Gigi in line for a coffee at Grounds for Rejoicing. Snippets of Jamie saying stuff that sounds scary out of context, overlaid with heavy filters to monsterize her: black-and-white, high-contrast, broken up by slashes like decayed celluloid. Jamie is disgusted looking at herself. Delia and Paola keep asking what's wrong, so she hands over the phone so they can watch.

Looks like McAllister Bushwick finally made his move.

In a way, Jamie is fascinated: one of her obsessions as a critic is the ease with which a clever narrator can turn an already-stigmatized person into a grotesque, an oleaginous specter. Jamie is getting a highly privileged window into the process of identity mutilation, in real time. On the other hand, oh shit oh fuck, she is trembling too hard to speak, the frozen sea-spray numbs her face, there's a sickly taste in her mouth, and she gags on the stench of decay. She's ruined. She's utterly ruined, and there's nothing for it but to devour what's left of herself, leaving no trace.

"Fuck this," Paola is saying. "They can't get away with this."

"Of course they can." Jamie stumbles over every word. "They always do."

"They barely have anything," Delia says in a soothing voice. "This video is pathetic and I promise it won't get much traction. Even with all the tricks they did, it's going to fizzle. The next few days might be rough, but you'll get through this."

Jamie doubles over, hyperventilating, hugging herself. "This is our fault. Serena and me, we brought this down. We were such fools. I never should have gone along with it."

Delia recoils. "What are you talking about?"

228 ⚘ CHARLIE JANE ANDERS

Oh. Jamie shouldn't have said anything.

"We did a spell." Jamie is still bent into a prong. "We put a curse on the man who made this video, and then he started showing up in my life."

Serena comes wandering back from her scouting expedition. "I saw a changing area not too far away, with one wall fallen down and the other walls rocked by green slime. It looked revolting, and utterly magical." She sees their faces. "What's going on?"

Jamie shows her mother the video, while also telling Delia and Paola about how JawBone messed up their lives, and the spell that she and Serena did.

"Oh wow. That is *hard-core*," Paola says, eyes wide and nostrils flared. "I never even thought of trying to cast a curse."

They head back to Delia's car, a newish hybrid that's a million times nicer than the dirtmobile, because clearly they need to get back to Boston. Jamie is dislocating, her mind wants to go back in time to five minutes ago.

"Why are you assuming our spell made JawBone come after you?" Serena asks as she climbs into the back seat next to Paola.

"Don't you think the timing is weird? How could it be a coincidence?" Jamie asks, though she knows Serena hates it when anyone answers a question with a question.

Jamie gets back in the front passenger seat, where she can watch Delia watching the road with her knuckles jutting around both sides of the steering wheel. Delia hasn't spoken since she heard about the curse.

Serena says this doesn't seem like a coincidence: predators like McAllister Bushwick don't quit. If you lived in a town where bears occasionally came out of the woods and assaulted your children, and you made a failed attempt at fortifying your home, would you assume any further bear attack was your fault?

"With magic, you don't get what you ask for, you get whatever you put your heart into. We put a lot of energy into focusing on McAllister Bushwick, and I should have known it would blow back on us." Jamie gazes out the passenger-side window at the rocky beaches and seagulls whipping past. "Bushwick had god knows how many nattering trans women to persecute, but he chose me."

Serena keeps poking holes in Jamie's reasoning. Paola is grilling Serena about curse-mechanics, like this is a cool new hack that she can't wait to try. Next to Jamie, Delia still hasn't said a word.

"Why are you playing 'blame the victim' on yourself?" Serena demands.

"I don't get it," Paola chimes in. "I mean, even if we ask for something good for ourselves, we're usually taking it away from someone else. Not always, sure. But if I get a gig, it means someone else didn't get it. I mean, I'm sorry if the spell backfired, but it was worth trying. Right?"

"Exactly," Serena says. "If anything, doesn't this prove we didn't hit him hard enough?"

"It wasn't worth trying," Jamie stares at Delia, like *Please say something.*

Jamie waits a long time, while Delia stares and drives.

"I can't say I haven't ever thought about cursing somebody," Delia says at last, without taking her eyes off the road. "I've had plenty of McAllister Bushwicks in my life, some of them quite recently. But I've always had this sense deep down that I shouldn't take it too far, or let anger shape my workings. Because in the places where humans tried to dominate nature and failed, there's something that feels generous toward us, as long as we ask nicely. And I don't know, humility seemed to be part of the equation. 'Strike down my enemies' never felt like a thing you should ask for in a place where your whole species was defeated. I'm not judging the two of you, but I would not have done that."

Jamie's neck hurts from craning, so she keeps her face forward. In the rearview mirror, she glimpses one of Serena's eyes: heavy-lidded, calculating. Serena knows she can't afford to alienate Delia.

"I don't see what any of this has to do with morality," Paola says. "Magic doesn't care about our human values."

Jamie keeps trying to look at Delia, and then something makes her look at the ocean instead. The shimmer-gray waves put her in mind of the goddess Athena, whose eyes are either "gray" or "bright," depending on which translation of Homer you prefer. Jamie hates to think of nature defeating humanity, because she doesn't want to believe there's a war going on: humans and nature are all on the same side, because we're part of one ecosystem.

Part of Jamie's mind is imagining the talk she's soon to have with Ariella, and all of the social media blowback and campus drama she's about to submerge in. It feels as though Delia is driving toward a stormfront, even though Jamie knows her problems are not localized in the greater Boston area.

"I don't think it has to do with morality per se." Oh shit, Jamie is doing her professor voice. "The only successful workings I've ever done have been super personal. Even if I'm trying to affect someone else, it always comes back to me, my relationship with that person." And here Jamie can't help remembering how much love she poured into blessing Ro, and how angry they were, and for the first time, she gets it. "Every spell I cast is about me, no matter what. So if I try to help or harm someone else, I'm bringing myself into it."

"Yes." Delia slaps the steering wheel gently. "Yes, exactly. You summed it up perfectly."

Once again, Jamie is great at helping other people understand why she is absolute garbage. If only this were an academic discipline, she could have a cushy job for life: Jamie Sandthorn, Chair of the Department of How Jamie Sandthorn Fucked Up Studies. They could hold brown-bag seminars.

"Can we at least spare some blame for the monster who keeps coming after vulnerable people?" Serena says with deliberate mildness.

Jamie stares at the ocean until she has a drowning mind. Now she knows exactly why Serena decided to leave the world and hide in a tiny schoolhouse: Jamie is fucked up. Jamie has fucked up. She was starting to like the way Delia looked at her, but now Delia will never look at her that way again, and she's already lost Ro. Her academic career is teetering. She's about to become detritus.

Center of gravity all askew and a moving target, clutching her sides with numb hands. She'll die alone, and maybe soon. Her face in the passenger window whites out as her breath fogs the glass.

The car turns and comes to a stop. Jamie looks up and realizes they've pulled into a rest area with a gas station and a Cumberland Farms. Delia fuels the car, then she and Paola go inside the store, leaving Jamie alone in the car with Serena.

Serena unsnaps her safety belt so she can scoot closer to the front. "I'm sorry. I know exactly what you're going through right now. I don't mind if you blame me, because that's what parents are for. But if there's one thing I hoped you had learned from me, it's never let anyone make you accept responsibility for the things that are done to you. You've been there for me so much lately, I want to be here for you now. Just tell me what I can do to help."

Jamie is turned sideways, still wearing a seat belt, her torso at odds with her legs—honestly the most apt metaphor you could imagine for her relationship with Serena. Jamie has to twist herself into a weird shape and look sideways in order to meet her mother face-to-face.

She feels like Laetitia Pilkington, living in disgraced squalor, having fever dreams where she's visited by the personifications of Death, Desolation, and Ruin.

All she says to Serena is, "Thanks, Mom. I'm in shock right now. I know we'll get through this." Jamie doesn't know that—at all—but it seems like the sort of thing you're supposed to say.

The rest of the drive back to Boston is quiet. She can feel Serena behind her, wrestling with the idea that she's in harm's way because of the spell Serena coaxed her to do.

When they're entering the urban outskirts, heralded by a big Star Market, Jamie finds herself telling Delia and Paola about the time when she and Serena blessed Teena Wash (without going into too much detail, of course). Partly to offer something to balance the scales, to show they didn't only do harmful magic, but also because it seems like an alternative to curses. But nobody seems in a headspace to take this information on board right now.

Delia drops Serena off first, outside her apartment building, which has vinyl siding with chronic rain damage, and the windows are small and clouded with grime. A chicken-wire fence surrounds a thin rectangle of dead grass and rusty gardening implements. Jamie can see how the schoolhouse was a nicer place to live, in some ways.

"I'll call you." Serena pauses with one leg out of the car. She seems about to say something else, then thinks better of it and climbs to her feet on the cracked tarmac.

"I can get out, too," Paola says. "It's easy for me to get home from here."

She looks at Serena, as if she wants to learn more about how to curse someone. Serena shrugs.

Delia looks at Jamie, then nods. "See you both later."

Soon they pull up in front of Markus's place, where he's letting Jamie squat on a cot in his utility room.

Delia pauses as she turns the engine off. "Listen. You messed up. It's true, it sucks. But we still have your back. Our witch union, or whatever we're going to be called. We'll have Serena's back, too. Serena already told us all, when we first met, that she had done some destructive magic and she was trying to do better. I'm gonna guess this Bushwick thing wasn't even the worst of it."

"No. Serena did worse spells than the Bushwick thing, but they're her story to tell."

"You're a good daughter." Delia shows the gap in her front teeth that makes Jamie melt a little. "I only talk to my mother in allusions that I know mean something different to her than to me. We have whole conversations where she thinks we talked about one thing, but I know I was talking about another thing entirely. That's how we keep the peace. I can't imagine sharing magic with my mom."

"Starting to think teaching Serena was the biggest mistake of my life."

"I wear my mistakes like my scars: proudly," Delia says. "They're credentials, because I learned better. Listen, you're a witch, and you've got powerful witch friends. Those fuckers can break their thumbs trying to come for you."

Jamie smiles down at her through the open car door, and it's not entirely a fake smile. "Thank you. Seriously."

She'd better call Ariella before the sun goes down and everyone goes full lizard brain.

·　·　·　·　·

That evening, Jamie sits in Markus's utility room, reading her well-thumbed copy of *The Cry* under the one dangling lightbulb. Her phone lights up with a text from Ro:

saw the video are you okay

Jamie almost types that she's fine, but she's vowed to stop lying to Ro. Instead, she tells as much of the truth as she can.

Both of Jamie's social media accounts have been battered by drive-by abuse, mostly the same few messages over and over. She's pretty sure it'll worsen, once the video gets picked up by heavier hitters. She's locked her accounts and turned off all her notifications, but it's hard to resist the urge to gaze into the abyss.

Meanwhile, Ariella finally spelled out what she's been hinting at for months: Rugby College is in trouble. Enrollment is plummeting, especially in the liberal arts, and the college can't afford a multimillion-dollar bond payment that's coming due, partly because the Quantified Text initiative was a fiscal sinkhole. According to Ariella, the English department might be shuttered, and the trustees could even close down Rugby College entirely—as soon as this fall. Everyone is freaking out. Tenured septuagenarians are honking like geese. So this wasn't a good time for one grad student to make a spectacle of herself, though Arielle keeps repeating that of *course* Jamie did nothing wrong. Still, there's talk of disciplinary proceedings, a temporary suspension, code of conduct violation, probation. Nobody thinks Jamie should be expelled, but this is a delicate time. The trustees are watching with their hundred never-blinking eyes. Jamie needs to lay low. Worst-case scenario: Jamie could end up scrambling to transfer to another institution with a bogus red mark on her record.

All in all, Jamie is thinking about starting an OnlyFans, which feels like a more sustainable career path than academia—her mother was a sex worker, and there's no shame in honest work.

Jamie explains all of this in a few texts. Ro asks her to meet them for a drink at the Thirsty Scholar, the silly pub that both of them love.

When Jamie arrives at the pub, Ro is waiting outside in the cold, instead of at a table inside. "Hey," they say. Jamie battles the urge to reach out and hug them, to lean into her side of a kiss. She hears choruses of bloody angels when she looks at their round face, but she just nods and smiles, tries to take it easy. They open the door and Jamie follows them inside, moving as though she has full-body tetanus from the strain of not acting like their wife.

Soon they're drinking pints of brown ale at a table near the back. Ro

234 Charlie Jane Anders

sputters with indignation: that fucker, that fucking video, hasn't he done enough harm? And why isn't Rugby College supporting her? The grad student union and the queer student groups need to step up. Jamie has already talked to Markus, who's equal parts scared and angry.

"It's just hitting me," Jamie says. "That video, seeing myself all distorted, it sparked my dysphoria. I haven't felt like that in years."

Ro gets it, in a way that few others can. "It just sucks," they say. "You go through life thinking your gender is a settled question, until something like this happens and you get hit with a reminder of how the worst people choose to see you."

"I keep thinking lately about this Sartre thought experiment." Jamie describes it: the man in the hallway, peering through a keyhole, watching in secret, until he realizes that someone is watching him in turn. "It's just weird, going from subject to object with no warning."

"It's not real. None of it is. They can't define you."

In this moment, Jamie can see her way back into Ro's arms. All Jamie needs to do is not tell Ro about the spell that she and Serena cast, and she gets to stay the innocent victim. Ro's protective instinct will kick in, and they'll probably be so keen to shelter Jamie that they'll end up bringing her home. She could have her marriage again. She could wake up happy and not dread going to bed. Except . . . she can't. She promised.

Ro sees Jamie shaking her head and raising her hands. "What?" they say.

"I have to tell you something. You're going to hate it."

Jamie explains the whole thing, how Serena talked her into putting a curse on McAllister Bushwick, and she's pretty sure that curse blew back on her. "If nothing else, it would be a pretty major coincidence if he went after first Serena and then me, years later. He never gave any sign that he knew who my mom was, and I made sure not to tell him."

"Oh." Ro leans way back over the booth divider, as if this information is literally knocking them backward. "Oh. I see."

"I swear that magic was not a big part of my life until recently. I should never have kept it secret from you, but I hardly thought about it, for months on end, until I started teaching Serena."

Ro showed up here ready to start a ruckus on Jamie's behalf, and now the two of them are back to the same dynamic they've had for the past few months.

"It means something that you told me the whole truth." They don't add the unspoken: *this time.*

For some reason, Jamie can't help thinking of Gavin and his injured ex-girlfriend, and Jamie's inchoate sense that Gavin was attempting another act of violence on her by turning her experience into a shitty story. If forced imprisonment is a form of harm, then trapping someone in a toxic narrative could be considered an actual assault.

"I don't expect to ever earn back your trust," Jamie says. "But that won't stop me from trying."

This could be the last conversation Jamie has with Ro for a long time. So she tells them everything that's going on in her life, including the witch social group that Serena brought together, Jamie's nascent friendship with Delia, and all the breakthroughs Jamie's made in her research. The only thing she leaves out is her attraction for Delia, since there's no point in mentioning something that's clearly going nowhere, and Ro can probably tell without her saying anything.

"I'm still kind of worried about Serena, because she's shown a scary disregard for boundaries and guardrails," Jamie says as she finishes her pint. "But thus far, I'm not seeing any sign that she's having as much luck getting any of these other witches to help her do harmful magic as . . ."

". . . As she did with you." Ro doesn't put any heat into that. They're just stating the facts.

"Right. Nobody else is going to have the baggage I have with her."

"So you feel responsible for this group, because they wouldn't exist without you," they say, and Jamie nods. "Is that why you said no when I asked you to stop doing magic?"

Jamie nods again. "Back then, I really thought Serena might have started a cult. Now I just worry that she might be a bad influence." Jamie tells them about Paola saying she didn't see anything wrong with cursing a person, and staying behind to talk to Serena.

Both pint glasses are empty. Jamie waits to see if Ro wants to order another round, until the roof of her mouth is unquenchable. No more drinks means no more conversation, possibly ever. Jamie doesn't have a right to expect anything.

Ro stands up, turning their skin neon-sepia from the lights in the window. Jamie tries not to let her face show all the teetering structures inside her, all the forms of desolation she will unfold if Ro walks away right now. But she is a terrible actor.

"I didn't have dinner," they say. "Did you?"

Jamie shakes her head. She's totally forgotten to eat, and beer on an empty stomach is probably not a great plan.

The two of them walk to the Indian place nearby. On the way, Ro says, "I keep thinking that you're not the person I thought you were, but that doesn't necessarily mean that I never knew you at all. Or that I can't know you now. I suppose there are many different ways to know someone. I'm still furious at you for hiding this from me, but I can't bring myself to make a clean break, after everything we've had together."

Jamie can't help saying it: "The sunk cost fallacy."

"Yeah. Except that feelings aren't a balance sheet."

They've reached the restaurant. Jamie is starving but also she can't conceive of ever eating again. Bollywood music reassures her that true love will always win, no matter how many misunderstandings, family disputes, and random catastrophes get in the way. They order, and soon they have two metal cafeteria trays heaped with veggies, dal, and rice.

"Doing magic has taught me a lot about entropy," Jamie says in a low voice as the music reaches a crescendo. "You spend enough time around decaying structures, you start to understand the hubris of building anything. Except sometimes you can tell that people really loved these clubhouses, tree houses, and sheds, for years. They got joy out of these places before they went to seed. Nothing stands forever, but some things are fucking glorious for as long as you can make them last."

Jamie is trying to find a way to say to Ro that they could treat this moment as a turning point, rather than an ending. The two of them could discover each other all over again—if they're willing to see a future with her.

"I need to find a way to forgive you, for my own sake if not yours," Ro says after they've listened to a couple of musical numbers in silence. "Not forgiving you is injuring me. But there's a cost to forgiveness, and I think it means that we can't be exactly what we used to be to each other. I can't tell you right now if we'll be friends or partners, or some third option."

Jamie is a thin shell around a hollow space.

She manages to say that she's good with whatever Ro decides.

"I think I'm not an easy person to understand, and you've put in the time to understand me," Ro says. "I have a lot of friends and colleagues and mentors, but none of them gets on my nerves the way you do. That's a good thing, by the way: I like the way you get on my nerves."

Jamie nods and looks down at her empty tray; somehow she's eaten without tasting.

"How will you know?" she whispers. "Take as long as you need, but how will you know what you want us to be to each other?"

Ro shakes their head. "There's no clear heuristic, is there? There's just how much I feel like I can trust you, and how much it hurts to let you in, and I think the only factor is time. I'll know when I know."

"Yeah." She gets herself some chai, mostly just to steam her face with milky spicy vapors. She can't bear the surge of hope, after she's already given up. "That sounds fair."

As they walk back to the apartment where Jamie used to live, Ro says, "Listen, you keep saying that your mother can't move past Mae's death, and that's the problem. But . . . I don't think you've dealt with it either. I was there, remember. I watched you mourn for a brief spell, then shake it off and try to keep moving. I think maybe all of this has been about that?"

Oof. Square in the chest. Even after the endless day she's already had, what Ro said still flips the table of her life, scattering everything. She would have sworn she was all wrung out, that she couldn't process any more paradigm shifts. But no. She's reeling all over again.

Of course.

"You mean . . ." Jamie feels so full, weighed down with sadness and tenderness—but meanwhile her brain is fizzing with the thrill of untangling the meaning of a narrative. "You mean that I've been trying to 'save' Serena because deep down, I know I haven't been able to process what happened to Mae? And this is just my messed-up way of offloading all my unresolved grief onto my living mother?"

"I'm just putting it out there," Ro says. "I know it's not my place, but . . ."

"It's absolutely your place," Jamie says. She reaches out a hand to Ro. She doesn't know what she'll do if they don't take it, but then they do, and it's so warm.

Jamie is realizing anew how much she's missed Ro's thoughtful heart. But also, she's remembering being on a hillside with a broken tire swing, speaking to Mae for the first time since her death. Why had Jamie waited so long to do that? Even in the silence of her own mind? Ro is right: this whole time she's been trying to heal herself. And going about it the absolute worst way.

"I think you're right," she tells Ro. "Thank you. For seeing me. Whatever . . . whatever you and I become, my life will always have a space for you in it."

"Same," says Ro.

For a brief instant, both of her hands are in both of theirs. Then the two of them sideways-hug, and she walks back to the dirtmobile.

15

Nothing is so delicate as the reputation of a woman: it is, at once, the most beautiful and most brittle of all human things.

—*EVELINA: OR, A YOUNG LADY'S ENTRANCE INTO THE WORLD* BY FRANCES BURNEY, 1778

One year before Jane Collier died, she and Sarah Fielding co-authored a metafictional novel called *The Cry: A New Dramatic Fable*. In *The Cry*, a woman named Portia tells the story of her relationship with a man named Ferdinand, along with the backstory of his family—but her narrative is constantly interrupted by a mob of hecklers called the Cry.

The Cry polices Portia's tone, accuses her of hypocrisy, and freaks out whenever she says that men should woo women by showing respect and being decent people, instead of bamboozling them with empty praise and silly romantic gestures. (In one hilarious section, the Cry insists that it's an abomination for women to learn logic and no man would ever want a "logical wife," but then it turns out that even the men in the Cry have no idea what the word "logic" means.) Most of all, the Cry only wants to hear stories about women who are jealous, manipulative, and vain. "Taunting ridicule is their strongest hold: once bereave them of that support to their conversation, and you would almost take from them the use of speech." It's the kind of book you could only write if you had firsthand experience of the "malicious sneer" of people who love to destroy others who are just trying to live their lives.

The Cry is exactly what Sarah Fielding was up against, when word got out about her dalliance with Charlotte Charke/Charles Brown. It's what tarnished women like Laetitia Pilkington and Eliza Haywood dealt with for years, as they wrote and performed and used all their wit to stay afloat. We want to think of the eighteenth century as an enlightened time—because of, well, the Enlightenment—but most popular writing from the time was vicious toward women and anyone living on the margins. Rape jokes were common currency: even Sarah Fielding included a nasty one in her 1760 novel *The History of Ophelia*. In 1736, Sarah was stumbling on the edge of social death, which meant starvation, disease, total squalor—how did she survive? What did Jane Collier do to help her?

Why is Jamie obsessing about mid-Georgian misogyny when her actual phone is overheating with the sheer number of people screaming abuse at her and accusing her of every crime? The question answers itself: this is how Jamie compartmentalizes. The awareness of the Cry—people remixing ugly videos of her, talking shit about her online—presses on the back of her neck like some squatting demon. It's like she told Ro: welcome back dysphoria, my old friend. So if she can't tune out the fuckery, she can at least channel that awareness into thinking about abusive dynamics in eighteenth-century England.

Jamie makes the mistake of glancing at social media: someone has posted an obscene A.I.-generated image of her. Trolls (bots?) are listing all the horrible things they would like to do to her. She turns off the screen hastily.

Nobody knew more about abuse than Jane Collier, if *The Art of Ingeniously Tormenting* is anything to go by. It's such a sly, well-observed catalogue of all the ways to shatter someone's self-esteem, to turn your home into a torture chamber, to engender despair. Jane hints that she had firsthand experience of being under someone's thumb, in that letter where she talks about flowers. Jamie can picture her now: wandering outdoors, seeking the right kind of desolation, finally pouring out her heart in the midst of ancient ruins . . . and receiving an answer.

There are so many clues about magic in *Emily* if you know where to look: not just the fairy tale, but also the moments where Emily explores an abandoned town near her house. Not to mention all the discussions of Nature, and Nature's gentle correcting hand, because back then nature signified a pastoral simplicity that was being lost as everyone moved to cities. This was the era of Rousseau but also of naturalists like Carl Linnaeus and Gilbert White. And then there's Goldsmith's hugely influential epic poem "The Deserted Village," which is all about nostalgia for the rustic simplicity of rural life. At one point, *Emily*'s narrator quotes Horace: *"Naturam expellas furcâ, tamen usque recurret."* Meaning, "You may drive nature away with a pitchfork; yet will she always return."

Oof. Jamie merely glances at her phone to check the time, and gets sucked back into the trash-maelstrom. As Jane explains in *The Art of Ingeniously Tormenting,* we outlaw the bastinado but allow the flaying of a person's mind.

So now Jamie is thinking of *Emily* as a story about nature, change, and chasing your own heart's desire in spite of everyone else's expectations. *Emily* is a book about the games we play along the cliff edge. About nature encroaching in the places that people have left behind to move to towns at the very start of industrial capitalism, and the changes that people can make in those places. It's about the trade-offs between security and self-determination, and Emily's struggle to find a way to have both.

Holy shit, did Jamie just find a thesis statement?

. . . . .

Sometime later, Jamie's phone blares with an ironic Bikini Kill ringtone. She picks up, and Serena starts talking before she can say hello. "How are you holding up? Do you need anything? What are we doing to fight this?" Jamie says she's hanging in there, but the internet is coming for her, and she's somehow both on probation and also teaching a class in two days. She and Serena agree to meet for coffee in an hour, at the 1369 on Mass Ave., because obviously they need to talk one-on-one.

Jamie takes the T instead of driving because she doesn't trust herself behind the wheel right now. This gives her too much time to look at her phone. A bevy of bottom-feeding sites have posted hot garbage about her, and a couple of queer publications have risen to her defense. Some perverse part of her is convinced these discussions cannot be as bad as what she's imagining, and maybe reading them will be a good reality check—but then she gives in and reads a few paragraphs, and it's worse than she could have guessed because she's not a dedicated vomitologist. She closes the tab on her phone—too late, her brain is already poisoned. Also, the same pundits who screamed that Wanda Bock's academic freedom was being suppressed are now demanding that Jamie be cast into a volcano, because freedom is only for those who hate the right people.

Warm yeasty-buttery air envelops Jamie when she steps inside the cafe. At a table near the front, Serena rocks forward and back in her chair, raven-like in a dark hoodie, with a phone tilted in both hands. Jamie hasn't seen her mother this frantic since when Mae was dying. Oof. Deep insistent throb. Jamie can't help thinking of what Ro said: *I don't think you've dealt with it. Maybe all of this has been about that.* Sometimes the truth takes you to pieces before it sets you free.

Jamie waves at her mother, then waits in line to get a large coffee and maple scone. She looks in all directions, twitchy, and she's pretty sure one person is staring, a retro-punk with a safety pin in their shaved eyebrow. Jamie tries to shrug off these minor-league haters, but anxiety slashes every thought to tatters. She might try and think, "I love scones," but it turns into "I love [ohfuckdeathdesolationi'mgarbage]ones."

The moment she sits down at Serena's table, Jamie realizes this was a mistake. This is the last person Jamie should be talking to, when she already feels like a penny in a fuse box.

When she's stressed, Serena talks entirely in rhetorical questions—and she is very, very stressed right now.

"Why does it matter what caused this situation? What kind of university doesn't support its graduate students in the face of a manufactured controversy? What happened to the search for truth? Who is going to stand up and say enough is enough?"

Jamie fills her mouth with scone, followed by coffee. The cafe is playing early 1990s alternative rap, Digable Planets or something.

"How are we going to fight this?" Each of Serena's questions drives an electrified spike into Jamie's adrenal glands. "I spent years organizing people, and I have firsthand experience of being smeared. The most important thing is: they push, you push back. How are you going to change the narrative?"

Jamie can't help snorting. "That phrase: 'change the narrative.' You might as well get swallowed by a beast and try to change its facial expression from inside its stomach." She looks her mother in the eye. "You know as well as I do that we helped to cause this."

Serena says when someone fucks with you, you don't stop to wonder if you might have deserved it. "Why are you second-guessing your own anger?"

A memory comes to Jamie. She was seven or eight, and she was crying for some reason—no idea why, at this point—and Serena leaned sideways and said that it wasn't going to work. Serena was convinced that Jamie was making a big production out of her distress to get an ice cream, or some toy. And Serena was not going to give in to emotional terrorism. Jamie protested that she wasn't pretending, she was really truly upset, and Serena said it didn't matter: you can be for real, actually upset, and still exploit your pain to get what you want. They were standing in front of a mall, facing a supermarket, a beauty store, and a pet store with a noisy window parakeet, a few feet away from people loading up their cars. The world dropped away as Jamie focused on her mother saying that sometimes you have to think about how your emotions affect other people. Jamie can recall six other occasions where she cried and Serena merely hugged her and offered comfort, but for some reason this one incident seeped into her psyche and became the basis for a rule. This whole time Jamie has been trying to get Serena to honor her own emotions, but there's a part of Serena that will always think of feelings as tools. Or weapons.

"You're the one who taught me to police my own emotions," Jamie tells Serena now.

"What does that mean?" Serena is fully a carrion bird, beak scooping and wings cocked, perched over roadkill.

Jane Collier's *Art of Ingeniously Tormenting* contains a whole section for parents who wish to torture their children, and a lot of it boils down to: wait until your children are fully grown, so you can mess with them as adults.

"I'm trying to tell you." Jamie grits her teeth. "You and I did this. We caused this. I'm still your teacher, whether you like it or not, so please trust that I know what I'm talking about." This is pointless; their conversation is going in circles. She tries to turn her own voice down to a low boil. "Please look past your own feelings and see that I'm having a crisis. I can't be taking care of you right now. The best thing you can do is give me space to figure things out on my own."

Serena is scowling and the temperature in this cafe has dropped, and Jamie feels as though everyone is staring at her.

"Just promise me, no more curses. They backfire, I've never been so sure of anything. Please promise me you won't mess around with curses anymore."

For a moment, Jamie is sure that Serena is going to play devil's advocate, or insist that they can't leave any weapon off the table. But Serena just nods. "If you insist. I hope you're wrong about the spell we did before, but either way, I'm sorry. I hope you know I would never do anything to hurt you on purpose. I'm still very sorry about what I did to Ro."

"Maybe you should tell Ro that," Jamie can't help saying. "You've told me twice now that you're sorry, but they're the one who really needs to hear it from you."

"You're right," Serena says. "I'll find a way to tell them soon."

The weather of their conversation has changed so suddenly, Jamie can't keep up—but now that she's not having to fight her mother, she's more acutely aware of the canker in her own bosom. The phone in her pocket feels heavier than usual, and she keeps fighting the urge to see what terrible things they're saying about her now. She doesn't know how bad this could get, or if it'll ever end—she's pretty sure nobody can find the address of the apartment she used to share with Ro, where Ro still lives, but what if she's wrong?

Serena is still talking. ". . . world is so fucking unfair. We turned cruelty and domination into our highest virtues, and . . ."

Something tugs at the edges of Jamie's peripheral vision. Three cold fingers just cradled the base of her skull.

Gavin sits near the doorway to the cafe, staring at her. Once she turns and stares back, he doesn't flinch or look away; he just smiles. He's holding something Jamie can't see, and she's sure he's filming her right now. Add that to the hours of footage he and his friends have already captured, but this time he's getting her and Serena together.

Jamie tries to ignore him, but she is fully Sartre's voyeur now, framed in a gaze she can't escape. Like sticky wispy strands brushing her skin.

Clatter commotion next to Jamie. Serena rises, moving plates and cups out of her way, and gives Gavin the ice-dagger eyes she used to be famous for. "You. Stay away from my daughter."

Gavin raises one hand with a fake-flustered look on his face. He is not flustered, he is delighted. This is better than he'd dared hope.

"Whoa, calm down, lady." Gavin still has something in his other hand, and now Jamie can definitely see a phone camera. "I'm just sitting here having a coffee. Which one is your daughter? Are you with Ms. Sandthorn? I'm one of her students. I stopped by to pay my respects."

"This is not what respect looks like," Serena says.

Jamie gets back in her own body, at least enough to nudge her mom and whisper, "Let's go."

Serena glowers. Jamie hustles her out the door, as fast as she can.

Gavin smirks as Jamie walks past. "I'll see you in class, Ms. Sandthorn."

Serena is still fixating on Gavin through the front window of the cafe. "Mom, stop it," Jamie hisses. "You're making things worse. Again."

Jamie marches Serena away from the cafe, down Mass Ave. toward the T stop. "Please, just go home. I need to be on my own. I'll call you."

Once Serena is gone, Jamie bends over, hands on crosswise kneecaps as if she's about to fake-Charleston. Not quite dry-heaving, but certainly breathing like a chain-smoker. Everything hurts so much, it seems impossible that Jamie isn't dying. Her mind tries to synthesize two loathsome self-images: the ugly caricature of her on the internet, and the real person who just stabbed her mother through the heart.

246   CHARLIE JANE ANDERS

Someone is standing next to her, looming over her. "Hey. Are you okay, Ms. Sandthorn?" Gavin asks.

Jamie straightens up, painfully. "Been a rough couple of days."

"Oh yeah." Gavin's face has never been more punchable. "I saw the video. People can be so mean."

"Give me your phone," Jamie says.

Gavin hesitates. "Why would you—"

"I'm going to delete the video you just filmed, or else we're going to go talk to the Dean of Students together. I have literally nothing to lose at this point. Give me your phone."

Gavin hands it over, still unlocked. Jamie goes into the camera app and deletes the video of herself and Serena having an inaudible argument, then finds and nukes two other videos.

"I just want to know," Jamie says, "why did you spy on me for McAllister Bushwick, of all people?"

Gavin had a guilty expression until she said that name, and now he just looks confused. "Who?"

"Do not fuck with me today," Jamie says. "You know who. McAllister Bushwick. You've been feeding him information about me."

But no. Gavin isn't that good of an actor, and he's too lazy to put on an act in any case. He genuinely has no idea what Jamie is talking about. It's not until she mentions JawBone that Gavin's face lights up.

"Oh. That guy! I remember him. Yeah, he's kind of old news." Now Jamie must be the one wearing a blank expression, because Gavin adds, "That guy lost his funding, because nobody cares about him. His whole deal was catching people on tape saying embarrassing stuff, and we don't need that anymore. We don't, like, need to gather a ton of evidence to show that someone is a problem. We just say they're a problem loud enough over and over, and it becomes true."

This is the first interesting conversation Jamie has ever had with Gavin, except maybe the eye patch thing. "Are you saying that because now we're living in a fully post-truth world, it's no longer necessary to collect damaging material on people?"

Gavin beams. "You get it. That Bushwack guy—"

"Bushwick," Jamie says.

"—he was old school. He was focused on getting *The New York Times* to pay attention to his scandals or whatever, which meant he needed evidence. But by now, the lamestream media has been trained, they know that any time we make enough noise about something, they need to cover it as a 'controversy,' regardless of whether it has any truth. Otherwise, they're censoring conservative voices, right?"

Jamie has to say it aloud. "This is why slashing funding for liberal arts is a suicide pact. If we don't have critical thinking—"

"You've taught me a lot about story structure and the development of the novel," Gavin says. "You're a good teacher, and I hope you stick with it, even though you're also a degenerate groomer. By the way, I submitted the eyepatch story to the literary magazine and they're publishing it next month."

"So if those videos weren't for Bushwick, who were they for?"

"We have a message board," Gavin says. "Me and some other conservative students. Just to vent about liberal professors trying to indoctrinate us. We all share videos and memes. One person photoshopped you to look like Shrek. It was pretty dope." He scratches his head. "What happens to the videos after they go on the message board, who knows? Maybe other people scrape them."

"Why do you hate me?" Jamie blurts out.

"Oh, I don't. It's just that instead of focusing on the canon of great writers, you taught a class about the history of the English novel that was all freaks and perverts," Gavin says mildly.

"The history of the English novel *is* all freaks and perverts!" Jamie realizes she's shouting, and the people on the street are probably staring. "Freaks and perverts created all the culture worth talking about. That's how it's always been. The people who have to go into the most desolate places and wallow in dirt just to find something, anything, that they can hold onto—" Now she's thinking about her mother. (And she's sounding like her mother.)

Jamie turns and walks away from Gavin, midsentence. She has no idea if he watches her go or not, because she's no longer looking at him.

· · · · ·

Daffodils poke out between wild grasses and the dried-out mulch of last year's fallen leaves: yellow heads lifted in song, just inches from the tarmac gutter at the edge of the two-lane highway. Are daffodils native to central Massachusetts? Or did someone lose some bulbs? No clue. But the moment she spotted them, Jamie knew she had to pull over, because these daffodils felt like a sign. Sure enough, she steps over the flowers and shoves past some tree branches, nearly tripping and going splat only once or twice, and then she sees it: a spot where some teenagers smoked up and built a secret stoner grove, then left to do whatever teen stoners do. Bong shards are scattered among the dead leaves, there's a grimy Gatorade bottle full of ashes next to some gnarly-looking poison oak. The perfect spot. Jamie kneels in the sod, taking great care to avoid any of the bong pieces adorned with pink skulls. The ashes flutter inside the bottle, and a squirrel runs along a branch nearly overhead.

Jamie fishes in her bag for something to leave behind.

And . . . she freezes. Her hand trapped between the zipper teeth.

Why can't she do magic anymore? Part of her has known deep down for ages that this is the case, and she hasn't wanted to worry about it. But now, in this spot, she's left wondering. What's wrong? If magic is need-based, as she always thought, then her need has never been greater. But when she thinks about reaching into her bag and pulling out any one of a dozen pieces of paper having to do with her dissertation, her job search, the ongoing inquiry into her conduct, along with some kind of offering, she suddenly cannot move. Anxiety spikes, her breathing speeds up, and she can't form a single thought. She's not sure if she can't move because of a panic attack, or if she's having a panic attack because she can't move.

She can only think of one explanation: deep down, she doesn't believe she deserves to want anything.

V

Lesbian, gay, bisexual, and transgender (LGBT) individuals often face challenges and barriers to accessing needed health services and, as a result, can experience worse health outcomes.

—KAISER FAMILY FOUNDATION WHITE PAPER, 2018

The hook, and it's the right hook for providers, is you're going to do a better job providing patient care. Did you really go into this profession to do a bad job?

—DR. KENNETH MAYER, QUOTED IN
"THE PROBLEMS WITH LGBTQ HEALTH CARE,"
HARVARD GAZETTE, MARCH 2018

Mae kept complaining about a pain in her lower stomach, which kept her up at night, twanging and twinging at inconvenient moments. Every time she mentioned it, Serena encouraged her to call Dr. Norchester, but Dr. Norchester had already told her that she only needed to lose weight and stop eating spicy foods.

Serena was putting out a thousand fires at the foundation right now—it was development season, plus they were joining a huge lawsuit against a real estate company—and meanwhile Jamie was coming home from college for a visit and bringing her new partner, Ro, and there were endless logistics to navigate. Once Jamie was out of the nest and no longer needed to go to school first thing in the morning, Serena had sworn she would sleep in, but instead she was rising earlier than ever. Her hands only left her computer keyboard to raise liquids to her face or to grind thumbs into her temples. Why had she ever wanted this ED job?

So she barely heard herself telling Mae, "I'm sure you're fine, it's nothing to worry about. Just have some acetaminophen and drink lots of echinacea tea, love." She didn't see Mae's face or body language as she spoke, because her face remained glued to spreadsheets, emails, and legal briefs.

For years after, Serena would hear herself saying *I'm sure you're fine,* without even looking the love of her life in the eye. And she would curse herself in the name of every star that dared to keep shining after Mae was gone.

. . . . .

Nobody had time to go pick up Jamie and Ro at Wesleyan, so they took a Peter Pan bus and Serena picked them up at the station. Serena made a huge show of bustling: hugging Jamie, clasping Ro's hand, hauling their duffle bags into the trunk, chattering about the weather and food options. Jamie towered over Serena now, and for some reason this came as a surprise yet again, Jamie having regressed in Serena's mind's eye during her absence. Ro seemed to find all of Serena's attempts at conversation exhausting, responding in monosyllables and head-tilts. Jamie compensated with bursts of random information about the clubs she was joining or helping to start at college, all the steam tunnels she'd explored.

When Serena started the car, she couldn't remember what music she'd been listening to—probably something mortifying, some Gen-X pop music or aging-lesbian folk-twang—but to her relief it was Le Tigre, the song about Hot Topic. She waited for the heater to come on so her hands would grip the steering wheel properly, then turned down the music and tried to find the breath to say, "Just so you know, your mama has been feeling under the weather."

Jamie had slid into the front passenger seat. She turned quickly and froze: a rabbit in a beam of light. "Is she okay?"

"Oh yeah," Serena said. "It's nothing, just a stomach thing. She's gotten a clean bill of health. She needs to take it easy for a while."

But when they got back, Mae was in high spirits, ladling fresh-made mulled wine and handing out cookies and tiny presents. Ro and Mae struck up a lively conversation about a book that both of them had read, and Serena caught the clove from her wine cup in her teeth, basking in the warmth of a well-occupied house. Jamie was telling Serena about eighteenth-century women writers, and the "matrimony trap" that forced women to marry petty tyrants or live in squalor. The gleam in Jamie's eye was like every time Serena stumbled on a great story or the perfect client: ravenous, fearless.

You spend your whole life wondering if anyone else experiences the same unnameable emotional states as you, only to see them in your own child—like a strange mirror in an ornate wire frame.

They had pizza for dinner, from the place with the square slices. Serena's phone kept fuzzing in her pocket with social-media updates (the myriad reasons for her to be outraged, the occasional reason people were outraged at her) until she silenced it. (The good thing about Twitter? Serena no longer obsessed about ratfucking from her enemies, she was too busy worrying about being torn apart by her friends.) Ro was trying to decide whether to go into applied statistics or economics, and Mae wanted to know the difference. Jamie had gone to some great protests and outstanding jam sessions, and she'd played her guitar at both, and nobody had complained (much). This wasn't even a holiday, just a weekend when Jamie needed to do laundry and Ro wanted to buy shoes, but an amber light coated the scene in Serena's mind, and she yearned obscurely for some ritual: giving thanks, singing songs, testifying.

"Do you think humans need ceremony?" she asked Jamie—god, her kid was so smart, you could ask her the goofiest questions and get a thoughtful response! how did this happen?—and Jamie paused to think about it, sipping the last of the mulled wine.

Jamie name-checked W. B. Yeats and two other people Serena had never heard of, then said yes, but only sort of. "I mean, ceremony is an elastic concept, right? It doesn't have to be tied to religion or politics, it doesn't need an officiant or any kind of fancy boss to make it signify. The main thing is a feeling of coming together, right? Of sharing something, even if not everybody agrees on what was shared. I don't know; sometimes I think the best ceremonies are the ones that nobody thought of as ceremonial at the time. People just started doing something spontaneously and everyone joined in, and only later did it become a thing. But the whole idea feels very culturally freighted."

Serena tried to ask Ro about Hayek, the right-wing Austrian economist, because everything was suddenly Hayek lately. They mumbled something about the Laffer curve and changed the subject.

Fancy cheese and nuts for dessert, since they'd already had cookies. Even if Serena hadn't figured out how to talk to Ro, this felt like the kind of family she'd always wanted and never gotten from her parade of siblings. That night, Serena and Mae held each other and whispered random endearments back and forth, giggling.

"I couldn't be happier if I was a basket of kittens," Mae whispered.

"I couldn't love you more if I was a butterfly and you were a field of bluebells," Serena whispered back.

They kept whispering silly nothings until they drifted off, and Serena thought maybe they kept whispering in their sleep. She would remember this warm feeling for the rest of her life.

Jamie didn't come back for another visit for months, missing the actual holidays, because there were road trips and extra classes and things. Serena and Mae were sad but they understood, and they had friends over instead. The next time Jamie visited it was almost Easter, one of those early spring days that fertilizes your daydreams with a lick of sun on your shoulders, a sweet taste on the wind, and the scent of cedar chips along every sidewalk. Ro didn't come with Jamie, and Serena tried not to read into it.

Serena noticed Jamie giving her parents an odd look, during a lull in the conversation. Had they said the wrong thing when she'd brought up her grad school ambitions? Was she psyching herself up to come out yet again, as nonbinary or demi or something Serena couldn't guess?

But then, when Mae had stepped away to get something, Jamie sidled up to Serena and said, "I'm worried about Mama. She seems like she's in a lot of pain, like every time she moves she's wincing. And she just seems more low energy. Is she okay?"

Oh. Oh shit.

Well . . . Mae had been needing more massages lately at the end of the day, but gentler because it was so tender. She still complained of aches and pains, but it had just become a new ritual where Mae complained and Serena sympathized. Dr. Norchester had given Mae a clean bill of health and she had cut down on the chili peppers. But Jamie was seeing Mae for the first time in months, and she was sure there had been a stark change.

After Jamie went back to college, Serena turned to Mae while they were watching Netflix and said, "Uh, maybe we should get you a second opinion. For your stomach pains."

Mae recoiled—was she about to protest, or even tell Serena to stop trying to micromanage her health? Then she said, "I guess, I mean . . . whenever I go to Dr. Norchester or that nutritionist they sent me to, they just talk past me and hustle me out of there. They won't even look at me, they just lecture me." She had the same tone as when she'd talked about Hettie's microaggressions. "I don't know, it feels like a waste of time. And like you said before, it's probably nothing."

"What if I went with you next time?" Serena said. "Maybe you need someone to advocate for you. I am very comfortable with being a pain in the ass for a worthy cause."

"I mean, can you?" Mae wore a look Serena had never seen before, in all their years together. Eyes wide, lips curled inward—like she was ashamed of how much she needed Serena's help, or like she had been burying her need in a deep gully. Later, Serena would come to think of this as the *I'm a burden* look. "I know you're all hands on deck at work, I know the Evensong case is coming to a crisis and all those people are in precarity and I don't want you to . . ."

"Are you kidding?" Serena said. "Nothing is more important. Nothing else comes close. I'm going with you to the doctor from now on. Listen, I'm not saying you can't advocate for yourself. I've seen you do it. No doctor in their right mind would mess with Mistress Ravenna." Mae smiled, but with a sad affect: she'd finally given up the dungeon a couple years earlier, and the reason she'd loved being a domme was because she couldn't be that person the rest of the time. "But sometimes it's good to have backup, right?"

Mae nodded, and a few days later she had made another appointment at the local clinic. Serena cleared her schedule, Evensong case be damned. She was going to show up for the woman she loved, no matter what.

She just hoped it wasn't too late.

· · · · ·

It was too late.

"If only we'd caught this sooner," said the oncologist.

"We might need to start talking about palliative care," said the patient care coordinator.

There was still a range of treatment options they could try, from chemo to radiation to some of the new gene therapies, but they were considered "heroic measures." Insurance would cover some of it, but only some, and only if someone (Serena) spent hours on the phone talking to claims specialists.

Basically, if they'd caught it back when Dr. Norchester was glancing at Mae out of the corner of his eye and telling her to lose weight, she'd have had a decent prognosis. Serena kept replaying all the moments she'd told Mae, *I'm sure you're fine,* instead of trusting her own wife and assuming the experts were as full of shit as they'd been every other time.

They had to tell Jamie. Neither of them could bear the thought of putting that on their kid, who seemed to be finding herself, building happiness, with Ro and her studies and everything.

"I can tell her," Serena said.

"No, I need to," Mae said. "But I'd rather not be alone when I do it."

Should they wait and tell Jamie in person? They could tell her to come home as soon as possible, because they had news, but then they'd only freak her out twice instead of once. Better to get it over with. In the end, they FaceTimed her, which meant they got to watch the light go out of her eyes in real time.

"Okay," Jamie said. She just kept saying that word: *Okay. Okay.* Though, of course, it was not okay at all. In this instance, "okay" meant a variety of things, including: "I understand," "The parameters of my whole existence have just shifted irrevocably," "I'm trying not to burden you with my emotions at a time when you are already overburdened with your own," and "I can't process what you're saying yet, but I'll be a wreck an hour from now."

"We're going to fight this," Serena said. "There are still plenty of options."

"Okay," Jamie said.

"I know this is scary," Mae said. "I'm scared, too. But I can throw a rock and hit five cutting-edge research hospitals around here. I'm going to get excellent care."

"Okay," Jamie said.

Serena chewed the inside of her mouth on both sides until it hurt to swallow.

She talked on the phone to the patient care coordinator, who often lapsed into the sort of airy, soothing voice you'd use on a nervous cocker spaniel. The cancer hadn't metastasized too far yet, and the oncologist believed there was still a slim chance—put it between 10 and 20 percent, depending on who you asked—that some mix of chemo and radiation could help slow things down.

But time was not on Mae's side, and her chances grew worse every day.

. . . . .

The best thing Serena could do for Mae, besides just being there, was to try and keep her mind off the pain and discomfort, and to make some more happy memories together. She took Mae out on one of those duck boats in Boston Common that they'd always been too cool to try. They went for dim sum with Jamie and some of their friends, at a place where they still brought the carts around and made marks on a piece of paper that went soggy with spilled tea. Serena took Mae for a weekend in the country, in a rustic one-room schoolhouse that the Fordhams said they could use whenever they wanted. At an antique store they found an old wooden duck, which made a perfect duck noise when you blew into it—it was made for duck hunters, apparently, but Mae took to using it to communicate. Serena would say something, and Mae responded entirely in realistic-sounding quacks.

"Tell me about the eighteenth century," Mae commanded Jamie. Mae was holding court in her favorite overstuffed armchair, wearing kitten slippers with a giant mug of tea. Jamie and Serena both perched on the edge of the fainting couch, ready to leap to their feet if Mae needed the least thing.

"Um, well, I'm still just getting started." Jamie ran both hands through her wavy-floppy hair. "This was a time when women's roles were shifting around, uh, because tons of people were moving into the cities, and the nature of housekeeping changed. All of a sudden? There was a huge population of women who couldn't find husbands. People started using the words 'spinster' and 'old maid' as insults in the early 1700s. So a lot of novels are about the problem of finding a suitable marriage for young women, who will be ruined otherwise. People mostly talk about a handful of books by men on this subject, but I'm finding a lot of women authors who had more interesting things to say."

"Uh-huh," Mae said. "So where were the queers?"

Serena cackled. "Trust you to go veering off the straight path."

"No, seriously, were there Boston marriages? As a Boston wife myself, I want to know."

"Well, um, I'm glad you asked." Jamie floofed her hair again. "So it was very common for unmarried women to become live-in companions to other ladies, which could be a very abusive situation but also could be very, um, companionable. Some women tried to create their own self-sufficient community in Bath, and actors got up to all sorts of shenanigans. Plus there were supposedly two lesbian bordellos in London, run by Mother Courage and Frances Bradshaw, and the dissolute and rakish Lady Harrington frequented them. Supposedly. Lady Harrington was a friend of Casanova, by the way."

"I want a lesbian bordello!" Mae protested. "Why did bloody eighteenth-century London have *two,* and we don't get to have even one? Serena, find me a lesbian bordello this instant."

"I'm on it." Serena mimed flipping through an imaginary Yellow Pages.

· · · · ·

The days crawled past in real time, but blurred in Serena's memory. Hours in waiting rooms, hours on the telephone with the insurance company. Jamie took a semester off from college to help with Mae, and some of their friends also came to help her do errands and sort through her possessions. The insurance company was denying gene therapy treatments as "experimental," and was also trying to wriggle out of paying for chemo, and in any case they had a massive deductible to pay off first.

They had set up a crowdfunding page for Mae's medical care and other expenses, resulting in a flood of donations on the first day from all their Boston-area friends, plus many of the people they'd brunched with in San Francisco. Numb as she was, Serena felt a pulse of gratitude, seeing all the names scroll past: all the people who remembered them, the lives they had touched. There were a few donations that Serena was pretty sure came from some of Mae's old dungeon clients. After that, the donations slowed to a trickle. Every couple of days, Jamie would go outside "to get some air," and every time she got back, she checked the donation page as if something must have changed while she was gone.

Even with the crowdfunding, there wasn't enough money. Mass General wanted thousands of dollars to start those heroic treatments, and Mae was adamant: they weren't going into debt. The patient care coordinator had forms ready for them to sign, there was a financial counselor who could talk to them, but Mae had read an article online about the lives ruined by medical debt, adding insolvency to injury. Serena called everyone she knew, but they'd all donated to the crowdfund already.

How was Mae doing? Hard to tell, it depended which day you caught her on. She was definitely in more pain than she let on, but she was still putting on a show of bustling as usual. Serena and Jamie kept trying to keep her spirits up, joking around, but soon discovered that she'd become the personification of that old it-only-hurts-when-I-laugh meme.

"I don't want to leave you with a mountain of debt," Mae said one evening when Jamie had wandered out. "You only just got the student loans squared away."

"You're not going to leave me with anything," Serena said. "We'll figure it out together, after you're on the mend."

"Cut the shit," Mae said without changing her subdued tone. "I've been listening to the same things you have, and I don't have the luxury of denial." She closed her eyes, screwed her mouth tight, and Serena could not tell if she was wincing from pain or resignation. "Believe me, I want to live to see

Jamie dazzle the world with her scholarship. I want to grow old by your side. It's all I want."

Mae shivered, she was running cold even on a warm day. Serena handed her a blanket.

Serena was kneading Mae's hand under the blanket, and she found herself pressing her face to Mae's outermost knuckles, like a child seeking benediction. "I would do anything. I would do literally anything. I would rob a hundred banks. I wouldn't trade you for all the money in the world." She kept saying things like this for a long time, until she hardly knew what she was saying.

She couldn't process the enormity of what was happening, death's ambush.

"Listen," Mae said, "I talked to Lottie." Their friend Lottie had been a nurse practitioner for a very long time and was a good source of no-bullshit medical feedback. "She said in my shoes, she would go for the hospice care. Please believe me that this isn't just about money or whatever, I'm doing what I've always done, trying to make the most of life."

Serena closed her eyes and for a moment she was pressed against a sticker-covered bathroom wall with Mae's fists clutching her hair and the front of her shirt. She'd never thought she could find love like this. It was too soon. She needed more time. She could almost turn the pressure of loss, bearing down on her, into Mae's hand pressing her against a dirty wall, until she opened her eyes again.

"I don't get," she said. Oh, her face was so wet now, her cheeks a double aqueduct. "I don't get why you're not angry. Those bastards. That doctor, he should have done his job. Why aren't you pissed off?" She'd already learned the hard way that Mae was not interested in filing a malpractice suit.

Serena still had her face to Mae's hand, and Mae gave her a gentle bonk on the chin. "You've known me this long, and you really think I'm not furious?" Mae was not crying at all, she was looking down with an expression that Serena slowly read as tenderly incredulous. "I want to scream, all the time."

"If you want to scream, you should scream." Then Serena quickly added: "But I support you dealing with this however you need to."

Serena was still kneeling, looking up into Mae's eyes, which were tearless but shining.

"You really don't get to tell me how to handle this," Mae said. "Listen, I keep thinking all the time. I keep thinking I can't control a lot of things right now. I can't control how long I have left, or what happens to you and Jamie after I'm gone. The only thing I can control is how my wife and daughter remember me, especially my daughter."

"Okay," Serena said. "But you know we've had years to build memories, right? Whatever happens next won't change that. Seriously, you can be a total mess, or freak out, and it's fine. I guess what I'm saying is, this is a fucking safe space, okay? You're not required to freak out, but you're allowed to, because you're with the people who know you most, and who will always hold you in our hearts, and . . ." Serena ran out of words.

It was sinking in that in the course of this conversation she'd gone from urging Mae to fight for life no matter what to imploring her to rage against the inevitability of death.

"Don't worry," Mae said, with a groan that Serena was pretty sure was mortification rather than pain. "I'll be a total mess soon enough. Just let me be perfect a little while longer."

"That's what I'm saying." Serena smiled through her tears. "You'll always be perfect."

. . . . .

Serena had been trying to work from home as much as possible, but she needed to go into the office for at least a few hours a day to deal with some stuff. The plaintiffs in the Evensong case were skittish as hell, especially after Evensong's reps tried to intimidate them, and they needed to confer with Serena personally. The foundation was taking on more nondiscrimination cases on behalf of gay couples. Plus the foundation was hiring a new paid intern, and they'd already narrowed it down to a few options, and Serena needed to meet with them. Raphael and Alice could cover for Serena—Alice was proving that she could've done the executive director job just fine, in fact—but Serena was supposed to be in charge, and everything was on fire.

"Go," Mae said. "We'll be fine here."

"I'll stay in case she needs anything," Jamie said.

So Serena went, promising to be back as soon as possible.

At the office, everyone lowered their voices around Serena and stared at the floor a few feet behind her, as if they wanted to show grace but didn't know how. The whole thing made Serena want to tell inappropriate dirty jokes and wreck the knickknacks on people's desks. She was an Archimedes screw full of brackish water, pumping stink and decay at an unbelievable speed. She was a visitor from the house of death, pretending that words had meaning and faces could smile without turning to grimaces. She was not really here.

Somehow she got through the client conference, letting her lawyer brain think and her mouth spout jargon. And then in the debrief, she just nodded, letting Alice talk.

Somehow two hours went by, profesh as hell, without Serena finding herself entirely paralyzed by the thought, *My wife is dying right now*. One thing was a dream, or the other was.

"I'm sorry, I know you're on compassionate leave right now," Alice said to Serena when they were both getting coffee in the tiny break room. She had gotten a cute bob and was wearing her best "nonprofit hipster" chic, a cashmere sweater and capri jeans, on her bony frame. "But thank you for coming in. If we didn't have the Evensong case blowing up . . . Anyway, sorry and thank you." Alice's hazel eyes looked kind in the fluorescent light, and she was at least willing to make eye contact.

"It's okay," Serena said. "I really appreciate you stepping up and doing such great work."

Almost time to run back home, but first Serena needed to talk to one of the leading contenders for the paid internship: a pale girl named Belinda with fuchsia hair and a chain between the piercings on her nose and left ear who was studying at BU or Boston College. This obvious trust-fund kid sat in the chair nearest Serena's desk, legs crossed in her thigh-length tweed skirt, expensive shoe dangling.

Belinda talked entirely in rote activist phrases, like a white paper in human form: "digital redlining," "generational wealth," "homeownership bias," "community partners," "reinvestment," "structural empowerment."

Serena found herself tuning out the jargon, which opened a space inside her for the howling superstorm she'd tried so hard to keep at bay. A scream filled her skull, her hands gripped the arms of her chair. She wanted to set everything aflame, hot enough to melt concrete. Warped glass between her and Belinda, who was still speaking someone else's words.

"Don't you agree?" Belinda asked.

Serena almost said yes, but something about the sudden eagerness in Belinda's voice worried her. "Agree with what?"

"That we need a new paradigm focused on radical redistribution of living space."

Serena suddenly could not stand to hear any more sterile buzzwords. "What I think," she said, "is that a tendency to impose top-down solutions has fucked over local communities again and again." She heard the tightness in her own voice but could do nothing about it. "Everyone deserves a place to live—including low-income people and the unhoused. Poverty shouldn't be a crime. I'm tired of watching people of color and queers be driven away from the places they helped to build. We need to change who we think of as a stakeholder."

Okay, so Serena was fully ranting now. Good—maybe this hipster kid would learn something, or maybe it'd provoke Belinda into saying what she actually thought, instead of parroting other people's words.

"So what about crime?" Belinda said. "Drugs, prostitution, they make people feel unsafe in their own neighborhoods."

Serena couldn't help snorting. Fearmongering about crime was the bleeding edge of bloodthirsty policies. Massachusetts was finally legalizing cannabis, like every other blue state, which meant cops could actually take harder drugs more seriously. As for "prostitution," who cared? "I'll tell you that if you had a sex worker in your building, you'd never even know, but it'd probably make you safer if anything. Sex workers are very good at security, because they have to protect themselves. You'd be lucky to have a sex worker for a neighbor."

"Oh, of course I agree," Belinda said. "I had neighbors who were doing satanic rituals, and they were the politest people."

How had this conversation gone from housing equality to satanist neighbors? Serena took a proper look at Belinda and noticed a faint smirk in one corner of her mouth. This conversation felt like a trap—maybe it had been for a while, and Serena had been too off her game to notice.

"It was nice to meet you, Belinda," Serena said. "We'll be in touch."

For about five minutes after Belinda left, Serena fretted that she had said too much. But screw it, she hadn't said anything she couldn't stand behind. Soon Alice wanted to go over the discovery motions in the Evensong case, and then Serena had to bail. On the way home, Serena picked up some fruit and flowers for Mae: kiwis and nectarines, peonies and pansies. Let her be surrounded by sweet pulp and blushing petals.

· · · · ·

"Tell me another scandal," Mae commanded, raising a hand imperiously from the bed, where she had begun holding court like a Dickensian matriarch.

"Oh," Jamie stammered. "Well, have I told you about Elizabeth Chudleigh? She attended a palace ball nearly naked, and the Princess of Wales threw a cloak over her. Everyone was about to banish her from polite society, but then the king held a masque in her honor a week later and kissed her in front of everybody."

Mae went *ooohh* and mimed eating popcorn. "So King George was hot for her?"

"Uh, yeah, he was." Jamie smiled. "She probably became his mistress. She always had a bunch of young women living with her as companions, and there's plenty of speculation about what she was doing with them. But also, she married two different men and they put her on trial for bigamy. She got away with it, because one of her husbands had just become an earl."

"Another one!" Mae demanded.

When Serena hustled down to the laundry room, Jamie was telling Mae about Hannah Snell, who disguised herself as a man, joined the Royal Marines, and fought in a battle where she was injured eleven times, with buckshot in both legs and in her groin. She dug the buckshot out of her groin herself, so as not to give herself away—but when she was discovered, she was celebrated as a hero, and became a celebrity.

Mae had decided that she wanted to spend as much time as possible listening to Jamie's stories of eighteenth-century hussies. Serena overheard snippets of the stories of Mary Porter, an actress whose chaise was attacked by a highwayman, only to whip out her pistol and hold him at gunpoint. The highwayman pleaded that his family was starving, and even though Porter was permanently disabled in the course of escaping from him, she later took up a collection and raised money for his family. There was also the Irish poet Laetitia Pilkington, who was disgraced by her evil husband— but got revenge by writing a bestselling tell-all memoir. Pilkington rented a room across the street from an exclusive gentlemen's club in London, where she bantered with the club's patrons, becoming one of London's most celebrated wits.

"It makes me happy," Jamie said, "to think that we're carrying on a struggle that's been going forever. There have always been crackdowns and backlashes, and people have always paid a heavy price for living their real authentic lives. They've left their stories for us to read, with all their trauma and sadness—but also joy! And community! There have always been women who spat in the eye of the patriarchy."

"Women like you and me." Mae squeezed Jamie's hand.

Jamie's face reddened: happy squirming. "Yes. Women like us."

The next day, Jamie went out to "check on a project," a regular errand lately, from which she always returned with mud stains on her knees and dirt under her fingernails. While Jamie was gone, Serena sat with Mae, who was in bed with a book splayed in her lap.

"We raised a good kid," Mae said.

"We did," Serena said.

"Thank you for not telling me how brave I'm being, or how well I'm dealing with this."

"I would never." Really, it hadn't occurred to Serena to say those things, because she wouldn't want to hear them in Mae's place.

"The truth is, I'm scared out of my mind, and I hate everything about this. Pointless thoughts keep barging into my brain, about all the books that'll come out in a year or two, that I won't get to read. Isn't that silly? To obsess about some novel that I probably would never have gotten around to anyway."

"It's not silly," Serena said. "The unfairness of this is so huge that it's hard to see the whole thing, you can only see pieces."

"I'm so glad I didn't listen to Wendy Preston when she warned me you were a bounder." Mae smiled, but her voice cracked.

Serena leaned her head against Mae's shoulder with great care. "I *am* a bounder. But I was captivated by your wit and beauty. I still am." Her throat tightened, in a different way than when she was ranting at Belinda. "I can't believe how lucky I've been. I never thought I would get to know someone like you, someone who brightens every room just by walking into it, someone who . . ." Oh well, Serena was crying again, in spite of all her resolutions. She really did not want to make Mae feel worse, or burden her with prospective grief.

"Keep going," Mae said. "I love hearing about how great I am." But she was crying, too, Serena could feel the spasms in her chest without looking up at her face.

Just then, Jamie burst inside, holding her phone. "Hey, Serena, Mae, you need to see this. My mentions started blowing up, it's really—you should see for yourself."

Serena found her own phone under a pile of medical notices and insurance crap, and looked at her mentions on social media. Oh. Oh shit.

· · · · ·

So there was an upstart right-wing organization called JawBone, which Serena had only vaguely heard of. YouTube had countless videos of the organization's leader, McAllister Bushwick, in a rumpled suit, drawling about the defense of liberty. Bushwick was the dark fringe of an approaching storm cloud, he was the untangling of all our best-loved skeins of mutual support and kindness, he was one long taunt. And now, he'd turned his attention to Serena.

They had audio of Serena's conversation with Belinda—heavily edited to feature Serena talking about sex workers, plus a part where they made it sound like she was saying we should let unhoused people use drugs in public. And . . . they'd gotten some video of Mae in her Mistress Ravenna gear, standing outside in front of the secret dungeon, bumming a smoke from a coworker. Whip dangling from Mae's fingers as if she were about to crack the cigarette from her friend's mouth. And there were racy photos of Serena and Mae from some party at Man Ray years ago.

The narrative was pretty simple: this housing activist was married to a "dominatrix" (who used that word nowadays?) and went to perverted events, and she wanted to force you to live among people having sex for money. Flimsy, pointless stuff, but ideal fodder for the outrage machine.

Mae stared at her own phone. "I look so happy in this video. I look . . . I look alive and healthy and full of joy in my work, and how dare those fuckers. How dare they?"

Serena didn't know what to say. Part of her brain was stuck on Belinda. Her trendy hair dye and piercings, her too-rote-to-be-true jargon. There had been so many signs.

Jamie had gone out again, wild-eyed and charging, as if she could somehow make this go away. Serena didn't have the headspace to wonder where she kept getting covered with mud.

"All I was doing was playacting, creating a fantasy, and helping people forget for one hour that this world is a sewer. It was the purest thing in the world. Now I can't even stand to look at myself." Mae threw her phone at the wall, the screen landed cracked. Her face was bright red, her whole body rigid and upright in bed. "Poison, it's all gone to poison."

Serena's phone warbled again: an email from Amelia Bayshire, the chair of the foundation's board. It said simply, "Call me when you get this."

Serena opened the keypad on her phone, but she couldn't make her fingers dial Amelia's number. She stared at the phalanx of numbers, three by three. Then she put her phone down, the number undialed.

"They can't fire you over this," Mae said. "They can't."

They can, and they probably will. But out loud, Serena said, "It's going to be fine. They'll chew us up and spit us out, and move on to the next victim."

Mae wrenched herself out of bed, threw on a robe, and kicked her feet into slippers. "Those worms. They can't stand to see anybody living their truth. Those, those . . ." She had reached the bedroom door and stopped her march, as if she'd forgotten where she was heading. "This can't be it. This can't be how my life is summed up, how people remember me. I refuse. I won't allow it. I can't." She slumped against the doorframe, and Serena rushed over in case she was a fall risk. Before Serena arrived, Mae straightened up again and headed for the kitchen. "I'm baking cookies."

"Cookies sound good." Serena stood in the bedroom doorway and watched Mae across the hall, pulling ingredients down from shelves, preheating the oven. Some stuff wasn't where Mae remembered, and she cursed. Serena wanted to tell Mae that video, this smear, would never define her, that her life had meant so much to so many people who would carry her with them forever. But she couldn't find her voice and she kept imagining the conversation she would have with Amelia Bayshire, and she was caught in a feedback loop.

Someone had left something in the oven, some scorched crust, and the stench of burning filled the whole room.

· · · · ·

Now, seven years later, Serena sits in her tiny apartment on a rickety folding chair, staring at her phone. Emails, texts, social media updates . . . they all say the same thing, featuring the same name: Jamie Sandthorn.

They're calling Jamie the Classroom Creeper. They're misgendering her and accusing her of predatory behavior, based on nothing. There are plausibly deniable threats of violence, like *Somebody ought to pay her a visit.* Everybody who predicted the attacks on Jamie would "blow over" was a fool.

There's a video making the rounds: Serena shouting at that student in the cafe, the leering fuccboi with the terrible hair. Serena sees herself wild-eyed, hissing *Stay away from my daughter.* People are starting to connect Jamie to Serena's long-forgotten scandal, to create a juicy narrative about a whole family of freaks. Time was, Serena would have found this amusing.

You made it worse. Again.

Serena takes a breath. She already knows what to do, has known for a long time. The strongest magic takes the most from you—when she did the spell that turned Ro into mist, she left behind her sister's diamond ring, instead of a piece of candy. She could feel the power in letting go of something she prized.

Now she gathers everything she has left, everything that still means anything to her.

The marriage certificate from the week after *Obergefell,* that she's cherished for years. Her law school diploma. Her wedding ring and all the jewelry Mae gave her over the years. The handmade birthday cards Jamie gave her as a child. All the tiny keepsakes of her family she's held onto. She ransacks her home for pieces of her life to offer up in exchange for Jamie's safety.

Serena looks around the studio she's been living in for the past few months, suddenly certain that she's seeing this place for the last time. "Well," she says aloud. "I never liked it here, did I?"

The bag containing all of Serena's keepsakes is terribly light on her shoulder. Her apartment door barely makes a sound as it clicks shut behind her. Everything feels inconsequential but final.

Serena borrows Lottie's motorcycle, riding until she reaches hiking trails through scrubby woods. The wind picks up, and Serena puts on a warm jacket she shoved in her bag. She'll find as many magical places as she can by moonlight.

Soon Serena crouches on the moss-spongy ground near a hollowed-out tree stump full of someone else's illegible love letters, staring at a picture of Jamie and muttering, *Please please, I don't care what happens to me, just save my girl.* Only a slight hesitation, and then the marriage certificate goes into the hole next to Jamie's picture.

Serena doesn't feel as though her marriage was just annulled—but she does feel smaller. Diminished. Reduced to a shabbier, more pitiful version of herself, someone that nobody would ever want to marry.

Good. Hopefully that means it worked.

Serena moves on to the next magical spot, and the next after that. She's got a long night ahead of her.

16

"Forget not the most dreadful lesson of all. Do you keep your spirits high and when you find a splendid prospect of Nature's reclamation, forget not to keep a humble mind," advised Lady W_____.

"But what if one has already given occasion to one's worse inclinations in the very bosom of Nature?" Emily demanded, for her mind was much afrighted. "How may one's transgressions be repaired?"

Upon Emily's asking this, Lady W_____ fell silent a very long time.

—*EMILY: A TALE OF PARAGONS AND*
DELIVERANCE BY A LADY, BOOK 5, CHAPTER 9

Jamie finally gives up trying to sleep at six A.M. and picks up her phone, only to see . . . nothing.

You know how sometimes there's an ear-blasting noise, from somebody's overtaxed woofers or street repairs, and then it stops? And that sudden absence of noise feels quieter than regular silence? That's how Jamie's phone is. There are no updates, nobody is texting or @-ing her on social media, nobody is screaming or sharing obscene memes. Jamie flinches a moment, as if her phone could deliver an electric shock, but then she googles herself and finds . . . nothing, beyond the boring academic-page stuff you'd have found a week ago. All of the negative articles about her on right-wing blogs have been quietly taken down.

Jamie's online presence has been scrubbed.

As if by magic.

There's a new email, sent late last night. It's from Serena:

Dear Jamie:

I can make this all go away. My love for you is strong enough to bend the universe and rewrite cause and effect. I would do anything for you, and I hate that I've caused you so much pain. Please tell Ro that I wish I could have apologized to them in person.

The truest love involves sacrifice. I really believe that. We have to let go of our most cherished baggage to make space for the people we love. When I first fell for Mae, I was carrying so much detritus— I had wrapped myself in my own useless legend—and Mae was more patient than I deserved, while I learned to let go of it. And then we had you, and I started to see what really mattered.

Mae's absence is a broken window, forever letting in torrents of rain. I could have saved her. I wouldn't even have needed magic.

Still, I'm grateful. I've gotten to spend a lot of time with you, and I'm so glad we reconnected this past year, even if I've brought disaster down on you. There's no excuse. I tried to protect you, and I hurt your partner. I tried to get justice, only to put you through the same shit I went through back in the day. But you know this already. So here's something you don't know.

I discovered a kind of magic you've never tried, and it's how I'm going to save you now.

If sacrifice is the spine of love, what can sacrifice do for spell-casting?

Jamie, you're still in your twenties. That's a time when starting over is easy. I'm going to do what I can to buy you a fresh chance.

Love,
Your mother

Jamie reads the email twice, a dense landslide coming down inside her as her brain wakes up. The second time, the email seems much worse, especially the mentions of "sacrifice." Jamie can't help thinking of Lady Sagacious in the fairy tale, and her too-costly bargain with the faeries. Jane made Sarah's scandal go away, but there was (almost) a heavy cost.

Jamie walks outside, so she won't wake Markus, and sits on a bench facing Herter Park, with a view of some stray geese and a dog chasing a Frisbee. She calls her one surviving mother. Serena picks up right away.

"I'm on a roll," Serena says before Jamie can say hello. "I've been doing workings, for hours now. You would think midnight is the best time, because of all that hokey pop lore, but I really felt something at three in the morning."

Behind Serena's voice, the line is noisy: wind, birds, the shrieking of distant machinery.

"You've been doing spells all night?" Jamie whispers, as if anyone could hear her on this secluded bench.

"I know I'm not the woman you thought I was. If Mae had survived instead of me . . ." Serena makes a rustling sound: she's doing a working right now. She's on her knees somewhere in a pile of rotted wood or fractured plastic.

"I thought we were done with self-pity, Mom," Jamie says.

In front of Jamie, a dog sits with its face uplifted toward a person's hand holding a treat.

"This isn't self-pity. It's self-awareness. Isn't there a difference? And yet, does it really matter in the end?"

The dog receives the treat, and Jamie has never seen a living creature be so happy to achieve anything. The human's hand ruffles the fur on the top of the dog's head, as the treat is devoured.

"Listen. You need to stop. You'll burn yourself out, doing this. Just like with the hat. Just like with Ro, and Bushwick. The kind of magic you're doing will blow back, and this time you'll hurt yourself. I wish you would believe me."

The dog and the human are gone. The geese flutter, shedding their fluff. People pay hundreds of dollars to have goose down in their jackets, but they launch petitions and letter-writing campaigns to keep it off the grass.

"Oh, I do believe you," Serena says. "That's why I'm doing all these workings on my own: I don't want anyone else to get hurt."

The spring wind bites harder. Jamie's gut tightens.

"What are you doing, Mom? What could you possibly—" Jamie is shivering, salt-faced. Death, Desolation, and Ruin loom over her shoulder, taunting. "Mom, don't do this. You don't need to do this to yourself. Mom, where are you?"

Serena doesn't answer. The geese have drifted away, and now Jamie has a view of grasses being combed by the river wind.

"Mom, just tell me where you are. I can't lose you. You can't do this to me. If you keep going like this, I don't know what'll happen, but it'll be bad. Mom. You're all the family I have left. Don't make me a fucking orphan."

Some teenagers are in the park now, passing around a two-liter soda bottle and chugging from it. They throw water balloons at nothing and shriek.

"Why should you care? Haven't I done nothing but hurt you?" Serena says in her self-aware-rather-than-self-pitying tone.

The teens hurl the empty soda bottle on the grass next to the skins of burst balloons. One of them has a bong, which reminds Jamie of daffodils and pink skulls. She feels queasy.

"Mom. Mom. Please just stop, let's talk about this. You already stopped the harassment, it's over. Please tell me where you are." At some point, Jamie started weeping softly. Words are a mess: too many consonants and diphthongs. Her every breath sounds like a series of gasps. "Mom, listen. I know you think this is all your fault, but it's not true. You hadn't dealt with your grief, not properly, but neither had I, and I brought that to you. I convinced myself you just needed to be hungry again, to move forward, when I should have found a way to mourn with you. I fucked up, too. Mom, I fucked up, too. I forbid you to take all the blame."

The teenagers lie on the grass, pointing at clouds and laughing at those random white puffs.

"You were right, I shouldn't have taught you to police your own emotions," Serena says. "Now you're just reflecting my own lessons back at me."

Jamie is drained, emptied out. But also, still heaving and shuddering, free hand gripping the edge of the bench.

"You can feel what you want, Mom. But don't do magic while you're full of self-recrimination. It's not going to go well."

"You don't even know the real reason you should blame me."

The phone goes dead.

Jamie stares at the dark screen. That was probably her last ever conversation with her mother, and they didn't even talk face-to-face. Jamie already missed Mae's last moments. She can't imagine what suicide by magic would look like, but she pictures something similar to what happened to Ro: Serena vanishing without trace, devoured by a vortex of bad faith.

Jamie hits redial. Serena doesn't pick up this time.

The only coherent thought Jamie can form is: *I need Serena to stay alive so I can scream at her about how much she's let me down.* Which is infantile logic.

The teens roll around as if they were on a hillside instead of level ground.

Jamie makes herself as small as she can with her lanky bulk. All she wants to do is sit on this bench, mourn and rage. But Serena needs her. And Jamie still needs her mother, too.

She takes up her phone again, and starts texting people.

· · · · ·

Soon Jamie is flanked on the bench by Delia and Ro, while Paola paces back and forth in front of them, kicking grass with her left shoe. Jamie had fully intended to get off this bench and meet everyone, but she couldn't seem to move her legs.

"We are so far outside my understanding of magic, I'm at a loss," Delia says.

"She actually scrubbed all of your harassment from the internet." Paola whistles. "That's way beyond what I thought was possible."

"But the cost is, what?" Ro sounds brittle. "She's going to undo herself? Make herself cease to exist?"

The memory of kneeling in the darkness, never knowing if she'd see Ro again, almost drives out the sense of their words.

Now Jamie looks at Ro, sidewise—they have a tender look in their eyes, but their mouth is pursed. They're wearing a neat brown blazer over a baby-blue turtleneck and pressed black pants, so they must have been on their way to teach undergrads.

"Well," Delia says. "We knew somebody was going to find the limits of magic at some point. We're going to need a code of conduct, but right this moment, we need to save our friend. Whatever she may have done, she's part of our community."

"Even if we can find her," Paola says, "what then? She's already worked a ton of sacrifice magic."

Ugh. That phrase: "sacrifice magic." It's a new coinage, as far as Jamie knows, but it instantly feels like part of her lexicon, something she'll be saying and hearing for the rest of her life. The exact same way "Covid" and "AQI" went from nothing to everything.

"There's no reliable way to undo a spell," Delia says. "Even if the caster changes their mind."

"You did it, right?" Ro says. "You told me she put your other mom's hat down and everything went gross, but then you fixed it."

"Yeah," Jamie says. "We got lucky. I don't think that'll work this time. Especially if she's done multiple spells, with bigger offerings."

Sacrifice magic. Makes her want to scream.

"Let's concentrate on finding her," Delia says. "Damage control comes once we can actually assess the damage."

Jamie realizes she's staring into space, not because of sleep-deprivation—it's the same trance she usually goes into when she's about to write a really good paragraph of her diss. Everybody stops talking, and Ro moves into her field of vision with a concerned look. "Sweetie, are you okay?" they ask.

They called me sweetie again.

But there's no time to melt. Jamie looks at her (ex?) partner. "I just thought of something that might help, but I need to make a pit stop and check something." She turns to Delia and Paola. "This won't take long."

"We'll start looking for your mom," Paola says. Delia nods.

Delia and Paola get into Delia's car and drive off. For a moment, Jamie is sure Ro will walk away, but they're still here. "What's our next move?" they ask.

"I know you don't like my mother, especially after what she did to you."

"I don't wish her ill. I don't want her to self-destruct, or do 'sacrifice magic.' I don't want you to have to live with this." They pause, then say it. "I love you."

"I love you, too." Jamie turns and rushes back toward the possibly doomed Rugby College. "We need to get to the library."

· · · · ·

Ro watches Jamie paw through all of her notes and photocopied pages, then reach for a heavily annotated copy of *Emily*.

"You're going to work on your thesis *now*?"

"I learned about this book thanks to magic," Jamie says without looking away from the pages. "I think I've always suspected, deep down, there was something magical about the story. Not the finding-a-husband stuff, but all the ruins and desolate landscapes. The fractured abbey, the Princess and the Strolling Player, all of it."

"So . . . Jane Collier was a witch."

"And she surrendered everything to save her friend—her life companion—Sarah Fielding. Sarah had gotten swept off her feet by a glamorous actor named Charlotte Charke, who played men's roles and lived as a man. They were caught at a sleazy tavern together, and Sarah's reputation was headed for the shredder. And then Jane did something, and Sarah's scandal was wiped away. Sound familiar? But this was early 1737, and Jane lived until 1755 and was healthy enough to write two books and co-write a third."

"So Jane did sacrifice magic, but then she fixed it somehow?" Ro pinches their own nose. "And she put the secret into *Emily*?"

"I think so. Hold on."

Jamie is flipping through the first edition of *The Fair Moralist,* following the trail of scribbles as Jane used this book for scratch paper. There's something obvious, something she's missed. Okay, so there's the magical map of Bath, with the daisy symbol showing all of the locations with spell-wreaking potential. And that daisy symbol appears next to a few other notations scattered throughout the book, so maybe these are Jane's scattered thoughts on magic? Jamie pictures Jane sitting there, trying to finish this beast of a novel, and processing the time she did sacrifice magic and almost died. An experience like that? It would find its way into every corner of your thoughts, even if you couldn't write about it in plain words.

What if the scrawls with the daisy icons are a key? Or a concordance?

"You're muttering to yourself," Ro says without a hint of disapproval.

"I am. Hold on, hold on."

Jamie squints and turns pages as gently as she can with her mother in death's vestibule. Okay, so, the daisy notations go: *mossy altar, direst extremity, tarnished crown, wreaths to invisible ministers, threads of lightning, absumed, gaming table, sacrifice cannot be abjured, rasa tabula, dilapidated tower, cureless malady, high moldering place, reciprocal clemency, obdurate power.* Her fingers tremble so hard she's terrified of shredding *The Fair Moralist.*

She gropes for her copy of the scandalously out-of-print Penguin Classics edition of *Emily,* which she hasn't quite memorized after all. Every moment that passes feels like a death knell. But there it is: each of those daisy notes points to a passage in the book, a string of secret messages, embedded in quotes in the middle of sundry monologues. Put it all together, and you get:

> I placed everything that I was on the mossy altar of love, and believed myself utterly lost. Instead, love saved and restored me. [p. 37] For I have long known that in the direst extremity, one may call upon something far greater than one's self—cry out in the ruins, offer up everything one has—and receive the most unlikely succour. [p. 72] My oldest, dearest friend had a tarnished crown bearing down upon her head, so constricting and saw-toothed, it would surely destroy her were it not removed—yet how? The crown clenched until it fused with her scalp, and I despaired of freeing her from its grip. [p. 137] Lucky, then, that I had spent so much of my life making a practice of solitude and offering wreaths to invisible ministers of decay along the fringes of desolation; I could never regret letting my feeble light go out, that a far brighter beacon might yet shine. [p. 160] Soon it was done, and my love was furiously angry at my un-asked-for generosity—like a tempest laced with threads of lightning—for it has often been observed

that an excess of kindness will wound a gentle heart more deeply than the harshest cruelty. [p. 182] Nonetheless, I had resigned myself to a slow wasting, being absumed by the land which I had loved so feebly; no lamentation could change what had been set in motion. [p. 184] Tiny miracles require only the smallest of tokens, but only life can buy life—or so I thought, but my love knew otherwise. Nature is not a gaming table, at which one winner inevitably means that others must lose, but rather something more bounteous and cryptick, whose reasons cannot be understood by mortal minds. [p. 240] Sacrifice cannot be abjured, yet can it be cured. [p. 241] I needed only to wish with all my heart for a rasa tabula, all the folly of the past swept clean and replaced by love's constancy. [p. 266] She and I came together, in a dilapidated tower overlooking a fen that swarmed with life; by this time, I was too weak almost to move, near to death. I was scarce breathing, and somehow she supported me up those crumbling steps until we took in the luminous prospect, the sunlight dappling the reflections of grasses in the shallow water. [p. 317] I told her there was no purpose to all this exertion, that mine was a cureless malady, that I regretted nothing; she bade me cease, and take her hand. [p. 378] I shall not speak of the object we left there, in that high moldering place; suffice to say, it was exceedingly precious to both of us, and yet we abandoned it gladly. [p. 440] The most insurmountable challenge was not surrendering our treasure; rather, it was cleansing our breasts of all ill-feeling, relieving ourselves of all our guilt and anguish, finding reciprocal clemency in each other's eyes. O, scorn death's embrace—climb toward life's promise instead! [p. 539] The most obdurate power of all comes from embracing the greatest softness. [p. 644]

It's . . . an instruction manual for people who have fucked themselves with unselfishly profligate magic. Jamie throws her already battered Penguin paperback onto the desk. "We need to go. I've got what I need."

As she rushes out of the library, Jamie tries to explain with scant breath. "I think I know how to fix this. How to heal her."

"Listen, you know that if it comes down to your life versus Serena's, that's not a contest," Ro says. "Serena has already had a whole life. You're just starting. And I don't want to lose you."

"Nobody is dying today. Nobody will be lost or forlorn. I won't have it."

Jamie gets a text. Delia and Paola have been trying the southern areas, near the Quincy Quarries.

"We'll try the north," Jamie says.

They get in Berniece the dirtmobile and start cruising toward the Medfordiest part of Medford. The whole drive, Jamie is trying not to overthink about her failure to cast an enchantment among the bong shards. What use is she going to be, even if they somehow find Serena? She glances over at Ro, who's staring out the passenger window, and prays that she's not using up the last of their goodwill. Jamie wishes she could just let go gracefully, but it feels like free fall.

No lamentation could change what had been set in motion.

Jamie hates the silence, so she puts some Miles Davis on the car stereo: *Bitches Brew*, all fragmented beats and layered janky grooves, the most magical music she's ever heard.

Sometime after "Pharaoh's Dance," Ro speaks up: "I never expected much from my family, so they never had a chance to let me down. And yet, I somehow know exactly what you're going through."

"Well," Jamie says without taking her eyes off the road. "You do know exactly what it's like to be fucked over by one of the people closest to you."

Why does Jamie feel this constant compulsion to remind Ro how much she hurt them? It's not just that she's punishing herself—she wants to make sure that if they choose to spend time with her, it's an informed choice. She doesn't want them to be lured into the familiarity of her companionship and somehow convince themself that what happened was no big deal. Because it fucking was.

Ro doesn't respond to Jamie's self-castigation, because there's nothing more to say about that. Instead, they say, "I want to help, but I don't know how I can. I won't assist you in doing witchcraft, and the thought of watching you cast a spell still squicks me. What did you have in mind?"

"I don't know. It means a lot that you're here." Jamie wants to cry on their shoulder, a lot. "You know me better than anyone. And you also know my mom better than most people, simply by virtue of having been part of my family for so long. I need you to be a reality check and keep me somewhat grounded. I'm realizing that magic is about putting desire into the world, but ironically it's very easy to lose yourself in the process. I can't really explain. It's one of those annoying paradoxes. It's like, the more you ask for what you want, the harder it is to see yourself clearly. And yes, I know that I said I was doing all of this to help my mother get in touch with her own feelings."

Jamie finds a sign for some hiking trails named after local indigenous peoples, and pulls over on the roadside dirt inlet. The dirt path is poorly maintained: rocky, cracked, overgrown in places, with tree roots jutting a few inches aboveground. Basically an accident dying to happen.

After fifteen minutes or so, Jamie notices a flash of red through the trees and goes to investigate. Someone was living rough in these woods, maybe. Scraps of red nylon cling to the branches, like a jacket or maybe some kind of blanket. "This looks like a likely spot. You can stay here, I'm going to investigate."

Ro says okay, and Jamie pushes through the branches toward the heart of the red-fabric swirl. When she reaches the center, she stops. And curses.

Jamie's own face looks up at her, with ants crawling around her eyes and nostrils. Total nightmare fuel, like *Un Chien Andalou.*

The ants swarm across a photo of Jamie, part of a printout of some conservative blog post about her with a headline about woke gender ideology and grooming, with a big X inked across it. The ants have been attracted by a piece of honeycomb that probably came from a farmer's market. Next to the printout is a patch from a queer leather bar circa 1992, with a picture of a bulldog wearing a cap and smoking a cigar. Jamie remembers Serena cherishing that patch as a token from a time in her life when she felt fully alive and embraced by community. She always said she'd sew it onto a vest or jacket, once she found the exact right article of clothing.

Jamie can't help backing away, as if she's looking at an unexploded nuke.

"Serena was here," Jamie tells Ro. "Pretty recently." She texts Delia and Paola, so they can stop looking in the wrong place.

They go back to the car and drive again. More Miles Davis, more brooding.

The next spot is the same: a nasty story about Jamie crossed out, with a necklace from Serena's first love, a young poet who helped Serena come out and then broke her heart. Some instinct tells Jamie not to mess with Serena's workings—Jamie could remove them, replace them with a spell of her own, but the best-case scenario would be that Jamie fails. The worst-case scenario . . . she can't imagine. She's never thought of magic as something to be maxed out, but she never thought anyone would do what Serena is doing.

I placed everything that I was on the mossy altar of love.

The next place has another picture of Jamie, with a handwritten letter from someone named Dolly, thanking Serena for representing her pro bono and saving her home from foreclosure. The place after that, a still from that horrible video accompanied by a plastic poker chip whose significance Jamie doesn't know. Jamie can't tell if she's getting closer to Serena or farther away—there's no way to know the order in which these spells were cast. Jamie shouts Serena's name a few times, but there's no answer.

Jamie is watching from a distance as her mother slowly kills herself. It looks like Jamie's face, over and over.

17

Toby said on many occasions that he could not, would not, pretend to a redemption that was not sincere. But, he added, he cared too much for the opinion of his fellows, who would most assuredly hate him were he to become too harsh a judge of their amusements. How could one be truly good, he asked, without being reviled?

Emily's only response, each time, was to say that people would no doubt despise Toby regardless of what he might do, though some wretches might endeavour to conceal their loathing for fear of reprisals. His only choice, she said, was whether he would need to hate himself.

—*EMILY: A TALE OF PARAGONS AND
DELIVERANCE* BY A LADY, BOOK 5, CHAPTER 12

Berniece the dirtmobile careens over craters and loose rocks. Jamie has to slow way down, to about fifteen miles per hour. She has a wobbly feeling, some odd mixture of dread and longing, she's not sure she can face this.

Ro pulls up a map on their phone: all the trails and nature preserves that a person can visit nearby, plus some other random stuff. "There's a field a few miles away where they held a music festival seven summers ago. Wow, I never really thought about how many of these half-natural spots there are, all over the place."

"Humans overreach. We can't leave shit alone." Jamie is trying not to out-wardly freak out, to tamp down the voice inside her saying it's too late, Ser-ena's already gone. She hates how slow they're moving.

"That's what I've spent my entire career trying to understand," Ro says. "As you well know. We can never have just enough. We always have to push further and harder, in a feeding frenzy of development and consumption. That's how you get cycles of boom and bust, and unsustainable develop-ment, because people can't recognize when something isn't working any-more, or they're chasing a broken dream."

"I never realized before." Jamie steers onto a narrow dirt path, and Ber-niece's suspension rackets. "I've been studying the beginnings of industrial capitalism, and you've been studying the tail end." New feeling just dropped: a prickle on the back of Jamie's neck. "I think we're getting close to Serena."

Ro nods with their whole torso. "What do you want to do?"

"I'm starting to realize that the number of situations in which someone can really know what they want, without a lot of static or complications, is pretty limited." Jamie drives at the pace of a toddler on a tricycle. "The world contains a stable high ratio of therapists to witches, and not only because witches are rare."

They've reached the end of the dirt road. Jamie doesn't see any car, so maybe Serena's not here. Or maybe she got here some other way. There's a thin dirt path, like a gravel trail, leading off to the right, to where the music festival probably was.

The invisible ministers of decay along the fringes of desolation.

Jamie grips the steering wheel and stares at that path. She should get out of the car and start walking, but she can't move. She's joint-fused. Slowly she becomes aware of her own atrial flutter, her shallow breathing. The feeling she had before, dread and longing twisting around each other, is stronger now.

"I will support whatever you decide," Ro says. "Like, if you just want to go get pancakes, and deal with your mother later. There's no law that says you have to run yourself into the ground. Or we can find someplace she hasn't touched yet and do a spell to protect and shield her." They see the look on

Jamie's face, and add: "I just, I want you to be okay. I don't want you to get hurt trying to fix this because you think it's all your fault. It's *not* all your fault, and you've owned the parts that are. You shouldn't self-destruct while trying to keep your mother from self-destructing."

Jamie thinks about it: she could just go get pancakes. Serena might be fine. There's no way of knowing what'll happen, because they're far outside Jamie's experience at this point. And maybe if she goes and shares food with Ro instead of rushing after Serena, it'll be the start of rebuilding their marriage. This is what a proper adult with healthy boundaries would do, probably.

And if Jamie goes down that path to look for Serena, maybe she'll be throwing away a final chance with Ro? They're not giving her an ultimatum, but this still feels like a choice. Ugh.

"Being a witch has been good for me." Jamie puts the car in park and turns off the engine. "You've only seen the bad side, but it's helped me in so many ways. You wouldn't have liked me much if I hadn't had magic to help me figure out stuff. And one of the things I learned was to trust my instincts. So I know what I ought to do right now, I'm just scared to do it."

Jamie opens the car door and gets out. When she walks the last bit of road to the dirt path, Ro is by her side.

A crumbling music stage sits at the edge of an overgrown field full of pussy willows and dandelions. At the foot of the stage is another printout: a nasty Facebook post about Jamie, with the keys to Serena's apartment perched on top. Jamie is sure that she and Ro have arrived too late yet again.

Until she sees a mound near the foot of the stage: tree roots, clots of earth, wide ears of fungus and moss. Inside this compost heap, someone has arranged scraps of dirty fabric in an S-shape.

Jamie doesn't realize at first that this bundle of rags is her mother.

As Jamie grows closer, she can make out a face poking out of the muck. Serena looks up with a calm, quizzical expression, as if Jamie just wandered into her living room. Serena tries to speak, but only a rasp comes out.

It's not like Serena is being swallowed by the earth—more like she's being reclaimed, like so many of the failing structures Jamie has crouched in front of.

A slow wasting, being absumed by the land.

Jamie stands over this heap and feels her legs trembling, her fingernails gouging her own palms, her neck tightening.

"Fuck you!" Jamie shouts, so loud it echoes around the field. "Fuck you. How the fuck could you do this? I have tried, I have tried over and over to help you, and you keep burning everything down, and just . . . Fuck you, Mom." She's gone hoarse, her face burns. This scream is all there is to her, is all she has left for Serena. She can feel Ro standing next to her, shocked and bewildered, because this is not what Ro thought they'd come here to do. "How the fuck? I knew on some level that you were just waiting to die, all these years, and now you're finally getting what you've wanted all along, and I hope you're fucking happy, I'm going to carry this for the rest of my life. I will never get over this, I will never. I could have gotten over everything else, but not *this*. How could you do this to me?"

Serena finds her voice with a huge effort, like her lungs are crushed under all this weight. "You weren't supposed to see this."

It's still sinking in. Serena is dying, poisoned by the magic Jamie taught her, and there's so much Jamie will never get to say, and Jamie will have an unfillable hole inside her forever. The loam smells rusty, but also too flower-sweet, like awful medicine.

"As if seeing it is the problem? You never think of anyone but yourself." Jamie finally drops to her knees, so her tears spatter onto her mother's face. She didn't even know she was crying. "I know with time I can integrate everything I know about you, but now I won't get that time, not with a living person. I already went through this once, but this time . . . I can't."

"I know how heavy that is," Serena says. "I'm truly sorry to lay this on you. I didn't see any other way."

Jamie realizes she's looking at a literal deathbed, even if it's made out of vegetation, fungus, and mud. There's no bedpan, no chirping machines, but Jamie is still suddenly nineteen years old, holding a limp clammy hand and reading aloud from a Rita Mae Brown and Sneaky Pie Brown novel, uncertain if Mae is awake enough to hear. Jamie entirely numb except for a persistent feeling of vertigo in her lower gut, the same three bars of "It's So Hard to Say Goodbye to Yesterday" looping in her head. Sourness clinging in the air, every visitor putting on a jovial somberness because nobody knew how to act around a dying person.

And now Serena is barely here, and it feels as though she's being devoured by a memory. Jamie remembers the exact moment at Mae's bedside when Serena shut down, when the fight went out of the mother who wasn't dying. All these years, Jamie has been telling herself that this shutting-down was grief tinged with resentment, but now she sees that moment anew. Serena was surrendering to guilt.

Serena told Jamie, *You don't even know the real reason you should blame me.* Feels like a decade ago.

Clarity arrives, and it's so heavy, like the lead vest they drape over you before X-rays.

I could have saved her. I wouldn't even have needed magic.

"Oh shit." Jamie stares at Serena. "You. You blame yourself for Mae's death."

"Shouldn't I?" Serena's face shivers even though the rest of her can't move. Jamie can't tell how much of the moisture on her face is tears, sweat, or dew.

"Why? So many things you could blame yourself for, but Mae's death wasn't your fault."

"I wasn't there when she needed me." Serena's voice is brittle, her eyes half-closed as if this hurts more than whatever is happening to her under all this mulch. "She kept trying, over and over, she tried to tell me that she was really sick, but I didn't listen. Worse, I gaslit her: *I'm sure you're fine, It's nothing, take some aspirin.* The doctors wouldn't listen to her either. The one time—the *one* time—she needed me to show up, I wasn't there. I could have made those doctors pay attention. It was the thing I was always good at, making myself a pain in the ass. But I waited too late. You're goddamn right I blame myself."

Jamie kneels in front of her mother's face. "*This* is what you've been holding onto all this time? The reason you couldn't move forward?"

"I'm sorry. I know I'm not who you thought." Serena manages to look in Ro's direction. "And I'm so sorry I hurt you. You deserve better."

Jamie finds Serena's hand in between two layers of dead leaves and filth, and clasps it. Ro takes Jamie's other hand.

"What do you want to do?" Ro speaks so quietly, Jamie can barely hear.

"I'm so scared, I can't do this. I can't." Now Jamie's entire sensorium is made of weight.

"I'm freaked out, too. This is bringing back a lot of trauma," Ro says. "But I won't leave. Do whatever you need to do."

Jamie looks at Serena, who gave everything she had left to protect her daughter the way she couldn't protect her wife. Yes, it's partly Serena's fault Jamie needed protecting, but Jamie needs to witch up and take responsibility for her part of it all.

She speaks the words she's never voiced before: "I forgive you, Mom. For all of it."

The roots and fungal blooms seem to fall away a little.

Serena looks almost affronted. "I haven't earned it, you shouldn't—"

"Doesn't matter. It's what I want. I forgive you." Jamie lets go of Ro's hand, and leans over to put her free hand on her mother's face. Serena's eyes glisten, reflecting the absurdly blue sky overhead, and Jamie can feel her struggling to breathe.

"You should just leave me. I want you to go—"

Fuck. Serena's hand slackens in Jamie's. Hopeless, already lost, nothing to be done.

Rotten air, stuttering breaths.

Jamie says the only thing she can think of.

"Mom. You will always be loved, no matter what. You will always be loved. You cannot mess up so badly that you will not be loved."

Serena's eyes widen. Her face shifts inside its veil of earth. "I didn't think you could possibly remember me saying that. You were so little."

"It's a formative memory, Mom."

Jamie gets it at last: *A rasa tabula. All of the folly of the past swept clean.*

"Listen, Mom. I want us to have a fresh start. All the shitty magic we both did cleared away. I think you want that, too, deep down, and I need you to focus on that want." Jamie glances up at Ro, who's perched on the edge of the stage, fidgeting.

"If you clear away all the bad magic," Ro asks, "will I remember what happened to me?"

"I don't know," Jamie says. "Probably depends. Do you want to?"

"Yes! That memory sucks, but taking it away would be another violation. And I wouldn't know you the same way I know you now."

"I think if you want to remember, you'll remember," Jamie says. "Now's the time to go back to the car though. We're about to do a spell."

Ro shakes their head. "I'm staying." But they keep their distance.

Serena is able to raise her head and shoulders a little, which means the crud definitely loosened around her. "I do want a fresh start," she says. "But I don't have anything to offer. I already gave it all away."

"That's okay," Jamie says. "I've got that covered. It's not a sacrifice, though. I wouldn't give up this part of my life for anything." She digs in her purse until she pulls it out: the tiny stuffed koala, made to cling to things like a clothespin, which Mae and Serena gave her on the first day of second grade. Horatio the Koala clung to Jamie's bookbag for years, then shifted to a bottom-of-the-bag friend when the grip lost its strength. Somehow Jamie never stopped carrying Horatio around.

Holding this object in her hand for the last time, Jamie gets a powerful sense memory of Mae and Serena holding both of her hands crossing the street, of Mae getting her an ice cream and saying not to tell Serena, but Serena had already gotten her a candy bar an hour earlier and she promised each of them not to tell the other one. Mae teaching her to sing some ridiculous ad jingle from her youth. She'd laughed so hard—Mae always knew how to make her laugh.

"Goodbye, Mama." Jamie is sobbing again, how does she have any tears left? Her whole body is one big shiver. "I'll always love you. Thank you for everything you did for me. I'll never stop thinking about you every day."

Jamie places Horatio in Serena's hand. Serena clutches it white-knuckle tight, like a talisman, which it is.

"Shit. Do I have to?" Serena says. Then, before Jamie can say anything, she adds: "Fuck. I'll never get over losing you, Mae, and maybe that's just how it is. I still don't know what family means without you. You were so gentle. You built trellises in people's hearts, not just mine, not just mine by any stretch—you built structures that will last as long as those hearts last.

I promise I'll keep flowers growing on the trellis in my heart, even on the days when I hate the world. Goodbye, my love."

Serena and Jamie had thrown a wake/funeral for Mae after she died, but neither of them really remembered much about it after. They'd spent the entire time taking care of other people, Mae's friends and randos from the community. The two of them had never quite managed to hold a quiet space for Mae, before Serena vanished into the schoolbox.

Jamie pulls Serena free of all the dirt and weeds, which now feel fertile rather than rotten. Something spectacular is going to grow in this place. Serena is coated with filth, her clothes and skin streaked and caked. They'll need to put down a towel in the dirtmobile and get Serena cleaned up before someone sees her and calls the cops or something, because right now Serena looks like someone who needs to be expunged from the city, lest she destroy property values. Serena can't walk unaided, so Jamie wraps one mud-heavy arm around her shoulder and supports her back to the car.

Serena can't stop apologizing to Ro. "There's no excuse for how I treated you."

"No," Ro says, "there isn't. But I'm glad you're okay." Ro seems like they're about to say more, but then they think better of it.

Jamie thinks about trying to track down every precious object that Serena scattered in the woods—but she's too exhausted, and Serena's a wreck. And she has a strong feeling that all of that stuff is gone, for good. Serena cleaned herself out, she'll have to start over with nothing. Sometimes you have to come back humble.

Turns out Serena didn't come here in a car, she borrowed a friend's motorcycle, which is chained to a nearby tree. She doesn't take that much convincing that she's in no state to ride a bike right now—Jamie promises to give her a ride back here in a day or so.

Ro is sitting in the passenger seat, next to Jamie, while Serena zones out in the back. The need to check in with Ro feels like an itch under Jamie's skin, and the ugly hiss at the back of her mind is whispering that now that they've seen her do magic, with her mother no less, they will flee. Jamie tells that cartoon snake to shut up: Ro already should've run away, and they haven't, and the only way she might keep them in her life is by being okay with whatever they want to do going forward. It's the "set them free" paradox that Sting immortalized in that annoying song: you can only keep people around by accepting that they have the right to bail at any time.

Fucking Sting.

Serena has fallen asleep in the back seat, curled up on a big beach towel with the seat belt still on. Jamie slows down so the potholes don't jolt her awake.

"That was not what I was expecting," Ro says, too quietly for Serena to hear. "The human compost pile was scary as fuck, but the actual spell-casting was . . . dorky."

"That's how it is," Jamie sighs. "It's dorky as hell. I wouldn't be into it otherwise." She keeps her eyes on the road; it would serve her right if they hit a deer and got wiped out right now. "I think I might need a break from magic."

"Don't quit doing magic on my account," Ro says. "I still don't know what I want us to be, going forward. And I wouldn't want to have a relationship that's based on you giving up something that gave your life meaning."

Jamie glances in the rearview at the back seat: Serena is still sleeping.

"I'm sure I'll come back to witchcraft in a while," Jamie says. "I just . . . don't think I need it at the moment. I had this huge identity crisis and academia gave me imposter syndrome, but the more I give up on my career, the more I remember why I love scholarship. And meanwhile, with this new group, 'witch' is becoming an identity instead of a hobby, and it's weird. I feel good about where I am."

"You do seem happier," Ro says. "You remind me of how you were when we first met, except without the mullet."

"The mullet was nice while it lasted."

Is Ro . . . flirting? Jamie can't tell. She doesn't want to get her hopes up.

Somehow they've made it back to Somerville, right by the Davis Square T. Ro jerks their head. "If you can pull over, I can get out right here." Jamie pulls over and they open the door.

Ro pauses, halfway out of the car.

So nervous. Like fourteen-year-old never-been-kissed, about-to-come-out-as-trans nervous.

"I need to make sure Serena gets home okay, and there's no after-effects," Jamie says.

Then Ro says the sentence that turns her to jelly. "If you're not done too late, maybe you could come over."

Jamie nods and smiles. "I'd like that."

· · · · ·

Serena sits on the secondhand sofa under the dirty front window of her studio apartment, cradling a steaming mug with two teabags inside. She has a quilt wrapped around her shoulders, like someone who was rescued from a house fire. She keeps shaking her head as if to say *No* to some unspoken question.

"My whole life, you've had this anger," Jamie says. "You channeled it into journalism and activism, and you've always tried to keep it focused on the people who deserve it, like McAllister Bushwick. Which is good. I think your righteous anger is a huge part of why I always looked up to you."

"Until I got angry at myself, for seven years."

"Yeah."

They both sit with this for a moment. The steam is gone from Serena's mug.

"I want to do the work." Serena looks out the window, then turns her steel-gray eyes onto her daughter. "Not just because I'm hoping you'll allow me to be in your life in some way, but because, I don't know . . . I want to live. I guess that's what I found out today: I really like being alive, and maybe I've been dishonoring Mae's memory this whole time. Being alive sucks—it hurts like a bitch—but it's better than the alternative. I get to keep learning and making connections and having more disasters to make up for, and isn't that something?"

Jamie has already cried more today than in the past several years. But oh, here's the itchy sting in the corners of her eyes, though this time around it's a quiet cry, decorous even. For some reason, Serena saying *I want to be alive even though it sucks* reminds her of Ro saying *I like the way you get on my nerves.*

All Jamie ever wanted was to remind Serena of herself, and now it seems she has. She feels grateful and proud and relieved—but also so, so tired. Today came way too close to being the worst day of Jamie's life, even with some stiff competition.

"That's great, Mom." Jamie hears herself speak those words and it's the sort of thing that you're supposed to say to a parent when she tells you that she's taking up flower-arranging or learning to make pewter jewelry that you'll pretend to like when you unwrap your birthday presents. *That's great, Mom,* is what you say to an arm's-length parent, someone you call dutifully once every month or three. Jamie thought teaching her mother would bring them closer together, but maybe Ro was right, and it's impossible to know your parents. Maybe their spiritual nakedness is as bad to gaze upon as the physical kind.

On the other hand? Jamie is a messy queer bitch who doesn't color within the lines.

"I want you to know I meant the things I said before." Meaning: *I forgive you for everything. You will always be loved.* "If I hadn't meant those things, your spell wouldn't have been broken." Jamie feels the floor under her feet, the chair-arms under her flesh-arms. She has the sensation of a fertile space opening inside her, rich soil and strong partial sunlight—a place where something spectacular is going to grow. "I'm officially resigning as your teacher. We've both seen each other at our most lost, and that means neither of us gets to tell the other what's up. At least, that's how I feel. I hope we can be honest with each other going forward. Not total honesty, because boundaries are good, but more than we had before."

Serena listens to all of this, nodding her head.

"You're a good teacher. I hope you keep teaching in some capacity."

"I think I'd like being a teacher better if I didn't have to be a professor. Plus every time I go into a classroom now, I'm going to be paranoid that one of my students is filming me in secret." Oof. Gavin.

"That reminds me." Serena perks up. "I'm still an attorney and licensed to practice in two states. I think while I was living in that schoolhouse, McAllister Bushwick was crossing some lines that could actually spawn a decent class-action lawsuit. Fraud, harassment, defamation. I'm going to see if I can start bringing his victims together."

Jamie nods. "I will help you to sue that man into a hole in the ground. With pleasure."

"You should get going," Serena says. "I'm just going to sleep for the next two days anyway. Honestly, I just hope you spend some time with Ro, without having to worry about me. I know it's complicated and none of my business, but I hope you work things out." Jamie hesitates, but Serena adds, firmly: "I promise I'll be okay. I'm not going anywhere."

Jamie glances at the clock on her phone. If she leaves now, she could be at Ro's place—the apartment that used to be her place, too—in time for dinner. She can no longer tell anxiety from hope.

"It's going to take time," Jamie says. "And it's not going to be like it was. I'm trying to be a witch about it. Even if I'm not doing magic right now."

"Maybe it's easier to be a witch about things if we both quit doing magic for a while," Serena says.

"I sure hope so." When Jamie reaches the door and turns to say goodbye, Serena is already asleep on the couch.

18

The day arrived for Emily's wedding to Mr. Langthrope, and she found herself unable to raise herself from her bed, so struck was she with a paralytick lassitude. Her mind and heart rejoiced at the notion of starting a life with this man who had earned her utmost respect and affection; yet could she not bestir her limbs. Some moments passed before she recognized the immobilizing effects of fear.

—*EMILY: A TALE OF PARAGONS AND DELIVERANCE* BY A LADY, BOOK 8, CHAPTER 1

For years Jamie has imagined marching into Hirschfeld Hall and up to the third floor. Striding past the department secretary, past the yellowing newspaper clippings of old *Hägar the Horrible* strips on the always-closed office doors of Professors Watling and Durkin (those tenured leviathans slumbering in the deep) until she reaches Ariella's office. In Jamie's daydreams, Ariella is sitting behind her desk, frowning at a giant crumble-spined hardcover of Lord Byron's plays, and startlement turns to delight as she first hears and then sees Jamie carrying a printout the size of a healthy baby. Jamie plunks it down on Ariella's desk and says, "*Ecce pomo!* Here is my dissertation, gaze upon my citations and rejoice." The printout, encased in some kind of cheap plastic binder purchased from the office supply store, makes a sound like a burlap sack of bricks cracking a shelf made of balsa or plywood. Ariella flings Lord Byron onto the nearest surface in her eagerness to dive into Jamie's eye-popping exegesis.

In reality, of course, Jamie is staying away from Hirschfeld Hall, out of hurt feelings as much as any lingering probationary bullshit at this point. And turning in her diss to Ariella is a simple matter of uploading a PDF to a file-sharing site and then emailing her the link with a one-sentence email whose word count consists mainly of pleasantries. Once the diss is with Ariella, Jamie almost gets up to walk around the block, but then a major fuck-it impulse sweeps over her. She opens another email window and composes a message to Gordon from Pimlico Books, saying that she's finished the book she told him about at that conference in Philadelphia, and she'd be happy to share a copy if he'd like to consider it for publication. She could retool it a smidge and turn it into a general interest book that jargon-averse people might pick up, one that might score a half-sentence mention in *The New Yorker, The New York Times,* or some other publication with "New York" in the title.

A few days after Jamie sends the diss to Ariella, the two of them meet for lunch at the Farmer's Glen, a restaurant where the menu tells you where every ingredient was sourced from, but you order at a counter and take a number on a stick. They huddle over a wrought-iron table with no tablecloth, trading small talk and gossip about the latest outrages on the academic-liberty listserv, and then Ariella says she's started reading Jamie's diss and it's really good so far. Jamie flushes with pride despite herself.

"I am so sorry for everything you've had to go through," Ariella says around the time their tiny salads, piled with Early Girl tomatoes, arrive. "It's disgusting that academic freedom goes out the window the moment a few donors get their jockey shorts in a twist. I want you to know I've been raising hell about this and I still believe you could have a great future. When you go on the job market, you will have me making calls and lighting fires on your behalf."

"Yeah, about that . . ." Jamie hesitates, because this is everything she thought she wanted: the dissertation finished, Ariella's approbation, a decent academic job maybe in the offing. But Jamie's wants have changed, as wants often do. "I'm not sure academia is going to be right for me after all."

As usual, the truth is sour in her mouth, but the aftertaste is refreshing. She tells Ariella about Pimlico Books, who seem interested.

"Oh. You're going to be a public intellectual." Ariella might as well have said "telemarketer."

"I do want to teach again. I enjoy it, when I'm not feeling unbearable pressure. I think I'd enjoy teaching way more if people weren't paying superyacht-money to find out about *Daniel Deronda*. We need the humanities, more than ever, but the systems we've built to commodify them are suffocating them."

Now Ariella just looks sad. They both ordered the same smoked-mackerel plate, and two ruddy fish pieces arrive at the same time, with green beans on the side. The fish is perfectly tangy, with the smokiness bringing out some rich seam of flavor.

"I don't like to think I've given my life to a giant scam," Ariella says. "But of course nobody ever wants to think that."

"I don't think it's a scam," Jamie says. "I just think money turns everything thoughtful into shit."

Well, that's a conversation-killer. Ariella keeps saying things like, *I'm here if you ever need any help,* or, *Please consider me as a resource.* Jamie is pretty sure these offers are sincere, and she'll absolutely take Ariella up on them.

Just before they part ways, Ariella says, "The one time I met your mother, she said something that's stuck with me ever since. She said that those of us who dedicate our lives to unburying hidden stories from the past should take care not to participate in burying vital stories in the present."

Jamie almost snorts. Rich words from the woman who spent years interring the heart of her own story. But all Jamie says is, "That sounds like something Serena would say."

· · · · ·

Ro and Jamie get drinks at the Thirsty Scholar, to be followed by Indian food around the corner. This has become something of a ritual—they tried hanging out at the apartment they used to share, on Russell Street, but it felt too weird to be inside a home from which Jamie had been exiled, and she couldn't help expecting Ro to say, *Why don't you just stay here tonight?*

Which they never did. Usually they get one drink each, and then thalis, but tonight Ro orders a second round and fixes Jamie with a solemn expression in the low lighting.

"I've made some decisions you need to know about," Ro says. "I'm moving out of our old apartment. I'm going to live with roommates, or possibly in a cheap studio. I need to live independently for a while. And I'm going to start dating other people. We always said we were poly, but we were too busy or too skittish to do anything about it. I'm ready to have more loves in my life. But I still love you, and I'm not giving up on us, and I want you and me to be partners again, officially."

Jamie can't take this in at first—the beer is trapped in her throat, she is fizzy-headed—until the gloom sinks in. This is how it goes. She won't ever live with Ro again, and they're actively dating other people, and she'll fade to an afterthought. She's so dreaded the moment when Ro would say they should just break up once and for all, but she wasn't remotely ready for this.

Ro gets uncomfortable with the silence and adds, "I couldn't see a way to go back to the way things were before."

Jamie stumbles over saying, "I get it. It's what I—"

"If you say 'It's what I deserve,' I will walk away and never speak to you again," Ro says. "This isn't a punishment, or a downgrade of our relationship. Just a new situation, one that might make both of us happy eventually. And I am honestly so tired of hearing you berate yourself. I know you're a submissive masochist, but your performative self-flagellation is not doing it for me. You fucked up; I'm not over it; groveling *does not help.*"

"O . . . okay." Oddly it's a relief to be told to stop groveling, even though everything else is still giving Jamie abandonment-scares. "I guess . . . I want to support whatever you're comfortable with. I just worry that us living apart and dating other people will be the next step in a slow, drawn-out breakup."

She doesn't add that it might be better to just rip off the Band-Aid in that case.

"It's really up to us. If we hold each other at arm's length, we'll drift apart for sure. But if we treat it as a new phase, that's what it'll be. I love you, Jamie Sandthorn. I am all the way in the tank for you, and I know I'll never find anyone else like you for as long as I live. I am officially recommitting to you, because I want to kiss your face every day. But . . . I'm also setting some new boundaries."

"Boundaries are good. I like boundaries. Just . . . don't date another witch, okay?"

Ro gives her an *are you fucking kidding* look.

The whole time during dinner, Jamie and Ro keep holding hands, when they don't need both hands to tear naan or scoop dal. Jamie amuses Ro by describing the look on Ariella's face when she said "public intellectual," and Ro talks about the latest fuckery in the Tufts econ department. By the time dinner's over, Jamie is scooched next to Ro with their arm around her, and she feels at ease for the first time in months.

· · · · ·

So. Ro is going to date other people, which means Jamie really ought to date other people, too. She has a whole maelstrom of dread, insecurity, and (yes, okay) excitement about this, but one thought comes insistently to the surface: maybe she'll need to start doing magic again?

She has dinner with Delia at a new Malaysian place just off Tremont Street, and over bowls of spicy, creamy laksa soup, Jamie geeks out about dating while magical, and what the rules are. After everything Jamie has just been through, she needs to be much more ethical about her spellwork, and she absolutely won't use magic to make anyone like her—but what if she could make a date go more smoothly, without annoying disasters? Meanwhile, she needs to figure out a non-heinous way to come out as a witch, to anyone she starts dating seriously. This is going to increase the pool of people who know about magic, possibly by a lot if word spreads, but she doesn't see any way around it.

Delia frowns. "I've dated rather a lot in the past few years. For me, I don't mind using magic to boost my confidence, maybe make myself feel a bit more attractive. When I feel sexy, I think it helps in general. But it's a blurry line, isn't it? We can't use spells to influence other people. This should be part of our code of conduct. Also, I have a rule: I don't date other witches. That's served me well."

Oh. Well, that's that. Jamie had already kind of guessed Delia wasn't into her, so this isn't exactly a surprise. Also, that seems like a good rule, and Jamie says so.

"I've only told one romantic partner so far that I'm a witch," Delia says. "And that was after a year of dating. I think it's the sort of thing where you really need to build trust first, on both sides, and you cannot rush that."

Delia shares some updates on the other members of the witch union, because Jamie's missed some meetings. Bee is experimenting with crafting, like making baskets that give a mild blessing to anything you place in them; nobody is sure if it'll work, but they're having fun trying. Paola is thinking about going to community college, and Jamie offers to help in any way she can. Yvette is trying to use magic to heal the coastline. Also, Delia has been using some of Martha's mindfulness techniques to help people in her therapy practice, without bringing actual magic into it.

"Thank you for not giving up on Serena. Or me. You and the others, you had every right to wash your hands of us after the messes we made." Jamie eats soup, to guard her mouth from rattling on.

"What I know about your mother is that she brought us together. We were all on our own, making sense of things the best we could, and she networked and poked around until we became a group." Delia stirs her soup. "Doesn't matter if she did that because she needed our help to be less of a disaster, the end result was a community that means a lot to me. That said, I'm grateful she didn't try to be our leader, because that could've been toxic."

"You were right when you said we'll need a code of conduct." Jamie laughgroans. "This thing we do, the 'Beige Arts,' can get much uglier than I realized."

Delia sighs. "I keep thinking about what Paola said: the number of magical places is going up all the time, and maybe soon Miami will be a whole magical city."

"I guess the only bottleneck will be people figuring out magic." Jamie is kind of thinking aloud. "I didn't realize until I spent time with you and the other union members, but all of us found magic the same way: we're oddballs who wandered desolate places and noticed something weird. And instead of shrugging and going on with our day, we decided to spend a lot of time exploring that feeling. Serena is an outlier: someone who was taught, instead of figuring it out on her own."

"You can't possibly be the first person to teach someone else magic, though." Delia's eyes widen and she makes a little sound in her throat, like she just thought of something. "The real issue is going to be if a malicious person decides to create their own coven, by training and indoctrinating a bunch of other witches."

Jamie nods. "Basically the thing I was scared Serena was doing with our group, at first."

"A dozen fanatical witches who all believe in the same nonsense could do some serious harm, even if a lot of it would blow back onto them." Delia shakes her head, like she's shaking off a bad dream. "It probably wouldn't work. We're not talking about a coven really, we're talking about a cult, and it'd self-destruct in no time. I think. I hope."

Delia takes a deep drink from her wineglass, because she just scared herself.

"I'm not worried." Jamie is *mostly* telling the truth. "What happened with Serena is a bit of a cautionary tale, but it also shows the limits of magic? She was so close to burning herself out, and probably even dying." Involuntary shudder.

"I've been thinking that we might be able to help with taking down that Bushwick guy after all," Delia says. Jamie raises an eyebrow, and Delia holds up both palms. "Not by cursing him! Nothing so extreme. But the fact that you and your mother were able to bless Teena Wash, whom you never met? I think our little group could do something similar for Bushwick's victims. Especially whoever he goes after next. Just . . . tilt the scales. Make it easier for someone to be believed and hold onto their life."

"I think that could do a lot of good." Jamie closes her eyes, tastes the wine she just drank. "If it stays focused on wishing the victim well, rather than dealing the asshole a setback." She opens her eyes and smiles. "You just gave me a big incentive to come back to meetings. And start doing magic again."

"Excellent." Delia raises her glass. "I think this could be fun, and having you more active in the group is a nice side benefit. To new friends."

"New friends," Jamie echoes.

Their glasses chime together, and they both drink. The two women end up finishing the bottle and getting into a debate about the Powerpuff Girls, and honestly Jamie hasn't felt so comfortable goofing off with someone in forever.

. . . . .

Delia's idea vibrates across the whole witch union, and within a few days it goes from a cool notion to a definite plan. Everyone has been hankering for a shared purpose, a way to become more than a support group. If this works, it could change everything. Even Wardin, whom Jamie still hasn't met, is on board. A buzz through the network, everyone chiming in with ideas: Bee has the perfect spot to do something big, Martha has some ideas for offerings. Paola has found the perfect blessing candidate: Faith Goodnight, who runs a brilliant abortion fund and has been smeared by JawBone but also a half dozen other orgs. Jamie gives as much advice as she can without oversharing about the Teena Wash thing—one reason Jamie's not sure if this will work is because it'll be hard for so many witches to keep from obsessing about the spell afterward. Barely a few days after Delia suggested the idea, they all meet, even Serena, around a batting cage that's been swallowed by vines and brambles, out near Route 44. Paola has printed a sympathetic Autostraddle article about Faith, and everybody has brought their own small item to pile up. Bugs cloud the air. Everything smells pungent like organic herbal tea. They all hold hands, Serena clutching Jamie's left and Delia grazing the right, and try to focus their minds on wishing good things for Faith. Nobody chants or even speaks out loud, but whispers and subvocalizations come from all around. Jamie murmurs something, like *Help her, give her strength,* and she hears similar things from Serena and Delia. Afterward, Jamie feels neither drained nor wired, just . . . calm. At peace. This felt right. She finds it easy to put the spell away in a pocket of her mind, but also she's sure this is the beginning of something much bigger.

. . . . .

Jamie wasn't there to help Serena move into her apartment in Alewife, so she makes extra sure to block out three days to help her move out. Wrapping every chipped bowl and illegible mug in layers of newspaper and sweaters, then wedging them tight inside the cardboard wine boxes they liberated from the loading dock at the Star Market. Every now and then Jamie has to pause and look at a quilt that used to drape across the old fainting couch in Wardmont, or a sweatshirt that Mae used to wear, but she no longer feels so weighed down when she sees that stuff. And Jamie knows if she stares at something for too long, Serena will appear at her elbow and say, "Do you want that? It's yours." Jamie already has too much junk, and Serena doesn't have enough anymore.

It's been a few months since the music stage, and Serena still isn't 100 percent. She gets tired, she has to sit down unexpectedly, and the muggy summer air is getting to her. The Silver Sneakers exercise classes for senior citizens have been helping, and she managed to get some physical therapy covered by Medicaid as well. Serena had to quit working at the bookstore, but the crowdfunding they organized to sue JawBone pulled in enough money to pay Serena's hourly rates for months—turns out a lot of people wanted to see that assclown and his crew go down. (They didn't use magic to boost the crowdfunding, but the witch union has made a habit of blessing Bushwick's victims and other victims of organized harassment, which is making them noticeably more prosperous, and some of that money has trickled into this lawsuit.) Serena keeps chortling about her plan to "pierce the veil" and get at JawBone's funders.

One day, Jamie will learn how to peel a roll of packing tape without either making bad tape-origami or sticking the remaining tape so tight she won't be able to get any more without digging in her fingernails. Today is not that day.

"Are you sure about this, Mom?" Jamie can't help asking, even though she's mostly pleased that her mom seems to be making plans and chasing dreams.

"At least for now," Serena says. "Nancy has a spare room, and I think the air in Taos will be good for me. I can't stand this humidity. I'll still talk to you whenever you want, and I can keep filing legal paperwork from there." She raises a throw pillow in both hands, staring, then tosses it in the "discard" pile. "Honestly, this is better. I need a fresh start, like you keep saying, and you need some space from me."

Funny thing is, Jamie doesn't entirely need space from her mother. Things between them have been good, better than ever before, now that all the weirdness has been lifted into the open air. The potential that Jamie glimpsed before, when they did a junk-food picnic and went antiquing, has become reality. She and Serena have been doing weekly brunches, going to the occasional drag show or poetry reading together, and hanging out with the other witches.

"I'm going to miss you," Jamie says. "A lot."

"Come visit," Serena replies. "We'll get tacos."

Jamie wraps T-shirts around dinnerware: artwork from old music shows and protest marches framed from below by the inner circle of each plate.

"I can't stop thinking," she says.

"That's a surprise." Serena snorts.

"I can't stop thinking," Jamie says more peevishly, because that was the start of a sentence, hello. "That I was in denial, when I kept insisting that this thing, the Beige Arts, wasn't about power. I mean, it's not *entirely* about power. But I think I just wanted to be harmless. To not be a bully, like that kid in third grade."

"Zeb." Serena rolls her eyes, because of course she remembers Zeb.

"I think I had it in my head that power is always selfish, or destructive. The wanting of it, or the exercising of it. I mean, power corrupts, but it also heals? I think you had the right idea, founding a community of witches. That's probably the only safeguard we really have in the end, community and accountability."

Jamie runs out of plates before she runs out of T-shirts.

"Maybe you have to distinguish between the power to control your own life, and the power to dominate others?" Serena cocoons a blender in bubble wrap. "Sometimes it's hard to tell, which is why there are so many shit-eating libertarians in the world. When you first showed me magic, it was like when I got my law degree: I felt like I had a handle on the world for the first time ever. But I think I have a nasty tendency to get carried away, to go too far, and I hadn't fully realized. I try to control things I shouldn't, and I don't control things I really ought to, and then I spiral with guilt. I suppose that's the human condition, isn't it?"

Jamie finds herself telling Serena about the fable with which Jane Collier concludes her satire *An Essay on the Art of Ingeniously Tormenting*: during the time when animals could talk, there was a poem about the agony of having claws sunk into your flesh, whose author was known only as "L." The lion, lynx, and leopard all claimed to be the author, because they were all experts on claws—but the true author was the lamb, because only a victim can describe what it is to suffer. This is Jane's way of saying that even though she's spent the whole book ironically cheering on the perpetrators of mental torture, her sympathies actually lie with the victims. But it's also a commentary on human nature.

"Anyway," says Jamie, "I guess what I wanted to say is that I get it now. I've seen your darkness. I came to terms with it, I think? And as scary as the past year has been, I feel like I've gained a measure of peace."

Serena roots silently in her pile of detritus for a while, and Jamie's not sure if the conversation is over or what. But then she pokes her head up and says, "There's no dichotomy, is there? Between power and self-knowledge? Fucking up is an excellent teacher, but so is not fucking up. I've learned a lot about myself from helping other people *and* from hurting other people, and I know which one I prefer. Anyway, what you said before, about community. That. That's everything." Something occurs to her. She draws upright and looks at Jamie. "Please tell me they're not still throwing a going-away party. I've eaten enough of Yvette's gluten-free pound cake already."

"It's going to be super chill, Mom. We're just getting pizza and sitting in the garden. People are sad you're leaving. Not as much as me, but still."

Serena grunts, as if she's partying under duress, but Jamie can tell she's pleased. "I'll be back for visits. I might even move back to New England in a year or two. I keep hearing Vermont is nice. Listen, you have to take some of this stuff. I won't need sweaters where I'm going, and there's no room in the van, and all of your warm things are full of holes. Come on. Take some sweaters. And scarves. And these gloves."

Somehow Jamie ends up with a garbage bag stuffed with her mom's winter clothes, despite all her vows to the contrary.

Serena laughs, startling Jamie as she's putting the garbage bag near the door. "I was just remembering the grungy goth phase you went through. You cleaned out this one Salvation Army. I don't even know what to call it:

you wore all black, but there were a lot of turtlenecks for some reason. And bell-bottoms? It was heinous. We were scared you were getting into something dangerous, just because those clothes looked like a cry for help."

"I wasn't ready to come out or transition," Jamie says. "I hated dressing like a boy, but I didn't know what else to do."

"Well, it was a relief when you started borrowing our old clothes instead," Serena says, pressing another warm jacket into Jamie's hands. "I'll never forget Mae's face when she saw you wearing her old Lesbian Avengers shirt. She felt so old all at once."

Jamie looks down at the jacket, which is sort of gray flannel with shark-tooth buttons. "Mae always dressed better than either of us."

Serena shakes her head and smiles. "She really did, didn't she?"

A bell clangs: it's coming from Serena's purse. She yanks it out and curses when she sees the screen, then stabs a button. "I don't have anything to say to you."

"Ms. Decker, I'm calling you to ask you to cease your frivolous litigation." Serena must have put the call on speakerphone, because Jamie hears McAllister Bushwick loud and clear. That voice still creeps her out, but not as viscerally as before. "Surely you must recognize this course of action will only—"

"I gather you saw the latest discovery filing." Serena grins. "We're going to keep going until it's all out in the open. You wouldn't believe what I've already found. We got audio of one of your secret training sessions. It's pretty juicy, and I'm looking forward to playing it in court."

"My lawyer says SLAPP laws . . . Ms. Decker, you must realize . . ."

"Your lawyer is the one who should be talking to me," Serena says. "You of all people should know it's a mistake to show weakness. In any case, you already have my settlement offer, which I consider more than generous."

"Your offer? Your *extortion attempt* will never—"

"Don't call me again until you have something to say." Serena mashes the red picture of an old-style phone, and the call goes silent.

Jamie shakes her head. "He sounded legit rattled. I can't believe it."

Serena cackles. "I can hardly believe it myself. His whole organization was based on exposing and humiliating people, so maybe it makes sense that his team all turned on him the moment we put the heat on? I've been amazed at the dirt we've gotten already."

"I'm proud of you," Jamie says. It feels different than when she was saying this sort of thing a year earlier.

Now they need to celebrate, plus they're almost out of things to pack, and the sun's still out, all of which means one thing: ice cream.

Serena wants to crash early, so Jamie ends up going to dinner at Ro's new apartment. Ro's sharing with two extremely nerdy enbies, Hayashi and Omar, who are used to Jamie being there all the time—Jamie crashes there, on average, three or four nights a week, and the other nights she's at the new place she's renting with Markus.

Ro is frying up some polenta in olive oil, with some garlic and rosemary, and it smells outstanding. They lean over to kiss Jamie and ask, "How's your mother?"

"She's good. She made me take too many hand-me-downs." Jamie hesitates, because she doesn't talk to Ro about Serena most of the time, except when they ask first. "I really think she's going to be okay. She seems . . . centered."

"I'm glad." Ro seems like they're going to say something else, but then they don't. They cook in silence for a while, with Jamie leaning over their shoulder, breathing the tangy vapors.

When dinner is over, Jamie clears up and does the dishes, and then Ro mentions that Hayashi and Omar are out until late, and Ro just got a new set of restraints that need to be broken in. Jamie's heart is a flying fish.

"Just sit there." Ro gestures at the sofa. "Close your eyes until I tell you to open them."

Jamie loses track of time almost immediately with her eyes closed. She smells the warm starchy garlic lingering in the air from dinner, and feels the soft corduroy of the sofa cushions under her hands and legs. She hears the light tread of Ro's feet, the bustle of preparation, the clattering of small objects, the whir of a distant air purifier. Normally, she'd feel antsy, waiting in self-imposed darkness, but she feels safe. Warm. She can wait as long as it takes for Ro to come back and show her whatever they're going to show her.

HISTORICAL NOTE

I've been fascinated by eighteenth-century English literature since college, but somehow that obsession took on a whole new life during the writing of this novel. I started out believing what I'd been taught in college: that the only novelists who mattered back then were men like Henry Fielding and Samuel Richardson. And then I discovered a whole wealth of brilliant women, and the Blue Stockings Society that surrounded them. Upshot: I'm even more fixated now.

The period I'm touching on here, in the 1730s and 1740s, is even more fascinating. The Restoration, starting in 1660, was a period of liberalism and wild partying, but by the early 1730s, the party was starting to come to an end. Most of the theaters got shut down in 1737, which helped contribute to a boom in novels and reading. Social norms and gender roles were suddenly more conservative, and the sexual double standard started coming down much harder on women.

It's a period of history that's well worth reading more about, so I'm going to provide some suggestions for places to look deeper.

First of all, to clarify: everything I talk about in this book is real—except for the novel *Emily,* which I totally made up. Also, the correspondence between Sarah Fielding and Jane Collier is entirely my invention, I'm afraid—very little of their shared correspondence survives to this day. But Sarah Fielding, Jane Collier, and all the other people I talk about were real, and all

306   HISTORICAL NOTE

the other works I mention. The quotes at the start of several chapters come from real works, except for the quotes from *Emily*.

If you want to know more about eighteenth-century women writers in general and have an hour to kill, I highly recommend watching the 2022 Foxcroft Lecture by Professor Karen Green, who breaks it down for you: www.youtube.com/watch?v=NOoKc8Cft8c.

Also invaluable as an overview is *Mothers of the Novel* by Dale Spender, which came out in the 1980s but remains utterly relevant today. I also got a lot out of reading *A Literary History of Women's Writing in Britain, 1660–1789* by Susan Staves and *The Professionalization of Women Writers in Eighteenth-Century Britain* by Betty A. Schellenberg.

Two biographies completely rocked my world, and I highly recommend them as fun beach reads. I became utterly obsessed with Laetitia Pilkington, whose garbage husband tried to destroy her, but who survived (literally) by her wits. I highly recommend her biography, *Queen of the Wits* by Norma Clarke. And if you want to know more about Charlotte Charke, you'll get a huge kick out of *Charlotte* by Kathryn Shevelow. Fair warning: both Laetitia and Charlotte went through some real hard times, and their stories don't have happy endings, but they burned so bright along the way.

Another book I highly recommend, as an endlessly entertaining source of juicy gossip about misbehaving women in the era, is *Companions Without Vows: Relationships Among Eighteenth-Century British Women* by Betty Rizzo. It's got tons of useful, engrossing information about Sarah Fielding and Jane Collier, as well as other authors like Sarah Scott. But it's also crammed with eye-popping anecdotes. Plus a fascinating dissection of the power dynamics between women of differing social and economic classes, and what happened to women who couldn't marry and weren't independently wealthy.

Want to know more about Sarah Fielding and Jane Collier? I sure hope you do. For a quick rundown of Sarah Fielding's life and career, check out Lucy Powell's eighteen-minute segment on BBC Radio: www.bbc.co.uk/programmes/m000sxbz. Also, Carolyn Woodward edited a new edition of *The Cry: A Dramatic Fable* by Fielding and Collier, with a brilliant introduction that gives a lot of information and insight. Linda Bree's survey, called simply *Sarah Fielding,* is also super helpful.

I also found two unpublished PhD dissertations quite useful, and they're both online: "The 'True Use of Reading': Sarah Fielding and Mid Eighteenth-Century Literary Strategies" by Mika Suzuki and "Sarah Fielding: Satire and Subversion in the Eighteenth-Century Novel" by June Jameson. Jameson also wrote a fictional autobiography of Sarah Fielding called *Sarah Fielding: Author of David Simple,* which adds some color and context to our fragmentary knowledge about her.

One thing I want to mention here: there's a weird theory among some scholars that Henry and Sarah Fielding had an incestuous relationship. This notion appears to be based on very scant evidence, but you'll definitely come across it if you dig into the literature. (Few scholars seem to think Sarah was gay, even though I'd argue the evidence for homosexuality is stronger than the evidence for incest.)

In case you want to dig deeper, other books that I found super relevant include:

- *Desire and Domestic Fiction* by Nancy Armstrong
- *The Matrimonial Trap* by Laura E. Thomason
- *The Other Eighteenth Century* edited by Robert W. Uphaus and Gretchen M. Foster
- *Richardson and Fielding: The Dynamics of a Critical Rivalry* by Allen Michie
- *Dr. Johnson's Women* by Norma Clarke
- *The Rise and Fall of the Women of Letters* by Norma Clarke
- *Cruelty and Laughter* by Simon Dickie
- *Circulating Enlightenment: The Career and Correspondence of Andrew Millar, 1725–68* by Adam Budd
- *The Rise of the Novel* by Ian Watt
- *Henry Fielding* by Donald Thomas

And of course, I read tons of books from the time: *The Adventures of David Simple* and *Volume the Last* by Sarah Fielding (Peter Sabor, editor); *The Governess* by Sarah Fielding (Candace Ward, editor); *The Female Quixote* by Charlotte Lennox (Amanda Gilroy and Wil Verhoeven, editors);

The Cry: A New Dramatic Fable by Sarah Fielding and Jane Collier; *An Essay on the Art of Ingeniously Tormenting* by Jane Collier; and *Millennium Hall* by Sarah Scott. I had previously read all of Henry Fielding and Samuel Richardson, along with some of Defoe and other male authors of the era.

If you really want even more context, here are some papers I made great use of:

Anderson, Emily Hodgson. "Women Writers in Eighteenth-Century Britain." Review of *The Professionalization of Women Writers in Eighteenth-Century Britain*, by Betty A. Schellenberg. *Huntington Library Quarterly* 68, no. 4 (2005).

Bowden, Martha F. "Jane Collier's Satirical Fable: Teeth, Claws, and Moral Authority in An Essay on the Art of Ingeniously Tormenting." In *British Women Satirists in the Long Eighteenth Century*, edited by Amanda Hiner and Elizabeth Tasker Davis. Cambridge University Press, 2022.

Bucknell, Claire. "Dreadful Apprehensions." *London Review of Books* 40, no. 20 (2018).

Dykstal, Timothy. "Provoking the Ancients: Classical Learning and Imitation in Fielding and Collier." *College Literature* 31, no. 3 (2004).

Mannheimer, Katherine. "A New Unmodern Eighteenth Century." *The Eighteenth Century* 55, no. 4 (2014).

Sabor, Peter. " 'Moral Romance' and the Novel at Mid-Century." In *The Oxford History of the Novel in English: Volume 1*, edited by Thomas Keymer. Oxford University Press, 2018.

Sabor, Peter. "Richardson, Henry Fielding, and Sarah Fielding." In *The Cambridge Companion to English Literature, 1740–1830*, edited by Thomas Keymer and Jon Mee. Cambridge University Press, 2006.

Woodward, Carolyn. "Jane Collier, Sarah Fielding, and the Motif of Tormenting." *The Age of Johnson: A Scholarly Annual* 16 (2005).

ACKNOWLEDGMENTS

I have taken some huge, ridiculous liberties with Jane Collier and Sarah Fielding, and I only hope people will forgive me—and take the time to learn more about the real-life works of these remarkable women.

Just like *Emily,* Rugby College does not exist—I decided to cram a bonus college in the middle of Allston, Massachusetts, basically occupying a chunk of the space that is occupied by Smith Field in real life. I went there in July 2023 and walked around, just picturing how the space would look with a transplanted Scottish castle and the Plaintive Gate in it. I'm terribly sorry to have erased a lovely playground in my fictional world.

So many people helped to make this book possible that I'm sure I will forget many of them. I apologize in advance if I left your name out!

Elizabeth Knauss generously spent a lot of time talking to me about this time period, and also read over my excerpts from *Emily,* as well as all my attempts at writing about the eighteenth century. Gary Gautier also gave me a ton of feedback about Sarah Fielding and Jane Collier. Ingrid Tieken-Boon van Ostade shared some insights about the correspondence of Sarah Fielding, and also shared some helpful articles with me.

Dr. Elizabeth Bates gave me helpful medical advice, and read over all the sections about Serena and Mae. Kristin Buxton got me some PDFs of scholarly articles, and so did my mother. Tam Frager talked to me about housing policy stuff. May-Lee Chai generously answered my questions about graduate school and graduate student teachers.

When it came to writing semicredible eighteenth-century prose, I relied heavily on Samuel Johnson's Dictionary online: johnsonsdictionaryonline .com. I also used Project Gutenberg's wealth of eighteenth-century texts to see how words were used in context. Also LibriVox's free audiobooks of eighteenth-century novels were invaluable to get the sound of the prose in my head.

I'm super grateful to all of my beta readers, who read some or all of this novel: Kate Erickson, Christine Boylan, Malka Older, Olivia Abtahi, Liz Henry, Annalee Newitz, Cecilia Tan, Emily Teplin, Eliza Clark, and Elizabeth Knauss. I'm especially thankful to Kit Stubbs, who "liveblogged" the book, sending me reactions and notes after reading each chapter.

Also, I'm eternally grateful to my agent, Russ Galen, for believing in this project when I first told him about it back in 2019, and for encouraging me to stick with it.

And last but definitely not least, thanks to the heroic army of folks at Tor Books who made this book, and so much more, possible. My indispensable genius editor Miriam Weinberg provided so many keen insights and helped me to refashion the eighteenth-century part of the storyline and rework the opening chapter—but more than that, Miriam brought this book to life in so many ways and helped make the magic real. Thanks also to Tessa Villanueva, Saraciea Fennell, Isa Caban, Khadija Lokhandwala, Will Hinton, Claire Eddy, NaNá V. Stoelzle, Dakota Griffin, Jamie Stafford-Hill, and so many other people at Tor who did so much to bring this book to the world. I'm so proud to be on your team, and so grateful to be able to work with you all.

Oh, and here's the music that formed the soundtrack for this book:

The Sweetwater Sessions by Jonatha Brooke
This Temporary Ensemble by 9m88
Temple by Thao & the Get Down Stay Down
sketchy. by Tune-Yards
The Omnichord Real Book by Meshell Ndegeocello
Black Terry Cat by Xenia Rubinos
Wildcard! The Jokers' Edition by Sananda Maitreya

Evolve by Ani DiFranco
Just Like That... by Bonnie Raitt
Wild Seed–Wild Flower by Dionne Farris
I'm a Dream by Seinabo Sey
Hunky Dory by David Bowie

And a few others—come by my house and I'll play you some music.

ABOUT THE AUTHOR

Sarah Deragon, Portraits to the People

CHARLIE JANE ANDERS is the author of *Lessons in Magic and Disaster*. Her other novels include *All the Birds in the Sky, The City in the Middle of the Night,* and the young-adult Unstoppable trilogy. She's also the author of the short story collection *Even Greater Mistakes* and *Never Say You Can't Survive,* a book about how to use creative writing to get through hard times. She's won the Hugo, Nebula, Sturgeon, Lambda Literary, Crawford, and Locus Awards. She cocreated Escapade, a transgender superhero, for Marvel Comics and wrote her into the long-running New Mutants comic. And she's currently the science fiction and fantasy book reviewer for *The Washington Post.* With Annalee Newitz, she cohosts the podcast *Our Opinions Are Correct.*